DRAGON'S KISS

HOWLERS MC SERIES BOOK 6

DRAGON'S KISS

HOWLERS MC SERIES BOOK 6

T.S. TAPPIN

Dragon's Kiss
T.S. Tappin
Published by T.S. Tappin
Copyright © 2022 T.S. Tappin
All rights reserved. In accordance with the U.S. Copyright Act of 1976, the scanning, uploading, and electronic sharing of any part of this book without the permission of the publisher is unlawful piracy and theft of the author's intellectual property. Thank you for your support of the author's rights and work.
This book is a work of fiction. Names, characters, places, and incidents are the product of the author's imagination or are used fictitiously. Any resemblance to actual events, locales, or persons, living or deceased, is coincidental.
Cover Design by: T.S. Tappin
Editing Services: Elisabeth Garner & Kimberly Ringer
ISBN: 9798358025363

Dedication:

*If you want something and you lick it, it's yours.
This is for the lickers.*

Other works by this author:

Under the name T.S. Tappin
Howlers MC Series:
Bk1: Axle's Ride
Bk2: Trip's B*tch
Bk3: Pike's Pixie
Bk4: Siren's Flame
Bk5: Bullet's Butterfly
Bk6: Dragon's Kiss
Bk7: Rebel's Fairytale

Tiger's Claw MC Series:
Bk1: Crush's Fall

Through Newsletter
Coming soon:
Rock's Reward: A Howlers MC Series Novella
Joker's Second Chance: A Howlers MC Series Novella

Under the name Tara Tappin
On the Clock: A Spicy RomCom Novella Charity Project

Acknowledgements:

My PIC: For pushing the *publish* button the first time for me. I Heart You.

My family: I appreciate your support and believe in me. You are my reasons why.

Kim: Squeee! It's finally here! Let's hope everyone else loves Dragon, too... just not as much as you. You licked him, so he's yours. HG 4ever!

Elisabeth: Your support, encouragement, and comma-lessons are essential to my writing non-process. I'll always work these streets for you! HG 4life! Huzzah!

Romance Riot: I've learned so much from all of you! Not to mention the number of times you've brought me to tears while laughing. You all are the best!

The HypeGirlSquad Discord: For keeping up my spirits each and every day, I thank you.

My Beta team: If not for you, none of this would make sense. Thank you for wading through the mess to find the good stuff.

My ARC team: Thank you, thank you, thank you for taking a chance with my work! You are one of the most important parts of the publication of my books. Without you, none of this would be possible.

Content Warnings

Dear Reader,

I want to make sure that no one is negatively influenced by my work, I decided to reupload my book files with content warnings about what you will encounter in this body of work.

The following are those warnings:

Death

Violence

Weapons

Possessiveness

Controlling behavior

Cussing/strong language

Explicit sex

War

Drug use

If you encounter something that isn't listed and feel it could trigger a reader, please email me at booksbytt@gmail.com

Thank you!

T.S. Tappin

T.S. Tappin

Chapter One

Kisy

Fuck. Fuck. Fuck!

Kisy repeated the mantra over and over as she hid behind the menu she was holding. She was at a restaurant across town, so she thought she was safe to actually go out and eat a meal that didn't come in a bag through a drive-thru window. Yet, there they were a few tables away, wearing their typical well-tailored suits and perfectly coiffed hair. One of the men had on a dark gray suit with a white shirt underneath and a diagonal striped, monochromatic tie of the same gray. The other man's suit was the same fit, but black, and his tie was a solid crimson. They were chatting and appeared to be distracted by their menus and not looking around. That was a minor plus.

The worst part of the entire situation was she had only been trying to be a good person and a responsible employee. Until ten days before, she was a property manager for a millionaire in Grand Rapids. She was at an event center to do her quarterly checks to make sure the owner's standards, as well as the state's, were being followed. When she stepped into that utility room, she expected it to be empty. She didn't expect to find a trio of men, one kneeling on the floor in front of the other two, with a gun sporting a silencer being held to his forehead. Kisy was proud of herself for not screaming, but she couldn't help the squeak that came out at the sight. No, she didn't cry out in shock... until a second later when the gun went off and the man on his knees slumped to the ground.

Kisy squeezed her eyes shut and tried to battle back the image of the man's body crumbling to the floor, the blood and gods-know-what-else leaking from the wound in his forehead, as she slid down further in her seat at the restaurant table. It was different seeing an execution in person than watching it in a movie.

Because she didn't want to end up as collateral damage in whatever situation she walked in on, Kisy bolted. Thanking the gods she was in comfortable shoes and not heels, she full-on ran down the side hall toward the front of the building, swung a right into the main hall, and didn't stop until she pushed through the front doors and slid into the driver's seat of her Ford Mustang. After starting her car, she threw it in drive and sped home, where she thought she'd be safe. How could they know who she was? She couldn't see how they would figure out her identity until she got a weird voicemail from her boss – her boss never called her as soon as she left an inspection before or sounded so urgent to get a briefing of her visit – and she couldn't find the binder she had been carrying during her inspection.

She didn't remember dropping it, but she must have. But what tripped her out more than anything was hearing a voice in the background of the beginning of the voicemail quietly mention something about that bitch's knowledge could bring down the entire fucking organization if she goes to the pigs. What organization? It couldn't be the property management company or the event company. It sounded like mob speak and that tripped her out. If her boss was part of the mob or some other illegal organization that was afraid of the cops, she wanted no part in any of it.

Trusting her gut, she packed a bag and grabbed the cash she kept at the house for emergencies. Then she took off to a hotel. She used her sister's driver's license to book the room, silently thanking her sister for losing it at her house months ago. She had the intention of bringing it back to Katherine, but her sister had already replaced it, so there hadn't been a need anymore. As Kisy sat on the bed, curled up in a ball, she prayed the men didn't dig too deep into her life and find her sister.

Kisy had finally called her boss back when she was in the hotel room. He didn't ask anything about her inspection. All he wanted to know is why she ran out of the building. When Kisy told him she had an emergency to take care of, he pressed and blatantly asked what she saw at the event center. Before she could answer, he answered for her. "You saw nothing. Do you understand? Nothing. Now, where are you?"

Kisy hung up the phone and blocked his numbers – cell, office, and home. She spent two days in that hotel room, pacing, scared to leave, trying to decipher what was going on and how in the hell she was going to get herself out of that mess. Then she got a call from the clerk at the front desk, who happened to be an old friend from high school, Elisabeth. She said men, who were dressed as Kisy had described, were headed upstairs in the elevator and made her feel uneasy. Elisabeth mentioned something about security being on their way, but Kisy didn't wait to find out for sure. After quickly hanging up the phone, she jumped up and tossed the few unpacked things back into her bag. As soon as she managed to stuff everything in the bag, Kisy grabbed it and her purse and made her way to the stairwell as fast as she could. They must have seen her go into the stairwell, because as soon as she reached the bottom, she heard them running down the three flights.

Paranoid, Kisy spent the next eight nights in her car at various campgrounds, eating from fast-food establishments and pinching pennies until she could come up with a plan. But all the fast food had made her feel bloated, which is why she decided to risk a sit-down restaurant.

Of course, the men in suits would walk into the restaurant she decided to eat at. Fuck her life.

The shaking started in her hands, causing the menu to flap in front of her. Great! That wouldn't draw any attention. She slapped it down on the table, desperate to stop the flapping. The sudden sharp noise caught the attention of the diners and servers around her. As their gazes studied her like she was the rudest person they ever encountered, or maybe that was just her anxiety, Kisy felt the shaking spread up her arms to her shoulders, her breathing becoming shallower.

Panic. She was panicking. *Shit!* She needed to get out. Now.

Doing simple math problems in her head in an effort to battle the panic attack, she pulled her wallet out of her purse, found a ten, and dropped it on the table. It was more of a tote bag than a purse. That's what happened when you were living on the run. You stayed prepared.

Trying to be as inconspicuous as possible, she stood and made her way toward the doorway that led to the bathrooms and the backdoor.

Don't run. Don't run. They'll for sure notice you if you run through the restaurant.

She was two strides from the open doorway when she heard, "That's her," come from the middle of the restaurant. The jig was up. And that's when she ran.

After she stepped through the doorway, made a left, and headed down the hallway, she pulled her jacket from her purse and yanked it on. She was almost to the bathrooms when she looked back to see if they were following her. Nothing... yet.

And that's when she slammed into a brick wall. When she looked up to see who she ran into, she was embarrassed to admit that her kitty clenched even in the middle of the life-threatening situation she was in. The man standing in front of her was the bad-boy of all of her deepest, darkest fantasies — tall, broad shoulders, a little wild-looking, a full beard.

"Woah," he rumbled out. *Fuck! That voice!* It was deep and just the right amount of rough. She wanted to hear it growl her name.

You don't have time for this, Kisy! Unless she used it to her advantage.

Thinking quickly, Kisy dropped to her knees and looked up at the stranger. "Please, just play along." Then she yanked open his jeans and pulled down his zipper.

She saw his eyes widen at her movements. He opened his mouth to respond, but quickly slammed it shut. She figured out why when she heard the heavy footfalls behind her. Praying her scheme worked, she leaned forward and buried her head in the stranger's crotch area. Was she actually doing anything? No! But the suits didn't need to know that. Hopefully, they would just assume the stranger and his woman were just being adventurous.

When the stranger let out a fake satisfied moan and gripped each side of her head, Kisy acknowledged she was a horny bitch as her kitty did more than clench, but she was also grateful that the stranger seemed to be doing what she asked.

"Where'd she go?" Suit one asked.

"Don't know, Man," Stranger growled. "I'm a little fucking preoccupied. Fuck. Yeah, Babe, just hold it right there."

Kisy couldn't miss the bulge that was growing up against her face. Apparently, the stranger was doing more than just playing along.

"Alley," Suit Two barked.

Then the footfalls got quieter as they made their way down the hall and out of the building.

Kisy breathed a sigh of relief and pulled her head back from him. The man smelled like the best ambrosia – pine, spice, and something a little feral. She wanted to bathe in the scent. Glancing up at him, she found him staring down at her with one eyebrow raised.

Kisy let out a nervous laugh as she climbed to her feet and slid her purse's straps onto her shoulder. "Uh... thank you. Really. I appreciate it. But... uh... I gotta go. So... nice meeting you." She turned to head to the front of the building, but the stranger stepped in front of her. Kisy looked up at him again. He had strawberry blond hair, heavy on the strawberry, that was a bit wild and down to his shoulders. The beard on his face was a bit long and copper colored. What stopped her dead was the intensity in his eyes. She would bet good fucking money that he could kill someone with a look if he really wanted to.

"Want to tell me what that was about?" he rumbled in a way she knew it was less of a request and more a demand. The word *Dom* slid across her mind, making the aforementioned Kitty purr.

"I just need to lose some obsessive followers," Kisy replied. "I really should go before they come back." Taking a chance, she reached up, curling her hand around the back of his neck and pulling him down to her as she lifted up on her tiptoes. She gave him a quick but firm kiss to the softest set of male lips she had ever kissed before. Then she dropped back down to her heels and went to step around him. He let her, but she noticed he was following her out of the restaurant. "What are you doing?"

Still following her, he ignored her question and asked one of his own. "Where did you park?"

"In the alley, unfortunately."

He let out an annoyed sigh. What in the hell does he have to be annoyed about?

"Why are you following me?" She stopped and turned to face him, worried she went from one set of thugs out to kidnap her and do whatever to a new stalker.

"Fine. Get on the bike." He pointed to a black Harley-Davidson motorcycle with a green and white design painted on the side of the tank.

She barked out a shocked laugh. "Yeah. That ain't happening, Slick."

Annoyance flashed in those intense green eyes as he stepped toward her, backing her up against the brick wall of the building. He lowered his head closer, keeping eye contact. In a low but tense voice, he ordered, "Get. On. The. Bike."

Kisy swallowed hard. "Yes, Sir," she breathed out, ignoring the fact that her entire body shivered at the tone he used on her, and not in fear, either.

He stepped back and held out an arm to the bike. Kisy swallowed hard again and took a step toward it. That's when she noticed the key in the ignition. Either this guy was trusting or everyone in the city knew better than to steal this man's bike. Probably the latter.

A part of her felt as if she could trust this man, but she had been stuck in self-preservation mode for ten days. That's what caused her to hop on that beast of a bike, start it, and take off before the stranger could lift a leg to straddle the piece of engineering beauty. Ignoring the honking from the car she cut off, Kisy sent up a prayer of thanks to her grandfather, who went out of his way to teach her how to handle anything he could think of that had an engine. She'd been riding motorbikes since she was a kid, the size of the bike increasing with her skill level. While the stranger's bike was big and heavy, she wasn't completely overwhelmed by it. In the hot mess her life had become, she was taking that as a win.

Dragon

As Dragon watched the little minx take off on his bike, part of him was extremely pissed the hell off. The rest of him was turned the fuck on, including his wolf, who was panting and pacing inside of him.

"Fuck. Did she just take off with your bike?" Bullet removed his sunglasses as he stopped his bike in the spot Dragon's bike had just left.

"Yes," Dragon gritted out as he slid on the back of Bullet's bike. If nothing else, the little minx was getting her ass spanked for making him ride bitch on his best friend's bike. "Follow her!"

Chuckling, Bullet took off in pursuit of the sexy bike thief. He could still hear Bullet's laughter two blocks down the road. Fucking tigers.

"By the way," Bullet shouted, "Brute and Ranger are following the suited shit stains."

In the whirlwind that was the little minx of a stranger, Dragon totally forgot about the men. That was unlike him. He was usually in complete control and kept his eye on the ball. If that was any indication of what this woman could do to him, he was in big fucking trouble.

The men they had been following were underlings to a drug-lord and human-trafficker named Donald J. Alito. Alito was the husband to a woman Bullet saved from the side of the road when her truck broke down. After some coaxing, Harlow, the woman Bullet saved, admitted that she was on the run from her husband and her uncle because she witnessed an execution they committed. In true Howlers MC fashion, they stepped up to help the woman and to make her safe again, which meant eliminating the threat to her life.

The pursuit of that brought him to Grand Rapids, Michigan, and following Alito and his men, which is what he was doing when the little minx dropped to her knees in front of him. Why the men were following her, he didn't know, but he wanted to find out. And he would find out, just as soon as he got his bike back.

T.S. Tappin

Chapter Two

Dragon

It took everything in Dragon to keep from launching himself off Bullet's bike until he parked it next to his own in the gas station parking lot. As he got off the bike, he glanced through the windows of the store and spotted the little minx waiting near the restroom door.

Dragon didn't even say a word to Bullet as he stalked toward the door to the gas station and shoved it, sending the door slamming into a display of boxes of crackers, knocking them over onto the floor.

Ignoring the shout of the cashier, Dragon stalked across the store, customers stepping out of his way. *Smart*. He stopped a couple feet from the little minx and took her elbow in his hand, so she didn't skitter out of facing her consequences for her little stunt.

His wolf was prowling and panting, a mix of desire and anxiety.

"Do you need to use the restroom?"

The little minx glared up at him. "Yes," she hissed.

Just then, the door to the restroom opened and an older woman stepped out, eyeing them warily. Dragon didn't blame her. He was intimidating on any day, but he was sure his aggravation was also written all over his face. To be honest, he wouldn't be surprised if she called the cops just because he looked like he was crazy.

Bringing his eyes back to the little minx, he gently pushed her toward the restroom. "Then go. I'll be right here. So, there's no point in trying to wait me out."

Her glare intensified as she stomped into the bathroom, made a show of yanking the door shut, and Dragon heard the lock engage.

In a minute, she was walking out of the restroom, still wiping her hands dry with a paper towel. When he again took hold of her elbow, she threw the paper towel at him. Dragon bit back his smirk.

Then he walked her out of the store and over to his bike, ignoring her every time she tried to yank her elbow out of his grasp. Dragon also ignored the smirk on Bullet's face. His best friend knew him too well.

"Get on the bike," Dragon said as he yanked his key from the bike. He heard Bullet snort a laugh at the move. With a huff, she got on, making his wolf let out a satisfied growl because she followed his order. Then he climbed on the bike in front of her.

"I'm bringing her with us. She's on the run from something. She won't tell me the details, yet," he told Bullet, since he was sure Bullet was wondering what he planned to do with the little minx.

"Hey! Stop talking about me like I'm not fucking here."

Dragon totally ignored her and continued, "But it has something to do with Alito's two lug nuts."

"Alito? Donald Alito?"

Dragon looked over at Bullet intently before he turned to look over his shoulder at the woman. "How are you connected to Alito?"

"And if I tell you? What do I get?" The snark in her tone, despite the quiver there, irritated him but also made him want to bend her over his lap, spank her ass until it was a pretty pink, and then play with her until she came all over him. *Damn woman!*

Instead of answering her question right away, Dragon let out a frustrated growl. "What I give you will either be a reward or a punishment. You'll enjoy both, but one is faster than the other. Pick your poison."

Dragon's gaze dropped to her throat and then her chest when the little minx visibly swallowed, and her breathing quickened a bit. Yeah, his little minx was thinking about his threat and liking it. He brought his stare back up to hers.

"He's my boss," she breathed, her eyes locked to Dragon's.

Dragon gave her a rare smile and growled, "Good girl." His wolf agreed.

Kisy's breath caught, and then a whimper slid from her lips. Dragon wanted to find the nearest bed and get right on delivering those consequences. Fuck, just the thought of spanking her ass had his jeans getting tighter. He didn't dare allow himself to think too hard about her response to him. If he did, he wouldn't be able to focus on the mission he was supposed to be on with Bullet and his other brothers.

But knowing that she was running from Alito's men and Alito was her boss, there was no way he could just turn her loose. He was going to find a way to make her safe, even if that meant he had to turn the mission over to someone else. If making her safe also ended with her tied to his bedposts and his face between her thighs... Well, he didn't think either of them would complain about it.

"What's your name?" Bullet blurted out and Dragon knew it was because of the long stare he was sharing with her and the whimper that escaped her lips. Bullet's question was liking snapping fingers right in front of his face.

The woman jolted out of her daze and looked over at Bullet. "Kaitlyn, but my friends call me Kisy."

Dragon bit his lower lip, still staring over his shoulder at Kaitlyn. "Mmm... yeah, Kisy fits."

"So, Alito is your boss? Why were the lug nuts chasing you?"

Kisy's gaze dropped down to her hands in between her torso and Dragon's back. "Uh... I don't think I'm ready to... answer that. I mean... I don't know either of you."

Dragon didn't like her sudden unease. It wasn't intentional, but he shifted from Dragon to *D* when he firmly but warmly ordered, "Look at me." He waited for her to lift her gaze to his before he continued, "I will do everything I can to protect you. You have nothing to fear from me or Bullet or anyone else wearing a Howlers MC cut. Tell me what you're running from, and I promise to make things right... or at the very least, make you safe."

There was a catch in breath, but then she let it all out. She told them her story. When she was obviously close to the end of her story, it struck Dragon how close her story was to Harlow's. Another woman on the run from a sick bastard who has no concept of the value of innocent life.

Dragon was feeling so much rage that he whipped around to face front and saw a flash of green light shine from his eyes before he was about to slam his lids shut. Dragon forced himself to suck in a deep breath through his nose and slowly exhale. And again.

While Dragon was getting his anger under control, he heard Bullet say, "You won't have to worry about Alito or any of his men for much longer. We promise you that."

"You don't understand," she uttered, voice full of desperation. "He's got a lot of money... and resources."

From the corner of Dragon's eye, he saw Bullet wink at her as Bullet said, "We do, too."

And that's when Dragon's phone rang. Dragon answered the call and put the phone to his ear. "Yeah?"

It was Axle, calling to inform Dragon that Harlow was gone and what they knew. When Axle said the words *Harlow's gone,* Bullet's face twisted, and a low roar came from his mouth as his eyes gave that gold glow and his fangs began to slide down.

When Dragon ended the call, he repeatedly tried to get Bullet's attention without drawing the attention of others. When that didn't work, he climbed off the bike and got right in Bullet's face. Bullet hissed.

It wasn't often Dragon experienced fear, but in that moment, he feared for his friend. If something happened to Harlow, he wasn't sure how Bullet would get through that or even if he would at all.

After another round of trying to get a response from Bullet, Dragon lifted his hand right between their faces and snapped his fingers.

Bullet jolted and blinked.

"We're in fucking public, brother. Pull it together." Dragon knew Bullet wouldn't want anyone to baby him, so he wouldn't do that. *Gentle insistence with a hint of demand.*

The hissing stopped, and Bullet closed his eyes, obviously making a significant effort to breathe and pull himself together. In and out. In and out. Over and over, until his fangs retracted.

While Bullet regained control, Dragon texted Ranger to get an update. After a moment, he got a voice message in response.

"There ya go, brother. Now, listen to me. She took off, they think. They are tracking her. As far as Axle can tell, she was trying to protect you... and the rest of us. They think he picked her up after she took off. But we'll get her back, brother. We *will* save your mate."

Bullet gave a nod. Through a raw, dry throat, he asked, "Where are Ranger and Brute?"

"They are trailing Alito's men. From what they can gather, after they lost Kisy, they called Alito and he told them to head to Warden's Pass, because that's the direction they are going."

"What?" Kisy started climbing off Dragon's bike. "I'm outta here. I'm not going *toward* them. Look. Thanks for the bailout back there at the restaurant, but I need to go."

"Kisy," Dragon said, sliding into D mode, and she stilled, "stay on that damn bike or you'll earn that punishment you just avoided. You're coming with us, because it's the safest place for you to be."

"We need to go," Bullet said.

Dragon met Bullet's stare and asked, "Are you in control?"

Bullet swallowed hard and gave a nod.

"Good. Let's go show these assholes what happens when you fuck with a Howlers ol' lady."

Kisy

After they rode into a small town she had never heard of, called Warden's Pass, Bullet kept on down the main road, but Dragon took a left. A few minutes and a few turns later, he turned down a cul-de-sac that had a two-story strip mall on the left, an auto shop and another two-story building on the right, and what looked to be an apartment building on the end. He turned into a lot between the auto shop and the two-story building, backing into a spot against the building and cutting the engine.

"What is this place?"

Dragon hiked a finger over his shoulder toward the side of the building. Kisy looked at where he pointed and saw a sign bearing the same logo that was on the back of the leather vest he was wearing—a wolf howling made of green flame. Above the wolf said *Howlers*. Below the wolf said *Michigan*, with a small *MC* on the side.

"Is this your headquarters?"

Dragon got off the bike and held out a hand to her. As she took it and he helped her to her feet, he answered, "Our clubhouse." Then he let out a loud whistle.

Two seconds later, a long-haired middle-aged man stepped out of the clubhouse and looked over. At first, the expression on his face was one full of *I will kill any threat*. Then it faded and he approached.

"Brother."

Dragon gave a nod. "This is Kaitlyn. She's tied to Alito. I need her safe."

"Consider it done. I'll bring her to Gorgeous to hang."

"Thanks, brother." Dragon and the long-haired man did some handshake-back slap thing, before Dragon threw a leg over his bike, started it, and took off.

Kisy watched him leave and narrowed her eyes at his back. He just left... without even saying anything to her. Just dropped her off with strangers. Not that *he* wasn't a stranger, but still!

"I'm Rex," the long-haired man said with a chuckle.

Kisy looked up at him. The man was tall, over six feet tall, and barrel-chested. His long hair looked to be blond but was turning white gray. The smile on his face was warm and welcoming, and Dragon said she could trust anyone wearing a vest like Dragon's. *A cut*, he had called it.

"Kisy," she replied. "Kaitlyn, but my friends call me Kisy."

"Well, nice to meet you, Kisy."

They shook hands. Then he led her into the clubhouse, explaining, "The women are hanging out in the cafeteria area. I'll introduce you to the president's ol' lady, Gorgeous."

"Ol' lady? That's not what it sounds like, right?"

Rex chuckled again as they crossed a room with tables, chairs, and a bar. "You're correct. It's a title of respect in our world. It means she's a sister to all of us — she's family — and the commitment between her and her biker is more serious than most people take a marriage."

Kisy nodded. Sounded pretty awesome to her.

On the other end of the large room, they walked through a wide doorway and into a room with long tables and lots of chairs. On the wall across the room was an extremely large screen television, where a romantic comedy was playing.

"Who is this?" a curvy blond asked with a smile as she walked over to them.

"This is Kisy. Dragon dropped her off."

The blond's eyes widened a bit. "Oh! Okay. Well, it's nice to meet you, Kisy. I'm Ashlyn or, as the guys call me, Gorgeous."

Kisy smiled at the woman. She seemed very nice. "Nice to meet you too."

"I got her," Gorgeous told Rex and slid her arm around Kisy's and began leading her further into the room.

Kisy looked over her shoulder to see Rex chuckling and stepping back through the doorway.

"Come on. I'll introduce you to the girls."

Dragon

Dragon found Bullet's bike parked about a mile down the road from the Aikman farm. He parked there next to it and got off his bike. After shifting to his wolf, he darted through the woods until he found Bullet, Axle, Trip, Pike, Striker, Siren, and Rock gathered at the tree line, discussing a plan to save Harlow.

In Dragon's opinion, they were wasting time. He shifted back to human and said, "Two groups. One goes in front. One goes in back. Humans wait outside for any runners and will have guns ready."

Bullet shrugged. "Works for me. But I'm going in as tiger. They will know fear before they die."

"Let's do this," Dragon said with a nod.

He saw Axle throw his hands up in the air in annoyance and turn around to head toward the edge of the field separating the woods from the house. "I guess we're going with their plan," he growled.

Dragon knew he and Bullet were walking on the edge of disrespect and would have to deal with Axle's annoyance at some point, but that was a later problem.

T.S. Tappin

Chapter Three

Dragon

Without waiting for the rest of them to get their shit together, Bullet and Dragon silently headed across the field, separating about halfway across. While Bullet headed to the back, Dragon moved toward the front of the house. He was carefully climbing the old wood steps, trying not to make noise and alert the assholes inside to their presence.

He managed to climb the steps and cross the porch to the front door without incident. Reaching out, he grasped the knob and slowly turned it, a little surprised when it turned easily. They hadn't even locked the door? *Idiots!* Not that locks would stop him, but still, it would have slowed him down a bit.

Taking a deep breath, he told his wolf it was showtime. Then he swung the door open and shifted. Scanning the room with his eyes, he saw Alito on the ground and two men to his right, one of the suited lug nuts and a guy in cargo pants. A third man, the other lug nut, was across the room, with a grip on Harlow's hair, yanking it back. He released a loud growl and noticed Bullet's tiger in the doorway just beyond where the man and Harlow were. Bullet let out a roar, his fangs on full display, along with the rage in the tiger's eyes.

"What the fuck?" one of the men called out as they finally noticed him there. "A fucking wolf!"

"Don't run. Predatory animals will hunt you down." This from the only man in the room not wearing a fucking suit.

"So just sit here and let them eat us?!"

Sounded good to Dragon. Without hesitation, he launched himself at the one in the cargo pants. As the guy tripped, trying to back away from the snarling wolf, Dragon was able to get a grip on the man's neck with his jaws. A few vicious tosses of his head and the man crumpled to the floor, dead.

As Dragon turned his attention to the suited man screaming his head off about what Dragon had just done, there was a commotion behind him. Trusting Bullet to handle it, Dragon jumped and landed on the screaming man's chest, bringing him to the floor, and tore the man apart until there was nothing left but scattered parts.

He was not ashamed to say he did the same with the first man when he was done, letting out all the rage and frustration he held inside.

As the club's enforcer, it was his responsibility to help Pike keep the club safe. It was his responsibility to keep their family safe. Yeah, he wasn't the only one, but he still took it personally when one of the brothers or their family members were put in danger. In just over a year, over a dozen had either been injured, in a dangerous situation, or kidnapped. It had to end. He had to find a way to end it.

Still working on decimating the two jackasses, Dragon heard a hiss from Bullet. He looked in that direction and saw Bullet snap his jaw together, letting the remaining lug nut know he wasn't playing any fucking games.

Lug nut let go of Harlow's hair and tried to turn to run for the front door.

Dragon launched himself in front of it to stop him, but it didn't matter. Bullet had vaulted over Harlow and had wrapped his tiger jaws around the man's head. With a yank, Lug nut's body fell to the floor, head-less.

They heard a moan from the left, and that's all it took for Bullet to spit out the head of Lug nut and turn his attention on Alito. Bullet and Dragon locked eyes for a moment and a deal was struck. They would make sure this motherfucker never hurt either of their women again. Bullet took one end of Alito's body. Dragon took the other. And they made sure he'd never be able to recover.

Bullet

After his rage drained out of him, Bullet noticed the blood on Harlow's face. He instantly shifted and moved toward her. Grabbing the front of his shirt and yanking it up to wipe off his face and hands, in case any blood was still there. When he reached her, he cupped her head in his hands and tried to see where she was bleeding from.

"Butterfly, you're hurt."

She was visibly shaking, and he was sure she was in shock.

He noticed a cut on her cheek but found a trail of blood above it. He followed the trail and saw a gash just inside her hairline.

"Are you injured anywhere other than your cheek and your head?" He started looking her over, running his hands over her body, looking for anything broken or out of place. When he glanced down, he saw what was attached to the heel of her shoe and winced. "Butterfly, I need you to trust me. Don't look down. I'm going to take off your boots. Okay?"

After a moment, she nodded at him, but she was still panting and shaking.

Bullet reached down and unzipped both boots, pulling them off her feet, and tossing them over in the corner. It would not help her to see her husband's eyeball stuck to the bottom of her heel, like a horror shish kebab.

"You... Dragon..."

"We're okay." He leaned forward and scooped her up in his arms. After giving her a kiss to her temple, he added, "We're just fine."

"I thought I wasn't... I thought..." She closed her eyes and took a deep breath. After a moment, she tried again. "I thought I wasn't going to make it out of here alive, but I was going to try. I just... I wanted him to suffer, but I couldn't take on all of them, so I did what I could."

Bullet chuckled as he carried her out of the house. "Well, what I learned is to not piss you off while you're wearing stilettos."

His worry about her began to ease as he watched her roll her eyes at him and gave a slight smile.

Yeah, she'd be okay.

"I do need to pee, Liam," she confessed.

He chuckled and promised to get her home as soon as he could.

Dragon

After shifting back, Dragon hung out by the front door and gave Bullet and Harlow some privacy, trying his best not to listen.

When Bullet scooped her up in his arms and headed for the back door, Dragon followed, but stayed on guard in case there was another threat they weren't aware of.

What they witnessed when they reached the bottom of the porch steps brought Dragon's anxiety right back up to explosive levels. Coming out of the woods at the back of the property and crossing the field, heading for the club members, were about a dozen people he'd never seen before.

While Bullet carried Harlow behind the line of Howlers that had formed in front of Axle, President of the Howlers, Dragon moved into position in that line, standing next to Pike. Together, they would protect their president. Guns out and aimed at the newcomers, none of the Howlers would hesitate to shoot if they felt it necessary in order to protect their club.

When Axle pushed his way past Pike and Dragon, both of them cursed under their breaths and shared a look. Dragon knew better than to push the issue with Axle in front of the newcomers. He was already walking on thin ice with his president. Questioning him in front of strangers? That was one way to get his ass handed to him. Dragon may be a big guy who could handle himself, but Axle wasn't their president *only* because he was a smart fucker.

The female in the middle was fit and muscular, athletic, with black hair she kept cut short and rich, dark brown skin. She was a beautiful woman, who was only more attractive when you saw the intelligence there in her eyes. That intelligence is what really set Dragon on edge. He knew not to underestimate her.

She stepped forward. "I'm Lira. It's nice to meet you, Orlan 'Axle' Weber. We were sent to help you out of the mess you've created. We were going to start with helping balance things for Harlow, but alas, it appears we were too late." The woman gave a forced smile. "But balance is the name of the game."

"Who do you work for?"

Her forced smile turned genuine. "I assure you that you don't know him. But he knows all of you. The God of Balance has an interest in making sure this war you're in with the Hell's Dogs doesn't result in shifters being outed to the humans."

Axle scoffed, and Dragon didn't blame him. God of Balance? What in the holy fuck?

Warily eying Lira, Axle asked, "And why would the God of Balance give a damn about a minor war between bikers?"

"The bikers in charge of the opposition have secret weapons of their own. Variulisis — a varium blocker, also known as an anti-shifting medicine — and feral shifters are going to make the scales even more unbalanced than they already were. But we'll get into that. So, you can doubt us all you want. You, however, do not have the power to turn us away. Only the gods can do that."

Still skeptical, Axle uttered, "The hard way or the easy way, we're fighting with you at our sides?"

Lira elbowed the female to her right, a curvy woman with olive skin, black hair that was long, and green eyes. "Look at that. He's smarter than he looks."

Trip snorted a laugh. "I think Gorgeous might argue about that."

Dragon looked over and caught Trip's gaze. Dragon just stared him down. The man was a fucking menace in times like this. He never knew when to be fucking serious. Trip rolled his eyes but gave a nod. Dragon returned his eyes to the exchange between Axle and Lira.

When Axle opened his mouth, as if to tell the woman to take her tall tale and shove it, Lira approached him, ignoring the fact that there were multiple guns aimed in her direction, stopping three feet away from Axle, and held out her hand to Axle. Raising an eyebrow at Axle she just waited. Dragon watched as Axle cautiously reached out and took her hand.

Suddenly, Axle looked freaked the fuck out.

Lira grinned at Axle and uttered, "They don't even know you were gone."

"What," he heard Pike ask. "What does that mean?"

Dragon wanted to know the same damn thing.

Kisy

As Kisy sat and watched the movie with the women, she wasn't paying any attention to what was happening on the screen. Her mind kept wandering to the weird things that happened at the gas station.

The light that came from their eyes startled her, but it couldn't have come from their eyes, right? Certainly, it had to have been a reflection from something else. Light doesn't just shine from eyes like that.

Then again, fangs don't appear in a human's mouth and the sounds they were making don't happen, either.

It had to be a stress reaction. She was making it up. She had to be. It was just what the brain did when it was stressed to the max. Right?

Kisy pushed the thoughts away. She couldn't deal with them. It would take more brain power than she had available. Sleeping in her car for days had amounted to very little actual sleep. That's it. She just needed sleep.

In an effort to block that all out, she looked around her at the women still in the room. Not long after she arrived, a copper-haired woman took all the kids and said she was bringing them to the kids' room for a sleepover. Kisy didn't know what that meant, but the woman seemed really nice. If she remembered correctly, the woman's cut said her name was Ginger.

Ginger's cut was different from Dragon's or Bullet's, though. Hers had a purple and pink logo with a tiger on the back and read *Tiger's Claw* instead of *Howlers*. A few others in the room had cuts like that, but none of them introduced themselves to her.

Gorgeous introduced her to what she coined *The Ol' Ladies*. There was Darlin', who was married to Trip, and was also Dragon's sister. Kisy could see the resemblance in their hair and eyes, but unlike Dragon, Darlin' was tall and thin.

She also met Pixie, who was just like you would expect her to be—petite, blond, short hair, sea-blue eyes. Her attitude wasn't small, though. She was outspoken and hilarious, but there wasn't a mean bone in her body. Kisy thought Pixie would be her type of friend if she was around her for more than the night. Apparently, she was with Pike.

Sugar was a sweet brunette. She said Siren was her man and she mentioned that the two of them balanced each other well. To this, Gorgeous giggled and said, "Yeah, she's gentle and sweet. He's hard and intense." And Sugar's cheeks turned a nice shade of pink.

Another blond introduced herself as Peanut and said she was with Striker. She was a knock-out and had the confidence to match, but she was somehow also shy.

Gorgeous mentioned that there were two other unofficial members of their little club—Mary and

Butterfly. She didn't ask what made them unofficial, but she remembered something Dragon and Bullet said about Butterfly being the one needing rescue. Gorgeous confirmed that Butterfly was Bullet's woman and told her that Mary was Rock's woman, but she lived on the other side of the state and hadn't made the move back yet.

Gorgeous followed that up with, "And then there's you."

Kisy looked at her, thinking Gorgeous had lost her mind. "Uh... I met Dragon and Bullet like two hours ago. I'm no one's *woman*."

She noticed Darlin' and Gorgeous exchange looks, but she didn't call them on it. Then Gorgeous smiled at her and said, "My mistake."

They were brief comments, but she picked up a few choice words about what her boss had been up to. After what she witnessed, learning that he had been into drug and human trafficking wasn't a surprise, but it still freaked her out even more. If the Howlers took him out, she wouldn't say a thing to anyone. She would consider that as them taking out the trash. She had a feeling there was more to the story, but she knew enough to make the determination to keep her mouth shut about however the Howlers chose to handle it.

Slowly, the women left the room, until she and Gorgeous were the only two remaining. Kisy caught Gorgeous yawning for the third time and said, "You can go to bed if you want. You seem tired. I'll be fine."

"If you're sure?"

Kisy nodded and smiled at her. "Thank you for being so kind to me. But, yes, I'm sure. Go to bed."

Gorgeous gave her a hug and left the room. Kisy heard Gorgeous talking to Rex for a moment, then Rex stepped in to ask Kisy if she needed anything.

"Nah. I'm good. If I want a drink, I know where the bar is."

Rex gave a nod. "I'll be doing patrols outside. If you need me, just open the door and give a shout."

"Will do." Once he was gone, Kisy was left on her own to wait for Dragon to return. Hopefully then, he would tell her what in the hell was going on and how she was getting back to Grand Rapids and her car.

Dragon

Knowing he was returning to Kisy and planned on giving her his room for the night, he texted Darlin' to see if she'd do a quick cleaning of the place. He kept things pretty tidy, but he had no intentions of telling Kisy it was his room. Why he wanted her in his room so badly, he wasn't going to examine. He just knew he did.

As he rode with his brothers back to the compound, he told himself to keep Kisy out of his thoughts as much as possible. Riding with a hard-on wasn't exactly comfortable. But his brain kept straying to her.

He breathed a sigh of relief when they finally approached the street that the compound was on. After they parked in the lot, Bullet and Harlow headed for their room, while Dragon went into the clubhouse to get Kisy.

Sexy Kisy, with the sweet curves and the audacity for fucking days. It took a lot to send him into bewilderment, but that little spitfire managed it. She had to be a foot shorter than him, and he could take her with one hand behind his back, but she managed to steal his bike and it boggled his mind. That was a hard thing to do. He was usually on top of things — sharp, and observant. Dragon, on his game, wouldn't have let her, or anyone else for that matter, drive off with his bike. He would have managed to pick up on what she was going to do and stopped her.

But he saw the way she shivered just a bit when he used his commanding voice. It wasn't a voice he used often, but there were usually orgasms involved. But when he used it on her, he noticed the way it went right to the heart of her. Or the core of her, if he was being accurate. Yeah, he noticed that shit.

And fuck him, if he didn't drool at the sight of her on her knees in front of him. His wolf had let out a growl and demanded they keep her. She had soft, blond hair with enough wave to make it look a bit wild. It wasn't the color, though, it was the feel of it in his hands as he held her head close to him. If that's the effect she had on him while he still had his jeans on, he was eager to see what would happen if, no what will happen when, she dropped to her knees in front of him while they were both fucking naked.

He yanked open the front door of the clubhouse and stepped inside as he thought about those wide, light gray eyes looking up at him, almost begging for instruction, and looking forward to defying those instructions. She might not even know it, but she was a sub. *His sub.* And without a doubt, he planned to be the one to make her aware of it.

"There you are!" Kisy rushed up to him, concern and relief on her face. "Did you find her?"

Relief swamped him at the sight of her. He was grateful he didn't have to go and track her down.

His wolf instantly began wagging his tail like a golden retriever and soaked up her attention. Damn mutt. "Yeah, Kisy, we did." He gently gripped her shoulders and gave them a reassuring squeeze.

"Is she okay?"

"Relatively. Her bruises and cuts will heal."

She let out a sigh of relief and dropped her gaze to his chest. "Good. That's good. Did everyone else get out... okay?"

Dragon nodded, but she wasn't looking at him, so he uttered, "Everyone who matters. Not sorry to tell you that your boss is no longer with us."

"Well, I heard some stuff while I was hanging here with the girls. I like them, by the way. They're pretty cool." She shook her head as if to reroute her thoughts to the right path. "And I learned some stuff about my boss. So, can't say I'm sorry to hear that, either."

"We have a conversation to have," he told her and waited for her to look up at him.

She didn't. She looked everywhere but at him. "Uh... I realize tonight is probably not the time to bring me back to GR, but I left my car and all my stuff at that restaurant. So, do you think you could bring me back there in the morning? Or maybe I could hire a cab. Or, I dunno, I'll figure it out." She stepped back a couple steps and his arms dropped from her shoulders. "But I do need a place to sleep. Can you direct me to the closest hotel? Or motel, even."

"Kisy," he said using *the voice*. Damn, he was using it a lot on her. That would have to change. He had to pull himself together. He had to make sure she was on board, but fuck, even his wolf was growling his dominance over her. He had never done that before.

Her eyes shot up to his face. "Hmm?"

"Sit down in that chair." He pointed at one at the closest table. He sent up a prayer to the gods that she actually listened to him. Once she was sitting, he turned the chair next to her and took a seat, so he was facing her. "First, the place to sleep. You'll be staying here. We have empty rooms. One of them will be yours… for now. Secondly, your stuff. I'll send someone to pick it up."

"That's not necessary."

"I wasn't done." He held her gaze firmly with his own. "We aren't done with the men that were working with Alito, so I can't have you running around out there, unsafe. You'll stay here where I can protect you or my brothers can protect you. We'll talk about why you seem to be closing yourself off to the feelings you might be having about your boss's actions and his death, but that won't happen tonight. What we're going to talk about tonight, is the fact that you hopped on my bike and rode off with it. You never take a man's bike without his approval."

Kisy scowled at him. "You're the one who ordered me to get on it."

"This isn't a debate."

She huffed out a sigh. "Fine. You're right. I shouldn't have borrowed your bike."

"Borrowed?"

An eye roll. "Okay, fine. Stole your bike."

Dragon let out a low chuckle. "Oh, Love, you sure are racking up the consequences."

"Consequences?"

Dragon just raised an eyebrow.

He could tell when the realization hit her. Her eyes widened a bit and her breath caught in her throat. He could even hear her heart beating, it was pounding so hard.

"Oh, fuck a duck," she breathed.

Dragon leaned toward her a bit, holding her gaze as he let his tongue run along his lower lip. "Nah, Love. I'd rather fuck you."

Chapter Four

Kisy

Kisy was not going to think about Dragon's words. No. Nope. Not gonna. If she thought about them, she was afraid she'd just strip and lay herself out on a table for him to do as he pleased. Every time he used *that voice* on her, she had to squeeze her legs together in order to ease the ache it caused.

"Let's get you settled for the night." Dragon stood and held out a hand to her.

Taking a deep breath, she refused to acknowledge how her hand shook as she reached out to take it. The list of things she wouldn't acknowledge or think about was getting pretty damn long.

"Where are we going?" she asked as she let him lead her.

"To one of the spare rooms."

Dragon led her down a hallway and took a left into another hallway. At the end of it, he pushed through a door, and they stepped into what looked to be a stairwell. Besides the obvious stairs, it was a simple brick room painted a utilitarian gray and had an open doorway to the left that looked to lead to a hallway. Across from the open doorway was another door that looked to be a fire exit. The floors were a white and gray checkered tile. Nothing fancy, but it did seem to be kept clean.

Still holding onto Dragon's hand, Kisy followed him up the stairs and into a hall. The tile of the stairwell gave way to wood laminate flooring. The walls between the numerous doors were a darker green. Kisy didn't count, but there seemed to be a couple dozen doors split between the two sides of the hallway.

Dragon didn't let go of her hand as they walked down the hall. She kept wondering which room would be her temporary home for the night, but he just kept walking. Then he stopped in front of the last door and pulled his set of keys from his pocket.

While he unlocked the door, she took the moment to study him. His wild hair and beard should freak her out a bit, and she was sure he kept it like that for that exact reason, but it didn't. It made her think of how he would look after being freshly fucked.

Without looking at her, Dragon uttered, "Close your mouth, Love, or you'll drool on yourself."

Kisy slammed her mouth shut and glared at him as she swatted his arm with her hand. Dragon's response was just to give her a slight smile and swing the door open.

He motioned her inside the room and followed her. While he closed the door, she looked around. She didn't know what she was expecting, but it sure wasn't what she found. The walls were a light gray and pretty plain, except for the Howlers logo mounted on the space above the bed. The bed was huge. It had to be a king. She loved the solid, dark green comforter. It went well with the logo, but it also went well with Dragon.

He could tell her it was a spare room all he wanted, but she already knew his scent and this room was Dragon's. The spice and pine was all Dragon. It was a scent she wanted to bury her nose in and just... *be*.

Dragon cleared his throat. "Bathroom." He pointed to a door on the wall to the left. "Closet." The door next to it. "Extra clothes in the drawers. Everything you need in the bathroom."

The clipped way he spoke sometimes made her wonder what he was trying to keep himself from saying.

"I'll be across the hall. Seven doors down from this end." His gaze met hers and he stared for a long moment. "If you need anything."

She wanted to ask him if *anything* included *him*, because the more time she spent with him, the more she wanted to climb him like a tree. There was just something about the way he held himself, the way he spoke to her that snared her. She didn't ask him, though. She had thinking to do. And she knew if she was in a room, at night, with Dragon, there would be no thinking.

Kisy dropped her gaze to her hands as she waited for him to either say something else or go.

After a moment, she saw Dragon's hand lift, and he slid his knuckle under her chin to tilt her head back up. As she stared up at him, he leaned toward her. She thought he was going to kiss her, and her pussy was cheering him on, and he did, but it was a sweet kiss on her forehead.

Her heart swelled at the gentleness he gave her, but her body was throwing a tantrum that it was her forehead that got the attention.

"Lock the door," he said in a low voice. Then he left.

Kisy huffed out a breath and plopped down on the bed. The stubborn side of her refused to lock the door. She knew she was pouting, but damn it. That forehead kiss was a damn tease after what he said to her in the clubhouse.

"Kisy," he said through the door.

"Fine," she shouted back and got to her feet. She stomped over to the door and forcefully turned the lock. "There! You demanding bastard!"

All she got back was a chuckle and a promised, "You have no idea… yet."

Dragon

It took a feat of raw willpower to get Dragon to walk away from his own room and go down the hall to the spare room. He was positive she didn't realize she was biting her lip as she listened to him tell her where everything was in the room. That little bite had him craving doing things to her that he hadn't cleared with her. Hell, he hadn't cleared anything with her.

They seriously needed to have *the talk*, but first, he needed to find a way to keep her in town. Once he knew she wasn't going anywhere, they could have *the talk* and he could finally find out what it was like to make her come harder than she'd ever come before. And that wasn't ego. He would put in the work to make sure it was fact.

Dragon had known since he was a teenager that he liked to be in charge in most aspects of his life, but he figured out in his twenties that being in charge in the bedroom was the only way he'd be fully satisfied. Over the years, he'd had women who sub'd for him in the bedroom. He'd even enjoyed them, but he always knew something was missing from the interaction.

Now he knew what it was — his wolf had always been passive. His wolf was not passive when it came to Kisy. His wolf was demanding and panting for her.

He used the key to the spare room and unlocked the door. One of the great things about being part of the 'security team' for the club was having a set of keys for all of the club's properties and to the unoccupied rooms in the apartment building. He didn't really want to have to tell Axle that he was being a pussy and staying in a spare room for the night. And that's what he'd have to do in order to get a key if he didn't have the set.

Pushing open the door, he took a deep breath in through his nose and pushed it out through his mouth, forcing his jaw to loosen. He had spent the last hour with his jaws clamped shut unless he had to speak, in order to stop himself from laying out his boundaries and asking for hers. He hadn't even broached the subject, because if he knew what she liked and didn't like, there would be no way he would be able to stop himself from stripping her bare and taking his time making sure she knew he could be exactly what she needed.

Fuck! He needed to steel himself and regain some control. After removing his cut, he hung it on the hook on the closet door and began yanking off his clothes. They felt too tight... too *restricting*. Once he was naked, he put his hands to the edge of the dresser and forced himself to take a few more deep breaths.

His wolf was snarling at him, demanding he walk back down the hall and claim their woman. *Their woman*. Yeah, he knew it. He knew she was his mate just by the way the sight of her on her knees hit him in the gut. Knowing his wolf was reacting to her only made it worse. But this? The *their woman* thoughts only clinched it.

For a moment, he thought about just giving in. He thought about walking down there and laying it all out. Telling her what she could expect from him. Telling her that he would respect her boundaries, but he'd also care for her, physically and mentally, and protect her. Promising her to honor who she was as a person and let her be herself, but also promise to watch over her health and safety. Revealing to her that she was his – his mate, his ol' lady, his sub – but he was hers – her man, her protector, her Dom. But he didn't.

They only just met. They needed time. He needed to know she was hanging around. He needed to know she wanted the same things as him and his efforts wouldn't end in heartbreak.

As he battled his wolf and his urges, he told himself that he could think about her and what he wanted to do with her, but he couldn't act on it. Using the willpower he was known for, the willpower he'd honed over the years, he looked at himself in the mirror over the dresser. Staring into his own eyes, he let himself wonder what would have happened if he would have kissed her lips and not her forehead, if he just pressed his lips to hers.

Just the thought of feeling her soft lips on his had his dick hard as a steel pipe. He closed his eyes and let his mind wander down that path as he reached down and wrapped his hand around his erection. Would she open up right away or make him work for it? His little bratty sub would definitely make him work a little bit. She'd wait, make him lick along her bottom lip, nip and suck on it, until she gasped. He groaned and stroked his cock, just imagining dipping his tongue in between those lips.

He could still smell the arousal that hit her as soon as he said he'd rather fuck her. It was like a wildfire mixed with the smoothest whiskey and a dash of sweetness. He wanted her scent all over him, especially his beard. *Fuck!* To have her ride his face? Fucking perfect.

His hand moved faster and faster as ways to get that scent spread all over his body flashed through his mind. His other hand moved down to cup his balls as the scene from the restaurant appeared in his mind again. This time, they were both naked and she was looking up at him as she wrapped her lips around the head of his cock and sucked him all the way in, letting the tip of him hit the back of her throat. His imagined Kisy slid a hand down her stomach, at his direction, and circled her clit with a fingertip. That's all it took. The look of pure pleasure in her eyes mixed with the fact that he was already on edge had him shooting his load all over the front of the dresser.

As the pleasure of his climax rolled through him, Dragon let his head fall back and breathed out her name.

After cleaning up the ridiculously messy remnants of his hand job, Dragon floated into the bathroom for a shower. He was feeling a lot lighter. His wolf was still demanding their mate, but his control was back. His limbs felt loose and a bit tingly, like he had received the best massage and drank a half bottle of whiskey. It was what he needed to keep himself in check.

He reached into the shower as a yawn rolled up his throat and had him stretching. Bed sounded fantastic. His brain tried to conjure up the thought of Kisy wrapped in his black sheets, but he shut that shit down right quick. He couldn't think of that, or he'd be right back where he was before he worked out his fucking urges with his hand.

Not waiting for the shower to warm, he stepped inside and let the cold water jolt him back to the present and his reality. He was *alone* in the shower and that was it.

He grabbed a bar of the soap they kept stocked in the rooms on the shelf just outside the shower.

It was the kind he always used. Slipping it out of the box and dropping the box in the trash bin just below the shelf, he snorted at the way the Claws had designed the place during the remodel. They knew how the Howlers were. That's why the space for the trashcan was so close to the shower. Otherwise, most of his brothers would have tossed that box on the floor and never thought about it again. And since the Claws didn't want to live with bugs, they were usually willing to clean the Howlers MC's rooms *for a price,* and they weren't cheap. But the Howlers were good with forking over cash to not have to clean toilets or make beds.

Dragon was not one of those men. Sure, he had asked Darlin' a few times to tidy up, but he kept things mostly picked up. He figured it was just part of the control he liked to have. If his room was orderly, his mind was the same. Well, unless Kisy was in the picture. Then his mind was all over the fucking place.

Once again, he slammed the door shut in his mind on thoughts of his little minx. Instead, he focused on lathering the soap into a washcloth and cleaning his body. He was done with that and washing his hair and beard when he heard the roar.

After a smirk of satisfaction that they rescued his brother's woman and that was why that mating roar was possible, Dragon threw back his head and let out a howl to let his brother know he was happy for them. His howl mingled with the howls and roars of his brothers. They were a family. When one was happy, they all felt that right down to their core.

Knowing what was coming, he rinsed his hair and shut off the shower. He needed to get dressed and head down to the clubhouse. But first, he needed to check on his little minx. That display of shifter camaraderie had to have freaked her out.

Kisy

Okay... she didn't imagine that. And if she didn't imagine that the building she was in had erupted in sounds that you would only normally hear in a zoo, then she probably didn't imagine the hiss and fangs at the gas station.

She was not ashamed to admit that she had been pressing her face into his pillow and breathing in that spice and pine scent when the first roar rang through the air. Fuck! He smelled so damn good. She wondered if it was a cologne or a soap or just because he spent a lot of time on his bike. Hell... with the sounds she was hearing... it could be... No. That shit wasn't real. It wasn't.

But she did hear the roars and the howls. She *did* see the fangs and hear the hiss. And then, there was that light from their eyes.

Kisy rolled back over and laid her head back on the pillow. She was torn between wanting to keep herself grounded and wanting to believe that she somehow stumbled into a romance novel where the men were good guys with a naughty streak, and *bonus,* could shift into wild animals and true love was an instinctual insta thing.

She was still arguing with herself when she heard the lock turn on the door and the door begin to open. There was a soft knock. For some reason, Kisy slammed her eyes shut and waited. Maybe she wasn't ready to confront what she just heard. Maybe she needed to examine things a little more before she told him what she knew, but either way, she pretended to be asleep and prayed that he would take it at face value and not step further into the room.

He must have, because the door shut again, and she heard the lock engage. After a few moments, she opened an eye and scanned the room. No Dragon.

Well... either she was in a building full of paranormal creatures, or she was losing her mind.

The worst part was she didn't know which one would be the bad thing.

Chapter Five

Dragon

Dragon was happy, not only for his brother, but also for Butterfly. Harlow had officially become Butterfly the moment she accepted Bullet for who and what he was. It was the way the Howlers let her know she was one of them, part of their family. That was what the gathering was about – officially welcoming her into their family.

Knowing what everyone was gathering in the clubhouse for, Dragon felt it important that he speak with Axle. It was a shock to him how close he had become with Butterfly, but their souls were evenly matched. There was a protectiveness they both felt deep that sealed a friendship between them. While with Sugar, he thought of her as a little sister and felt the need to be gentle, with Butterfly it was more a recognition of fierce strength. Like him, she was a warrior.

Axle didn't even let Dragon open his mouth to speak before he rolled his eyes and nodded. "You coming for all the perks of my job or just this one?" Axle asked, but his president didn't hold any animosity toward Dragon. He knew that. Axle was just giving him shit because Dragon had handed out more property cuts than he had.

"Nah, Pres, you got a shit job keeping our feral asses in line. You can keep it."

As Axle chuckled, Dragon motioned for the prospect behind the bar to hand him a beer. He could acknowledge the kid had a name, but the prospect hadn't earned that yet. If he wasn't a shifter, he wouldn't even be in the clubhouse for the ceremony.

Once he was handed the beer, Dragon leaned back against the bar and took a drink. While they waited for the lovebirds to arrive, the room filled with conversation. His brothers were talking to each other and their women. The women were talking to each other and the Howlers. The Claws trickled in and mingled with everyone. One of their prospects joined the Howlers MC prospect behind the bar.

Everyone knew the moment Bullet and Butterfly walked in. A cheer started near the back and worked its way through the place. Dragon looked over and saw them standing just inside the room from the back hallway.

Dragon watched Butterfly's face as Trip pushed his way through the crowd to greet her. She looked happy and grateful, but she also looked overwhelmed. He hated that she was so shocked that people could love her without hurting her, but he was honored to be a part of her finally receiving that.

"There they are," Trip called out as he pushed forward from the crowd and cupped her face in hands, ignoring the hiss from Bullet. "Welcome to the family, Butterfly." Then he wrapped her in a tight hug. Dragon knew part of that was to annoy Bullet, but mostly, it was to give her the comfort Trip knew she needed.

When he set her down and stepped aside, Dragon stepped forward. He gave her a hint of a smile to let her know he was happy for them. "You are a pain in the ass, but you're *our* pain in the ass." Then he hugged her.

"You really don't have to touch my woman," Bullet grumbled.

Dragon just rolled his eyes as he pulled back and reached behind him. Axle stepped forward and handed Dragon the cut.

"I keep stealing this job from Axle, but our president can just deal. After hearing your story and having that... moment with you, I feel like I've earned this. He agreed, so he gave me the honor. And it is an honor, Butterfly." He smiled at her again.

After taking a deep breath and meeting her gaze again, he raised his voice a bit and said, "By tying yourself to Bullet, you tied yourself to us and to our pack. By having his back, you have ours. By protecting him, you protect us. By loving him, you love us. We're a package deal. And we understand we're getting more out of the deal than you are. You will never need for anything for long. You will never want for anything for long. You will never suffer again. And if for some reason you do," growling and hissing filled the room, giving a voice to what Dragon was feeling, and bringing tears to her eyes, "the one who caused it will suffer far more for their efforts. I'm honored to call you my sister." He held out the leather cut he was holding.

Her hands trembled and tears ran down her cheeks as she reached out and took the cut from his hand. With a smile, she choked out, "Thank you, Dragon. You're very sweet."

Dragon scowled at that. He wasn't sweet, but he wouldn't argue with Butterfly over it.

She ignored the chuckles and scoffing laughs from the rest of the room as she held out the cut in front of her and looked it over. After taking it in, she slipped it on, and the sobs came pouring out of her.

Dragon didn't know what to do. Why was she crying? He thought the tears were from happiness, but sobs? Sobs of happiness?

Not knowing what else to do, he scooped her up in his arms and held her close to his chest. After a moment, she looked up at him and the sobbing stopped, but she started laughing.

"Are you okay? Are you having some kind of... breakdown?"

She rolled her eyes as she reached up and wiped the tears from her face. Dragon released her and took a step back, taking that as a confirmation that she was okay.

"I'm wonderful," she assured him. "I'm just happy to have all of you. This means more than you could ever know."

Dragon cleared his throat and blinked a few times in an effort to stop the tears that threatened to form in his eyes. Then he scowled. He hated getting emotional. "Why do women cry when they're happy? It's so damn confusing." He turned and stormed through the crowd to the bar.

Dragon heard Bullet chuckle and whisper to Butterfly, "Well, well, well. I think you just made our resident badass tear up."

Then he heard Butterfly respond, "He's such a softy."

That's when Trip burst out with laughter, choking on the drink of beer he'd just taken. Served him right for being such a traitorous bastard. Best friend, Dragon's ass.

As Darlin' pounded on Trip's back, she giggled and uttered, "He really is just a big softy, but he's going to scowl if you mention it."

"Because it's not fucking true," Dragon called out to his sister from the bar. "Damn it! I need to shoot something."

Then the whole room was laughing.

Dragon downed the rest of his beer and motioned for another one.

"Shots," Sugar called out, sounding tipsy.

Trip called back, "You sound like you've had enough."

Dragon looked over his shoulder in time to see Sugar flip Trip off. "I seem to remember you telling me it's tradition. And we will honor tradition, Trip. Don't make me tell your brother!"

Siren wrapped an arm around her shoulders and chuckled. "I'm pretty sure you just told the whole state of Michigan."

"I fucking love them," Butterfly told Bullet as Axle headed her way with three shots in his hands.

"They love you, too," Bullet replied against her hair.

And that was the fucking truth.

Kisy

Kisy was sitting in the middle of Dragon's bed, hugging his pillow to her chest and contemplating the situation she found herself in, when the door opened again, and Dragon stepped into the room.

"Why are you up?"

Kisy threw a glare at him, just because.

He arched a brow in response.

She huffed out a breath. "I'm not tired."

"Why are you still in your clothes? Get comfortable."

"Is that an order?" Yes, she was baiting him, but damn. She was still reeling from his words and that damn kiss to her forehead.

Another arched brow. "Do you want it to be?"

Kisy didn't dare answer that question, because the truth was... *Yes!* She wanted him to order her to take off her clothes. She wanted him to take off his own. She wanted *him*.

Dragon sat down next to her on the bed, facing her, and reached out. He took one of her hands from the pillow and wrapped it in his own. "I have to take off. I don't know how long I'll be gone, but you'll stay here. You're safe here, and I need to know you're safe."

"Why?" She looked up and met his gaze.

His brows drew together as if he didn't understand her question.

"Why do you need to know I'm safe?"

The confusion melted from his expression and was replaced with something that she couldn't identify. He leaned toward her, slowly, holding her gaze until his face was a few inches from hers. Then his gaze dropped to her mouth.

She couldn't stop herself from biting her bottom lip. It was either that or climb into his lap.

Dragon let out a quiet growl. Then he closed his eyes and took her mouth in a slow but scorching kiss. He didn't bother with brushes of lips or sweet caresses. He sucked her bottom lip between his and nipped at it. When she gasped at the pleasure of it, he tilted his head further and took her mouth the way she had wanted him to do earlier that night. His lips were firm but warm. His tongue swooped in and caressed her own, letting his piercing play along the interior of her mouth. He didn't just fuck her mouth with it, Dragon used his tongue as a tool to not only arouse her until she felt like her body was on fire but also to explore and learn.

Before she knew it, her head was being held in his big hands, and he was pulling her even closer, letting her know he was in charge but was also enjoying the kiss as much as she was.

Just as she was about to give in to her urges and climb into his lap, Dragon gave her one last, slow kiss and backed away.

His voice was deeper when he spoke again. "Just stay here and stay safe. You can go anywhere in the compound but stay in the compound. If you need anything, just ask and someone will get it for you. I'll talk to Darlin' about getting you some clothes." Then he stood and headed for the door.

"Wait."

Dragon stopped at the door and looked over at her. "We'll talk," he said and gave her a wink. Then he was gone.

How was she supposed to sleep after that? She wasn't going to be able to, not for a while. Kisy decided to get up and go see if any of the other women were awake. At least she wouldn't be alone.

She thought about bringing her bag, but decided it wasn't necessary. Her gut told her to trust the Howlers, and that's what she was going to do. They hadn't given her any reason not to trust them. If anything, they had proven they could and would keep her safe by handling the situation with her boss and his cronies. So, no, she wouldn't carry around her bag.

Climbing to her feet, she approached the dresser and pulled open one of the middle drawers. Tees. Just what she was looking for. She exchanged the shirt she was wearing for one of Dragon's dark gray tees. She took off her jeans and switched them out for a pair of basketball shorts she found in the next drawer down. She didn't have her flip flops, so she'd have to go barefoot. Oh well.

After grabbing her phone from her bag, she stepped out into the hallway and closed the door behind her. She didn't have a key, but she'd ask one of the women about it. With that thought on her mind, she headed down to the clubhouse.

When she entered the main area of the clubhouse, she saw a handful of Howlers scattered through the room and a few of the women hanging out and laughing at the bar.

At first, she didn't recognize the woman talking to Darlin' and Sugar, but then, the woman turned her head to look over at Bullet. That's when it hit her. Harlow Alito. Bullet's Butterfly was Harlow Alito. *Holy shit!*

Dragon and Bullet's anger about her boss made so much more sense. The woman her boss was trying to kill wasn't just one who saw too much like herself. It was his wife. How could any man plan to kill the woman he vowed to spend his life loving? Of course, that would inspire such rage inside men like Bullet and Dragon – good men, honorable, protectors. Add in the feelings Bullet obviously had for Harlow and it was no wonder the Howlers were so adamant about making her safe. She was their family.

Kisy slowly made her way toward Harlow. "Harlow?" Unsure of how the woman would react to her being there.

Harlow turned and looked at Kisy. "Yes?" She looked confused.

Then Kisy remembered that while she had seen pictures of Harlow with Mr. Alito in his office and had spoken with her on the phone a number of times, Harlow wouldn't know her face. They had never officially met in person.

"Oh. Right. You wouldn't know my face." Kisy let out a nervous laugh. "I'm Kaitlyn Neilson. I ran the management company for—"

Harlow nodded. "My late husband." Harlow didn't even flinch and Kisy didn't blame her. With understanding in her eyes, she approached and hugged Kisy. "What are you doing here?"

"Well, I was on the run because I saw some of Mr. Alito's men shoot a man. I used Dragon as a distraction. Then I stole his bike. He's a bit upset about that, but he was also worried, so he brought me here. Why I'm still here? I don't know. He insisted."

"Wait." Trip turned and looked shocked at Kisy. In fact, everyone had gotten very quiet around them. "You stole *Dragon's* bike?"

Kisy shrugged. "He left the key. And I was on the run. In my defense, he ordered me to get on it! It's not my fault the key was in the ignition!" She didn't know why she was defending herself to this man. It was none of his business, but she was tired of people acting like she hit him. She only took it for a few minutes.

Trip's gaze shot to Bullet. At the same time, they let out loud laughs.

"She's not lying," Bullet confirmed.

"That's fucking fantastic," Trip uttered through his laughter. "Oh, just wait. Fuck! Just wait!"

"Great," Darlin' sighed out, but she also had a smile on her face.

"Tell me she's staying around," Trip said to Bullet. "Please. I need this." His face was turning red with the force of his laughter.

Bullet shook his head but continued to chuckle.

Staying around? Kisy twisted around to stare at Trip. He must have lost his damn mind. "I can't just stay around here. All my stuff is in GR."

"I don't think that's going to matter," Darlin' told her. "Don't worry. The guys will make sure you and your stuff are reunited."

She wasn't the one who was insane. These people were.

Harlow smiled at Kisy. "It's so good to see you. And I'm sorry you had to see what you did. But you can trust Dragon and the rest of these guys. If you're thinking about hanging around, maybe we could have a girls' day or something. Get to know each other on a more personal level."

Well, that sounded okay to Kisy, so she smiled back. "I'd like that. But besides some sparks with Dragon, I don't know if staying around here would be a good idea. I mean... considering that I have to figure out my life now that I'm basically unemployed."

"You need a job?" Keys took a couple steps toward her. "I can help with that."

Kisy spent the next hour telling Keys about her job history and skills. But it took only ten minutes before he offered her a job at their property management company, Howlers Properties.

"The job is yours. I just have to run it past Axle. That won't be a problem, though." Keys seemed a bit out of place compared to the other Howlers, until he met her gaze, and a fierceness filled his eyes. "We don't like seeing women struggle, and we don't like when men are the reason they're struggling. I promise you, it won't be a problem for Axle."

The look in his eyes stated clearly that he may be a nice, kind guy, but he was also a badass who didn't have a problem taking care of business.

Chapter Six

Dragon

The next thirty-six hours were full of chaos for Dragon.

After leaving Kisy in his room, looking like a wet fucking dream, he headed out with Brute and Ranger. Together, they would look into the addresses Keys found. They found the address where the tracking was coming from through Keys's I.T. skills. They had cleared two addresses in Lansing and were headed to Grand Rapids when he got a call from Axle telling him that someone was tracking Butterfly's calls through her best friend.

Dragon made the decision to go directly to the newfound address instead of looking into the addresses from their original mission. It was to a property with a luxury RV on it, and he spotted

Butterfly's shitty uncle and his cronies. From what he could tell, it was their base of operations. He passed that information along to Axle.

Axle sent back up in the form of Striker, Siren, Keys, and Rebel. The plan was to wipe out as many of the shit stains as they could, but he was given word that Butterfly wanted to be the one to end her uncle. In Dragon's mind, she had earned that right and he'd do what he could to make that happen. Bullet wouldn't be a part of their strike group, but he would be close by with Butterfly in order to bring her in when they were done.

That was what happened, but there was a surprise visit by another group of bikers. Most of them got away. They may not have killed them all, but they made a dent. They also scared the shit out of the survivors by shifting in the middle of the fight. In the chaos of the gun fight, Striker and Brute were hit. Brute shifted to his bear in a rage and all bets were off.

After they cleared out all the riff raff, except for the uncle, they gave Bullet a call to let him know they were ready for Butterfly to do what she pleased.

Dragon was so damn proud of Butterfly, though. She walked into the RV with her head held high. She faced her last demon and slayed it like a motherfucking boss. Every Howler in that RV got a little choked up at her strength and their pride for her, but none more than Bullet.

Even though the Howlers all looked at the mission as necessary for the safety of a member of their family, Dragon knew Butterfly held some guilt for Striker and Brute getting shot. Brute would be fine. His shifter healing ability would have him right as rain in a matter of days. Striker was human, though, and his recovery would take a lot more time. The update from Siren was that there was a significant chance that Striker would lose some or all use of his hand and possibly his arm. Only time would tell.

But Striker was alive and would stay that way. When Dragon stopped by the hospital to check on his brother, Striker told him in no uncertain terms that he would take ten bullets to keep Butterfly safe and he had no regrets.

It was going to be hard for Butterfly to accept that level of support, but she was just going to have to get used to it, because that was exactly how every member of the Howlers felt, and he'd guess most of the ol' ladies would say the same. Not that the Howlers would allow that shit, but the sentiment still stood.

Yeah, the last thirty-six hours were chaotic. Dragon was fucking thrilled to be home as he pulled into the parking lot and backed his bike into a spot on the side of the clubhouse.

Dragon wanted a hot shower, a nap, and Kisy. However, the last would have to wait until the time was right. He wondered how her previous day was spent. He hadn't heard from her. If he was being honest, it bothered him that he hadn't heard a word after that fucking phenomenal kiss they shared.

That was what was on his mind as he crossed to the far side of the apartment building, entered the stairwell on the opposite side of the building from the clubhouse, and climbed the stairs. He'd stop in at his room and check on her before he went to the spare room to shower.

He knocked on the door, feeling like an idiot for knocking on his own damn door. After a few moments, the door opened, Kisy scowled at him, and slammed the door in his face.

After he heard the lock engage, she called out to him, "I know you have the key and will just open the damn door since this is your damn room."

Dragon chuckled to himself and pulled his keys from his pocket. Kisy was a smart cookie and figured shit out, apparently. He shrugged at the thought and unlocked the door. Pushing it open, he looked around it and found her sitting on his bed with her arms crossed over her chest.

"Angry with me?" Dragon shut the door behind him and matched her pose, crossing his arms over his chest.

"Ya think?" she said with snark and rolled her eyes. "You kissed me like that and left. No word. No expected return date. Just vanished. Okay. You told me you were going. But *still*."

"You could have called."

Her eyes bugged out at him, and he wondered if she was going to find something to throw at his head. He realized he wasn't wrong when her attention shifted to the nightstand and the empty plastic cup that was sitting there.

"If you throw that cup at me, I'm adding it to your list of consequences." He didn't use *the voice* on her. He didn't have to. His meaning was clear. He watched as Kisy pondered his words and must have decided it wasn't worth it since she didn't throw the cup.

"How would I have called you, Dragon? I don't have your number."

The truth of her words hit him like a brick to the head. She was right. He didn't give it to her. He let out a *fuck* under his breath and dropped his gaze to the floor. "Shit. You're right. I'm sorry." Then he looked over at her again and held out his hand. "Give me your phone. We'll fix that."

She shook her head. "I don't want your number."

"Kisy."

"No. It's fine. Keep your number."

Dragon resisted the urge to roll his eyes. "Kaitlyn, give me your phone." He saw her shift a little in her seat. Biting back a smile, he pulled out *the voice* and demanded, "Give. Me. Your. Phone."

She kept glaring, but the little bite to her bottom lip gave her away. She wanted his orders. She wanted it badly. With a fake huff, she grabbed her phone from where she left it on the bed and brought it to him.

"Thank you," he said and took it. With efficiency, he entered his number and made sure to call himself, so he would have her number, without having to make the humiliating move of asking Keys to get it for him. Then he gave her the phone back. "Now, to be clear, you can call me anytime, day or night, and I will either answer or call you right back. Are we clear?"

She bit that lip again and gave a nod.

"Good." He bent down and gave her a quick kiss on the lips. "I need to shower. We'll get lunch after."

"Nope," she said and turned on her heel. Kisy returned to her spot on the bed. "I'm having lunch with Keys."

"Keys?"

"Yup."

Dragon's wolf finally woke up from his slumber at that. It snarled, and Dragon felt like doing the same. He also felt like tracking down his brother and beating him until he understood Kisy was Dragon's. End of Story. He didn't do that, because Dragon was beginning to understand his little minx, and something told him she was baiting him.

"Keys?"

She nodded and shrugged.

"Oh. Okay. Enjoy lunch."

Then he turned and left the room.

When he made it to the spare room, he texted Keys.

>Lunch better be for a reason other than the fact that Kisy is a fucking beautiful woman or I will hunt you down.<

The text response was immediate.

>Job paperwork. Giving her job at H. Prop. I know she's yours. We all do.<

There was hope blooming in Dragon's heart. Would it be as simple as she was offered a job and decided to stay? Fuck, he hoped so. As long as she was in town, he would be able to win her over and claim her. She was meant to be his and he'd put in the work. Before he got too hopeful, he texted for clarification.

>She took a job?<

A few moments passed, then he received a text back from Keys.

>She wants more information. Nothing official yet. Will let you know if she accepts.<

All Dragon could do was send some prayers up to the gods. It would be a blessing if he didn't have to try to talk her into staying before he even broached the subject of their preferences.

>Good man<

After sending the last text, he headed into the bathroom to shower. Telling himself to hold off on any further advances until he knew for sure she was staying around. There was no sense in getting addicted to the taste of her lips if she wouldn't be there in a matter of days.

His wolf growled at that, but Dragon knew it was for the best. What he planned to build with Kisy was too important to fuck up just for a kiss or two. He wanted a *for life* arrangement. Not a *for now* arrangement.

Telling his wolf to have patience, Dragon turned on the water and began to strip.

Chapter Seven

Two days later... **Kisy**

Lunch had been interesting. The offer Keys gave her was just over what she was making at her job with Alito properties, but the workload was also lighter. Alito properties had been a demanding workload, requiring her to have long hours, well beyond a nine to five, and she always felt like she was behind. She broached the subject of hiring assistants to Mr. Alito, but he shot it down and said they'd *reassess* in six months.

The Howlers Properties seemed to have quite a list of properties in Warden's Pass, but it wasn't such a demanding job that it would require such compensation. When Kisy brought that up, Keys waved it off and said they paid what their employees were worth. She got the impression there would be no discussion on that.

Besides the pay scale, the benefits were fantastic. Insurance and paid time off, extensive enough to let her know they weren't only smart business people, but they were also progressive in the way they compensated their employees. The flexible maternity leave was a benefit she definitely didn't have with Alito properties. It was six weeks, and Mr. Alito expected you to be on your game the day you returned. Not that she ever had a need for maternity leave yet.

Keys also hinted at other benefits that would come with time. She was still reeling over the pay and the listed benefits that she didn't even ask about what that meant.

He didn't demand an answer, either. He told her she could think it over and get back to him whenever. She appreciated that. Not feeling pressured gave her the opportunity to think things through. Of course, she wouldn't take too long. Kisy wouldn't want to keep them from filling the position if she wasn't going to take the job.

Whether or not she took the job all depended on whether or not she decided to stay in town. And *that* was dependent on different factors, the biggest of which was a tall, burly biker with a perma-scowl and a stare that set her panties on fire.

Right after he gave her that earth-shattering kiss, she would have said she needed to stay in town because something was starting, and it was something she wanted to explore. Now, days later, she wasn't so sure. Since he returned, there was nothing. Not. One. Thing. Even after she tried over and over to get a reaction out of him, to break that steel shell he erected around himself.

She made sure to give him flirtatious looks at every opportunity, even when he was talking to his brothers or when she was talking to them. Kisy made it clear that she was open to it, but the most he gave her was an arched eyebrow.

Her car and belongings were brought to the compound the same day he returned, but she hadn't put on any of her shirts, instead choosing to wear his tees, even to bed.

Kisy also insisted that he sleep in his own bed. When he started to argue that he was fine in the spare room, she told him she would go find a motel or something because she refused to take his own bed from him. That was the only time she got a reaction out of him. He turned his head quickly and slammed his eyes shut, but not before she saw the hint of green light.

Feeling like she finally was getting somewhere, when it came time for bed, she only wore his tee, but Dragon kept to his side of the bed. Two nights of sleeping next to each other - and nothing.

Her Hail Mary was that morning when she noticed the mess of clothes she'd left on the floor. She got out of bed and bent over to pick them up, knowing full well that she didn't have panties on, and he'd see everything. She heard a growl, but by the time she looked over at him, he was on his feet and pulling on his jeans.

Kisy didn't know what else to do.

Maybe she should decline the job and go back to Grand Rapids. She was sure she'd find a job somewhere in the metropolitan area.

Standing on the sidewalk in front of the clubhouse with Butterfly and Bullet, that was the thought running through her head as she watched a grumpy Dragon wash and then dry his bike. He was scowling at it like the bike did something to his dog.

"He's been a royal pain in the ass for days," Bullet complained as he stared over at Dragon across the parking lot from them.

"What's wrong with him?" Butterfly asked.

"I don't know. And I'm sure he won't enlighten us." Bullet kissed Butterfly's lips, gave Kisy a nod, and headed for the clubhouse.

"We need to get him to loosen up," Butterfly commented as they both watched Dragon stalk off toward the apartments. When he passed them, he didn't even acknowledge them, which only pissed Kisy off more.

For days, she had been trying to get his damn attention, and he was withholding it from her for some reason. If she couldn't flirt her way into him giving her a reaction, maybe pissing him off would do the trick. Hell, even if it didn't get a reaction out of him, playing a prank on him would make her feel a little better. "We should paint his bike some girly color like pastel pink." Kisy grinned. "With glitter."

Having been washing his bike with Dragon, Trip had walked up to them and uttered, "Ladies, as much as I would love to see the look on Dragon's face if you did that, I would hate to have to attend your funerals. So... how about I make a suggestion."

"Boo." Kisy gave a pout. "Taking all of our fun."

"Not all of it." Trip grinned. "What you need to do is..."

Dragon

After taking a quick but cold shower in an attempt to cool his fucking libido, Dragon wrapped a towel around his waist and exited his bathroom. While washing his bike, he kept getting distracted by the sight of Kisy standing off to the side, chatting with his family. His eyes were drawn to her, over and over again, until he wanted nothing more than to growl a warning at everyone to leave them alone.

But that was just fucking rude. It wasn't anyone else's fault that he was having a hard time controlling his desires for the first time in his life. He needed to take her, but he wouldn't go there with her until they had the necessary conversations. A casual sex situation was never going to happen between them, not even to slate his hunger.

With other women he had been able to have a fling or a long weekend… but not with his mate. And Kisy was definitely his mate. His wolf was barely kept contained when she was around. The demand to claim her was constant and insistent.

And that was the fucking problem. Until they had the necessary conversations, he wasn't sure he could pacify his wolf while he fucked her. But if he knew she was his and he was hers, and they agreed to that, he could tell his wolf to be patient.

He just needed to know if she was going to accept the job and stick around.

Dragon thought over the best way to start the conversation with her as he dried his body and got dressed. He was still contemplating that as he headed back outside, with the intention of taking Kisy for a ride on his bike.

When he stepped outside and glanced around, he didn't see her, but his eyes landed on a ball of fur sitting on the seat of his bike. Confused, Dragon walked over to it and picked up a tan teddy bear wearing a fake leather vest. He turned it around in his hands, and that's when he saw the piece of masking tape on the left lapel. Written on it in feminine handwriting was *Dragon*.

He wondered who in the hell did it until he heard the sound of two women giggling and a traitorous motherfucking chuckle. Whirling around, he found Trip standing with Kisy and Butterfly just outside the front door to the clubhouse. All three of them were laughing so hard they had tears in their eyes.

Dragon pretended to lunge toward them, which made all three of them scramble to go back inside, still laughing like a pack of fucking hyenas.

Scowling harder so he didn't let the smile grow on his face, Dragon opened his saddlebag and slid the teddy bear inside.

Later that night, he opened the closet in his room and put the teddy bear in a box he had on the top shelf with all of the pictures he had of him and Dani over the years. The box also held the watch his father gave him when he turned twenty-one and the poem his mother wrote him to tell him what she expected out of him as a man. Yeah, that teddy bear was meant to be in that box with all of the rest of the stuff that meant anything to him, but he was never going to let Trip know he kept that fucker. He'd never hear the end of it.

Kisy

Still giggling and holding onto each other's arms, Harlow and Kisy stumbled into the main room of the clubhouse. Trip was right behind them.

"What did you do?" Darlin' demanded as she stood up from the chair she had been occupying and put her hands to her hips.

Kisy knew she should come to Trip's defense, saying that he didn't do it alone, but she was beginning to understand that Trip did enough on his own to probably deserve Darlin's assumptions.

"I didn't do anything," Trip replied, sidling up next to his mate and pulling her into his arms. "It was all them. All I did was watch."

"Hey!" It was Kisy's turn to put her hands to her hips. "And buy the bear. And give us the idea in the first place. And wasn't it you who found the masking tape and marker?" There was no way she was going to let him just push all the blame on her and Butterfly.

"Trip," Bullet uttered on a sigh, "he is going to kill you."

Trip waved off Bullet's warning. "Nah, he wouldn't hurt his namesake's father."

"Hurt?" Darlin' raised an eyebrow. "Yes, he would. Kill? Maybe not."

"He's just a big ted—"

"I swear to the gods, Trip," Dragon began as he stormed into the room, "if you finish that sentence, I'll make sure you aren't able to make any more babies. Hell, you won't even be able to try."

"But then how would Darlin' get her nightly satisfaction?"

And that was when Dragon took off, chasing Trip around the clubhouse like two little boys playing tag.

Through the laughter that had erupted in the room, Bullet sighed again and shook his head. "I'm going to end up playing pall bearer for one of them."

Butterfly giggled. "At least it will be entertaining until then."

"There's that." He gave her a wink.

Kisy giggled at Butterfly and Bullet's comments as she made her way over to the bar to get a drink. Well, there was a reaction. Dragon didn't sweep her off her feet, but he wasn't as unfeeling as he liked to pretend he was.

Later that day, the women had decided to meet up at the tattoo shop owned by the Howlers and the Claws. Butterfly had invited Kisy, saying it was something to do with ol' lady tradition. She was just happy to get some bonding time with the women that she was quickly coming to love. They were strong and supportive, but they were also funny and not the least bit scared of the men in their lives. Yeah, Kisy was excited to call them her friends.

As they waited for the others, Kisy bounced a little on her toes and asked Butterfly, "So, you and Peanut are getting your tats?"

Butterfly nodded. "Yeah. Since Peanut is bartending now, instead of dancing, she was ready to do it."

"Where are you getting it?" Sugar asked as she walked up.

"I thought I'd get it high on the top of my thigh." Butterfly grinned. "I'm just going with Bullet's Butterfly."

Peanut approached as Butterfly finished her words. "I'm getting Striker's Snack." She giggled. "He named me Peanut because, like them, I'm his favorite thing to eat."

"Yesssssss, Queen." Kisy gave Peanut a high-five.

Kisy hooked her arms in the elbows of Butterfly and Peanut. "Are you ready, Bitches? I don't have a reason to brand myself with the Howlers MC logo, but I'm getting something."

Butterfly and Peanut snort laughed as they headed into the shop.

Dragon

When Axle sat down next to him at the bar, Dragon let out a deep sigh. He knew he wasn't going to like whatever conversation Axle wanted to have. Either he was going to rip Dragon a new one for the numerous instances of disrespect he'd shown in recent times, or he wanted to gossip like a teenage girl.

"So... why haven't you claimed her?" Axle asked and motioned to the prospect for a beer.

Gossip like a teenage girl, apparently. The men of the Howlers MC were some of the worst when it came to gossip. If one of them found out about something, they *all* found out. It was ridiculous, but he knew his president wasn't going to let this go, either.

Dragon sighed again and took a drink of the beer in his hand. "She hasn't decided if she's staying. I want it to be her choice without me being the reason."

Axle made a noise of understanding and took a drink of his beer. "So, you're going to let your mate just move away and you're not going to do anything?" Sliding off the stool, Axle gave Dragon's shoulder a squeeze. "Sounds like you're scared, Drag. I wouldn't expect that from you."

Dragon clenched his jaws as his wolf snarled at him. Not only was his wolf pissed at being called scared, but his wolf also agreed with Axle when it came to Kisy. And of course, Dragon wouldn't just let Kisy leave without doing anything.

Shit. He needed to figure it out.

Chapter Eight

Kisy

Giddy. That's the only way Kisy could describe what she was feeling as she left the tattoo shop and crossed the street to the clubhouse. The women were still there, but she couldn't wait to show Dragon her tattoo. It was something she always wanted to do and hadn't had the opportunity.

Was it weird that the first person she wanted to show was someone she had only known for a few days? Maybe, but it didn't change the fact that he was who she wanted to show. She wanted to show him a part of her that went deeper than attraction, deeper than superficial.

Moons were special to her. Her grandmother used to tell her about how the moon was just as important as the sun, but too many people forget about the moon and all its power. They used to bring a blanket out into the yard on clear nights and lay out on their backs, taking in the moon and stars for hours. It was their little ritual that she hoped to pass on to her children and grandchildren someday.

She wanted to share that with Dragon. With a bit of anxiety about his response and whether she'd have the opportunity to have that conversation, she yanked open the door to the clubhouse and stepped inside.

Kisy was getting fed up. Kissing her like that and then cutting her off was damn cruel, in her opinion. He either needed to let her in or end things. She couldn't stay in limbo for much longer. She had decisions to make, and those decisions hinged on whether she had something to hang around for.

Spotting Dragon sitting by himself at a table in the corner, Kisy headed that way. She took a deep breath in order to prepare herself.

Sure, she wanted to share her tradition from her grandmother with him, but she also wanted him to have a reaction to her body, to act on the attraction that had been burning between them from the beginning.

As she approached the table, his green eyes locked on her rolled down leggings. To get the tattoo, Ginger had her roll the top of her leggings down low on her hips. They weren't as low as she stopped in front of Dragon, but they were still showing more of her skin than normal. And on her left hip was a white bandage, protecting the new tattoo.

"I did something," she said with a giddy smile.

The corner of his mouth quirked. "I see that," he said in that naturally deep voice of his. "What did you get?"

"I got a moon. It's got some small stars around it. It's... it means something special to me."

She thought he was going to ask why it was special when he opened his mouth a bit, but he closed it again.

"Want to see it?" she asked.

"Sure," he said.

With hope still lingering that he'd give her *something* to go on, Kisy peeled back the bandage and showed him.

His gaze dropped down to her tattoo, then returned to her face, his expression unchanging. "It's nice."

Nothing. He gave her *nothing*.

Kisy narrowed her eyes on him and huffed out an annoyed breath. She turned on her heel and stormed over to the bar to order a drink from the young man behind manning it. While she waited for the beer, she glanced around and saw a few of the Howlers just down the bar a few feet and Axle talking to Skull on the other side of her.

A stupid and amazing idea struck. This was it. If Dragon didn't react to what she did next, Kisy would turn down the job and return to Grand Rapids to start over.

After receiving her beer, she turned to Axle and Skull. "Hey. You guys want to see my new ink?"

"Always," Skull said.

Kisy figured that made sense because the guys arms were covered in tattoos. Same with Axle.

Axle gave a nod and his features softened as soon as he faced her. He always did that, toned down the badass when he spoke to one of the women.

The two men took in her tattoo after she pulled back the bandage and gave her compliments on the design choice as well as commenting on the line work Ginger had done.

The three of them chatted about tattoos for a bit, with the guys explaining a few of theirs to her. It was nice. Kisy liked that the men were willing to bond with her just like the women. It made her feel at home with them. If only Dragon would do the same.

When Axle got a call, he and Skull excused themselves and headed down the back hall.

Kisy took a drink of her beer and strolled down to the other Howlers – Ranger, Trip, and Siren. "Hey, boys," she said with a wide smile.

Trip grinned back. "Hey, Kisy. I see you got some ink."

Siren gave her a nod. Ranger glanced over her shoulder before his eyes met hers and he smiled.

"Yeah," Kisy replied. "Want to see?" She reached down and peeled back the bandage again.

"That's kickass," Trip told her. "Can't go wrong with a classic like the moon."

"Very true," Siren commented.

Ranger looked over her shoulder again before he took a step back and bent down to see it. "Ginger do this? She's always been great with detail work."

Dragon

Sitting in a chair in the clubhouse with his arms crossed over his chest, Dragon watched as Kisy showed that fucking moon tattoo she got on her lower abdomen to yet another of his fucking brothers. He wanted to remove their eyes with a rusty fucking spoon.

It was time. They needed to have *the talk* and lay down some damn boundaries.

Boundary #1: No showing your panty line to my motherfucking brothers.

As he started compiling a list of things he wanted to bring up during their talk, he told his wolf to calm the fuck down. Dragon couldn't approach her to have *the talk* while he was walking the edge.

When Ranger bent down to *get a closer look,* he rose to his feet and stormed across the room. He reached them in three strides and glared at his MC brother.

Ranger grinned and let out a quiet chuckle. "I get it, brother."

"Get what?" Kisy looked back and forth between them.

"It's time," Dragon said and bent down. He lifted her with his shoulder to her abdomen, throwing her over his shoulder, but careful not to hit the fresh tat. Then while his woman pretended to be outraged, he stalked toward the front door of the clubhouse.

It wasn't until the front door closed behind him that he heard his brothers let out the hoots and hollers they had been holding back.

Kisy

Finally! Kisy was fucking ecstatic when Dragon threw her over his shoulder and stormed out of the clubhouse. While she pretended to object, she looked up and winked at Ranger, Siren, and Trip. The grins she got back let her know they were well aware of what she had been up to.

When he brought her out to his bike, she was a little surprised. She had expected him to carry her up to his room at the compound.

"Where are we going?"

Dragon stilled in his movement to get on the bike in front of where he placed her and growled, "Shut. it." Then he finished his movement and started the bike.

Knowing she was about to get exactly what she wanted, Kisy chose not to push him on that. Instead, she just wrapped her arms around his waist, smiled, and pressed her cheek to his back. *Fuck!* She loved the smell of the leather of his cut mixed with the spice and pine that was Dragon's scent. The smells, being pressed against his hard body, and anticipation had her panties soaked... and that was before he revved the engine and took off.

Axle

After getting a phone call while talking with Kisy, Axle, and Skull headed to Axle's office. Earlier that morning, Axle had called his father for advice. He was trying to portray confidence in front of his brothers and everyone else, but he was worried. What they were facing was more than Axle ever expected.

His father, Joker, was the previous president of the Howlers. Even though he was a retired member and no longer living in the area, Axle was hoping he would know something or have a strategy that Axle hadn't thought of. As he sat in his office chair and listened to his father tell him they didn't have any new information, Axle's chest felt tight.

"We're coming back to town. We're not riding, though. Don't need to get caught by the Hell's Dogs along the way. Since we aren't sure where they are or if they're all together, it isn't safe for us to be alone during such a long ride."

"Dad, I don't want Mom here during this," Axle interjected.

"Well, Son, I'll let you tell her that when we get there," Joker replied on a chuckle. "She may not have given birth to you, but you're her boy, and she will be there for you whether you want her to be or not. Tell Trip. We'll rent a vehicle at the airport."

"We can pick you up."

"Nah. You have enough on your hands. Some advice?"

"Always."

His father became serious when he said, "Call Hawkin. Tell him the truth. Ask for help. If he's anything like his predecessor, he will help."

Axle was surprised by that advice. It wasn't a secret that his father held no affection for Hawkin or the previous owner of Milhawk Investigations. "I don't know, Dad. He's... pretty strait-laced."

Joker snorted a laugh. "Call Hawkin." Then he ended the call. Axle may be the current president of the Howlers, but that didn't mean his father would treat him differently than he always had. Sure, when it came to making decisions for the club, Joker would yield to Axle, but he was still his father.

Axle sighed and sent a text to the owner of Milhawk Investigations, requesting a meeting.

Sitting in the chair across the desk from Axle, Skull asked, "What did Joker say?"

As he waited for a response from Hawkin, Axle answered, "The retired members are coming home. He also said to call Hawkin."

Skull looked at Axle like he lost his mind. "Hawkin? After the way he made it clear he wouldn't break any laws for us?"

Axle gave a nod. "Dad says to call Hawkin. I'll give it a shot. If nothing else, I'm confident he'll keep it to himself if he declines to help us."

"Help us with what?"

"Whatever he can," Axle said on another sigh. His shoulders and back were tight as hell. He needed a massage from his mate and sleep. "Fuck, Skull. We need every bit of fucking help we can."

His phone vibrated in his hand. He opened the text string and read Hawkin's response.

>Two hours. M.I. HQ.

<

Chapter Nine

Kisy

When Dragon pulled into the two-stall garage of the ranch style home and did a swoop around, so the bike was facing out, Kisy's eyes were wide and looking around at everything.

From what she saw of the house on the drive in, it was a dark gray siding with lighter gray brick on the bottom half of the house. There wasn't much landscaping design or ornamentation in the front yard, but the lawn was cut, and nothing looked like it was neglected. The front door looked to be the lighter gray, as well as all the trim she could see.

The garage was clean, as if it was rarely used. Kisy wondered how often he came to the house or if it was even Dragon's.

Dragon cut the engine and pressed a button on his keychain. The rolling door of the garage slid down and an overhead light came on. She thought that it was nice that the light came on automatically without having to stumble through the space to find a switch.

After Dragon threw his leg over and got off the bike, he faced her and held out his hand. Kisy took it and swallowed hard as she took in the intensity in those sexy green eyes. She wouldn't run from it, though. She had wanted that intensity focused on her for days. It was finally time for her to get what she wanted, and she was ready.

Once she was off the bike, Dragon kept a hold of her hand, only adjusting his grip until his fingers slid between hers. He led her to the light gray, plain door on the side of the garage, unlocked it with his key, and swung it open.

Dragon let go of her hand and motioned for her to enter in front of him. When she climbed the two small steps to the door and stepped inside, his hand was pressed gently to the small of her back, sending tendrils of pleasure through her body.

She stepped through the door and into the kitchen of the house. It was all white and light gray. Nothing decorative or even small appliances on the counter space, except for a coffee pot. There were no magnets on the stainless-steel refrigerator. There were no dishes or pans sitting anywhere that she could see. There weren't even any washcloths or hand towels hanging to dry on the edge of the sink. What Kisy saw inside the house was a whole lot of nothing.

Using that hand on her lower back, Dragon led her to the other half of the open space – the living and dining area. The space had shiny wood floors and light gray walls but still nothing decorative. In the dining space, the only furniture she saw was a black rectangular table and four chairs. The living room had a black couch and a coffee table, but Kisy didn't even see a television.

"Is this... your house?"

Dragon dropped his keys to the dining table. As he slid off his cut and hung it on the back of a chair, he answered, "Yes."

"There's nothing in it," Kisy said.

Dragon gave a low chuckle. "There is and you'll see it. This floor is waiting for my woman to do what she wants with it."

"This floor?"

Dragon pulled out a chair on the side of the table and motioned to it. "Sit."

Kisy did as he told her and sat down in the chair.

She watched Dragon as he sat down in the chair at the end of the table and got comfortable at an angle, spreading his legs and hanging on arm over the back of the chair.

"You'll see the basement." Then his green gaze locked on hers. "First... we have some talking to do."

Kisy swallowed hard. She had an idea what to expect the topic of conversation to be, but she had stuff she wanted to clear up with him first.

"Are we doing this or what? I mean... are we together? I've been waiting for any indication of where this was going from you before I tell Keys if I'm taking the job or not. If we're not, I don't want... I don't want to see you with someone else. I mean... I know I don't have a right to say that, but–"

"Kisy," Dragon stated, immediately ending her ramblings.

She pressed her lips together and waited.

"I was waiting for you to decide if you were staying." He gave her a slight smile. "It seems we need to have this conversation for more than the original intention."

"So, we're doing this? We're together?"

"It's what I want. That's the only way you can stay in Warden's Pass, Kisy. The type of relationship I need might give you pause, but I don't think it will. I've seen the way you react to my orders. I can smell how your body responds to my voice."

Kisy felt the heat infiltrate her face. Her breathing picked up as she watched Dragon slide into the person he was when he used *the voice*. "You're a Dom," she breathed.

Dragon gave a nod. "And you're a sub."

"I've… not… I've never *really* had a relationship like that. I mean… I've dabbled, but…"

"Kisy, every Dom/sub relationship is different. We decide the rules. That's the point of this conversation. I will make it clear to you what I expect. You can accept or decline, and we'll make sure that what we agree to is acceptable to both of us. We start that by agreeing to general rules. For instance, I'm not looking for a full-time sub who never makes decisions for herself."

Kisy blew out a breath. "That's good. I'm not known for taking orders well."

Dragon gave her a grin. *An actual grin*. "I'm aware."

Kisy smiled back. "You like that?"

Not answering her question, Dragon ran his tongue along his bottom lip, his piercing flashing. "In your everyday life, I will only expect you to follow my orders when it comes to your health and safety. If you don't, I can get creative in how I respond to that."

"So, you won't give me orders... in my everyday life, unless it has to do with my health and safety?"

"I'll give orders. The only ones I expect you to obey are the ones regarding your health and safety."

Kisy grinned. "That's good. And other times?"

Dragon's gaze traveled over her body and back up to her face. "You will follow my orders. You will do what I say and only what I say. You will not come without my permission. You will call me D. You will pick a safe word and we'll discuss a safety motion if we decide that gags are okay. These are only the beginning of the rules."

After giving a nod, Kisy forced herself to breathe in and out slowly. Her body was getting hotter and hotter with each word that he spoke. Her panties were pretty much useless, and she was surprised her nipples hadn't burst through her bra and shirt they were so hard.

"I expect you to drink water, stay hydrated. I expect you to keep yourself healthy – eat and take care of yourself."

She made a face at the word *water*.

"Kisy, water is what keeps your body able to enjoy all the fun things I plan on doing to it."

Dragon put his elbows to his knees and leaned toward her. "You will drink the water."

"Fine," she grumbled and crossed her arms over her head. "Are we going to have a contract like on *that* movie?"

Dragon shrugged. "We could, if you feel we need to, but I don't think we need it."

"That seems… so… impersonal."

"Then we make decisions and make sure we are both clear on them."

"Like what decisions?"

"What is your safe word? Something you'd never say during sex."

Kisy blurted the first word that came to her mind. "Koala." Okay, it wasn't the first word, but it was the first word that didn't have anything to do with sex with Dragon.

Dragon gave a nod. "Are there things you know for a fact you are not into or don't want to try?"

"I'm… I'm not into… like humiliation stuff… or anything that would make me bleed or like scar me. I'm not huge into pain, but some is okay… ya know like… spanking."

"I'm not into making you bleed. That's not an issue. I have no desire to humiliate you. No fire. No needles. No cutting instruments. No bodily fluids except those expected during sex. What about wax or breath control? Clamps?"

Kisy squirmed a little in her seat at the thought of Dragon pouring hot wax on her naked body. "Uh... wax is okay. I'm not sure about breath control. Clamps? Maybe."

"Good." Dragon reached out and caressed her cheek with his fingertip. "We'll put the clamps and breath control into the maybe list and revisit later. Are there things you need me to be aware of? Any absolutes, acts or words?"

"Like positions?"

Dragon grinned again. "Love, you will be in a variety of positions. I mean do you like toys to be used? Do you like to be tied up? Do you like anal play? Is there anything you've always wanted to try but never have?"

"Yes," she blurted and tried to ignore the burning reminisce of his touch on her cheek. It was like he was still touching her, and it made her ache to have those fingers in other places.

"Yes? To what?"

"All of that."

Dragon rose to his feet and held out a hand to her. "I'll put together a list of what we agreed to and anything we haven't discussed. We don't need a contract, but I think it's important that it's clearly laid out what is acceptable and what is not."

Kisy took his hand and stood on shaky legs. She briefly wondered if he would balk at her climbing him like a tree right then and there, but she tamped down the urge and just let him lead. "Okay."

"For tonight," he began and held her hand as he led her across the room to a door just before a hallway that led off the living room, "I think we have enough to explore. Remember that you can always stop me. I don't care what we're doing or how far into it we are, you can always stop me. Just say your safe word and everything stops."

"I know," she said and waited for him to open the door. When he didn't, she lifted her gaze to his face.

Dragon lifted a hand and cupped her cheek in his palm. "I promise to always take care of you, Love, in bed and out."

Kisy lifted her free hand and covered his where it rested on her cheek. "I promise to always take care of you, D."

She saw a flash of green light from his eyes, then they closed, and his lips slammed against hers. He stole her breath with the force of his kiss, and she wouldn't have cared if she died right then and there. All too soon, he pulled back and laid his forehead to hers, eyes still closed.

"We have more to talk about," she panted.

"Yeah. Tomorrow."

"No. Tonight. But I want to see this other floor."

Dragon straightened and eyed her curiously, but he didn't say anything as he opened the door, flipped a light switch on the wall, and started down the stairs. Still holding onto his hand, she followed him down.

The stairs were a light gray carpet, and she was beginning to hate the damn color. Like seriously? Of all the colors of the world, that's the one they chose to splatter all over the house?

When they got to the bottom, she realized that he probably had little to do with the rest of the house, if he was in charge of that room. And she didn't see Dragon asking anyone else to decorate this room.

Everything was black. The walls, the floor, the furniture, the linens. In the middle of the wall on the other side of the open expanse was a large platform bed with an added metal frame that jutted up over the bed and connected to the wall a few feet above the headboard – a four poster bed for a biker Dom. The sight of the metal loops and hooks scattered along the edges of the frame made her heart race at the thought of all the ways Dragon could use them to keep her exactly how he wanted her.

On either side of the bed were plain square nightstands, each with two drawers. On the side wall to the right of the bed was a black, simple cabinet, but it was closed, so she couldn't see what was in it. Across from the cabinet was a floor to ceiling curtain that was hanging from the ceiling about a foot from the wall. Of course, the curtain was black.

"What's behind the curtain?"

Dragon stepped further into the room and slid his hands into the front pockets of his jeans. He looked over his shoulder at her and winked. "Have a look."

She *so* wanted to look, but she had something she needed to address with him. If they were going to do this, honesty and communication had to be paramount. She needed to know the truth. Really, she was pretty sure she already knew, but she needed it verified.

Kisy walked around him and turned to face Dragon. "I'd rather talk about something."

Looking down at her, Dragon just raised an eyebrow.

"Tell me why your eyes can shine green light." She crossed her arms over her chest and waited. When he looked away from her and over to the side, Kisy huffed out a breath. "And why Bullet can have fangs and hiss like a house cat. And why you growl like a pissed off pit bull when someone gets too close to me. I'm pretty sure I know why. I just want you to verify it." For a moment, there was nothing but silence. Kisy wasn't going to let this go. "Dragon, if we're doing this, we need honesty and communication. You want me to trust you and be honest with you. Then I need that in return."

Kisy refused to take back her words. She needed the truth. *They* needed him to tell her the truth.

His gaze shot back to her and Kisy could read the slight fear in his eyes.

"Dragon," she stepped forward and pressed her hand to his chest, "I'm not going anywhere."

She watched as he let out a long, slow breath and gave a nod.

"I can growl like a *wolf* because I can shift into a *wolf*. Bullet can hiss like a house cat because he's a tiger shifter. And if you tell him I told you that before I get his approval, there will be consequences." He hiked a brow and stared at her for a long moment.

She nodded and waved off his concerns. "Yeah. I get it."

"And the light happens when our emotions get pushed to the edge. Extreme emotions."

Kisy nodded and applied what he explained to what she knew. "Okay. So, when the light bright situation happened at the gas station, it was from rage?"

Dragon shook his head and huffed a laugh. "Light bright," he mumbled.

"And at the compound... in your room, it was because of—"

"I *extremely* wanted to fuck you," he said, firmly.

Kisy swallowed hard at the intensity in his green gaze. Her hand slowly slid up his chest on its own. "So... you're shifters?"

He nodded.

Then Kisy was jumping up and down and giggling, pumping her arms in the air. "I fucking knew it! I walked into a paranormal romance novel! I knew it!"

Dragon's eyes narrowed and he shook his head. "A what?"

"A paranormal romance novel! Ya know... where ordinary women fall in love with sexy badass men and find out they can turn into predatory creatures and are willing to kill all of her enemies, come home, shower, then fuck her brains out."

"Oh. Well... yeah." Dragon shook his head again, this time in humor at her. His slight smirk had her convinced he liked her craziness, which was good because he hadn't seen anything yet.

"Can I see?" She stopped jumping and waving her arms, before she pressed her hands together in front of her. "Please?"

Dragon flashed a grin, then he rolled his eyes and two seconds later, a large russet colored wolf stood in front of her. The head of the wolf came up to her chest. It was huge. But what drew her attention wasn't the size of the animal. It was his eyes. They were the same bright green as Dragon's.

Kisy blew out a breath and smiled. "It's really you." She lifted her arm and ran her fingers through the thick scruff right behind his ear. It was somehow coarse and soft at the same time.

The green light shining from his eyes shocked her. In a blink, Dragon was standing in front of her again, his eyes still shining.

"You're playing with fire," Dragon growled. No, not Dragon. That was all *D*.

Kisy bit her bottom lip as she stared up at him. After a moment, she released her lip and asked, "Yeah? How?"

T.S. Tappin

Chapter Ten

Dragon

Dragon's wolf was going crazy, pacing and growling. He had been since Dragon scooped her up and carried her out to his bike. But when she lightly dug her fingers into the scruff behind his wolf ears, his wolf demanded he mate her and mate her right then. It was like the man in him lost all reason. He shifted back in an attempt to regain his ability to think.

When she bit her lip and stared up at him, he knew she liked having him on the edge. Oh yeah, Kisy was the one, his mate, the sub he needed.

"Strip," he growled at her and watched as she swallowed hard.

It didn't take long for her to snap into action though. Those knee high black boots she had on were yanked off and tossed to the side. Her leggings and panties followed them. But when she went to remove the tee she had borrowed from him, he reached out and took hold of her hands. "No. Leave it on."

Kisy released the fabric and stared up at him, ready and waiting. Dragon reached behind him and yanked his own shirt off, dropping it on the floor.

"On the end of the bed, facing me, on your knees." As she turned on her heels and headed for the bed as he instructed, Dragon emptied his pockets on a small table next to the stairs and removed his boots and socks. Taking deep breaths and exhaling slowly, he regained his calm. He didn't want his first time with her to be fast and furious. He wanted to learn her and wanted her to learn him.

If his wolf had his way, Dragon would be inside of Kisy, and his mating mark would already be on her shoulder.

Feeling calmer and more in control of his urges, Dragon turned and looked over at Kisy. *Damn*, she was beautiful. Her slightly wavy hair falling around her face and her gray eyes, reminding him of when she was on her knees in front of him in that restaurant.

Slowly, he made his way across the room and stopped in front of her. Lifting his arm, he ran the back of his knuckles across her cheek and down the side of her neck, watching as her chest heaved with each breath she took. His little minx was already ready for him.

He turned his hand, palm down, and dragged it down her chest and between her breasts. Her breath caught when he paused there. Then he slid that hand up and wrapped it around her throat, not tightly, just enough to let her know who was in charge.

He met her gaze with his own and watched as her eyes turned pleading. Gone was the brat. His sub was in full attendance.

"Do you know what you did to me when you dropped to your knees in front of me at that restaurant?"

"Yes," she whispered.

He bent down and licked along her bottom lip. When she opened to him, he didn't take what she was offering. Instead, he nipped at that bottom lip, making her squeak out a moan.

"Back up two strides," he ordered and released her throat.

As she did as he ordered, he reached down and unbuttoned his jeans. Her gaze dropped to his hands. Oh so slowly, he pulled down his zipper and opened his jeans.

"You owe me," he told her as he pulled his hard cock from his jeans. He knew when she saw his Frenum piercing on the underside of his dick, because her eyes widened, and she bit on that bottom lip again. "It's time to pay up, Love."

Her breath caught again as she bent forward onto her hands and came face to face with his erection. "Can I... Can I touch you?"

"Yes," he replied, his voice grittier than normal.

His wolf was snarling and snapping inside of him. Not at Kisy. No. His wolf wasn't happy with *him*. As far as his wolf was concerned, their mate was right there and needed to be claimed. It was pure determination that allowed him to shut his mind off to his wolf. He needed to focus on Kisy. His wolf would only distract him.

Kisy lifted one hand to wrap her fingers around the base of his cock. At the same time, she opened her mouth, and her tongue came out. She circled the tip a few times, before she ran that tongue along his piercing and then wrapped those pretty lips around him. She moaned as she sucked him in a couple inches, pulling back, and sucking him a little further.

Dragon slid his fingers into the hair on the side of her head and pushed it back, giving him a better view of her face as she took more of him with each downward stroke. *Fuck!* She felt even better than he expected her mouth to feel. Hot. Slick. Her little tongue danced along the underside of his cock, playing with his piercing, sending shocks of pleasure up his shaft.

As much as he wanted to let her suck him to completion, they had plenty of time for that, and he wanted inside of her. He gave her a few more minutes, taking in how fucking beautiful she was with her lips wrapped around him, before he cupped her jaw and gave a slight squeeze, letting her know to pull off. His good little minx did as he wanted.

"I can't give you anything. Shifters aren't able to transmit human diseases." He ran his fingertip along her bottom lip. "But we can get full-human's pregnant. Condom?"

"I'm on birth control," she breathed against the wet tip of his finger.

"Okay. Good to know. But do you want me to use a condom?" Something flickered in her eyes. He wasn't sure what it was, and he wasn't going to let it pass without finding out what that look meant. "What's going through your mind, Love?"

Still bent forward, holding herself up with her hands, she swallowed hard and blinked a few times. "No... No man has ever... asked if I want them to... after they learn I'm on birth control."

Dragon cupped her jaw and gently pulled her up until she was on only her knees. He bent down and pressed his lips to hers, letting them linger there. "This is all about what you want, Love. Do you *want* me to use a condom?"

She swallowed hard again, then a sweet smile lit up her face. "No," she replied.

He gave her another kiss, before he wrapped his arms around her and lifted her. With one hand on her ass and the other wrapped around her waist, he walked up the bed on his knees and laid her out on the bed.

Still on his knees, he grabbed a hold of the tee and slid it up her body. Her arms rose above her head as he continued. He pushed the tee up her arms until he reached her wrists, then he wrapped it around her wrists and tied it to the ring in the middle of the headboard.

When she tried to pull her hands free and realized she was tied up, her legs twisted together, and a moan slipped out.

"You like that," he uttered with a slight smile and dragged his hands down her arms, over her shoulders and chest, until he was able to cup her soft, full breasts in the palms of his hands.

"Y-yes," she stuttered as her head pushed back into the pillow, arching her back, pressing her breasts into his hands.

"I want to spend hours on these," he told her and gave her breasts a squeeze, rougher than he intended but not hard enough to hurt her. "And I will. But for now, I want to feel you around me."

"Please, D," she moaned and pressed her thighs tighter together.

"Spread for me, Love." He moved out of her way, only backing up enough for her to do as he ordered.

With her legs spread wide for him, he got his first good look at her core. The tip of his cock was dripping with pre-cum at the sight. With hesitation, he bent forward and licked her from bottom to top, ending with a swirl and flick to her clit with his piercing, making her jump and moan.

He crawled up between her thighs, kissing along her body as he went, dragging his fingertips up the inside of her leg.

"How ready are you for me, Love?" He shoved his jeans down a bit more to give him room, wishing he would have thought to take them off, but there was no way he was climbing off the bed to do that when he was finally between her legs.

"R-ready," she blurted. "I'm always ready for you, D."

Without another word, Dragon rolled his hips and slid inside of her, slowly but steadily, until he was fully-seated inside of her.

"Wrap your legs around me," he growled as he tried to not let the overwhelming pleasure he felt overtake him and have him coming from the first stroke. Never had a woman been able to undo him the way she did.

He kissed along her jaw before drawing his teeth down her neck. When he got to the spot where her neck met her shoulder, he sucked the flesh into his mouth as he pulled back his hips and slid back in. He didn't let go of her skin as he repeated the action with his hips over and over, lowering his body so his torso rubbed against hers with every thrust. The dusting of hair on his chest rubbed against her nipples and his pelvis caressed her clit, making her cry out.

He finally released her flesh but didn't pull back. Against the underside of her jaw he growled, "Don't come until I tell you to."

"But... D," she moaned.

"Do. Not. Come." He reached down with one hand and slapped her ass cheek, making her core squeeze him tight.

He quickened his thrusts and slapped her ass again as he kissed his way up to her lips. Taking her mouth in a deep, wet kiss, he put more force into each thrust until the slapping of their skin echoed through the space.

When he released her lips, he kissed a path across her cheek to her ear. He loved the way she responded to him, open and expressive. His Kisy wasn't afraid to let him know exactly how good he made her feel. It was heady to finally have someone who caused the same sensations in him. With every thrust, she cried out in pleasure and his climax built in his balls.

When he felt the tingle that told him he was about to blow, he whispered in her ear, "Good girl. Now, come for me, Love."

Her head flew back into the pillow as her arms pulled on the tee that bound them and her cunt milked his cock. Dragon pulled back to watch her face as his eyes shined green light and he shot his come deep inside of his mate.

When his pleasure crested, his eyesight gave way to a blank whiteness and his hearing narrowed to the pounding of his heart. He couldn't breathe. He couldn't think. It was as if her core had sucked everything from him.

Slowly, his breathing and eyesight returned to him, followed by his hearing. What he saw when his sight returned was his Kisy grinning up at him, sated.

He returned her grin, before he kissed her lips. Then he slid out of her, groaning at the feeling of her slick passage caressing his sensitive dick. He climbed off the bed and went to the cabinet. After opening it, he pulled out a few wipes from a container he kept in there, next to a stack of hand towels. He used one to clean himself, making sure to clean the area around his piercing well. Once he was done, he returned to the bed.

Kisy just watched him, her eyes glassy and sated. "What else you got in there?"

He smiled. "You're welcome to explore." He laid next to her and used the wipes to clean her, taking extra time to caress her clit.

She whimpered and bit that bottom lip of hers.

"Fuck," he breathed and took her mouth in a deep kiss. When he pulled back, he stared into her pretty gray eyes. "Every time you bite your lip, I want to slide my cock into your mouth."

The tip of her tongue slid along that lip. "So do it."

Dragon dropped the wipes and went back to her clit with just his fingertips. "Love, we're just getting started."

Kisy

The sight of Dragon's head between her open thighs combined with the feeling of his tongue piercing flicking her clit and two of his large fingers curled inside of her made Kisy positive she was about to die. *Death by too much pleasure.* Perfection.

Her climax had been building for long moments and threatening to explode, when Dragon lifted his head and looked up at her.

"Do. Not. Come."

Kisy whimpered, desperately trying to hold it off. She just watched as he kept his gaze on her but lowered his head, his tongue slid out of his mouth and flicked her clit again. Her legs twitched and her stomach clenched.

But Dragon didn't finish her off. No. He kissed her inner thigh and climbed off the bed, running his hand over his beard and intently staring at her core. When he turned around and walked away from her, showing her his gloriously muscled back and firm, naked ass, Kisy wanted to throw something at him. That was impossible, though, because her hands were still tied.

She could stop everything by using her safe word. Dragon would return and untie her, but she didn't really want it to end. She was enjoying every second of their lovemaking, even when he brought her to the edge for the third time in the half hour after he fucked her for the first time. After letting her come and Dragon finding his pleasure inside of her, he removed the rest of his clothes and began his sensual oral assault.

Dragon walked over to the area right next to the stairs and over to a small kitchen area. She hadn't even realized that was there. She looked around to see what else she missed, anything to distract her from the throbbing of her clit and the twitching of her inner thighs and saw two doors on the wall that also had the curtain.

After opening and closing the refrigerator in the kitchen area, Dragon turned around and headed back in her direction, a bottle of water in his hand. He walked around to the side of the bed and sat down. Running the fingertips of his left hand up her inner thigh, slowly, Dragon's gaze traveled over her naked body and up to her face.

"Let's talk about consequences."

"Now?!" She knew her voice was squeaky, but she couldn't care. Her clit was throbbing to the point it was almost painful. She needed to come, not have a conversation.

Dragon twisted open the bottle of water. Slipping one hand under her head and lifting, he brought the bottle to her lips and ordered, "Drink."

She did what she was told and took a few sips from the bottle.

As he helped her drink, he calmly said, "You earned a few consequences. Starting with stealing my bike. Then your little stunt of bending over and showing me your sweet pussy when I wasn't able to take you up on your offer."

When she opened her mouth to protest, because he absolutely *could have* taken her up on her offer, he raised a brow at her and she slammed her mouth shut.

"Most importantly, Ranger had his motherfucking face too damn close to where I wanted to be... and that's not fucking acceptable." He gave her another drink of water, before he took a drink himself and twisted the top back on the bottle. After setting it on the nightstand, he maneuvered his way between her thighs, his lips hovering over hers.

"D," she whispered against his lips.

"In future, my brothers don't need to see any tattoos that would be covered by a pair of shorts. Understood?"

She nodded and for the first time since they arrived, she worried about how her tattoo was fairing. "I totally forgot about it!"

"It's fine. We'll clean it and take care of it in a minute. Answer my question."

She nodded again. "Understood."

"Good." He nipped her bottom lip. "Now, since you've been such a good girl, do you want your hands tied or free when I fuck you?" His eyes glowed that green light as a sexy as hell grin grew on his face, making her pussy clench in response.

"T-tied," she replied.

"Mmm," he sounded against her lips before he took them in a deep kiss as he slid his hard cock inside of her on a hard thrust, instantly sending her into climax.

Lights exploded behind her eyes as her body shook and her core tightened around him. Dragon didn't pause in his movements. He just pulled out and slammed back inside of her, over and over, prolonging her pleasure. She wretched her lips from his when she threw her head back and screamed.

Even through her screams, she could hear Dragon growl, "Yeah, Love, ride it out," as he continued pounding into her.

T.S. Tappin

Chapter Eleven

Axle

When Axle arrived at Milhawk Investigations with Skull and Pike, they entered the large lobby to wait for the Claws representatives to arrive. Michael "Mick" Hawken, owner of Milhawk Investigations, leaned back against the receptionist desk when they walked in. As usual, Hawkin had his employees, Beckett Major and Teagan Banks, with him. Since the business was technically closed, Hawkin voiced that they could meet in the large lobby to discuss any help M.I. could give the Howlers and the Claws.

Hawkin was just under six feet tall with assessing brown eyes that missed nothing. Often clocking everything without letting you know that, he tucked that information away for when he needed it. He wasn't a bulky man, but he wasn't lanky, either. Hawkin was strong physically, and no one would doubt that, but his biggest strength was his mind.

At first glance, you would assume he was just an older man who took care of his body, but the truth was he hid his almost genius level intelligence behind that well-defined body, shaggy salt-and-pepper hair, and gray soul patch.

Being CEO of Milhawk Investigations didn't mean you'd find him in a suit, either. He always wore black jeans or cargos, a black tee, and black boots. If it was cold or he needed to hide his weapons, he might slip on a black jacket. His less than professional wardrobe was part of the reason Axle felt comfortable around him.

If you chose to underestimate him, it was a choice you would regret. If he didn't make you regret it, one of his crew most certainly would.

"Just the six of us?" Hawkin had his arms crossed over his chest as he leaned back and rested his ass on the front side of his assistant's desk. That assistant happened to be Pike's mate, Pixie, or as Mick knew her, Alyssa.

"Crush, Pinky, and Nails will be here soon," Skull answered as he took a seat in one of the steel and brown leather chairs along the side wall of the lobby.

Axle sat in a chair directly across the space from Hawkin. Pike stood by Axle. Banks and Major stood across the room from Skull. Axle smirked at the way all of them had walls at their back. Even Hawkin had a wall just a few feet behind that desk.

"I can start explaining what's going on while we wait for Crush." Axle leaned forward, resting his elbows on his knees. "Is this room listening?"

Hawkin flashed a smile before he looked over at Banks and gave a nod. Banks rolled her light brown eyes. She was a handful of inches shorter than six feet tall, with long, dark brown hair that had a natural wave to it. Her standard outfit was a black muscle shirt and a tight pair of black jeans, a ponytail and very little makeup. She was pretty, and she looked sweet, but she could take any man in that room, without breaking a sweat. Then she rounded the desk.

"Ears and eyes are off," she said after pressing a few buttons before returning to her spot on the wall.

Axle didn't take offense. It was what Axle would do if he were in Hawkin's position. "We eliminated the charter who kidnapped Trip's ol' lady, Darlin' and my siblings, tried to kill us, tried to force Pumps to go back with them, and also ran drugs through our state. We also eliminated three of the major drug players in SW Michigan, one of whom kidnapped Butterfly, Bullet's ol' lady, *did* kidnap Sugar, Siren's ol' lady, and was also trafficking women and working with another chapter of the Hell's Dogs MC."

"That's a lot of ammo you've just given me," Hawkin said with narrowed eyes. "I could go to the police with that. You know that, which leads me to believe you want something from me and are trying to build trust."

"Other chapters of the HDMC have teamed up with a few Reapers MC chapters and supposedly the UpRiders." Axle met Hawkin's gaze. "We have a war breathing down our necks. And we need all the help we can get."

Hawkin turned his head and looked over at Major. The two of them just stared at each other, but Axle knew what that meant. He often had silent conversations with his brothers.

While they waited for Hawkin's response, the door opened and Nails walked in, looking around before she stepped aside to let Crush and Pinky enter. As sergeant at arms, it was her job to protect her president. Axle always liked Nails. She was great at her job.

"Catch me up," Crush said as she slid into the chair next to the one Axle was sitting in.

Nails flanked Crush the same way Pike was flanking Axle. And Pinky sat down next to Skull.

"I caught them up on what has happened between us and the HDMC as well as Alito and the shit stains that took Sugar. I also told them we're facing a war and need as much help as we can get. That's when you walked in."

"Get him," Hawkin said to Major.

Beckett Major was a very built and broad Black man with a bald head and stood well over six feet tall, dressing much like Hawkin, except Major's jeans were blue instead of black. Crush had told him once that Major was a man that many women wouldn't turn down, so Axle took that to mean he was attractive.

Major gave Hawking a nod, before he turned and approached a door off the back wall of the room. After punching a code into a keypad, there was a click, and Major pulled the door open.

Growls and hisses rang through the room as Riles and four other UpRiders MC members walked through the door Major had just opened.

"Weber," Hawkin warned, "not here. Listen to them."

"Why should we? They are partnering with our enemies." Axle knew he was close to the edge of shifting. His wolf was prowling and snarling inside of him. The weight of protecting the club and their families was crushing him. Being faced with the people responsible for the suffering of people he loved only made it harder to bear.

Riles shook his head. "No, Axle, that's not true." He ran his hand through his hair and huffed out a breath. "I made a promise to you guys, and I meant that. I'm here to keep that. I just found out what some of my members are doing. They aren't working under my orders or the orders of my VP."

"If you can't keep your members under control," Skull said as he stood, "then we'll eliminate the club and be done with it. We've already had this fucking talk with you."

Riles glared at Skull. "*My club* has nothing to do with the HDMC. We have five members who were left over from BM's days, who were on board with what he was doing. As soon as I found out what they were planning on their *tubing trip*, the rest of us rode down to warn you."

"Why didn't you come to us?" Crush asked, arms crossed over her chest as she leaned back in the chair, looking like she didn't have a care in the world.

Shifting his attention to her, Riles answered, "Because I wasn't sure of the reception we'd get, and we can't defend ourselves against both of your clubs. So, I came to the one place I knew would give me an opportunity to have a sit down with you, without allowing you to just take me out. Hawkin wouldn't allow that in his office, and you have too much respect for him to do it here, anyway."

"How did you know about Hawkin and the respect between us?" Axle eyed Riles as he waited for an answer, watching for any indication he was lying.

"I've known Rex since he was a prospect," Riles answered and gave a shrug. "I was around when Joker met with the former owner. Rex mentioned that Hawkin wasn't as tight with the Howlers, but there was mutual respect."

"If that's what you want to call it," Banks mumbled.

Hawkin shot her a look, but he couldn't hide the smirk.

"We already knew UpRiders were working with the HDMC," Axle said with a shrug.

Riles nodded. "They don't know that these two are on my side." Hitching a finger over his shoulder, Riles motioned to two young men, both a good six inches taller than Riles.

One of them had a head full of long, black hair, tied back at the nape of his neck. His eyes were a light blue and assessing like Hawkins. He was smart, Axle would bet on it. He looked to be fit and a bit on the muscular side, not as big as Axle or Skull.

The other kept his brown hair almost completely buzzed, but he had a bushy, full beard on his face. His eyes were a medium brown. He looked to be the more muscular of the two but not by much. This one could have been Skull's younger brother with the same build.

Riles continued, "They are willing to infiltrate the traitors and feed us information."

"How do you know you can trust them?" Pike asked from over Axle's left shoulder.

"I practically raised these boys. I knew their dads before some shit happened. My club was unaware of what I'd been doing, but I was at every damn game, every birthday, every Christmas."

"We didn't go without because of Riles," the long-haired one interjected. "He asked us to keep that quiet when we asked to prospect, so we did... out of respect for him."

The other one nodded. "We'd do anything for Riles... because he's earned that loyalty."

Riles stared at Axle. "I hate what is happening. I want to fix this, but I need some help. If we cut out the rot, we can rebuild the relationship the

UpRiders MC once had with your club and the Claws."

"We'll talk it over. Where are you staying?" This from Crush.

Riles gave a nod. "I haven't arranged that yet. We got into the area a few hours ago."

"They were telling me what they know when you texted me, Weber," Hawkin explained.

Axle looked over at Skull. "Arrange rooms for them at the hotel. Tell Mama Hen we don't want her there for a couple nights, and we'll have someone run the place for her."

"Tell her I'll send a few of the Claws," Crush said and stood. "Give me an hour and they'll be there."

Skull nodded and pulled his phone out of his pocket as he walked out of the room with Crush, Pinky, and Nails.

"If you even so much as stain a pillowcase, I will destroy you," Axle told them, meaning every word.

In the parking lot outside of Mama Hen's hotel, The Hen House, Axle and Crush straddled their bikes and watched as Skull and Pinky talked to Mama Hen in the lobby. Pike and Nails were standing off to the side on their phones.

"I think we have to send Rex in," Axle told Crush. "He's more familiar with Riles."

Crush let out a sigh. "I trust what he was saying. I just don't know if I trust the younger men to be able to pull this off. I think we should send Ranger with Rex. See if he can get them tips on not standing out like sore thumbs."

Axle smiled. "Good thinking."

"I know I'm a woman, Axle, but that doesn't mean I'm incapable of common sense."

Axle looked over at her and raised an eyebrow. "You're crankier than usual."

Crush flipped him off. "We're facing war. It's likely that we won't make it out of this without damage. *That* makes me cranky."

"Lucifer doesn't have anything to do with your bad mood? I heard you turned him away and he told you he was going to Heat then." He watched as her jaw clenched and her grip on the handlebar tightened. Axle lowered his voice so only she could hear and said, "He didn't go. He went to Bobby's and got hammered. Bobby called, and I sent Rock to go get him. He's sleeping it off in the spare room at the compound. Our floor."

She gave a slight nod and tried to hide her sigh of relief.

"What are you waiting for?"

Crush's head turned sharply, and she glared at him. She opened her mouth, no doubt to lay into him about minding his own damn business, but she clamped her mouth shut when Pike and Nails approached.

"Vixen, Ivy, and Ginger are going to guard the room. Shortcake is going to run the desk. She filled in when Mama Hen went on vacation."

"And I called Rex. I assumed you wanted him involved in this," Pike informed Axle.

Axle nodded. Pike knew him well, so Axle didn't take offense to his assumptions.

"Well… let's hope we aren't letting roosters into Mama Hen's house," Crush deadpanned.

Axle and Pike snorted laughs at the corny joke. Nails just grinned and shook her head.

T.S. Tappin

Chapter Twelve

Dragon

Dragon was beyond content. He was downright giddy as he woke up wrapped around a naked Kisy, her back to his front. With his leg shoved between hers and one of his arms under her head, he wrapped the other arm around her waist and cupped her sex with his hand. He pressed his nose into her hair and drew in her scent. *Vanilla*. Her scent, her curves, her personality — All of it was exactly what he was looking for and he wanted to wake up just like that every morning for the rest of his life.

His wolf whined, still pushing for a mating bite, but Dragon told him to be patient. Kisy was in their bed, in their life, and staying in town. They had time to tackle all of that later.

He nosed her wavy hair away from her neck and pressed his lips to the skin there, slowly dragging them up to her ear. "Morning, Love."

His hand cupping her sex felt her reaction to his voice. As she slowly came out of her sleep, he slid a finger between her folds and circled her clit. Nipping her ear, he lifted his leg, causing hers to open, giving him easier access.

"D," she breathed and turned her head toward him.

"What do you want, Love?" He gently kissed her lips and kept up the circles with his fingertip.

"You," she answered as her hips began to work with his finger. "However you want."

Dragon grinned against her lips. Pulling his hand away, he ordered, "Roll onto your back."

Kisy rolled onto her back and stretched her arms over her head. When she kept her hands there and looked up at him, waiting, Dragon let out a growl of approval. Yeah, she was made for him, and he was made for the little minx of a woman in front of him.

Sliding his arm out from under her head, he sat up and moved his attention down her naked body to the tattoo on her lower hip. It looked good and was healing well. He bent down and did what he did the night before. After their lovemaking, he cleaned her up and licked the tattoo, using the shifter healing properties in his saliva to quicken the healing process. If he had to guess, another couple of hours and it would be healed. He made a mental note to pick her up some oil to keep the skin healthy.

He looked up her body to meet her eyes. Her beauty and trust hit him like a punch to the gut. Swallowing hard to push down the emotion she caused in him, he shuffled off the bed and scooped her up in his arms.

She squeaked and wrapped her arms around him. "Where are we going?"

"Shower," he replied, and crossed the room, taking the first door. He stepped into the large bathroom and approached the spacious glassed-in shower. After setting her on her feet, he reached in and started the water.

Kisy went to step in, but he wrapped his free arm around her waist to stop her. Holding his other hand under the falling water, he checked the temperature. He turned the handles, adjusting the temperature of the water until he had it just right. Then he bent his head down and kissed her bare shoulder.

"Get in," he told her.

As she stepped inside and under the spray, he opened the linen closet across the room and pulled out two larger towels and a thinner, smaller one for her hair. He set them on the small table just outside of the shower before joining her.

Kisy

As Kisy stood under the shower spray and let the water drench her hair and run over her pleasantly achy body, she let her mind wander to thoughts of how amazing the bathroom was to look at. The various grays and black color scheme was sexy, a statement of power while still remaining relaxing. She wondered how Dragon decided on the color scheme.

She loved that not only was there a shower large enough for the both of them, but there was also a tub that was deep enough for the two of them to soak together. Across from the door, she saw a little room with a door that held the toilet. Privacy was good.

The double sink vanity made her smile. She wouldn't mind sharing space with Dragon, but a double sink gave her room to have space of her own. When he designed the space, he clearly kept the needs of the woman who would use it in mind.

How she got so lucky, she didn't know, but she was really beginning to think that everything that had happened in recent years of her life was leading her to Warden's Pass, to Dragon. Maybe it was too soon to make those determinations, but she didn't think so.

She tried to remember the last time she felt the intensity of connection with someone other than Dragon, but she couldn't come up with even one instance. It was as if his personality and her own were molded around each other, filling holes, completing and complementing each other. She liked the idea of having someone who was made for her and of being made for someone.

Her eyes were closed, and her head was tilted back, a smile on her face, when she felt his hands grip her hips.

"Fuck. That's a gorgeous sight."

Kisy opened her eyes to look and see what he was referring to. She figured he was eyeing her body, but he wasn't. He was gazing at her face with those intense green eyes. She realized he was referring to her smile. Tears filled her eyes as she smiled wider and put her hands to his chest.

Dragon lowered his head and pressed his lips to hers. After a kiss, he kept his lips to hers as he said, "I promise to do what I can to put that look on your face as often as I can."

And that was when she fell the last little bit. She was in love with Dragon... and she didn't even know his real name.

"What's your real name?"

Dragon straightened and cocked an eyebrow. He used his grip on her hips to lift her and press her back against the smooth stone wall. "Dexter Dole."

Kisy giggled as she wrapped her legs around his waist and her arms around his shoulders. "Your name is Dexter?"

Dragon smirked at her. "Arms up." When she complied, he nipped her bottom lip. "Yes, but no one calls me that."

"Can I?"

"Right now? No."

Kisy grinned and folded her raised hands together. "You're D, right now. I know. I mean outside of this."

Dragon nipped her chin and kissed his way down her neck. "Not Dexter. Dex."

She moaned as his tongue did a swirl where her neck and shoulder met on the left side. "I like that."

"Yeah... there's a reason," he murmured against her skin. "We'll talk about that later. For now, I want you to focus. Don't come until I tell you." Then he reached between them and lined himself up. "Scream for me, Kisy." He slammed into her, immediately setting a steady rhythm.

Kisy's head fell back, feeling so full. She focused on the way his skin slid against hers and how his mouth was working on every inch of her he could reach. As the moans escaped her throat, she contracted her internal muscles, trying her best to get those noises from him.

"Fuck," he growled, and a green light washed the space. She knew she was successful.

"D," she breathed and tightened her legs on his hips.

"My little Kisy is asking for consequences," Dragon said against the skin of her clavicle.

"I am?"

Instead of answering her, he quickened and hardened his thrusts, tilting her hips enough to make sure he was hitting just the right spot. Each thrust sent waves of pleasure to wash over her, making her scream and moan.

Dragon reached between them and circled her clit with his thumb. "Fucking come for me, Kisy."

The command in that deep, gravelly voice made her body explode with pleasure. Every muscle in her body clenched. Her back arched toward him, her head falling back even more in the process.

A few thrusts later, still in the middle of her climax, she heard Dragon's growl of pleasure as he emptied himself inside of her.

As she returned to her body and awareness, Kisy felt Dragon ease himself out of her and set her on her feet. Leaning against the wall, she tried to catch her breath as she watched him. His movements were not as controlled as they usually were as he grabbed a washcloth and a bar of soap. In his face, she could see a peace and contentment that wasn't there when they first met. She wondered if she had anything to do with that.

"I think I'm falling for you," she uttered and watched as his head turned in her direction and that green glow shot out of his eyes again.

He visibly swallowed. Then in a vulnerable voice she had never heard from him before, he said, "Don't stop yourself. You'll eventually be where I am."

Kisy was still reeling from Dragon's words as he dried her body fifteen minutes later. He had used that washcloth and bar of soap to clean every inch of her body while she washed and conditioned her hair. She was surprised he had conditioner, but she probably shouldn't have been. He seemed to anticipate her needs pretty successfully.

As crazy and wild as he kept his hair, she doubted he ever used conditioner, so she was positive he bought it for her.

When she was cleaned off, he did a quick but thorough cleaning of his own body, demanding she not leave the shower. She listened and just let her eyes take in the beauty that was Dragon's wet body.

When he was done, he stepped out of the shower and wrapped a white towel around his waist before holding out another white towel for her to step into. He secured it around her as he wrapped her hair in the smaller towel. She was impressed he knew how to do that and make it where the towel wouldn't slip. Then he removed her body towel and set about making sure every inch of her body was dried with loving caresses of the terrycloth against her skin.

She had never felt so loved and cherished in her life. He was the sweetest bossy badass that she ever met.

Kisy wanted to bask in it, but she was distracted by the words he'd said. *You'll eventually be where*

I am. What *exactly* did he mean by that? Was he falling for her? He implied he was further along, but he couldn't mean... No, he couldn't mean that. They had just met.

Then again, she knew she felt love for him. Why couldn't he return that? She had only said *falling* instead of *fallen* to lessen the freakout she had been expecting. Maybe they were feeling the same way. She wasn't sure if she should be freaked or not.

"Stop thinking so hard," he said as he took her hand and led her out to the bedroom.

She shook her head to try to dislodge the thoughts but was only mildly successful. "I can't put dirty panties back on," she commented as she reached for her leggings. Pulling them up her legs, she shrugged. "You'll just have to deal with me going commando."

A growl echoed in the room as a green light washed over the space. She turned her head and looked to find him staring at her ass in the leggings.

"Like the view?" she asked.

"You fucking know I do, Love." He yanked on his jeans and fastened them. "We'll be stopping at the compound to get you panties. The fuck I'll let you walk around and let anyone see your ass like that."

Kisy giggled as she pushed her hips back and swung her ass from side to side.

"One," he stated, firmly.

"One what?"

"If I get to three, you'll learn what." He gave her ass a smack before turning away from her and heading for the other door in the room. When he returned, he had two of his tees. He handed her the black one with the Howlers MC colors on the front, then he yanked the plain gray one over his head.

Grinning, Kisy put on the shirt. She liked the thought of earning whatever three got her, but she also liked the idea of wearing his club's insignia. It was like a branding, a claiming, a declaration of his possessiveness, but also her support for him and his chosen family. With that on her mind, she wondered if it would be too much to wear a Howlers MC tee every day of her life.

"Where are we going after the compound?"

Dragon finished tying his boots. "Breakfast… or I guess lunch, since it's almost eleven, now. Then I figured I'd show you around the town."

Still grinning, Kisy approached him where he sat on the bed. She cupped his face in her hands and was happy when he didn't reprimand her for touching him without his permission. She knew some Doms insisted on it only happening with permission, but she didn't know if she could handle that rule.

Looking up at her, he waited for her to speak. Instead, she lowered her head and kissed his lips. "I've already reached where you are, D."

Chapter Thirteen

Kisy

When Kisy slid into the booth at the diner, she looked around and took in the dated but homey interior. The booths were a faded brown, and the tabletops were scuffed, but everything felt so welcoming. She liked it.

"Why didn't we go to the diner at the compound?"

Dragon slid in on the other side of the booth. "Because we'd have a dozen sets of eyes and ears on us," Dragon replied as he motioned over a waitress. "She needs a glass of ice water. She'll have an omelet with a side of wheat toast and bacon. I'll have that, too, with a full order of fried potatoes, crispy not burnt. Give me a glass of water and a glass of orange juice."

As the waitress nodded and walked away, Kisy raised an eyebrow at him. "I will?"

"You need to drink more water."

"Okay." Kisy put that aside for a moment. "And the food?"

Dragon just stared back at her. "I've watched you pick at your food and not really eat. If you're going to keep up that fucking amazing body of yours and not lose all of the softness that I fucking love, you'll need food and a good amount of it." He leaned a little closer and met her gaze head-on, his voice dipping low. "Because I plan on fucking you as often and as long as I can."

Kisy pressed her thighs together to stop the throbbing of her clit. She swallowed hard and gave a nod. "Okay," she breathed.

"Good girl." His lips twitched as if he knew exactly what effect his words had on her.

"Dragon," Kisy heard a woman call out from behind her. She turned her head and saw an older woman with teal hair and a pleasant smile heading their way.

When the woman got closer, Kisy's heart skipped a beat. "Auntie Hen?"

The woman came up short and moved her gaze to Kisy. A grin spread across her face. Then Kisy was pulled out of the booth and into her aunt's arms. "My precious chicken! Girlie, what are you doing here?"

Kisy hugged her aunt tight. She missed Auntie Hen so much. "I'm moving here," she told her. "What are *you* doing here?"

"I've lived here for about ten years." Her aunt pulled away enough to cup Kisy's head in her hands. "It's so good to see you. And you're moving here? That's the best news I've heard in years! Your mother won't like it, but oh well."

"And when have I ever cared what she thought?"

Auntie Hen chuckled and kissed Kisy's forehead before she released Kisy. "True. I'm so glad you'll be close. We'll have to have some girl time." Then her aunt looked over at Dragon and raised her brows. "Mind telling me what you're doing with my beloved niece?"

Dragon shrugged. "Plan on keeping her. You okay with that, Mama Hen?"

Kisy watched as her aunt approached Dragon's side and patted him on the shoulder. "Good man."

"Join us," he said and slid out of the booth. He took Kisy's hand and pulled her until she was standing closer to his side of the booth. Motioning her into the side he had been sitting on, Dragon called out, "Peggy, Mama Hen needs to order."

Kisy slid into the booth, giving him a glare at his demand that she sit with him. She would have anyway, but that wasn't the point. "I can't even choose where I sit?"

Auntie Hen snorted a laugh. "Have you met the man, Chicken? Of course, you can't."

Kisy watched as Dragon's face split into a grin. Her heart skipped a beat at the sight. *Damn*. She'd do anything to make him look like that again.

Dragon

After they ate, Dragon gave Kisy a quick tour of Warden's Pass, including showing her where her office would be. When they were done with the tour, he took her on a long ride, allowing him to just enjoy having her wrapped around him.

He loved her. There was no denying that. It wasn't just that his wolf was drawn to her or that he was attracted to her. It was so much more than that. He loved her look. He loved the way she thought things out. Her sense of humor and how her laugh filled him with warmth. And her stubbornness and lack of fear of him kept him on his toes. He needed that. He would be bored if she just followed him around like a loyal puppy.

No, he wouldn't like that. He wanted the passion that came with the challenge. It fired his blood and spiked his adrenaline, making him eager to see how he could make her pliant. It had nothing to do with making her do what he wanted, though. She wanted to do what he told her to do, most of the time, but she also realized that it was much more fun when she didn't just give in.

The thrill of the chase without the chase. As a wolf, he appreciated the appeal of catching his prey after having to work for it.

Fighting his grin, he turned onto the street that held the compound and then into the parking lot of the clubhouse. He backed his bike into his usual spot and killed the engine. After he climbed off his bike, he held out a hand to her.

When she took it and let him help her off the bike, he gave her a wink. She was fucking gorgeous in his Howlers MC tee. If he could get away with keeping her in the house and only allowing her to wear that by itself, he fucking would.

"Thank you for showing me around. I'm slowly figuring out where everything is. I think I want to visit the salon sometime soon." She motioned with her hand to the salon they had in the strip mall that held the diner and tattoo shop. "I want to dye my hair. I'm tired of the boring. I don't usually keep my hair like this." She kept hold of his hand as he led her into the clubhouse. "I only dyed it my natural color because I was being chased and didn't want to stand out."

Dragon growled, along with his wolf, at the reminder of her running for her life. The thought of that would never *not* make him want to set the world on fire.

"So, dye it," he told her and gave her hand a squeeze. "I noticed you wear contacts, too."

"Is there something wrong with that?" she asked, cautiously.

Dragon stopped walking just inside the clubhouse and turned to face her. He cupped her cheek with his free hand. Gazing into her eyes, violet after she changed at the compound earlier, he told her, "If you want to change your hair color, eye color, nail color, cover your body with tattoos, whatever… you do it. Understand? There's nothing you could do to make me not want you. Got it?"

When Kisy bit her bottom lip and nodded, he knew she wanted to drag him into a bathroom and suck him off. He caressed her abused lip with his thumb. "Later, Love," he growled. "I'll be down your throat."

The whimper that came out of her made his wolf do the same. Fuck, this woman was everything he ever wished for. He lowered his head until his forehead hit hers. Then he tilted it to the side so he could take her mouth in a deep, wet kiss, using his piercing to tickle the roof of her mouth. She whimpered again at the touch, this one he swallowed down his throat as he pressed her against the wall next to the door.

A throat being cleared from his left made him pull back and glare at the face of his president.

Axle just grinned and said, "I need to bring you up to speed, and Keys wants to talk to Kisy."

Reluctantly, Dragon backed away from Kisy and took her hand again. Following Axle into the main room of the clubhouse, Dragon saw several of his brothers standing around. All of them were giving him knowing grins. He just flipped them off, causing all of them to laugh.

He released Kisy's hand but faced her. He gave her a quick kiss and uttered, "Stay in here. I'll be right back."

"Yes, Sir," she said and gave him a cheeky salute.

Dragon raised a brow at her. "Two." As her mouth dropped open, he turned and followed Axle down the hall to his office, calling out over his shoulder, "Drink some water."

He heard her mumble, "Bossy bastard."

Kisy

After sticking her tongue out at Dragon's back, Kisy turned around to find a group of obscenely attractive bikers grinning at her. *Fuck.* The sheer amount of male beauty and muscle in this club should be illegal. It was truly unfair to anyone attracted to men. Seriously, how were they expected to maintain reasonable thinking skills when *that* was looking back at them? *Impossible.*

Keys waved Kisy over. She mentally wiped away her imaginary drool and approached the table where he was sitting. There were two laptops and a stack of papers in front of him. When she took a seat across from him, he slid over the stack of papers.

"Just a few things to tie up."

"I didn't take the job, yet."

Keys rolled his eyes. "Well, the scene at the front door didn't say you were moving away and never coming back, so I felt it safe to assume."

"Smartass," she commented as she looked down at the paperwork.

Keys chuckled. "But was I wrong?"

She flipped him off.

"Didn't think so." He chuckled again. "I really like you, Kisy."

"That's good. Because the whole damn club is stuck with my ass and my sass. Congratulations."

Bullet slipped into the chair next to her. "That's good to hear, Kisy. Butterfly will be happy to hear it, too."

Kisy began filling out the forms. She glanced over at Bullet and smiled. "I hate that we had to go through what we did, especially Butterfly, but I'm glad that it brought us together."

"She is, too. It will be good for her to have a real female support system."

"Happy to be a part of it." Kisy flipped to the next page. "So... what kind of cat are ya? I saw the fangs and heard the hiss. If I had to guess, I'd say tiger. You're long and lanky. Well... not really lanky, but anyway, yeah. I'd guess tiger."

Bullet let out a loud laugh. "You'd be correct."

"Mental note: Tease Butterfly about Tony time."

That pulled laughs out of most of the men.

"Thank the gods," she heard Trip call out behind her. "She's going to test him at every turn." Kisy assumed he meant Dragon, and he wasn't wrong.

"If I didn't, his life would be boring."

"His life?" Bullet quirked a brow. "Plan on hanging around for a while?"

"Until he tells me to leave."

With that, the laughter died down. She wondered why until she looked into Bullet's eyes and saw nothing but gratitude shining back at her. If she had to guess, she would say that they accepted her and wanted her for Dragon. That meant more than she could ever tell them, which is why she practically dove at Bullet and wrapped him up in a hug.

"You trying to get me killed, Kisy?" Bullet asked with a quiet laugh as he hugged her back.

Dragon

Once in Axle's office, Dragon took a seat in one of the chairs across the desk from his president. He wasn't surprised to see Skull and Pike already in the room. Dragon assumed the talk would have something to do with the war and having them in on the talk was expected.

"We met with Hawkin last night," Axle said as he sat in his desk chair, rested his tattooed forearms on the desk, and clasped his hands together. "We explained the situation and were going to ask for any help he could provide, when he brought out five UpRiders from his back office area."

His wolf's fur stood on end at that information, and a growl slipped out of Dragon's mouth.

Axle gave a nod. "I know. We all felt that way. But…"

As Axle explained how Riles found out that a faction of his club was planning to work with HDMC, and that he was coming to warn them, Dragon began to understand the situation. He could see how Riles would be hesitant to approach the Howlers without a buffer. With the intel they had about the UpRiders working with HDMC, Riles would have been met with hostility.

"We have them staying at the Hen House," Skull stated, making Dragon's wolf even more pissed off.

"Are you fucking insane?" Dragon glared at Skull. "If those fuckers are lying and something happens to Mama Hen—"

"We asked Mama Hen to let us run the place for a few days," Pike interjected, probably trying to stop Dragon's anger before it got to the point of no return. Pike knew the intense protectiveness Dragon felt for anyone connected to the club.

Dragon took a deep breath and let it out slowly. In a calmer tone, he uttered, "Not only is she important to us, she's Kisy's actual aunt. She was already family, but now she's *family*."

Axle cocked a brow. "Voting on ol' ladies has been pushed aside lately, but are you asking for a vote?"

Dragon met Axle's gaze and replied, "I'm telling you that she's my ol' lady, even if she doesn't fully know it yet, and I'd be happy if you guys approved of that. In the end, if you didn't, wouldn't make a fucking difference."

Pike chuckled. "So, we were right. She's your mate."

"Fucking yeah, she is," Dragon said, and didn't fight the smirk that grew on his face.

"Congrats, brother," Axle said. "By the way, it's an unofficial vote, but the brothers all approve of her."

"Yeah." Skull nodded. "We like her."

"Good." Dragon sighed. "So, what are we thinking with this war shit?"

"We tentatively trust them, but we also keep our guard up," Axle said. "We need all the help we can get. And honestly, I think Riles is telling the truth. I sent Rex in to talk to him. He knows Riles the best. He says Riles is torn the fuck up that his club is causing us problems again. I believe him."

Dragon nodded. He did, too. "We need to figure out where they are setting up base and what their game plan is."

"Maybe the young bucks from the UpRiders will be able to fill in some holes," Pike commented.

Dragon sure the fuck hoped so. His wolf was ready to destroy the world if it meant keeping his family and his woman safe.

T.S. Tappin

Chapter Fourteen

Kisy

Later that evening, they were still at the clubhouse. Dragon and Kisy had dinner with the clubs and had moved on to drinks. Kisy was hanging out with the ol' ladies at a table in the corner, while Dragon was standing at the bar, drinking and talking with Trip and Bullet.

She was sipping on a Moscow Mule, because every time she took a full drink, Dragon looked at her and raised an eyebrow. After she finished her second drink, he said something to the sexy black man behind the bar, who showed up at her table a few minutes later with a glass of water.

In response, she ordered another drink. She drank that whole glass of water because she was already on *two,* and she wasn't sure she wanted to find out what happened when she got to *three*.

Okay, yeah, she did, but they weren't in his room of fun. They were in a room full of people, so the chance that he would tie her up and have his way with her was slim.

She was letting her gaze slide up and down his body, taking in every muscle hidden by his clothes, remembering what his body looked like naked. She was enjoying her time with the women, but he looked good enough that she was considering faking a headache just so he'd take her out of there and they could be alone. A grin grew on her face at the thought of what would happen as soon as she got him to a bedroom, but it quickly disappeared when she saw an outrageously sexy woman ease up to Dragon's side and put her hand to his chest.

In a blink, Kisy was across the room and shoving the presumptuous woman away from Dragon. "Hands fucking off, Bitch!"

The woman caught herself on a table and straightened on her ridiculously high heels, before she turned a glare on Kisy. Kisy watched as all of the Claws in the room lined up behind the woman. The woman's eyes shifted over Kisy's shoulder, and Kisy glanced back to find all of the ol' ladies lined up behind her. Her heart clenched at the show of solidarity.

A hiss cut through the room, bringing Kisy's attention back to the woman. A set of fangs and glowing bright blue eyes greeted her.

"Bring it, Bitch," Kisy taunted and readied herself. She may get her ass kicked by a shifter, but she wasn't about to back down.

"Kisy," Dragon began, but he shut up when she turned a glare on him.

"No fangs or claws," Axle stated. "Crush, tell her."

From just behind the woman, Crush let out a deep sigh. "She's human, Pumps. Fair fight."

The woman, Pumps snarled. Then she retracted the fangs and took a step toward Kisy. "I'm about to teach you not to put your hands on people."

"When you learn that fucking lesson, I might listen. In the meantime, I'm going to teach you what the fuck happens when a bitch thinks she can put her hands on my man." Then Kisy launched herself at the woman, tackling her to the ground, taking down a few Claws in the process.

Kisy didn't worry about them. She knew the Howlers and the ol' ladies wouldn't let them jump in. This was between her and Pumps.

Before Pumps could get her wits about her, Kisy held her down with a hand to her throat. Fisting her other hand, she swung repeatedly, hitting Pumps in the eye, the jaw, the nose. Pumps grabbed a hold of Kisy's face and was pushing her back, while Pumps's other hand tried to block Kisy's blows.

Kisy felt something crunch under her fist just as a set of arms wrapped around her waist and she was yanked off Pumps.

"Let me go," Kisy shouted and fought to get free of the steel bands around her waist.

"I'm not letting you fucking go," she heard Dragon growl in her ear.

"I wasn't fucking done!"

"You made your point, Love," Dragon replied, and she swore she heard pride there.

Then her ass was on the bar and Dragon was in her face. His eyes scanned her body, settling on her right hand. His brows drew together, and a growl came out of him. She glanced down at her hand and saw split knuckles and blood.

"Fuck." It wasn't until she saw it that it started to throb.

"Yeah. Fuck." Dragon gently lifted her hand so he could look at it better. "I don't think you broke anything."

"Good." She hissed when his breath hit an open wound.

Dragon scowled at her hand. "Ice! First aid kit!" His barked order was immediately answered. A baggie of ice and a large white box was set on the bar next to her hip.

Kisy tried not to let tears gather in her eyes as Dragon cleaned her wounds. He was trying to be gentle, but there was no way to clean them without them stinging.

As he put ointment and bandages on her hand, Axle walked up next to them. Kisy looked over at him, ready for him to yell at her for picking a fight with Pumps, but she was also ready to tell him she didn't regret it.

What she saw on his face was barely contained amusement along with a raised brow. "Your man? Who said he's yours? Dragon tell you that?"

Still feeling sassy, Kisy leaned down and licked Dragon's face from bearded jaw to temple. "I licked him, so he's mine."

And for the second time that day, Kisy caused all the men in the room to laugh.

As his brothers continued to howl with amusement, Dragon finished bandaging her hand and lifted his head. He met her gaze and smiled. "Love, you can stake your claim whenever you want. You're right. I'm yours." He kissed her lips. "But you just reached three."

Then she was over his shoulder and was being carried out of the clubhouse for the second evening in a row.

Dragon

It was time. As Dragon opened his bedroom door at the compound, his wolf was prowling inside of him, panting, ready. Dragon felt the same way. He stalked into the room, slamming the door behind him, and approached the bed. After tossing her on the bed, he started to undress himself.

As he hung his cut on the hook on the back of the closet door, he instructed, "Get naked. In position on the end of the bed."

"I gotta pee," she squeaked out.

"You've got two minutes. I expect you to be in position. Use the time wisely."

She streaked past him to the bathroom.

Dragon untied and removed his boots. As he yanked off his socks, he planned his strategy. First, that mouth of hers was going to be put to work. She had been sassy all day, and while he loved every second of it, there were *consequences* for that sassiness.

He reached behind his head and took a hold of the neck of his tee. Yanking it over his head, he tried to decide if he would let her come before he was inside of her or make her wait. He was unzipping his jeans when he decided she needed to wait.

When he was fully naked, Kisy ran out of the bathroom, naked, and climbed onto the bed. Immediately, she got on her knees on the end of the bed, arms raised in the air over her head. *Fucking perfect.*

Dragon strolled over to stand in front of her. Her eyes fell to the erection that was eager to get inside of her in some way, anyway. He cupped her chin in his palm and tilted her head up until her eyes looked up at him. Then he ran his thumb over her bottom lip and growled, "Good girl."

Her whimper was a bolt of pleasure through his cock. He had to talk to her before he fucked her, but his cock and his wolf didn't understand that.

Taking a deep breath and letting it out slowly, Dragon pulled himself together. He continued the stroking of his thumb on her lip. "Do you know what mates are?"

"Like… soulmates?" she asked against his finger, her breath stirring his arousal again.

"In my world, the shifter world, a mate is considered more sacred than a wife or a husband. It's someone our animal side is drawn to. Someone that matches us, completes us, has a hold on us.

It's a lifetime gig. Some matings don't work out if there's an addiction or one of the pair is a horrible person, but that's extremely rare."

"What are you saying?"

"Love, you're my mate," he told her as he looked into her eyes and let her see the truth of his words. "I've wanted to claim you since the moment you ran into me."

"What... what does the claiming... entail?"

"Lovemaking. Orgasms. And a bite," he moved his hand down to gently grip the spot on the left side of her neck where it met her shoulder, "right here."

"Oh! Like the scar that Butterfly has!"

Dragon nodded and breathed a sigh of relief. It was the one thing he had been unsure about. He wondered if the thought of the scar would deter her. Obviously, she wasn't disgusted by it. That was a good sign. "Yes. That's Bullet's mating mark on her."

"Does it hurt?"

"I've heard the stronger the match, the more pleasurable it is. So, my guess is no."

"And... you want to mark me?"

Taking a hold of her hands, he lowered them until they rested on her thighs. "Yes."

She shrugged. "What's stopping you?"

He gave her a smile. "Love, you have to agree to it."

Her eyes widened, and she giggled. "Oh." When her laughter faded, she gazed up at him and said, "I love you, D. Mate me. Claim me. Or don't. I'm not going anywhere."

His wolf howled inside of him. Dragon let out a growl of approval as he cupped her head in his hands, his fingers sliding into the wavy hair on the back of her head. He bent down and took her mouth in an almost savage kiss. He bit and licked his way into her mouth, fucking her with his tongue, teasing her with his piercing.

When he had her squirming, he yanked his mouth free from hers and straightened. "Suck me," he ordered, his eyes bathing her in green light.

Kisy didn't hesitate. She bent forward and braced herself with a hand on his thigh, using the other hand to grip him as she licked and flicked her way around the head of him, making sure to pay extra attention to his piercing.

Dragon allowed his control to slip. This one time, he let himself just enjoy. His mate was about to suck his cock into her mouth. Soon, it would be buried in her pussy, and his fangs in her neck, making her his. He didn't need to be D. He just needed to be in the moment.

D would never fully leave him, though. As soon as she was done giving his erection a good few strokes with her mouth, D would be back.

Kisy opened her lips and wrapped them around the head of his cock. Looking up at Dragon with her violet eyes, she slid him inside her mouth, caressing the underside of his shaft with the tip of her wicked tongue. After a few inches, she pulled off him only to suck him in again. Repeating the process, taking him in further each time, until the head of his erection hit the back of her throat. Then his Love really got to work. She didn't stop until he was about to explode and forced her to pull off by yanking a little on her waves.

"Arms in the air," he ordered.

Instantly, she lifted her arms in the air above her head. Letting go of her hair, Dragon dropped to his knees on the floor in front of her and pressed a light kiss to the skin between her breasts. "Before I mate you, you have *consequences*."

"Wait. For what?"

"One." He circled her right nipple with the tip of his tongue for a moment, before he bit down, not enough to hurt her, but just enough to heighten the sensitivity. She whimpered as he blew on the wet nub. "Taunting me." He kissed across her chest to the other nipple. "Two." He gave the other one the same treatment. "That sassy salute." He kissed and licked down her abdomen until his beard was rubbing against the hair on her mound. He circled her navel with his piercing, looking up at her lust-filled gaze. "Three." He nipped the skin there. "Not trusting me to take care of that situation with Pumps. You got to trust me, Love."

"I do," she whined, her chest heaving with the strength of her arousal. He knew how turned on she was because he could smell her arousal gathering between her thighs. "I just... she *touched* you."

Dragon chuckled against her skin as he kissed his way down to her mound. "Spread your knees more." After she did as he ordered, he replied, "That wasn't the first time, Love. But it sure as hell will be the last. And it would have been the last without you going all Rocky on her. I would have made it clear."

"Well, do it faster next time," she said with a sassiness that had his cock twitching.

He tsked. "My Love likes to rack up *consequences*." He stuck his tongue out and flicked her clit, making her jump. "Wonder how many times I can make you *almost* come."

"Oh, shit," she breathed as the realization of what her consequences were going to entail.

"Remember, no orgasm unless I tell you to."

"I love you," she panted.

Dragon leaned forward and circled her clit with his tongue, slowly. "Love you, too, Love. Now, be a good girl and take your punishments."

As Kisy whimpered, he dove in, using his tongue and fingers, and worked her pretty pussy and clit until he felt her walls contract on his fingers. He backed off and kissed along the crease of her thigh and hip while he listened to her panting and her heartbeat.

Once she was mostly breathing normally, he dove back in, this time using his beard and his fingers. The scratching of his beard against her clit had her immediately panting and moaning.

When her inner walls began to contract on his fingers again, he backed off and ordered, "Lay back on the bed. Head on the pillow. Arms up."

He kept a close watch on her as she frantically obeyed his orders, ready to catch her if she was too shaky and started to fall off the bed.

The pride he felt for her when she made it and stretched her arms over her head filled his heart and made him grin. When he crawled on the bed, she opened her legs for him. "So eager," he commented, and nipped her inner thigh.

She moaned her pleasure at the act, making him do the same to the other thigh.

Dragon laid out on his stomach and slid his arms under her thighs. Wrapping them up and around her thighs, he pulled her toward him until she was close enough for him to bury his tongue in her cunt. While he fucked her with his tongue, he used the thumb of one of his hands to circle her clit. This time, it only took a few circles and a few thrusts for her to contract.

He backed off and released her, causing her to let out a cry of frustration. Grinning, he climbed up over her, kissing his way up her body, until he was able to look down into her eyes. "Such a good girl," he said, low, and ran his nose along the side of hers. "I'm going to fuck you now."

"Yes," she replied, desperately.

"When you orgasm, I'm going to bite you."

She nodded eagerly.

"Then you'll be mine and I'll be yours."

"Do it. Please, D."

He nipped her chin. "No—"

"No coming until you say so. I know. Just please..."

Dragon bit back his chuckle and reached between them. He lined up his erection and slowly slid inside. His wolf was prowling and growling his approval. Kisy threw her head back and let out a long, loud moan as he filled her.

"Fuck yes," he groaned into the curve of her shoulder as he pulled out and slid back in. "Arms and legs around me, Love."

She did just that, wrapping him up tight, digging her heels in his ass. "You feel amazing," she panted.

In response, Dragon pounded into her harder and faster, loving every squeak, every moan, every whispered plea from her beautiful lips. He lifted his head enough to press his forehead to hers, gazing into her eyes.

The love shining back at him had him choking on the emotion it stirred inside of him. Never did he think someone would look at him that way. He had seen the women look at his brothers that way, and he always felt joy for them when he saw it, but he never allowed himself to wish that for himself.

"I love you," he whispered as he felt her limbs tighten.

"I love you, too," she whispered back.

"Come for me, Love," he ordered as his fangs slid down and his eyes dimly lit the room in green.

Two thrusts later, he felt her contract around his cock. He slammed inside and stayed there as he struck, sinking his fangs into her flesh.

As her pussy milked his cock, he felt her fill his heart, complete his soul, fit into that spot inside of him that had always been empty.

When her body finally loosened, he withdrew his fangs from her flesh. He threw his head back and howled as he finished inside of her sweet body.

He dropped his head back to her neck and was licking away her blood, sealing the wounds, when he heard the answering howls and roars of his brothers.

Then his sassy Love was giggling while his cock still twitched inside of her.

T.S. Tappin

Chapter Fifteen

Kisy

After the fastest shower she ever took, Kisy held Dragon's hand as he led her back into the clubhouse. Unable to keep the grin from forming on her face, she didn't even try. She was Dragon's mate, and he was hers. She couldn't wait until she could get her tattoo like the other ol' ladies had. What would hers say?

Kisy was thinking that over as the room erupted in cheers and whistles. Then she was being passed around between the brothers as they each hugged her, ignoring the growls Dragon was giving them. He was never going to like other men touching her, even if he considered them family.

She just giggled and welcomed all the love they were giving her. It was their way of officially accepting her into their family, and there was nothing but joy in her heart in knowing that.

Once they were done passing her around, she was set on her feet in front of Dragon. Then Trip was pushing his way through the crowd with a giant grin on his handsome face.

"It's my turn," he declared.

Standing next to him, Axle rolled his eyes. "It's supposed to be my fucking job, but whatever."

She heard Dragon chuckle behind her, but she kept her gaze on Trip.

The goober cleared his throat obnoxiously, then he looked more serious than Kisy had ever seen him. "My brother reluctantly gave me the honor to do this. And it *is* an honor, Kisy." He gave her a wink. After taking a deep breath, he raised his voice a bit and said, "By tying yourself to Dragon, you tied yourself to us and to our pack. By having his back, you have ours. By protecting him, you protect us. By loving him, you love us. We're a package deal. And we understand we're getting more out of the deal than you are. You will never need for anything for long. You will never want for anything for long. You will never suffer again. And if for some reason you do," growling and hissing filled the room, "the one who caused it *will suffer* far more for their efforts. I'm honored to call you my sister and my accomplice." With another grin lighting his face, he held out the leather cut in his hands.

On the left side of the cut, right where it would lay over her heart, were two patches. One read *Dragon's OL*. The other patch read *Kisy*.

Kisy bounced on her toes. "Squeeee!" Then she snatched the cut from Trip's hands and slid it on.

Trip chuckled. "Right on, Kisy!"

The room erupted in cheers and celebration as Dragon slid his arms around her from behind. In her ear, he whispered, "Later, I'm fucking you with just this on, Love."

She turned her head to look at him over her shoulder. "Will you wear only yours?"

He nipped her earlobe and chuckled. "If you wish, Love."

"Righteous," she breathed.

"Shots," Butterfly called out and headed their way with shot glasses on a tray.

Kisy giggled as Dragon let out a growl.

"You better chase those with water, Love, or... *consequences*."

Kisy bit her lip as she looked back at him. "That's not the threat you think it is."

His eyes flashed green light for a moment. Then he replied, "One."

After partying with their family and returning to their room at the compound, Kisy changed into one of her sleep shirts while Dragon undressed and relaxed on the bed with his back to the headboard.

Kisy climbed on the bed and settled between his legs, leaning back against his chest and abdomen. When Dragon's fingers immediately began to play with her hair, she smiled. He seemed to love touching her hair.

"Tell me about you," she said, grabbing his free arm and pulling it around her waist.

"Not much to tell that you don't already know."

Kisy rolled her eyes. "I mean it, Dex. I want to know you."

"You do." He gave her a squeeze. "Fine. I took care of Dani when my parents decided to retire. The older generation of the Howlers were stepping aside and handing over power to the younger generation. But they knew that it would be too tense to have the older generation in town. It's the alpha bullshit. Mostly, it was the knowledge that his dad and my dad would have a hard time adjusting to Axle being in charge. To avoid any conflict, they decided to retire to Florida and form a retired members chapter down there. Axle and I were young, early twenties, but we were raised in the club."

Kisy tried to imagine Dragon and Axle in their young twenties and failed miserably. She'd have to ask the women if they had pictures.

"At the time, Trip and Dani were still in high school. It was no big thing for Trip when his parents moved. He was already pretty active in the club, and Axle had been in charge of him for years. My parents knew Dani wouldn't want to move, so they just left her in my care. I didn't mind. She's my sister. I'd do anything for her. So, yeah, I was fine with it, but I wonder if that bothers Dani."

"Feeling abandoned?"

"Yeah." He let out a sigh and rested his chin on the top of her head. "I wonder if she thinks they didn't care enough to stick around."

She knew it was none of her business, but Kisy felt it important to gently point out, "If she does feel that way, those feelings are valid."

"You're right." He let go of her hair and wrapped his other arm around her, holding her close. "She went through high school with her big brother acting as her father. I don't regret it, any of it. But looking back at it now, I was probably too hard on the boys around her. Maybe if I wasn't, she might have connected with Trip a long time ago. Would have saved her some heartache."

Kisy giggled. "You don't mind that he's with your sister, do you? You just rag on him because you can."

Dragon chuckled. "That's our secret, Love."

"I think that experience of raising her triggered something in me. I was already protective of the people I loved, but that went into overdrive."

Running her hands along his forearms, she whispered, "It's okay if you can't do it all by yourself. It's literally what the club is for."

"I can tell what our future's going to be like."

Kisy smacked his arm. "What does that mean?"

Another chuckle. "It means you're not going to let me carry the weight by myself."

"Of course, I won't. We're mates."

She grinned when he let out a growl. Then he was nosing her hair out of the way and caressing their mating mark with the tip of his tongue. Pleasure shot through her, stealing her breath, her pussy clenched in response to the wave of sensations that flooded her system.

"D," she breathed.

"We're mates," he confirmed. "I've always been the quiet one. The watcher. The protector. I'm the unmovable force between my loved ones and the people who would hurt them. I was the same way in elementary school. Axle and I would take on a crowd to protect someone smaller. So, Love, you know me."

"I could have used you on the playground."

"Why? Were you bullied?"

"Girls are catty," Kisy replied and shrugged. Thinking about her childhood, it wasn't the childhood bullies that made her sad. The way her mother treated most situations made her disappointed in her. "Actually, I could have used you at home. My dad was passive. He was the fun parent, but he was silent when it came to real issues. We couldn't cut our hair the way we wanted or dress in the latest styles or have sleepovers."

"What?" Dragon sounded irritated.

She shrugged again. "My mother felt like we needed to be quiet and fade into the background. She worried that our friends would influence our behavior. The only time we were allowed to spend time with friends outside of school was when we went to stay at our aunt's house. She used to let us have sleepovers in secret." Kisy smiled fondly at the memories of those fun nights. "My mom found out when I was thirteen and my sister was ten. The fight between the two of them was explosive. Things were said on both sides that couldn't be taken back. We weren't allowed to see her or talk to her anymore. Then she moved, and I didn't see her again until today."

Dragon lowered his head and pressed his cheek to the side of her head. "I'm sorry that happened to you, Kisy."

"Our brother was able to pretty much do what he wanted because *boys will be boys*. Mom didn't let up on us until my sister tried running away when she was twelve. Then we were allowed to have sleepovers, but only at home. Dances were out of the question. So, I still went, but I had to sneak out of the house to go."

"Do you have a relationship with her?"

Kisy shook her head and shifted until she was sitting sideways in his lap. She rested her head on his shoulder. "I hear from her on holidays and my birthday, but the conversation usually ends in a lecture where I tell her I have to go and hang up. I talk to my sister regularly. It's on and off with my brother. It usually depends on what's going on in his life. I hear from him more when he needs advice or support. If he's happy, I never hear from him."

"What about your dad?"

"He's useless. He'll never push back against my mother, so I don't bother trying, and he doesn't reach out on his own. I'm okay with that." She turned her head and smiled up at him. "If we ever have kids, I understand that you'll want to keep them safe, but we can't lock them in the house. They need to have space to figure out who they are."

Dragon nodded. "I get that. We might need to negotiate when it comes to dating."

She giggled. "Are you agreeing to have kids with me?"

He cocked an eyebrow. "Are you my mate?"

"Yes."

"Do you want kids?"

"Maybe."

"If you want kids, we'll have kids. I love kids." He cupped her cheek in his hand and gave her a soft kiss. "Haven't you figured it out yet?"

"What?"

"I would do damn near anything to make you happy, as long as you're safe and healthy."

Grinning up at him, she asked, "Are you real?"

Dragon ran his nose along the side of hers. "I was just wondering the same about you."

Dragon

Dragon woke up with the vanilla scent of Kisy's hair filling his nose. It made sense because he had been sleeping with his face buried in her soft waves and his body wrapped around hers.

They talked for hours about their pasts and their dreams for the future. They continued to chat and learn about each other until Kisy fell asleep with her head resting on his shoulder, soft snores coming from her beautiful lips. It was the cutest sound he ever heard. For a while, he just listened to the sweet sounds and held her close.

When his eyes started to cross, he shifted them in bed until they were laying side by side. He buried his face in her hair and fell asleep, his wolf content and calm inside of him.

But now he was awake, and so was his cock. He ran one hand from her abdomen down and over to her hip, then back up to cup her breast through the sleep shirt she had on. In her ear, he used *that voice* and said, "Love, it's time for your consequences."

Kisy grumbled but she stretched, rubbing her body against the length of his. "Consequences?"

His wolf gave a satisfied growl and urged him to take their mate.

"Yes. I'll allow you to use the restroom. You've got three minutes."

"What time is it?"

"I would guess around four in the morning."

She groaned and stretched again, causing his wolf to whimper at the sight.

"Love. Three minutes."

His words must have sunk in because she catapulted off the bed and ran to the restroom. Dragon chuckled as she slammed the door, and he heard the sink turn on. A few moments later, he heard the toilet flush and the sink turn back on. Then the door opened, and she stepped back into the room.

Dragon rolled and sat up. He was sitting on the side of the bed, facing her, with his feet flat on the floor. He crooked a finger at her to beckon her over. Her steps were tentative, but he could see the anticipation in her eyes as she crossed the room and stopped in front of him. The expression on her face made his wolf growl.

Reaching out, he ran his hand up the back of her naked thigh and cupped her bare ass. Looking up into her eyes, grayish-blue since she took out her colored contacts, he asked, "Do you know why you earned consequences?"

She shook her head. "No, D."

"You don't?" He raised an eyebrow.

Her eyes widened. "Uh... the shots?"

Dragon gave a nod and gripped her ass in his hand. "Yes. Do you know how many shots you took?"

As he waited for her to answer, he reached out and ran his other hand up the back of the other leg.

"I... uh... I don't know. Four?" Her voice raised in question.

"Six," he corrected. "While you were taking those shots, you were awfully sassy and complained when I suggested water. What did I tell you about orders regarding your health?"

Kisy bit her bottom lip and didn't reply.

Dragon pulled his hand away and gave her ass a slap. She gasped and pressed her thighs together. "What did I say?"

She visibly swallowed. Her chest moved with the increase in her heart rate and breathing pattern. "You expect me to follow them."

"And did you?"

She pressed her thighs together again. "Not willingly."

"Not willingly." He pulled her hands from her and motioned to his lap. "Lay over my lap."

"D."

"Take your consequences."

Kisy bit her lip again, but she couldn't hide the small smile that graced her pretty face as she moved and did as he instructed.

His wolf was panting and pacing with anticipation, but Dragon tried to ignore the animal, needing to focus.

Once she was settled, Dragon pulled up the hem of the nightshirt and revealed her bare ass. He ran his hand in circles over each cheek, warming the skin. He waited for her to fully relax. When she did, he pulled back his hand and swung it forward, making firm contact between her ass cheek and his palm.

She gasped and jumped.

"Count them. Out loud."

"One," she breathed.

He pulled back his hand and did the same to the other cheek.

Her breath caught. Then she uttered, "Two."

When she settled, he spanked the first cheek again, harder than the first time.

This time, she let out a moan and pressed back into his hand. "Three."

He rubbed the skin in gentle circles. "Damn, your ass looks so fucking pretty red from my hand," he said in a growl, and his wolf did the same.

He pulled his hand back and smacked the other cheek, even harder.

The moan that came from her lips was even louder as she pressed back into his hand and wiggled her perfect ass. "Four," she said, loudly.

Dragon continued to give her slaps, loving the way she reacted to each one. The sounds coming from Kisy and her leaning into each smack had him riled up. His wolf was prowling and growling, demanding he take care of her in every way.

Dragon rubbed the reddened skin for a moment, before he slipped his hand between her thighs and found her wet and ready for him. "Love, I think you liked that."

"Yes," she moaned as he slid a finger into her hot core.

He bent down until his mouth was close to her ear. "Good girl. Now, ride me."

He barely got his boxer briefs pushed down before she was straddling him and sinking down onto his hard cock. She rested her hands on his shoulders and pressed her forehead to his as she lifted and dropped on his dick, her moans warming his lips with every motion.

"You're so fucking beautiful," he told her, cupping her face in his hands and pulling her hair away. "I could stare at you forever."

"Do it," she replied. Her hands slid into his long, wild hair and fisted, slightly pulling as she lifted and dropped, over and over.

Dragon moved his hands to her hips and helped her. He lifted her off him and slammed her back down. "One hand on your clit. Make yourself come for me, Love."

Kisy whimpered as she did as he asked.

Fuck. He didn't even need to see her skin to have her turning him the fuck on. She was gorgeous, perfect, and in love with him for some unknown fucking reason. He'd never let her regret that. He would do everything in his power to make sure she knew he appreciated her and the chance she was taking on his grouchy ass.

When her core tightened on his cock, he wrapped his arms round her and rolled them until she was on her back on the bed. Holding himself up on his elbows, he began pounding into her. As she cried out his name, he lowered his head and gave his now-healed mating mark a suck, making her cry turn into a scream of pleasure.

He released her skin and growled, "I fucking love you." After slamming into her one last time, he let his climax wash over him. His wolf threw back his head and let out a satisfied howl.

T.S. Tappin

Chapter Sixteen

Next day... Kisy

Her ass was tender. As Kisy walked into the clubhouse, she tried her best to pretend nothing was different, but she knew she was failing miserably. She tried to stand off to the side, but Dragon pulled out a chair for her and raised a brow at her when she didn't immediately move. The little smirk on his face made her want to slap him. Instead, she sat, trying not to wince when her tender muscle took her weight.

"What did you do to her?" Darlin' asked from across the table, sitting next to Butterfly, both of them sipping on juice.

Obviously ignoring his sister, Dragon bent down and gave Kisy a kiss on the temple. "I'll be back in a while. Drink water. Get some food. Just let them know at the diner to put it on my tab."

"I can pay for my own food, Dex," she snapped and glared at him over her shoulder.

"But you fucking won't," he replied, and had the audacity to grin. Then he was leaving the room, heading down the back hallway. Over his shoulder, he shouted, "Water."

"Coffee is bean water," she called back and watched as he stopped in his tracks and turned to look at her.

"What was that?"

Kisy grinned. "I said I love water."

He returned her grin, but he mouthed, "One." Then he turned back around and disappeared down the hall.

Kisy instinctively wiggled in her seat, but she instantly regretted it when her ass protested the action.

"Seriously. Are you okay?" Darlin' was looking at her with concern on her face.

Kisy nodded. "Yeah. I'm fine. Sore muscles."

Butterfly was in the middle of taking a drink of her juice. She suddenly slapped a hand over her mouth and bolted from the table. They watched as she rounded the bar and spit her juice into the sink. Then she threw her head back and let out a loud laugh. "Sore muscles! Yeah, I bet." On her way back to the table, she commented, "Why do I have a sneaky suspicion you have a new love mark in the shape of Dragon's hand on your ass?"

Kisy narrowed her eyes on her friend. "Why would you guess that and not that I fell on my ass?"

Butterfly rolled her eyes. "Because it's pretty damn obvious that Dragon is a Dom."

"No!" Darlin' covered her ears with her hands. "La la la la I don't want to hear this la la la la I don't need to know my brother is a freaky freak in the bedroom la la la la la even if I am happy for my new friend la la la I don't want to know!"

Nodding, Kisy looked over at Butterfly. "I'm impressed she was able to do that in one breath."

"Trip must really like her breath control."

Kisy snorted a laugh as Bullet slammed something down on the bar and huffed out an annoyed sigh. "Why do I always walk in on these fucking conversations?"

Dragon

As Dragon followed Axle into Milhawk Investigations and through the building to a large conference room, Dragon wondered how the war council would work when there were so many leaders in attendance — Axle, Crush, Riles, Hawkin, and Lira.

He wondered if there would be a fight for dominance. Would the five of them be able to put aside their need for control long enough for them to defeat the assholes who were threatening their lives?

Dragon couldn't speak for Lira's need for control. He only met her for a few moments at the farmhouse. From what he knew, she was the leader of the champions. He was curious about the champions, especially since Axle said they were made up of members from many different groups. He wanted to know the hierarchy, the makeup, the responsibilities of the members.

Axle mentioned something about assigning each champion a shifter partner so they could help – however they planned to do that – more efficiently. Maybe he could get some of that information from a partner.

When they entered the conference room, Dragon noted it wasn't actually a conference room. It was the unused, open space of the warehouse. Unlike most unused warehouses, it was clean and well lit. That was a plus.

Directly across from the door they entered through, Lira and her champions were lined up. To Dragon's right was the Milhawk investigations team as well as Riles and his few UpRiders. His wolf was instantly on guard. To the left was Crush and the Claws.

In the middle of the room was a conference table large enough for the leaders and their seconds. Dragon hung back with the rest of his group, while Axle and Skull took seats, along with the leaders and their seconds from the other groups – Crush and Pinky, Hawkin and Major, Riles and Eagle, and Lira and a woman Dragon wasn't familiar with.

Like Dragon, the rest of the members of the other factions hung back in their respective sections, watching and ready to act if necessary. Dragon had a thought that the treaty between them wouldn't work if they didn't learn to trust and pick a unified leader.

As his eyes raked over the members of the other groups, he checked in with his wolf to see if his wolf had any negative reactions to any of them. Surprisingly, his wolf was calm.

That had to be a good sign. *Right?*

⋆⇌⥂⋐⋑⥃⇋⋆

It was decided that Axle and Lira would be in charge of the war movements, with Hawkin and his crew only coming in if necessary, or if they had intel on the movements of the other side.

Dragon could understand Hawkin's hesitancy to be involved. Laws were going to be broken. Hawkin tried to avoid that. But Hawkin was also the type to always side with good over evil and despite their differences, Hawkin knew the Howlers and the Claws were good people.

"Who is watching your women and children?"

Dragon's attention was tweaked at Lira's question. He looked over at the woman and saw that she was looking directly at Axle.

Axle stared back. "Half of the Claws and a handful of the Howlers. Do you need names?"

Lira smirked. "No. I was just curious."

"Your curiosity doesn't give me the warm fuzzies about this partnership," Crush said in her typical deadpan voice, making the Howlers and Claws chuckle.

Lira continued to smirk, but her second replied, "I thought the majority of you were fuzzy."

Trip snort laughed.

Ranger grinned at Dragon. "I think I like her."

"Relax, soldier," the second said with a grin. "I don't go for your type. I prefer my partners to have bigger balls and wear them on their chests."

"Which god do you represent?" Ranger asked. "I need to know which one I'll be praying to tonight."

Axle chuckled but said, "Shut it, Ranger. We need to finish the meeting, not find you a date. And no, we can't do both."

"Pres, not all of us have women waiting at home for us."

Trip laid a hand on Ranger's shoulder. "Yeah, Bro. Have a heart."

"Right," Ranger agreed, nodding. "I just want love."

Dragon shook his head. "The two of you are going to get yourselves or the rest of us killed, someday, with your fucking mouths."

Trip and Ranger both opened their mouths to retort, but Axle turned around in his chair and gave them the look that told them he meant business. "Not. Another. Word." Both of them snapped their mouths shut. Smart.

Lira waved a hand over her shoulder and her crew stepped forward and lined up. "Let's sort out these partnerships."

For the next thirty minutes, Axle and Crush worked with Lira to place champions with members of the Howlers or the Claws. Dragon was surprised that his wolf was watchful but remained silent. He ended up partnered with Ordys.

The Latin man approached and held out his hand to Dragon. "Hey. Ordys De León."

Dragon shook his hand, giving the shake extra grip, letting Ordys know that Dragon didn't give a shit if the man was a champion to a god or demi-god or whatever the fuck. If the man posed a threat to the Howlers or the Claws, Dragon would take him out.

"Dragon."

"Your real name is..."

"Not your business." Releasing the man's hand, Dragon took in the man's appearance. Golden brown skin. He was around six feet tall, making him almost as tall as Dragon. He wasn't bulky, but Dragon could tell he was thickly muscled under the long-sleeved navy t-shirt he had on. His hair was dark brown, as was his eyes and full beard. Unlike Dragon, Ordys kept his beard groomed, even if it was a few inches long.

"I'm a champion for Raghnall, God of Sapientiam."

"God of what?" Dragon had no idea what Ordys had said.

Ordys smirked. "God of Wisdom. Look. I think we should spend some time getting to know each other. In battle, it will help to know each other's strengths and weaknesses."

"You expect me to tell you my weaknesses?"

After a shrug, Ordys replied, "You can tell me, or I can contact Raghnall and ask him to find out. Your choice."

"Whatever." Dragon turned and headed out of the building. "You have wheels?"

"Yeah. Where we going?"

"I'm fucking hungry. Meet you at TC's diner."

Kisy

Kisy was just leaving the HTC merchandise store with three bags full of Howlers gear when she saw Dragon pull up and park his bike in the lot for the clubhouse. After climbing off his bike, he headed her way.

He looked so fucking good. His hair was wild as always, but he had a pair of dark sunglasses on his face, making him look even more badass than usual. Add in the dark jeans, dark gray tee, and cut... *hot*.

"Hey," he said as he reached her and bent down to kiss her lips. "What's in the bags?"

Kisy bit her bottom lip and shrugged. "Some stuff."

Dragon chuckled. "Stuff or *stuff*?"

Grinning, Kisy replied, "Both."

He gave a nod. "Did you eat?"

Damn it. She knew she was forgetting to do something.

"Love," he said in *that voice*. "Two."

Kisy rubbed her thighs together to ease the ache the sound of his voice caused. "I might have gotten distracted."

"Come on." He took the bags from her hands and returned to the store. She watched as he spoke to the woman behind the counter – a Claws prospect – and asked her to stash the bags behind the counter. Then he took Kisy's hand and led her down the block to the diner.

When they entered, Kisy looked around. Most of the tables had a Howler or a Claw with another person she didn't know. "Something going on?"

Dragon stopped next to a booth with a Latin gentleman sitting at it. He motioned for her to take the other side of the booth. She slid in and Dragon slid in next to her.

"Yes," Dragon told her, "and I will explain it in more detail later, because you need to know what's happening. For now, you're going to fucking eat like you should have earlier, while I talk to Ordys." He motioned for a server and Kitty approached.

"Kitty," Dragon began, "I'll have my usual. Get Kisy that, but a half order. Add a water. Ordys, you want anything?"

"Just a piece of pie — your choice in flavor — and a cup of coffee, please?"

Kitty looked over Ordys. The look in her eyes said she liked what she saw. "Ever had a piece of Kitty's pie?"

Ordys raised a brow but smirked. "I'd be up for trying that."

"Great. Pecan pie for lunch. Kitty pie for dinner… and a late-night snack." Then Kitty strutted back to the kitchen in her jean short-shorts and her cropped white tee that had TC's Diner in purple on the front. She did that wearing heels that had to be five inches.

Kisy was impressed. Get him, Girl!

Ordys looked back and forth between her and Dragon. Then he smiled. "I take it this is your woman."

Dragon laid his arm along the back of the booth seat and nodded. "Yeah. Kisy, this is Ordys De León. He is a champion to the God of Wisdom."

Kisy's eyes bugged out. "Exsqueeze me?"

"I'll explain later."

"Uh, no. You'll explain now!" Kisy turned in her seat to face Dragon. She knew she looked crazy, but she couldn't process his words.

Dragon turned his head and met her gaze.

"I'll just make this easy." Ordys clasped his hands together on the table and addressed Kisy, "There is The Creator. Then there are the God of Life and the God of Death. They had children – the Gods of Balance, Wisdom, Negativity, Positivity, Action, and Chaos. The God of Wisdom is my direct god. His name is Raghnall. Dragon's direct god would either be Rue or Mattyx, the Gods of Negativity and Positivity. They are the gods of land shifters and water shifters. My god is the God of, ironically enough, dragon shifters."

"What?!" Kisy shifted until she was up on her knees in the booth seat and leaning on the table on her elbows, totally enthralled by what Ordys was saying. "Real dragons? Like the small dragons in the south or like *dragon* dragons?"

"Yes. He's the god of all dragons. But I can shift into a full-size, fire-breathing dragon at will, just like your man can shift into... what?"

"A wolf," Dragon bit out.

"Oh. Okay." Ordys nodded.

Kisy giggled. "That's so fucking cool! Like can you fly? And if so, what do your wings look like?

Do you have scales or just like tough skin? Are you green? Are you like cold-blooded? Do you lay eggs? Can you fly? Wait... I already asked that."

Ordys grinned. "We have to be careful, though. Have to make sure our masking is intact, so the world doesn't learn the secret."

"I want to go for a ride! Can I?"

"No. You. Fucking. Cannot."

At the sound of Dragon's gritted declaration, Kisy realized what it looked like. She was leaning over the table, having a conversation with Ordys. But to an observer, it wouldn't be out of the question to assume it was flirting. She quickly returned to her seat and leaned into Dragon.

"You're right. That wouldn't be a good idea. Sorry. Got caught up." She lowered her gaze to the table, feeling bad that she might have hurt Dragon's feelings or made anyone doubt her commitment to him.

Then Dragon was lifting her chin using his knuckle. She looked up into his eyes, seeing nothing but love there. "It's okay, Love. But... *three*."

A chuckle came from across the table. Dragon looked over at Ordys with narrowed eyes. "Problem?"

Kisy looked at Ordys to see him grinning. "Nope. I just realized your dynamic and... kudos. Just happy for my partner and his mate."

Feeling like she needed to help smooth this over after her actions, Kisy wrapped her arm around Dragon's waist. "If you two are going to be partners, you should learn to be friends. Ordys, tell us about you."

"That's a great idea, Kisy. I'm in construction. I do various jobs, but mostly, I am lead contractor. I have a degree in architecture, but I'm more of a hands-on type than a creative. I also have a master's in history and a bachelor's degree in economics. I like learning."

"Wow," Kisy commented.

"I have four sisters. No brothers. None of my sisters are champions. They have a different father, but I love them with everything I am. I like baseball and reading. What else do you want to know?"

Kisy looked up at Dragon to find him still staring at Ordys with narrowed eyes. She poked Dragon in the abdomen. When he looked down at her, she gave him a smile. "I'm assuming you were assigned together, right?"

Dragon nodded.

"Then Axle will expect you to make the best of this, right?"

Dragon sighed and gave a nod. Then he returned his attention to Ordys. "I'm enforcer for the Howlers. I'm a legacy. My father was the previous enforcer. I have a younger sister. She's mated to one of my club brothers. I have no college education and am not a fan of reading, but I help run the club's businesses. As for hobbies, you don't want those details."

Kisy's cheeks heated. She definitely enjoyed Dragon's *hobbies*.

"I'm a grouchy bastard. That won't change."

Kisy sighed. "He's really smart and one of Axle's most trusted. Yes, he's grouchy, but it's because he thinks he's responsible for the safety of everyone in the club and their families. He takes it personally when he doesn't keep them protected."

Ordys looked from Kisy to Dragon, his humor gone. "So, I imagine this war situation is feeling heavy for you. Dragon, you aren't—"

"If you say I'm not responsible for this, I will tear your throat out," Dragon said through clenched teeth.

Ordys inclined his head. "Noted. But… you're not."

"Anyway," Kisy blurted before Dragon made good on his threat, "where are you staying?"

"I'm not sure yet. I heard there is a hotel not far from here."

"You should let him stay with us at the house," Kisy suggested. "Do you have furniture in the room on the main floor?"

"There's a bed," Dragon said, but he didn't look happy.

"Dex, if you keep him close, you know he's not stabbing the club in the back," Kisy suggested, but shot Ordys an apologetic look.

"Fine," Dragon bit out.

Chapter Seventeen

Dragon

After their lunch at the diner, Dragon and Kisy showed Ordys around Warden's Pass in Ordys's 1955 Mercury Montclair. It was just as much for Kisy's benefit as Ordys's. Kisy's tour had been hindered by the fact that they were on his bike. There wasn't a chance for him to point out much to her. In the car, he was able to be more detailed.

Once he felt Ordys and Kisy were familiar enough with Warden's Pass that they could find their way around, he gave Ordys his home address and told him to meet them there around eight for dinner. He decided they would grill out for dinner, and that would give him more of a chance to feel out Ordys.

Kisy was right. They needed to come to an understanding and trust each other, but that didn't mean he was going in blind. He would watch out for red flags. Hopefully, Ordys's intentions were pure, and Dragon wouldn't need to end the man's life.

Fucking dragons. As a shifter, it shouldn't surprise him, but he was baffled that there were actual dragon shifters. What other creatures were out there, he wondered. He figured he could ask Ordys, but he wouldn't. He knew Kisy would eventually. She was so damn curious.

He loved that about her, just like he loved everything else that made up the beautiful, sassy woman. She was always surprising him. He never knew what was going to come out of her beautiful mouth. Their life together would never be boring.

The amount of joy he felt in his heart was almost more than he could take. He felt like it was about to burst open and leak out everywhere. How had he ever lived without her energy and dramatics in his life? He didn't know, but he knew he wouldn't be able to live without it again.

That was what was on his mind as he led her down into their room, making sure the door was locked behind them. She had sassed him, as usual, and he was looking forward to her *consequences*. He knew she was expecting edging or spanking or even telling her to use her mouth, but he had something special in mind for her. And with Ordys out to meet with Kitty, he wanted to hear her.

When they reached the bottom of the stairs, she headed for the bed. Dragon slipped off his cut and hung it on the hook on the wall.

"Love," he said, firmly.

He watched Kisy stop in her tracks. "Yes, D?"

"Naked. I have a craving to make love to my mate."

He had been thinking about making love to her for hours. Not dominating her and fucking her. *Making love* to his mate. Face to face. Gazing into that beautiful face. And that was what he was going to do.

That didn't mean he was excusing her behavior. No. He had plans. He was just going to put them off for a bit. Let her think he forgot. Let her wonder when he would remember. Let her wonder what he would do. Then he'd give her the *consequences* she had earned.

Kisy did as he asked and stood near the end of the bed, staring at him, waiting for instruction. *Fuck.* He liked that.

His wolf growled inside of him and began to pace, anticipation coursing through him and making him feel a bit wild. So was the man.

Dragon let his gaze wander over her body as he disrobed. When he was naked, he approached her and cupped her face in his hands. She had in her teal contacts. It made her eyes almost glow. Running his thumb over the skin at her temple, he lowered his head and pressed his lips to her right eyelid, then to her left.

Kisy's breath hitched.

"I like your contacts. They make your eyes shine. If you want more, let me know. I'll buy them."

Kisy looked up at him and smiled. "I have a variety of colors, but the teal and the purple are my favorite."

"What did you buy today?"

"Howlers gear," she told him. "And some other stuff."

"Stuff for me?"

She bit her bottom lip. "Yeah."

He let out a growl. "You can show me later." Pressing his lips to hers, he shifted her toward the bed. "On the bed on your back. Arms up," he whispered against her lips.

When she immediately did as he instructed, his eyes began to glow, making her body tinted in green. He fucking loved how obedient she was when they stepped into their room.

He started at her feet. Kissing and licking her arches, moving from one to the other and back. Doing the same, he worked his way up her ankles, calves, and thighs. By the time he reached her core, she was panting and shifting restlessly on top of the comforter. His wolf was doing the same inside of him. He skipped over her core and moved to her abdomen. Continuing up until he reached her lips.

After a few gentle kisses, he asked, "How wet are you, Love?"

"F-find out," she breathed.

With a smile on his face, he reached between them and let his fingertips caress her pussy, dipping in before continuing up to circle her clit. Wet and hot, she was ready for him.

"Just this time, you come when it hits you, Love," he told her as he lined himself up and began a slow glide inside of her. "Understood?"

"Y-yes," she answered, pressing her inner thighs to his hips.

"Legs around me, Love." He slid his hands up her arms until he could thread his fingers with hers and grip her hands. Kissing her lips, he began a steady rhythm, curling his hips just right at the end of each thrust.

She wretched her mouth from his. "D," she moaned as her hands squeezed his and her heels dug into his ass and lower back.

"Yeah, Love, let me hear it," Dragon growled and shut down the glow so he could see her face clearly. Her cheeks were flush, and her eyes were shining at him, filled with love and pleasure.

Intensifying his thrusts, Dragon watched as Kisy threw her head back and let out a loud moan.

"Look at me," he told her.

Her head straightened as her panting quickened, her chest heaving against his own, making her breasts rub against him.

"You feel so fucking good," he growled and nipped her bottom lip. "So tight and slick... hot. I'm fucking addicted to you, Love."

"S-same."

He lowered his head until his mouth was at the mating mark he left on her neck. He gave it a good suck and felt her core begin to contract. Within a few seconds, she cried out his name and her limbs tightened around him.

Dragon quickened his thrusts and laid his forehead to hers, watching her eyes as her climax crested and slowly faded, leaving her sated and smiling softly. That look set off his own climax.

Slamming home, he whispered, "I love you," as he emptied himself inside of her.

She ran her nose along the side of his and replied, "I love you, too, D."

After a relaxing bath where they cuddled and Dragon caught Kisy up on everything that was going on with the war, Dragon helped her out and dried her off. He helped her brush her hair and pull it back in a ponytail, liking that she giggled the entire time he wielded that brush.

She made the mistake of questioning his abilities, since he never did much with his own wild hair. Dragon proved her wrong.

"I can't believe you know how to do that," she said as she examined his handiwork in the mirror, a simple ponytail high on her head.

"Believe it." Wrapping a towel around his waist, he headed out to the bedroom and over to the curtained section of his bedroom wall. Pulling back the right side of the curtain, he opened a small drawer attached to the wall and pulled out two packages that were still in their plastic containers and tied together. He fixed the curtain and removed the smaller package, setting it on the nightstand.

"What's that?"

Dragon looked over at Kisy and saw that she was looking at the package in his hand. Grinning, Dragon didn't answer her. He rounded the bed and opened the cabinet. On the third shelf down, he had a few bottles of lube. He grabbed the oil based one and shut the cabinet doors.

"D?"

He noted the slight worry in her tone and could understand that. She was beginning to catch on that it had something to do with her *consequences*.

Turning around to face her, Dragon opened the plastic package and pulled out a buttplug. It was the same teal as her contacts. He held it up so she could see it.

"Tomorrow, when you go to work, you will have this in. And you will keep it in, all day, until I remove it. Understood?"

Kisy visibly swallowed. "It's my first day."

"Yes."

"What if that distracts me and messes up my work?"

Dragon grinned. "I happen to know the boss, so I think you'll be forgiven."

"D."

"Love," he said, and raised an eyebrow at her.

Kisy stomped her bare foot on the floor. "Fine."

"If you don't want it, I won't do it. You know how to stop everything. What's your safe word?"

Kisy sighed. "Koala."

"Are you using your safe word?"

"No." Her gaze met his. "If I wear that all day, are you going to take my ass tomorrow night?"

Dragon growled and his eyes glowed for a few moments. "Yes."

Kisy rubbed her thighs together, and Dragon's gaze dropped to her nipples to find them hardened. Yeah, his Love wanted it.

Kisy

It was her first day at work, and Kisy was full of butterflies. Butterflies and a buttplug. It wasn't the first buttplug she ever used, but it was the first one lovingly and sensually inserted by the man she had fallen in love with. The way he spent almost an hour relaxing her, stretching her, kissing and touching her, made her breathless to think about.

She enjoyed the process as much as she would enjoy having him claim that part of her later that night. She liked anal sex, always had, if the person she was engaging in it with knew what they were doing. She had no doubt Dragon knew what he was doing.

Kisy was trying to pay attention to what Keys was saying as he introduced her to the building staff and showed her around the building and her office, but all she could focus on was the delicious pressure inside her ass shifting with every step she took.

A knowing look crossed Keys face and he smirked. "You're not going to be very effective today , are you?"

"It's Dragon's fault," she blurted and then covered her mouth with her hand. She hadn't meant for that to come out, but it wasn't wrong.

Keys chuckled. "Dragon mentioned something about you getting a pass on fuckups, today. I'm not going to ask why, because I want to keep my life. So today, just try to familiarize yourself with the list of properties and what type of property they are."

"Can we... uh... not tell Dragon that I..."

Another chuckle. "Yeah. Consider it a professional privilege."

"Thank you," she breathed and smiled back at him. "And I can call you if I have any questions?"

"Yup. Especially about the security systems. If it's about the properties, you can call me or Trip. We are the ones who are the most familiar. You could also call Dragon. He fills in for Trip when Trip's otherwise engaged and is considered the Staff Manager."

"Good to know," she replied and waved as Keys headed for the door.

Once he was gone, she approached her desk chair and looked around her small but beautiful office. It wasn't much, just a desk and chair for her, two chairs for visitors, and some shelving units. She liked that it wasn't typical white, but instead was painted a medium gray and had teal accents on the various knickknacks and decorative doodads that were sprinkled on the shelving units. There was a tiny howling wolf statue made of green glass and several teal planters with small cacti. Even the guest chairs had dark teal stripes in the dark gray upholstery.

The bottom half of the shelving units were pull-out filing drawers that locked. She briefly wondered where the keys were until she pulled open the middle drawer of her desk and saw a set of silver keys in the corner.

Taking a deep breath and preparing herself for the monumental task of learning a new set of properties, Kisy sat down and bit back the moan that wanted to come out of her mouth as the plug shifted. She scooted her chair in and opened the folder Keys had left on top of her desk that he said was an overview of the properties they owned.

She was halfway down the page when the plug began to vibrate. Her pussy instantly contracted and her back arched. She couldn't believe how strong the sensations were. If it continued for much longer, she'd be orgasming at her desk.

Just when she thought it would was unavoidable, the vibrating stopped. Kisy sucked in a lungful of air and whimpered as she reached for her phone and sent Dragon a text.

>You have a remote. Don't you?<

The answering grinning emoji was confirmation enough.

She wanted to be annoyed, but all she could think about was Dragon talking to his brothers about club business while pressing the button to turn on her vibrating butt plug, and that thought sent her into a fit of giggles.

She didn't stop giggling until two minutes later when the plug started vibrating again.

Dragon had edged her before, but never like this. With her hands tied behind her back and her body bent over the end of the bed, she let out a frustrated groan when he pulled the vibrator from her pussy and stopped shifting the plug in her ass. The second he stopped, the climax that had been building in her lower abdomen started to fade.

"Patience, Love," Dragon said into her ear with amusement in his voice.

"D, that was five orgasms you have denied me." She tried to press her thighs together for some friction against her clit to bring back the orgasm, but Dragon was standing between her spread legs.

"You earned each of them," he replied and ran a hand from her ass cheek up her spine to get a grip of the hair on the back of her head. Without hurting her, he used it to turn her head and gave her a gentle kiss on the lips.

"How? I didn't do anything."

"Love, you asked if I'd ever consider sharing you with another man. That earned you more than I've given you, but I suppose we can call it even. But I need you to hear me when I say this." He dropped his head and gave the mating mark on her neck a suck. When he released the flesh and looked into her eyes, he growled, "If you want more than one hole filled, they will be filled by me and only me. Do you understand?"

When she didn't reply right away, Dragon slid that vibrator back into her pussy.

"Yes," she moaned and arched her back, trying to force it deeper.

"Are you sure you heard me, Love?"

"D!" She gasped as it brushed her g-spot. "Yes! Yes, I heard you! I understand!"

She heard him chuckle against the skin of her neck. "Where do you want me, Love?"

"My ass, D."

Dragon pulled the vibrator from her core and backed away from her. Instantly, the cool air of the room hit her fevered flesh, making her shiver a bit. She knew better than to move from the position she was in. As much as she liked it when Dragon spanked her, she still had the plug in and was too on edge to fight an orgasm while he doled out love taps.

"I'll try to warm this for you, Love."

Then she felt his fingers brush her skin near her ass and the plug was slowly slid out. As soon as the plug was free of her ass, his fingers slid in, covered in what she suspected was lube. True to his word, he had tried to warm it and mostly succeeded.

As he stretched her more with his fingers, he bent over her back and whispered into her ear, "When I take this, I will finally have all of you. Do you know how hot it is that you're willing to give me all of you?"

"D," she breathed.

He pulled his fingers out of her. Then she felt the bulbous head of his cock pressed against the stretched hole. As he pressed in slowly, popping through that ring of muscle, a green light shined from behind her and he uttered in a guttural tone, "I fucking love you, Love."

"Love you," she moaned as he slid in until he bottomed out.

When he slid back out until only the head of his cock was inside of her, she felt the vibrator slide back into her pussy. A thin sheen of sweat coated her body. Dragon began fucking her in both holes on a counter rhythm that send shocks of pleasure coursing through her body. She gasped repeatedly, desperately trying to hold off her orgasm until he said the word.

He must have sensed her struggle since two strokes later, he growled, "Come for me, Love."

She exploded, white light blinding her as her body tensed and released, tensed and released, stealing her breath and thought. She felt him slide in and the vibrator slide out. As she faded into blackness, she heard him call out her name.

Kisy didn't know how long she'd been out for, but when she opened her eyes, she saw pink terry cloth. Blinking slowly, she tried to bring her eyes into focus. When she could finally see clearly, she lifted her eyes to find that Dragon was standing on the side of the bed with his hands on his hips.

"Welcome back, Love." Then he motioned to the towel wrapped around his hips. "Did you happen to toss something red in with my white towels?"

Kisy couldn't help it. She snorted and rolled over in bed, laughing so hard tears filled her eyes.

Chapter Eighteen

One week later... Kisy

Dragon was being an overprotective, demanding asshole, Kisy decided as she glared at him in the middle of the clubhouse. She knew it was going to be a problem as soon as she got a text from Butterfly saying that Axle had given the order to lock down the women and children.

She had been getting ready for work in their room at the compound when the text came through. After she was dressed, had done her hair, and applied minimal work makeup, she found that her car keys were missing from her bag. Irritated, she went looking for Dragon and found him in the clubhouse talking to Trip, Bullet, and Ranger.

"Dexter Dole!" She stepped in the middle of them and glared up at her mate, hands on her hips. "Where in buttfuck are my keys?"

"Well, that's a new one," Ranger commented.

Trip chuckled until Kisy shot a glare at him. That shut him up and she returned her glare to Dragon.

Dragon raised an eyebrow at her and said, "First... *One*." He paused to let it register in her head, no doubt, but she was too irritated with him to care. "There's been a situation. Axle has ordered that all women and children stay at the clubhouse and apartments until it is resolved."

"Uh... no. I have a job," Kisy replied. "And I intend on performing that job, since I'm getting paid to do so."

"We're your bosses, Kisy," Bullet said, but it was in a calming tone.

Kisy was too far gone to be calmed. "Save it. You have your own woman to contend with, since she told me you and Axle could kiss her ass if you think you are keeping her from volunteering at the children's hospital today."

She heard muttered curses behind her as Bullet stormed out of the room. Kisy glanced over at Trip. "Seen Darlin' today?"

Trip's brows drew together. "Why?"

"Because if I had to take a guess, all of the ol' ladies are of the same mind. But I could be wrong since she has Cane." Cane – also known as Little

Man — was Axle Dexter Weber, the infant son of Trip and Darlin', named after his proud uncles.

Trip also cursed under his breath as he pulled his phone out of his pocket and walked away.

Once he was gone, Kisy shifted her gaze to Ranger. "You just hanging around for the show?"

Ranger grinned at her. "If I had popcorn, it'd be perfect."

She ignored him and looked up at Dragon. "I'm not staying here. I'm going to work." Out of the corner of her eye she noticed her keys sitting on the bar top. She tried to snatch them up, but Dragon was quicker.

He slid them in his pocket and said firmly, "You are staying here. End of story." Then he walked away.

"Bossy bastard!"

Dragon lifted a hand and held up two fingers above his shoulder. She knew what that meant, but again, she was too far gone to care.

"It really is for the best. At least during the day when the brothers can't be with you. It's easier to protect all of you when you're together," Ranger told her and gave her a pat on the back before he too walked away.

Furious, Kisy started to pace in front of the bar. She was about to turn and head in the opposite direction when she saw what else was sitting on the bar top. A set of keys with a familiar keychain. It was a gunmetal gray leather diamond with *World's Most Badass Uncle* stitched in Howlers MC green. Dragon's keys.

Knowing full well that she was breaking rules, and pissed enough not to care, Kisy grabbed the keys and ran for the parking lot.

Dragon

When Dragon finally caught up to his little minx at the property management office for Howlers Properties, he stalked into the building, past all of her curious coworkers, and headed for her office. After he stepped inside, he shut the door behind him, slowly and deliberately turning the lock, his eyes locked on her the entire time.

"Dragon," she breathed in an anxious but excited whisper as she stood from her desk chair and stepped to the side.

"On your knees, Love," he growled.

"I'm at work."

His eyes flashed green light at her. "You're about to get to work. On. Your. Knees."

As he watched her do as he instructed, he crossed the office and shut her blinds. He stalked over to where she was kneeling while he unfastened and unzipped his jeans.

"I thought I told you not to steal my bike."

She looked up at him with a flash of defiance in her eyes – purple contacts. "You stole my car keys."

Dragon grinned. "Love, if you wanted my cock in your throat, all you had to do was ask." He shoved his jeans and boxer briefs down to mid-thigh and fisted his erection. He tapped it on her bottom lip. "Open."

She glared at him, but he noticed the way she was trying to rub her thighs together. She wasn't fooling him. Even if he told her he forgave her – which he had – she'd still want to suck his cock. It was their little game.

Kisy opened her lips. Her hot little tongue came out and tickled his piercing.

Dragon groaned and slowly fed his erection into that sweet mouth. Kisy's defiance immediately vanished. She began sucking his cock with an eagerness that would get her a reward as soon as she was done. Forward and back, Kisy swirled her tongue around the tip. She used the perfect amount of suction. And when he gave her the okay, she reached up and cupped his balls in her soft hands, squeezing them just right.

"Damn, you're great at that, Love." He slid his fingers into her waves, now a white blond after her trip to the salon, and fisted his hands. Just as his thighs began to twitch, she deep-throated him and triggered Dragon's climax.

Pleasure shot up his spine and through his limbs. His vision and hearing blinked out, and the world was nothing but ecstasy and Kisy's wet, hot mouth. As he came down and slid himself out of her mouth, he stared down at his mate, loving the proud little smile she had on her face as she fisted his still hard cock. Still sensitive, Dragon shivered at the contact.

"I love you," she said, softly.

Dragon's heart skipped a beat, and his wolf howled inside him. He dropped to his knees in front of her, his hands still fisted in her hair. With his forehead pressed to hers, he whispered, "I love you, too, Love." The kiss he gave her was sweetly gentle. "Which is why I wanted you safe at the compound."

"D, I have to have a life. I can't just be locked down whenever you guys think there might be danger."

Dragon sighed and pulled back so he could look into her eyes. "We wouldn't lock you down unless there was more than just a possibility. We're facing a war, Kisy. And this mark," he let go of her hair and ran a finger over the mark he left on her neck, "tells them that you belong to me."

"I know... and we'll talk more about that, but I have a question."

"Okay." He put himself back in his jeans and refastened them while he stared at her and waited for her question.

"Why is it that all of your brothers with full-human ol' ladies have tattoos on their necks declaring that to the world, but you don't? You ashamed of me?"

Dragon grinned. She was jealous. "No. Of course I'm not. I make most of the decisions in this relationship, but there is one decision that is and will always be yours to make."

"And that is?"

"When I mark my body with your name, you will always be the one to decide where it will be and how it will look. It's your mark on me."

A grin grew on her beautiful face. "I can design it?"

He gave a nod.

"I want it on your neck."

"We'll get it done soon."

She bit her bottom lip. Then she released it and said, "I want the Howler's logo with your kiss print. But you'd have to put stuff on your lips to do that."

He kissed her and replied, "Haven't you figured it out?"

"You'd do anything in your power to make me happy," she whispered, repeating words he'd said to her before.

"Anything," he confirmed. He smiled. "Now... pants, panties, and boots off. Ass on the desk. I'm hungry."

Rebel

Rebel had always loved the library. His life was shit, always had been. Well, it was shit until he fell in with the Howlers. But the library had always been an escape for him. He could dive into the worlds of J.R. Ward's Black Dagger Brotherhood, George R.R. Martin, Tolkien, Ann Rice, Stephen King, and Agatha Christie, giving him a reprieve from the hell that his life had become.

When Gorgeous approached him about going on a run for things to occupy the ol' ladies and children while they were on lockdown at the clubhouse, he jumped at the chance. She asked for books, cards, games, and puzzles. When he left, she was setting up the big screen in the cafeteria so the ol' ladies could watch some chick flick, but he knew they would get tired of movies and shows before too long.

He parked his truck outside the library and got out. As he approached the front door, he locked the doors to his truck, making sure no one could steal the goodies he had already picked up. The excitement that he had as a child every time he stepped foot in a library was still there as an adult. He stepped through the door and felt the flutter in his gut, the rush through his veins. Within the four walls were galaxies of wonder and adventure, passion and drive, friendship and lessons. Everything you ever needed to know could be found in a book.

He wasn't one of those guys who scoffed at romance novels or called them porn. Rebel knew the truth. Those books held more truths and solved more mysteries about women than men were aware of. If they knew how much easier it would be to please their women if they just examined her bookshelf, there would be far fewer divorces.

Which is why he didn't blink an eye when the ol' ladies requested the smuttiest smut that ever smutted. They thought he'd be embarrassed. Rebel was not a smut virgin. He couldn't wait until he showed up with the best of the best books, maybe even some that they hadn't heard about.

As he passed the desk, he saw a drop-dead gorgeous woman sitting behind the counter, reading one of the new paranormal romance books he had his eye on. He didn't realize it had come out yet. It was by Kimberly M. Ringer. He already read her entire The Five Angels Series and had high hopes for Astral's Bonded. The world in The Five Angels Series was so complex and interesting, he'd read the three-book series in a week.

He was about to ask the librarian how the book was so far, when he was distracted by a soft meow coming from his left. When he looked, he saw the cutest all gray cat perched on the top edge of the bookshelf. He slowly walked over and just as slowly lifted a hand to let the cat give him a sniff. Rebel was not at all surprised when the cat hissed and jumped down, taking off across the library. The cat smelled the wolf in him. Dogs and cats were not so trusting of each other.

Still chuckling about the cat, he looked over at the librarian and instantly jumped into action at the color of her face. She was choking!

Bri

Astral's Bonded was getting good. Well, not getting good. It was good from the first paragraph, but it was getting to a detailed sex scene, and Bri was here for it. She already had a laugh out loud moment in the library when she read the scene with the pink hand towel. Her friend told her she would, and they weren't lying. If only she could find a man like Kolton to model a hand towel for her.

Yum.

On that thought, she put a couple more gummi bears into her mouth from the stash she kept in the bottom drawer of her desk. She might have a problem. Was a five-pound bag of gummi bears in her desk enough to be considered a problem? Well, whatever, she liked her gummies.

She was engrossed in the scene, picturing each and every dip and crevice of Kolton's body, when she was jolted out from her imagination by the meow of the library cat, Bleu. She looked up at Bleu's typical spot where she liked to perch her tush and found a hot biker reaching up to pet the cat. When he lifted his arm, his tee lifted with it, exposing a good five inches of defined abdomen that made Bri's mouth water. *Did I manifest a hot man into existence?*

Not wanting the biker to catch her drooling on herself, she swallowed, totally forgetting the two gummi bears, and one got wedged in her throat. She instantly began to panic when she tried to cough and couldn't dislodge the candy. Bri couldn't breathe! Her vision and hearing started to fade, either from the lack of oxygen or from the panic, she wasn't sure.

Shoving her chair back, she tried to think of what to do, but all she could think was I'm choking! I can't breathe! I'm going to die by gummi bear!

She didn't know how long it was before she felt a pair of hands grip her sides and force her to her feet. Then a strong set of arms wrapped around her, one hand grabbing the other fisted one, before beginning abdominal thrusts. A few thrusts in, the cherry red gummi flew out of her mouth and stuck to the end of a bookshelf ten feet from the opposite side of the desk.

As she sucked in air as quickly as possible, she heard a low, slightly graveled voice ask, "You okay, Ruby?"

Embarrassed, Bri quickly removed herself from his hold and began fidgeting with anything within reach in an attempt to hide her shaking hands. Her throat hurt, her stomach wasn't feeling the greatest, either, and her ego had taken quite the hit. For fuck's sake! A gummi bear!

"Uh... yes," she choked out. She reached for her bottle of water and took a drink, trying to clear it. It still felt off. "Thank you. You saved my life." Finally, she pulled herself together enough to look up at him and almost swallowed her tongue.

Bri! Get yourself together before you choke again!

His hair was medium blond, long on top, and brushed straight back. The sides were darker and cut close to the scalp. The eyes looking at her with concern, but also amusement, were a dark green and brown blend. A full reddish-blond beard surrounded smirking lips and ran along his jaw. It was a few inches long, but well-groomed. She didn't see a bunch of random hairs sticking out every which way. It suited him, though.

Instantly, her brain inserted him in the pink towel scene, and her nether regions shouted *Huzzah!*

"Your color was going back to normal, but now it's red again. You still have something in there, or are you embarrassed, Ruby?"

"Why do you keep calling me Ruby?" she asked, breathily as she tried to get herself under control. What was going on with her? It had to be the books. She was in heat and desperate for a good story. She just wished she was the leading lady for a change. That explained why she was inserting this man into her fantasies after only meeting him moments before.

"It's the pretty red of your cheeks. At first, it was because you were choking, and I didn't know your name. But now, it's because your cheeks become a charming shade of red when you blush."

"Bri." She cleared her throat and stuck out her hand. "I'm Bri."

He took her hand and gave it a nice squeeze. "Rebel. It's nice to meet you, Ruby." He gave her a half-smile.

And she was blushing again. *Fuck!*

Chapter Nineteen

Dragon

After Kisy climbed up on the edge of her desk, naked from the waist down, Dragon tried his best to make sure she had no doubt of his feelings for her. He loved her, all of her. He needed her in his life. And he wanted her every second, even when he was pissed off.

He kissed, licked, and nipped her until she threw her head back and moaned his name like they were alone in their bedroom. Kisy didn't give a second thought to what her coworkers would think. She probably would, later, but she'd learn that she wasn't working for a typical company.

Dragon continued to kiss and lick her thighs and her abdomen as she came down from her orgasm. Then he stood and took her sweet mouth in a kiss that lasted a good ten minutes. He could kiss her and touch her all day, but they both had shit to do.

After a while, he pulled out of the kiss and laid his forehead to hers. "Your car is outside." He pulled the keys from his pocket and set them on the desk next to her hip. "Promise me that when you get out of here, you will head right to the compound. No stops. If you need anything, text me what it is and I'll make sure it's there, waiting for you. Unless intel says otherwise, we'll probably get to stay at the house tonight, but I need you to be at the compound until I'm free to be with you at all times."

Kisy gave a nod. "We aren't going to have this fight tomorrow, right?"

Dragon let out a low growl. His wolf did not like the fact that their mate was in danger, and let it be known by the prowling and growling he was doing inside Dragon. "If we get intel on a confirmed plan, you will be at the compound with the rest of the ol' ladies. But... for now, I guess I won't fight you on it."

"I love you."

"I love you, too." He kissed her forehead and stepped back. Gripping her hips, he lifted her off the desk and set her on her feet.

As she got dressed, he looked around and found his keys hanging on the hook by her office door. He slipped them off the hook and into the pocket of his jeans.

"What are Ordys and the others doing today?"

Dragon let out a sigh. "They are meeting with Axle and Crush. Axle and Crush had some questions about everyone's abilities, and we weren't getting much information, individually. But it's only fair that they tell us what they can do, since they seem to know everything about shifters."

"That's true." Kisy fastened her jeans and approached him, wrapping her arms around his waist. "But I also think you guys need to be a little more trusting. They didn't have to come help."

She looked so cute, staring up at him, sated and happy. He bent down and gave her a quick kiss. "You're right. Get to work. Remember. No stops."

"Yes, D," she uttered, causing him and his wolf to growl.

Axle

Axle had spent thirty minutes on the phone with his father, getting all of the flight information. He tried again to convince his father to let the Howlers pick them up, but Joker wasn't having any of it.

Joker was coming with Griff and Thrash the following afternoon. Joker had somehow convinced his ol' lady, Tweetie, to stay home with the other ol' ladies. Axle promised to keep Joker updated as to the movements in the meantime.

Once he got off the phone, he and Crush made their way to the cafeteria where they were meeting with Lira and the other champions. Skull, Pinky, Pike, and Nails were already there.

When they entered the room, Axle was surprised that it was so quiet. Usually there was talking going on when there were group events in their building. The silence was a bit unnerving to Axle.

There were four rectangular tables in use, each were able to sit six to eight people. Three of the tables were filled with champions. At the fourth table, Lira and Marya sat with Pinky and Skull. Pike and Nails were standing off to the side, watching.

Axle and Crush took the seats between Skull and Pinky. He gave Lira a nod. "Thanks for getting all of the champions together."

"We're here to help," Lira responded.

Crush crossed her arms over her chest and relaxed back. "In order to be effective, we need to know what weapons we have at our disposal."

Lira gave a nod. "That's understandable. What I need you to know going into this conversation is that each of the champions gets to decide what they are comfortable doing. We will not be forced to use powers we aren't comfortable using."

Axle shrugged. "That's understandable."

"Great." Lira took a deep breath and looked behind her. Two women raised their hands. "Along with Marya and Myself, Rebekkah and Mezanya are Aileron Aegis champions. That means we serve Colvyr, the God of Stratera — the God of Balance and Calm, usually just referred to as the God of Balance."

"The guy in the boat shoes that I met."

Lira faced him again and nodded. "Yes. Our specialty is of the air. We are bird shifters. We have enhanced speed, agility, strength, hearing, and sight."

"Bird shifters?" Crush sat up and looked intrigued, a slight smile on her face.

"Yes," Lira chuckled. "Hawks, eagles, and ravens, mostly. Some falcons. We're a bit larger, just like you guys and your animal forms."

"That's kinda kickass," Crush admitted with a shrug.

"Ordys is the lead champion of the Sagacity champions. Along with Rozzat and Vega, he serves

Raghnall, the God of Sapientiam – the God of Wisdom and Thought, also referred to as the God of Wisdom and Judgment."

Axle looked over and saw Ordys, Rozzat, and Vega each give him a nod.

"They are dragon shifters. Their specialty is, as you can probably guess, fire. They have enhanced strength and speed, but they're also cunning and pretty good at persuasion. That's why their biggest weakness is their ego."

"Dragon shifters," Pike uttered from behind Axle. "That's insane."

"Maybe," Ordys began with a chuckle, "but it's true."

Lira smiled. "Next, we have two sets of champions, the Dolor Ayre and the Pangloss Eyne. They are closely connected, since their gods are twins. Rue is the God of Negans, the God of Negativity. Mattyx is the God of Positivum, the God of Positivity. Their champions are the ones that would be considered your gods, since their champions are shifters of the water and the earth." She turned her head and nodded to the table behind her and to her left. "Luna, Sky, and Orion are Dolor Ayre. Sol, Storme, and Aurora are Pangloss Eyne." Each of the champions gave a wave as their name was said. "Along with either pessimism or optimism, they have enhanced strength and hearing, but they are also really great at tracking, as you probably already know."

Axle wasn't surprised by any of that. It was basically any of his shifter brethren on steroids.

"Then we have Iri, Winona, and Chantel." She nodded to the table where the three champions were sitting. "They are Stehppes and serve Teko, the God of Accio — the God of Action. Storms, shadows, stealth, and security systems are their thing. Locks mean shit to them. I think you all might have some of their skills in that department. They are impulsive. But they have been pretty firm on not using their storm and shadow powers. It fucks with the weather systems." She shrugged as if she didn't quite understand that, but she also didn't care to. "They have the strength that the rest of us do."

Crush nodded. "And what type of animal or whatever do they have?"

"Snakes and reptiles," Iri said from his spot at the furthest table.

"Kickass," Pinky commented from next to Pike.

"And lastly, we have the Atax Aya. They are the vampires and other hybrids, only vampires here, though. Steve, Spike, Poindexter, and Aires." The middle table shot grins their way, showing off the fangs they let slide down. "They serve Aella, the God of Chaos. They are the spirit or energy god and can affect your energy, your spirit. Atax Aya are the masters of persuasion, manipulation, rumors. They aren't allergic to garlic or the sun... or even religious relics and are just like shifters, except they don't change form. Their eyes glow red, and their fangs come down, along with having enhanced hearing, strength, smell, etc."

Marya took a deep breath and said, "Basically, we have much the same abilities as you. Ours are just more enhanced. The abilities we have that you don't, we try not to use because it can have a wider influence on the world around us."

Axle nodded. After glancing around at the champions again, he uttered, "Thank you for sharing that information with us. We appreciate your trust. Now... let's get down to planning this war as much as we can with the limited information we have."

Kisy

As much as she loved it when he got into edging her, she felt like her heart was going to give if he denied her another orgasm. Her body was covered in sweat, her skin was over sensitized, and her clit was throbbing from the denied releases.

Earlier, when they finally made it to their bedroom, Dragon demanded she strip and proceeded to blindfold her. After he led her over to their bed, he tied her up where she was kneeling on the end of the mattress. Rope was tied to each of her wrists and fastened to the upper corners of the bedframe, forcing her to keep her hands above her head. Between her knees was a hard metal bar that prevented her from being able to close her knees.

Once he had her the way he wanted her, he began his sensual assault on her body, using his fingers, tongue, and teeth. He kissed and licked and nipped his way over her body, bringing her to the edge, again and again. But each time she was close, he stopped and walked away. She wasn't sure how far away he was, but she heard him talking on the phone.

She opened her mouth to throw sass at him, but he pressed a finger to her lip, silently ordering her to keep quiet. When she stopped hearing him speak, she held her breath and listened, trying to catch any hint as to where he was or what he was doing. But she didn't hear a thing.

After what felt like forever, she felt his skin against the front of her, his hard cock pressed into her abdomen. Just as she felt his breath on her lips, she felt him insert a vibrator into her pussy and turn it on. This time, he completely ignored her clit, instead he focused on her g-spot. But she was already so primed that it didn't take long for her to be at the edge.

"Love," he whispered, his breath caressing her ear as he withdrew the toy, "did you learn your lesson?"

"Wh-what lesson?" She took a deep breath, trying to calm herself.

"That you shouldn't steal my bike."

Kisy couldn't stop the corner of her lips from twitching into a slight smile. "Then you shouldn't steal my keys."

There was a brief rush of air that accompanied a hard slap of her ass and a sexy growl.

"You love to test me, don't you, Love?"

Kisy bit her bottom lip, knowing what that did to him, and did her best to shrug. She wasn't sure if she actually did it, until he cupped her breast in his hand and said against her lips, "It's a good thing I like it."

Now she was shaking from the latest orgasm denial and mentally cursing his name. It was driving her crazy, and he knew it. Through the edging, he proved he knew her body as well as she did. He knew which spot would make her moan and which spot would make her scream. He knew how to make her beg and he knew how to make her sigh. The man was a god when it came to playing with her body.

"D," Kisy moaned and laid her head back, closing her eyes and focusing on fighting back her orgasm. She couldn't come until he gave her permission, and he hadn't said anything even close to giving her that.

"Did you learn your lesson, Love?"

That fucking bike! He was still handing out *consequences* for her taking his bike. She forced down the bitchy comment she wanted to sling at him, and instead replied, "Yes, D. I won't take your bike."

Her arms suddenly felt looser, allowing her to drop them down at least a couple feet, but the slight freedom didn't last long. Moments later, he flipped her over until she was bent over the foot of the bed. He removed the stretcher bar, but kept her legs spread using his own thighs and knees.

"There's my good girl. Now, come for me," he whispered into her ear as he slammed into her well-primed pussy. The pace he set stole the breath from her lungs and sent her soaring.

The next thing she knew, she woke up plastered across his torso as he slept. She smiled as she stared at his face, taking in how peaceful he looked while unconscious.

Dragon may be the baddest enforcer around and the grumpiest bastard in town, but to her he was everything she needed and wanted. He was her equal, her partner, her *mate*.

Chapter Twenty

Rebel

Rebel didn't know what Ruby drank. He couldn't remember seeing a drink on her desk when he had been at the library the day before. He didn't want to be wrong, though, so he went with a cup of iced tea and a cup of coffee. In the paper bag he was carrying, there were a variety of creamer cups and sugar packets from the gas station, along with a bag of the best gummi bears he'd ever tasted. It was corny as hell, but he wanted an excuse to talk to her again.

Stepping through the library doors, he looked over at her desk, but she wasn't there. Frowning, he approached and set the bag and drinks on the top. Then he went on a search for Ruby.

It didn't take long before he found her down one of the aisles, on her hands and knees on the floor, reaching behind the couch that was there.

His wolf panted and whined inside him as he watched her for a few moments, loving the way her cute ass wiggled with her movements.

"Come on, Kitty. You're not supposed to be in here."

"Need some help?" Rebel asked.

Startled, Ruby jumped and scurried back from the couch. She whipped around until she was sitting on her ass and looked up at him. "Rebel!"

"Glad you remember my name." He smiled at her and motioned toward the couch. "Need help?"

"I've been chasing that cat around here for months. I don't think you'll be able to help, but you can certainly try."

"Watch for him to run through," Rebel said. Then he walked over to the other end and crouched down. He eyed the sliver of space behind the couch and the wall, maybe eight inches wide, and saw the cat a few feet from him. He reached an arm back there, with no intention of grabbing the cat, but instead with the intention of herding the cat toward Ruby.

It worked. As soon as his hand was within a foot of the animal, it hissed, turned, and darted for the other side.

"Got you!"

Rebel straightened and saw Ruby holding the cat. The way she was petting the cat's head made him and his wolf a bit jealous, but he told his wolf to chill. Then Ruby stood and headed for the exit. Rebel followed her and watched as she released the cat outside, several feet from the door. When she came back in, her cheeks were red, and she avoided meeting his eyes.

"Thank you for your help."

He took a step closer to her and used a knuckle to lift her chin. When her eyes shifted to him, he gave her a smile. "Hi."

The corners of her mouth twitched. "Hi," she replied, quietly.

"I didn't know if you were a tea drinker or a coffee drinker, so I could have screwed it all up, but I brought you some stuff." He cringed at the rambling and stepped back. "I... uh... left it on your desk."

"Really?" Her face lit up as he spoke. Then she almost skipped over to see what he brought her. She opened the lids of the cups and smiled. "Nice.

Nice. Um... I prefer hot tea, but in a bind..." Then she yanked open the bag.

When she just stared down into the bag, he thought he royally fucked up. His wolf growled at him for being an idiot and possibly ruining their chances with her. He went to take the bag from her hand to toss the offending gift, but she yanked it out of his reach and looked up at him with the most sparkling grin he had ever seen.

"Gummi bears!" She set the bag down and threw her arms around him. "Thank you! That's my favorite snack!"

The feel of her body pressed against his sent Rebel's mind to places it probably shouldn't be while in a library. And of course, his wolf was all about marking her right there on her desk.

After a far too brief hug, Ruby stepped back and dropped her arms to her side. "Oh... sorry. I shouldn't have done that without your permission or... I don't know... I don't really know you."

Rebel grinned at her. "For the record, you have my permission to touch me in any way you feel the need to, especially when you're thanking me."

And just like that, her cheeks flushed again. *Fuck!* He loved that.

"So, I was thinking," Rebel began and cleared his throat, "would you be interested in maybe grabbing some tea or some coffee with me sometime? I mean, my club has a lot going on, and it would probably be a week or so before I could, but... would you be interested in doing that... with me?"

What the fuck, Rebel? Why are you stammering like a teenager asking a girl to the prom?

There was that grin again. Ruby gave a nod. "Sure. Yeah. I'm here most nights until around eight. Just come by when you have a firmer grasp on your schedule."

Rebel breathed a sigh of relief and told his wolf to be patient. "Good. Yeah. I'll do that."

"Right. Well, I should get back to work. Uh... was one of these for you?" She motioned to the drinks.

He shook his head. "All for you. Talk to you soon." Then he headed for the exit. He had just pushed open the door, when the thought hit him that he was there to grab more chapter books for the tweens of the club. As he turned back around to head in, a cat darted past him.

Fuck.

Keys

Keys was in a meeting with Axle, Skull, Pike, and Dragon when Axle got the call from Riles that he had information to share. From what Keys understood, it was paired with a warning that the women were in danger.

After Axle sent out a notification that the women and children who weren't already at the compound needed to go there immediately, the Howlers mounted their bikes and rode out for the hotel to meet up with Riles and the UpRiders to get exact details.

The women wouldn't be alone, though. Half of the Claws were there as well as Rebel, the prospects, and Rebel's cousins – Ross and Ryker. Since they were staying at Rebel's house, they were also targets.

Crush, Pinky, and Nails went to have yet another *conversation* with Lace about pulling her shit together. The last thing they needed was to worry about a member on a bender. But with the latest intel, Keys was positive the women would be heading back as quickly as possible.

As the Howlers pulled into the parking lot, Riles and two other UpRiders came running out of the building. Riles looked freaked the fuck out, in Keys's opinion. Riles was almost to them when Keys started getting notifications one right after another on his phone.

Pulling the device from the side pocket in his cut, he made eye contact with Axle. He knew what the sound was for, since he had assigned a special notification to the security systems at all of their properties. That was the sound of disturbance at the properties that had Howlers or their family on staff.

"Fuck," Axle growled.

Keys pulled up the application that gave him access to the cameras and cursed. His heart started racing at the devastation he was seeing on the screen.

"What is it?" Axle demanded.

"The... there was an explosion at HPM and at... Heat."

"What?" Dragon was off his bike and coming for Keys at a determined clip.

"That's what I was coming to tell you," Riles said, panting. "They are targeting your properties, especially ones where the women might be."

Before he could finish his sentence, Dragon was already back on his bike and roaring out of the parking lot, no doubt on his way to check on his mate.

Emerson

Being Ashlyn's brother-in-law had pros and cons, Emerson thought. Sure, it meant his wife was the most beautiful woman on earth and he had a ready-made family full of kickass men and women, but it also meant there were more times than would be considered normal where their family was in danger. This was one of those times.

After ending the call with Axle, Emerson went looking for Georgia in Axle and Ashlyn's house, where they were staying until their house was done. He found her in the bathroom getting ready for the day. She was fully dressed, which was a good thing, but it looked like she just started her hair. She was just going to have to deal.

"You need to head over to the compound," he told her, loud enough to be heard over the blow dryer.

She stopped blow drying her hair and looked over at him, confusion on her face. "What? Why?"

"Axle's calling all the women there. Lock down. I guess they heard of a possible threat."

Georgia huffed out a breath. "Okay." She unplugged the blow dryer and began to put her blond hair up in a ponytail. "Are you ready to go?"

"I'm going to go meet up with Axle and see how I can help."

"Uh... what's going on?" She finished putting her hair up and turned to face him.

He cupped her beautiful face in his hands and pressed a kiss to her lips. Her light blue eyes were filled with concern, and he hated that he was about to give her news that would shatter her world.

"I don't know all of the details, but there were some explosions. Some Howlers-owned buildings were taken out. It's unclear if anyone was harmed."

Her gasp killed him. "You aren't going to put yourself in danger, Em. I won't let you. You can't."

Emerson laid his forehead against hers. "You and the Howlers are my family. I need to defend my family, Gigi. What kind of man would I be if I didn't?"

Tears filled those beautiful blue eyes, and her chin wobbled, but she gave a nod. "Will you see if Axle needs anyone to guard the compound? I'd feel better with you doing that than… whatever Axle and the guys are doing."

Emerson wanted to say no, but instead he gave a nod. "If that's where Axle puts me, I'll be okay with that. Promise me you'll go straight to the compound. No stopping anywhere."

Georgia sniffled. "Okay. I will."

He pressed his lips to hers and wrapped his arms around her. "I love you," he whispered against her lips.

"I love you, too."

Five minutes later, they were locking up the house and heading out to their vehicles. Georgia's car was parked in the driveway, and Emerson's motorcycle was parked at the curb, approximately forty yards from Georgia's car.

Emerson threw a leg over and straddled his bike, waiting to leave until she was safely on her way. He watched her climb in her little car and close the door. He started his bike at the same time she started her car.

The deafening explosion rattled his soul. Parts from her car flew into the air and landed all over the yard. The fireball was massive and hot enough to incinerate everything in and around the car. The heat of it hit him even from a distance, making his eyes water, but he was paralyzed with fear, unable to turn away.

His wolf began howling inside of him as his heart shattered. She was gone. He knew it. He could feel it. She was no longer in his soul. That space she had filled inside of him was empty once more. It was as if someone had ripped out the deepest part of him and destroyed it in front of him.

He wasn't sure how he got halfway across the lawn to the car and on his knees in the grass, but that's where he was when he opened his mouth and let out the longest, most horrible sound he'd ever heard.

Emerson no longer had control. When his wolf pushed to come to the surface, he didn't even fight it. He just gave in.

Keys

Dragon had just urgently taken off from the hotel parking lot. They were going to go after him, but Axle wanted to get as much information out of Riles as they could get before they took off to meet up with Dragon at the Howlers Properties.

Keys got another notification as Axle spoke with Riles.

Watching Emerson fall apart on the front lawn of Axle's house was almost as bad as the explosion that pulled that emotion out of the young shifter.

With a lump in his throat, Keys looked into Axle's eyes and said, "Georgia."

"Is she okay?"

Keys couldn't say it. He couldn't make the words come out. He shook his head and handed Axle the phone.

It was at that moment that the rental car pulled up and the retired members — Joker, Thrash, and Griff — climbed out.

"No!" Axle tossed the phone back to Keys and let out a howl that shook the bike Keys was still sitting on.

"What?" came from multiple people, but the loudest two voices were Trip and Joker.

"Georgia's dead," Keys managed to choke out.

Anger and devastation coursed through the group of men like a poisonous gas, weakening and slowly killing them.

"Meet up with Dragon. I'm going after Emerson." Axle's voice was more growl than human. Before he could take off, Joker hopped on the back of Axle's bike.

Joker looked over at Trip. "Go with the others. I'll update you."

Trip's eyes were wide and full of tears and his jaw was clamped tight. He gave a nod.

Then Axle took off, peeling out of the parking lot.

Skull cleared his throat and ordered, "Let's go find Dragon."

Crush

Crush was pissed the fuck off at Lace. She wasn't the worst Crush had ever seen her, but she was definitely drunk. With bloodshot eyes, Lace swayed and stumbled through her apartment. Who knew what else was in her system? After everything Rock and the Claws had done over the years in an effort to get her clean and sober, Lace was once again throwing it all away. It made Crush want to cut her loose from the club, but Lace was family and Crush just could do it. Crush, Pinky, and Nails decided they would just bring her back to the compound and let her sleep it off while the rest of them answered the emergency text Skull had sent her.

>Explosions at HTC owned props. Gigi dead. Maybe others.<

She didn't know everything, but she knew enough to gauge that the war was upon them and shit was already messy. She didn't know Georgia well, but she liked her. The men of the Howlers loved that girl like she was their blood baby sister. This was going to destroy them. It was most likely going to be up to her and the Claws to keep everyone on track to take care of those responsible, because it was quite possible the men would be distracted with grief.

Crush and the girls were crossing the parking lot of Lace's apartment building across town from the compound when it happened. Shots rang out from a row of trees at the back of the lot. Crush took cover behind a car and pulled her gun from the holster inside her cut. As she looked around to check on her crew, she found Lace on the ground a few feet from the rear end of the car. She had blood coming from the left side of her abdomen.

"Lace," Crush shouted and tried to get to her, but if she did, she would put herself in the line of fire. "Lace!"

Pinky had dove behind the car on the other side of the lot. Lace was between them. Crush wasn't sure where Nails was at. Then she heard it.

"Fuck you," Nails shouted. Her yell was followed by a series of shots.

Crush lifted up enough from her crouch to look over the trunk of the car, just in time to see the bullet go into Nails's left thigh.

Pinky rushed out to catch Nails as she fell. Not willing to let her members continue to be harmed, Crush rushed out and stood in front of them.

"Get them out of here, Pinks."

"I can ride," Nails forced out through gritted teeth.

Crush faced the woods, ready to defend her crew, but the shooting ceased. Eight men stepped out from the tree line and stopped.

The one in the middle looked like he was having the time of his life. His hair was shaggy around his craggy, bearded face. "Give yourself up and we'll leave your members alone," he said with a grin.

Crush didn't trust him for a second. "Get them out of here, Pinky," she repeated.

"I need a car."

Lace moaned and tried to reach for her pocket. Crush didn't dare look back to see what was happening. Then Pinky said, "Awesome, Lace." There was more moaning and some grunting. "Boss, her car is one car past you. I have the keys." The words were said low enough that she could hear it with her shifter hearing, but the assholes wouldn't be able to.

Crush started marching forward, praying Pinky would get Lace and Nails into Lace's car and out of the lot before the men started firing again. She was surprised when the men let her club sisters go without any further resistance. The men just watched with their guns pointed at them.

As soon as her girls were gone, Crush darted for her bike, which was parked closer to the men than to her. She was almost to it when she was tackled by at least two men. A third man kicked her gun out of her hand.

As she struggled to get the men off her, another man walked up and looked down at her. His patch said *Craggy Bastard* Through a chuckle, he said, "Stop fighting." Then another man stuck her in the arm with a needle, and Crush could feel her tiger begin to fade.

T.S. Tappin

Chapter Twenty-One

Dragon

There was no way that was real. It was all Dragon could think as he stared at the bonfire that was Kisy's mustang in the middle of the property management building's parking lot. The car was so engulfed in flames that there was no way someone could have survived that.

Dragon would know. He had set an explosion or two in his day.

His wolf was howling over and over inside of him at the sight of the burnt vehicle that had once been his mate's pride and joy. As fear of a future without her fogged his brain, Dragon tried to put the facts that he knew into their proper places of the full picture, but he couldn't. Anger filled him, followed by the deepest sea of grief he'd ever experienced. Even his wolf was losing it. Neither of them could fully grasp what was in front of them.

His Kisy. His mate. His Love.

Not willing to accept what was in front of him, he hopped off his bike, not giving a damn if the thing fell over behind him, and raced into the building. He searched everywhere, every office, every bathroom, every closet... hell, he even looked under each of the desks. Nowhere. He couldn't find her anywhere.

He heard footsteps behind him and swung around, hope flaring in his chest that it would be Kisy, but it was Trip and Bullet. The expressions on their faces brought tears to his eyes. He started to vigorously shake his head.

"Drag," Bullet said, softly.

"No," Dragon responded, still shaking his head, not giving a shit as the tears started to fall. "No!"

"I'm so sorry," Trip choked out.

"No!" Dragon turned and grabbed the edge of the desk to his right. With everything in him, he flung it up in the air. As papers and computer equipment fell around him, he threw his head back and let out a howl. By the time he stopped, he was in his wolf form.

As he bolted out the door, he vaguely heard cursing and running footsteps behind him. He couldn't worry about that. He had one goal — kill every last mother fucker who had anything to do with this.

After rounding the building, he took off down Main Street, looking for motorcycles. They had to be close, and he'd find them if it was the last thing he did. His wolf darted around cars and past people walking down the sidewalk. There was a green haze over his vision. He knew that should cause alarm in him, but he couldn't remember why. All he could remember was that Kisy was gone, and he needed to avenge her.

Rebel

Rebel knew it wasn't the safest way to travel, but he couldn't think of another way to get all of the women and children from one place to another without using a vehicle the enemy would recognize. Praying the ride would be smooth enough and relatively problem free, he and his cousins helped the women and children out the back door of the clubhouse and up into the back of the box truck they used to relocate women and children who were abused. The Claws were still at the compound, keeping an eye out for anyone or anything suspicious. One of them had already come out and started the truck to make sure no one had tampered with it. He had fought with Foxy about that, but in the end, she flipped him off and walked out.

She had a point. What was the difference if he did it instead of her? If it was set to explode, one of them would be dead, and while that would be tragic, it wasn't more or less tragic if it was her instead of him.

He didn't want the bikes of the Claws following them and drawing attention, so it was left to him and his cousins to protect their most precious family members – the ol' ladies and the kids.

Talk about pressure.

The Claws didn't fight him too much on that, since his explanation of why he didn't want them to come was interrupted by Lace's car flying into the parking lot and Pinky jumping out, shouting for help.

Rebel wanted to go find out what was going on and help out if he could, but he was given a mission, and he wouldn't fall down on the job. Letting the Claws handle whatever that was, he climbed in the truck and pulled out of the lot.

When he was trying to think of a nearby, safe location to take them that wasn't owned by the Howlers, the only place that he could think of was the library. It might have had something to do with his wolf's incessant need to make sure Ruby was safe, even though there was no reason anyone would think of her as having a connection to the Howlers. He didn't examine that too closely. He just trusted his gut and headed for the alley behind the library.

Stopping right outside the emergency exit door, Rebel cut the engine and turned to look at Ross sitting in the passenger seat. "Stay here and stay alert. I'm going to open the emergency door, but I gotta let the librarian know what's happening."

Ross gave a nod as his eyes already began to scan their surroundings with his hand gripped tight around the gun, Rebel had been teaching him to shoot for weeks.

Rebel hopped out of the truck and quickly made his way around to the front of the building, keeping an eye out for anything that might be off. Not seeing anything, he yanked open the front door of the library and stepped inside.

Glancing to his right, he spotted Ruby in a row just beyond her desk area. She was quietly slipping books onto the shelves. Breathing a sigh of relief, he approached her.

Startled at the sight of him suddenly appearing next to her, she jumped, dropping the book she was holding and placing a hand to her chest. "Sheesh! You scared me."

Rebel cringed. "I'm sorry. I keep doing that, don't I?"

"It's okay." She waved it off and bent down to grab the dropped book.

Rebel forced his eyes to look straight ahead. He didn't have time to be ogling the gorgeous librarian. He had a mission.

"Do you need more books?" she asked as she straightened.

He cleared his throat. "Uh. No, but I do need to ask you a favor."

"If I can help, I will."

"I can't explain everything now, but I'll tell you what I can. I just... I'm in charge of keeping all of the women and children connected to our club safe. I need a safe place to hang with them that isn't connected to the Howlers. I know it's a large ask, and I won't blame you if you say no, but I promise to make it up to you. I just need to bring them through the emergency exit, if that's okay, and hide them out for a while. Would that be—"

"There's a conference room down the hall. It's nothing fancy, but it has a table, chairs, and a television. The emergency door has an off switch on the bottom, so you can disable the alarm."

Not thinking, Rebel cupped her face in his hands and pressed his lips to hers. "Thank you," he breathed as he pulled back.

Her cheeks flamed red, and Rebel realized what he did. His stomach dropped at the stupidity of his actions. "I'm so sorry."

Ruby let out a nervous laugh. "Please don't apologize for kissing me. That would just take the pleasure out of it."

Rebel grinned.

After raising an eyebrow, she asked, "Don't you have some women and children to hide?"

"Oh, shit! Yes!" Then he was jogging through the library.

Trip

It took a half hour to find and subdue Dragon in his wolf form. Luckily, he hadn't killed anyone, but there had been a moment when Trip thought he would be Dragon's first victim. Thrash and Griff pulled up behind him and Bullet with their rental car, just as he and Bullet were able to talk Dragon into relaxing enough to stop the snarling and lay down. That's when the whimpering began, and tears leaked out of his green wolf eyes.

Trip's heart was bleeding. First, Gigi. Then Kisy. *Fuck*. It would take a fucking miracle to keep the club from going absolutely insane. The only reason he was keeping himself from falling apart was he knew his brothers and his sisters were going to need him.

Axle and Ashlyn were going to have a hard time with it. Emerson was probably just as bad as Dragon. Top had been in a relationship with Gigi's mom before she died, during which he spent enough time around Gigi to establish a bond. All the brothers loved Gigi long before Ashlyn came into the picture. Then Kisy burst into Dragon's life, and they all fell in love with her, too. Yeah, this was going to devastate the club.

It took some coaxing, but they finally got Dragon into the backseat of the rental, still in his wolf form. Thrash and Griff would drive Dragon back to the compound, and Trip and Bullet would meet them there. They would lock Dragon up in the cell in the basement until he was able to shift back.

After making their way back to the compound, Trip and Bullet entered the clubhouse. Thrash and Griff had already managed to get Dragon into the basement without much incident. Trip imagined it had to do with Griff being Dragon's dad.

"He's okay," Griff commented as Trip approached him, his voice even rougher than its normal gravelly bass. "Well, as well as he can be, but he hasn't shifted back."

Trip ran his fingers through his hair and let out a deep sigh. "People saw him... his eyes were glowing."

Griff nodded as his brows drew together. "We're going to have to deal with that once all of this is over."

Trip's phone went off. He pulled it out and saw a text from Axle.

>Chased Emerson to Markum Park. In bathrooms. Need vehicle<

"Rock," Trip shouted and looked around. A few moments later, Rock came out of the back hall and headed toward Trip. "Axle needs a vehicle at Markum Park, at the bathrooms."

"On it," Rock said and caught a set of keys that Ranger tossed him.

Ranger drove an old Bronco when he wasn't on his bike. Since he lived permanently at the compound, the Bronco was parked out back. It would be the perfect vehicle for transporting a distraught wolf shifter.

As Rock rushed out to meet up with Axle, Trip noticed Pike pacing on the other side of the room. He had his phone in his hand and was staring at it. Pike's other hand was gripped in the hair of the back of his head. Trip saw Pike's brows drawn together. He looked not just worried but panicked. He approached his brother. "Pike, what's wrong?"

"I haven't heard from Pixie." Pike blew out a deep breath. "I... I texted her... before all of this happened. She was... at work. I told her to come here. I don't know if she made it."

"Did you text Rebel?"

"He's not answering. I don't know what to do."

Trip gripped Pike's shoulder and gave it a squeeze. "The only other explosion we know about was Heat, and it was empty. I'm sure she's with Rebel."

"They took Crush," Pinky said as she approached them. "After shooting Lace and Nails, they took Crush. She let them so I could get Lace and Nails out of there."

"Shit," Trip bit out and looked around the room at the rest of his family. They were being hit from all sides, devastated, injured. How were they supposed to win this when they already lost so much?

And where in the hell were the champions?

Kisy

In an abandoned office building on the edge of town, Kisy glared at her captors as they tied Crush and Pixie to some office chairs. Thinking about how she ended up in her position drove her nuts.

It was her fault. When she got the text from Dragon to head to the clubhouse as soon as possible, she had told the rest of the employees to head home on a paid leave. One of her coworkers, Sarah, waited to walk out with her, even though Kisy had insisted she go. When they walked outside, there were five bikers, wearing cuts that didn't have the Howlers or the Claws patches.

Kisy instantly stopped in her tracks. Sarah had been distracted while she dug her keys out of her bag. They grabbed Sarah and held a gun to her head.

"Take her," one of them said, pointing to Kisy. "She's one of their ol' ladies. We might be able to use her. Have this one set off the bomb." He nodded toward Sarah.

Bomb? Kisy didn't know what they were talking about, but she knew they were the enemies that Dragon was worried about. If they thought she'd go without a fight, they were fucking wrong. While they were discussing what they were going to do, she slipped her hand into her bag and pulled out a can of pepper spray.

She was only able to catch two of them in the eyes before being disarmed. One of them grabbed Kisy, holding her arms behind her as another was still holding a gun to Sarah's head while she sobbed and begged to be let go. The last biker took her bag and pulled out her keys.

"You are the reason she's about to die," he said and pointed at Sarah.

Even as Kisy fought to get free, and yelled at all of them, they dragged Sarah to the car and forced her in. One of the men turned their gun on Kisy and ordered Sarah to start the car. As she fumbled with the keys, the bikers quickly backed away from the car.

Kisy kept yelling at Sarah to not do it and to let them kill her, but Sarah wasn't listening. She was running on fear. Kisy prayed that they were somehow wrong and there was no bomb, but as soon as Sarah turned the key, the car exploded.

Feeling the heat from the blast, Kisy cried out for Sarah and for the Howlers. She knew they'd come for her, and they would put themselves in danger to try to save her. But what shook her to her core was how easy it would have been for her to be the one to come out to the car and turn the key, expecting to drive to the compound. Her life had been saved by a few minutes of convincing her employees to leave early.

Was it saved? Or were they just going to kill her when it was most damaging to the Howlers?

A few moments later, a car pulled up to the edge of the building, far away from her burning car. The bikers forced her into the backseat. She fought them the entire car ride, but she hadn't managed to get away. Then they forced her into an office building across town.

From what she could see as they entered the lobby, the two floors were open, with the walkways, balconies, and stairs in full view of the entire building. Around the open center were cubicles on both floors. Judging by the dust on all the flat surfaces and trash strewn across the floor, the building had been empty for a while. There were desk chairs tipped over and desks shoved into strange positions. The only area that seems to be mostly free of trash was the staircase.

The men practically dragged Kisy up the stairs because there was no way she was going willingly. Once on the second floor, they tied her up to a metal handrail that ran along the top of a glass railing that lined the interior balcony.

Pixie and Crush were about five yards from her and were being tied to visitor office chairs, the kind they lined lobbies with. As the men finished tying them up, Kisy met Crush's gaze and winked.

Crush gave her a confused but curious look. Kisy just waited. Once the men figured the women were secure, they walked off to the side and began talking. There was a group of eight bikers, but a few others had been there and left. She wasn't sure how many were in Warden's Pass, but she counted eleven total who had passed through the office space since she had been brought there.

Kisy remembered Dragon mentioning how good the hearing of shifters was and figured she'd give it a try to get a message to the women. While the men were talking, and not paying close attention to the women, Kisy said low, "I can get out of the ropes."

Crush nodded.

She didn't want to reveal her cards too quickly, though, so she waited. Maybe twenty minutes later the majority of the bikers left, leaving three men to watch the women. When one of them got a little too close to Pixie and put his hand to her baby bump, Kisy bit back her words of disgust and went to work on the knots securing her hands to the handrail.

It didn't take long for her to loosen them enough to pull her hands out. While the other two were smoking over by the stairs, looking at something on a phone, Kisy got to her feet and walked over. She stood next to the handsy biker. After a moment, she said, "You know Pike will kill you for touching her, but he'll cut your hands off, first."

The man jumped back and loudly cursed. Then she was grabbed and dragged back to the handrail. The other bikers came over and helped him tie her back up.

Kisy met Crush's gaze and was treated to a slight smile and a nod of appreciation.

T.S. Tappin

Chapter Twenty-Two

Axle

Two hours after they were first notified of the explosions, Axle stood outside the cell in the basement of the clubhouse and stared through the barred door at his club brother and his brother-in-law. His heart hurt so much that it had become numb. He supposed he needed that while he dealt with the disaster and devastation his family was facing. If he had to fully feel the pain of their loss, he wasn't sure he'd be able to keep himself together. The Howlers and the Claws needed him to stay tight.

It was the first time in Axle's time with the club that they had to use the bars instead of just shutting and locking the door to the room. Until that moment, he wasn't sure why his father had put the bars in. Now, he understood. They weren't for human prisoners. They were for out of control shifters.

The reason he was down there was because his father had been guarding the room with Griff and had come up to tell him that Dragon had shifted back.

Axle looked over at Griff. "Has he said anything to you?"

"No, I fucking haven't," Dragon growled out.

Axle shared a look with Griff before he shifted his attention to Dragon. Dragon wasn't looking in his direction, instead staring at the ground between his feet as he sat on his ass on the concrete floor with his knees up and bent. His arms were bent and resting on his knees, his face hard and expressionless.

"I'm so s—"

"Don't fucking say it." Dragon's gaze shot up to meet Axle's. All Axle could see was an ice cold rage. "Let me fucking out of here, so we can kill them all and make sure Kisy didn't die for nothing."

Axle gave a nod. "You can't just run off half-cocked, Drag. We need to plan. The champions are upstairs. We need to figure out how this is going to go down before we go after them."

Dragon didn't reply verbally. He just gave a nod.

Axle looked over at Emerson, who was still in wolf form and laying on his side. The wolf hadn't stopped whimpering since they brought him in, and it was the saddest sound Axle had ever heard. "Stay in here, Emerson. Just relax. We'll make them pay."

Emerson gave a weak howl and went back to whimpering.

Axle unlocked and opened the barred door as Dragon got to his feet and crossed the room. When Dragon stepped through the doorway, Griff grabbed Dragon by the back of the neck and pulled him into a tight hug. He was letting his son know he was feeling Dragon's grief, even if he hadn't met Dragon's mate. Griff's son was hurting, and that was enough for Griff to know Kisy was something special. It was just the way in the biker world.

Axle led them up the stairs. When they made their way into the main room of the clubhouse, Lira approached him.

"We know where their base is, and we have a plan, but we need to make sure everyone knows what to do. I've sent Vega over to the library to help Rebel. He said he'd ask about Pixie, since Pike still hasn't heard any news."

Axle nodded and shouted. "Everyone in the cafeteria!"

Kisy

Kisy had to admit that she was enjoying fucking with these bikers more than she should be. Every time they got too close to Crush or Pixie, she got out of her ropes and distracted them. Finally, they used a set of handcuffs, instead of the rope. Apparently, they were tired of her shit. Since it had been four times she got out of the ropes in an hour or so, she could understand their frustration. She figured Dragon would be quite proud of her.

She wasn't allowing herself to think about what Dragon might be going through with her nowhere to be found and her car a pile of rubble. She couldn't think about it, or she'd fall into a pit of anger and sorrow. She needed to stay sharp and try to get them out of this.

Unfortunately, as that thought crossed her mind for the third time, the biker who seemed to be in charge ordered the other two bikers and another two men who had just arrived to get Pixie and Crush ready for transport.

They had untied them from the chairs, but when they tried to tie Crush's wrists together, she fought them. It wasn't until they held a gun to Pixie's belly that Crush stopped fighting. Kisy wondered why Crush didn't shift, but she couldn't ask with all of the assholes in the room.

She expected them to come uncuff her from the handrail, but they didn't. As they walked out, the leader – the patch on his cut said *Rage* – sneered at her as he bit out, "Have fun dying here." He flashed fangs as he let out a hiss.

Fuck! They're shifters?

"What?" Kisy pulled on the handrail. "What do you mean?"

"You're too much trouble. More trouble than you're worth." Then he jogged down the stairs and out of the building.

Kisy was dumbfounded. She knew she had been annoying. That was the point. She didn't think they would just leave her. They wouldn't have left her if they expected her to live. They would have shot her on the way out. That meant they didn't expect her to get free.

Well, fuck that.

As soon as she heard their bikes and the car pull away, she started searching the handrail for any weak spot she could use to her advantage.

Under the cylindrical metal handrail were stabilizing posts every three feet, separated by transparent glass panels. The posts were attached by two screws. As she examined the post on her right, she noticed one of the screws looked loose. She scooted over to it and used her fingernail to turn the screw.

It took some work, and the process destroyed her nail, but she was able to get both screws loose enough to disconnect them from the cylinder. She slid the small chain of the handcuffs along the bar until she was free of the handrail.

With a sigh of relief, she rolled onto her hands and knees and climbed to her feet. Sending a prayer up to the gods that she wouldn't fall down the stairs or run into any bikers she didn't trust, Kisy ran down the stairs and out of the building.

Once outside, she looked around and saw the top of Auntie Hen's hotel over the trees to the left. If she had to guess, the building was only a few blocks away. Sending up another prayer, she headed for the hotel.

The hotel ended up being eight blocks away, and Kisy hadn't paced herself. She needed to get to safety and get word to the Howlers as soon as possible. There wasn't time for her to keep a measured pace.

When she finally made it to the hotel, Kisy was panting so hard she could barely speak. She stumbled into the lobby and over to the desk where her aunt was standing. Auntie Hen rounded the desk and caught Kisy as she collapsed. "Howlers," she wheezed.

Crush

When Crush saw where they brought her and Pixie, she was pissed. If they hurt Bobby just so they could use Bobby's Bar as a place to torture them, Crush would kill them with her bare claws and enjoy stringing their intestines up like Christmas lights.

She told Rage as much as he manhandled her through the back door of the building and down the hall to the main room of the bar. Seeing Bobby sitting on the floor in front of the bar, Crush took a calming breath. He looked scared and quite pissed, but he also looked unharmed.

"Let him go," she ordered on a growl.

Rage rolled his eyes. "I know you can't shift, Bitch."

That fucking shot they gave her had prevented her from shifting, but it hadn't suppressed many of the other shifter-given skills. Her strength was dimmed, but not completely gone. Her eyesight and her hearing were perfectly fine, which is how she was still able to hear Dragon's howl of despair earlier when it was obvious Kisy and Pixie hadn't heard it.

It had to be the Variulisis they were warned of — a shifting blocker that had adverse effects on a shifter over time if they were given repeated doses of it. No one knew how long the drug stayed in your system, or at least, no one knew and had been willing to share that information with them.

"That doesn't mean I can't kill you with my bare hands." Crush turned and got in his face. "Uncuff me and we'll take care of this."

"Not a chance," Rage replied, a smile growing on his face. "How's my nephew? Heard he rushed in to save my boys."

Holy shit! Crush took a step back and stared at him. *Could it be?* She studied his facial features, and it only took her a moment to see it. *Fuck!* Rage was Rebel's uncle. *What had they done to him to get him to join the HDMC? Better question — how was he okay with trying to eliminate a club his nephew was a member of?*

"Yeah, that's right. Looks like the pretty kitty is finally catching on." Using her shock against her, Rage swung his leg around and knocked her legs out from under her. Once she was on the ground, he forced her over next to Bobby and ordered,

"Now, don't be a fucking problem or I'll have to kill you."

"Let Bobby and Pixie go, and I won't put up a fight," she promised. She knew it wouldn't work, but she had to try.

"I'm not letting an ol' lady go," Rage stated and let out a belly laugh. "I'm not that fucking stupid. She's more valuable than you are."

"The Howlers will not negotiate with you. They will kill you for even looking at her with the wrong expression on your face. But fine, just let Bobby go."

Rage stared at her for a long moment. Then he asked, "How do I know he won't just run to the Howlers and tell them where we are?"

Crush turned her head and made eye contact with Bobby. "If they let you go, promise me you will not go to the Howlers or anyone the Howlers know and tell them anything. If you do, I will personally make sure you pay for that. Do you understand?"

Bobby visibly swallowed and nodded his head. "Y-yes. I-I won't say a-anything or g-go to them or a-anyone."

Crush looked back at Rage. "You've killed one of their women, kidnapped two more, caused havoc for them and for the Claws, by taking their president. What in the hell do you need a bar owner for? Just let him be. Hell! He didn't even know shifters existed until you opened your mouth about my shifting."

Rage shrugged. "Fine. Like I care." He motioned toward the front door with his hand. "Go."

Bobby hesitated for a moment and looked at Crush with apology in his eyes.

"Don't worry about us. Go."

As tears filled Bobby's eyes, he climbed to his feet and bolted out the front door before Rage could change his mind.

Crush looked over at Pixie, who was standing with one of the other bikers just inside the room. She looked okay, but her hands were covering her baby bump, protecting the bundle inside.

The biker next to Pixie took her bicep and forced her into a chair. Then one of the bikers locked the front door and stood in front of it to block the exit. Two more blocked the hallway that led to the backdoor.

Crush still didn't know what the HDMC planned to do to them, but at least she avoided having Bobby's death on her conscience.

Axle

Standing in the cafeteria, waiting while his brothers went through the motions of assigning weapons and readying them for use, Axle was surprised when his phone rang, and *Mama Hen* showed on the screen. A deep feeling of dread filled his gut as he pressed *answer* and put the phone to his ear. With everything that had happened that day, he prayed to the gods it wasn't another hurt member of their family.

"Yeah?"

"Axle, my boy, my niece just stumbled into my lobby and collapsed in my arms. She said to call you, but that's all she could get out."

Axle's heart skipped a beat. "Kisy? Are you sure?"

"Boy, I know what my niece looks like."

"What?" Dragon pushed his way through the crowded room and was looking at Axle with wild eyes. "What about Kisy?"

"Does she look hurt?"

"Just winded, I think. She has handcuffs on her hands, but I have a universal key, so I can get those off while you're on your way."

Axle's brows drew together. "How? How do you have…?"

"My past is *mine*, Boy."

Axle was smart enough to not push. He just replied, "We're on our way."

After he ended the call, he met Dragon's eyes again. Dragon was barely hanging on. He wasn't sure if he should tell the man his woman might be alive or go check for himself, first.

"I know what you're fucking thinking, Axle, and fuck that. I heard you say her name. Tell me what the fuck is going on."

Axle sighed. "That was Mama Hen. She said Kisy just showed up there."

He barely got the sentence out before Dragon was running for the front door.

Kisy

Sitting in the lobby of Mama Hen's hotel, Kisy rubbed her wrists and watched the television mounted in the corner. It was showing the local news. As the front door to the hotel opened, a news story came on the screen about multiple accounts in the area of people turning into animals.

She wasn't able to hear the rest because she was lifted up in a set of familiar strong arms and held tightly to a chest she had kissed every inch of. Her legs dangled inches off the ground as Dragon held her.

"Love," Dragon choked out with his head buried in her hair. "Thank the gods. Love." His body shook once with a sob.

"I'm okay, Dex," she softly replied and stroked her hand over his strawberry blond hair, fisting her hand in it at his nape.

He pulled his head back to look in her eyes. He had managed to fight back the tears, but his eyes looked wild, and the fear in them had yet to fully subside. "Don't ever fucking make me think you're dead ever again. Understood?"

Kisy snorted a laugh. "Dex, I didn't do it."

"Don't sass me in a time like this, Love," Dragon said in *that voice*.

Kisy smiled and let go of his hair. She cupped his bearded face in her hands and gave him a soft kiss. "I'm not sassing you, but if you feel the need to spank my ass later, I won't object. But maybe we should focus on getting Crush and Pixie back from the asshats for now. And that," she pointed at the television screen, "might be a problem."

Dragon's head turned to look at the television. Then he growled, "Fuck."

"Don't worry about it for now," Axle said from the doorway. "We'll handle it after we get the girls and end these motherfuckers."

T.S. Tappin

Chapter Twenty-Three

Kisy

After they returned to the compound, Dragon wouldn't take his hands off her, but Kisy didn't mind. Even as his brothers each briefly told her how happy they were to see her safe, Dragon had a hold on her hip or her shoulder. There was a brief moment of waiting while Axle took a phone call. From what she could tell, it was about where Crush and Pixie were taken. She saw him mouth the words *Bobby's Bar* to Skull during the call.

Sitting on Dragon's lap, she answered all of Axle, Dragon, and a woman named Lira's questions, while the rest of the Claws, Howlers, and Champions stood around the room, waiting for orders. Dragon had briefly explained that she was the leader of the group of champions that were helping the Howlers and the Claws. Kisy liked the way the woman stood her ground with the men and didn't let them take over the conversation. It made her respect Lira, even if she barely knew her.

There wasn't much that Kisy could give them. She only knew where they had been held, Pixie's state of being, and the fact that Crush didn't seem to be able to shift.

When the subject of why she was left behind was brought up, Kisy just glossed over it. She'd tell Dragon later, but they needed to be on their way to get the girls.

"I was too annoying," Kisy said and shrugged. "I guess they didn't think I was worth the trouble."

She heard a growl come from her mate and rolled her eyes.

"I'm going to have someone drop you off at the library with the rest of the women," Axle commented, and motioned someone over.

Kisy pushed Dragon's hands off her and stood. "Uh... no. I'm going with."

Axle looked over at Dragon and said, "No."

Kisy shifted so she was standing in front of Dragon, blocking Axle's view of her mate. "I'm right here. Talk to me."

"Drag," Axle growled, "we don't have time for this.

"Great. Then don't argue," Kisy said with a saccharine smile. As she spoke, she saw Lucifer out of the corner of her eye. He was quietly making his way out of the building. Their eyes locked for a moment, and Lucifer gave her a wink right before he left her view.

"Kisy," Dragon said as he straightened from the chair he had been sitting on, "you aren't coming with."

"I won't live in a damn cage, Dragon. I wasn't able to get them out. I failed them. I'm going to make it right."

Axle opened his mouth to say something when Pinky pushed her way through the crowd to stand next to Axle. She met Kisy's gaze. "If you were to prospect for the Claws, Axle wouldn't have a say on whether or not you could rescue your president." Then she held out a black leather cut, smirked, and raised an eyebrow. "You in?"

Kisy's attention jumped from Pinky to Dragon as she quickly thought it over. Without saying a word, Kisy reached out and took the cut. As she slid it on, she noticed the resignation build in Dragon's gaze. He was pissed, but he acknowledged she needed to make her own decisions. It wasn't something he would accept without a fight, but they didn't have time to fight about it at that moment.

As the other Howlers began to strap on their weapons in preparation to leave, Pike stormed through the room and stopped by their little group. He was already tricked out his gear.

"I'm not sitting here listening to this shit any longer. I'm going to get my mate. Do what the fuck you want," Pike stated as he headed for the front door.

Siren and Trip both followed him out without saying a word. From what Kisy knew, they understood Pike's fear. Ranger stopped by Dragon, gave Dragon's shoulder a squeeze, and shrugged, before he stepped past them to leave.

When Pinky took a few steps toward the door, Kisy followed her. Dragon would just have to deal, and so would Axle. She heard footsteps behind her. When she looked over her shoulder, she found a line of Tiger's Claw members following her out in support of their vice president and their newest prospect.

As Kisy was climbing on the back of Pinky's bike, she looked over at the front door of the clubhouse. Filing out of the building were the rest of the Howlers MC members, with Dragon, Skull, and Axle bringing up the rear. Her gaze connected with

Dragon's for a long moment, before Pinky started her bike, only waiting a moment for Kisy to brace herself before taking off out of the parking lot.

Lucifer

There was no way Lucifer was going to sit around any longer while his woman was held captive by some piece of shit bastards. Hell fucking no. He was going to get her. It didn't matter that she hadn't admitted that she was his woman yet. They both knew she was, and that's all Lucifer needed.

While the Howlers were arguing with Kisy about whether or not she would help rescue the girls, Lucifer slipped out. After pulling his old HDMC cut out of his saddlebag, he put it on. When he had put it in there, he wasn't sure why, but now he was glad he had. Ready to go, he hopped on the bike he recently bought from Bullet and headed out to where the two UpRiders told them the women would be.

One look at those two young UpRiders and Lucifer knew they could be trusted. They were like him. They put their faith into a group of men and had been let down. They wanted to belong to a good group of like-minded men with decent morals. Half of their club was exactly that, unlike the club that Lucifer had joined.

Lucifer had been sold a pack of lies when he prospected for the Hell's Dogs MC Indiana. He didn't find out the full story of why they were doing all the shit they were doing until he met the Howlers — until the Howlers and the Claws saved his life. And he would continue to repay that kindness to the Howlers and the Claws for the rest of it.

That was the thought on his mind as he pulled into the parking lot of Bobby's Bar. He slow-rolled to the back, looking around as he went. Taking in everything and looking for a sign of trouble. When he got to the back of the building, he parked near the rear door and killed the engine.

Taking a deep breath, he felt for his gun in the holster under his tee in the back. Feeling the outline of his handgun, he was reassured. He *would* rescue his woman.

He yanked open the back door and came face to face with another HDMC member who aimed a gun at his chest. Lucifer couldn't tell which chapter the man was from, but it didn't matter anyway. He took a chance and held out his hand. The man dropped his gun hand and slipped his gun back into his holster, then he shook Lucifer's hand.

"I was sent to relieve you. They want you at base," Lucifer told him.

"Me?" The eagerness with which the man stepped past him disgusted Lucifer. He didn't even ask Lucifer any questions.

Once the guard had disappeared out the back door, Lucifer headed down the hall and met two more men at the archway to the main room of the bar.

The two of them looked him over. Then they turned around and looked over at another man. One of them uttered, "Slice, they sent a new one."

Lucifer waited for them to wave him through. He stepped past the two men and looked around. He spotted Pixie, first, sitting on a chair at the closest table. She looked okay, but irritated. That didn't surprise Lucifer. Pixie was feisty.

Crush was sitting on the floor near the bar. She looked pissed, but her face was paler than usual. He didn't like that. His gaze met hers.

"You good?"

"I'd be better if I was with my club."

As Lucifer nodded, Slice blurted, "Who the fuck are you?"

Lucifer grinned as he yanked his gun out of his holster and aimed at the man's head. "I'm her man, and you fucked up." Then he pulled the trigger.

After taking him out, he turned and quickly dispatched the other two before they could pull their wits together to do anything about it.

Then he went to work on untying the girls, Crush first. Once Crush was freed, he gave her his gun and went for Pixie's ropes.

"You good, Pix?" Lucifer rubbed Pixie's wrists to help her circulation.

"Yeah, just fucking pissed," she gritted out and stood. "Bunch of fucking assholes."

"I agree," Lucifer said, and chuckled.

"Let's get the fuck out of here. I only have my bike, but we'll figure it out."

Crush bent down to one of the guards and yanked a set of keys from the prick's pocket. "I'll take his."

Lucifer shrugged and took his gun back. He led the woman down the hallway to the rear door. He carefully opened it and stepped out, gun up and ready. No one.

He lowered his gun and waved the girls out. He was approaching his bike when the sound of a large pack of bikes roared into the lot and around the building. When the Howlers and the Claws stopped and killed their engines, Lucifer loudly said, "Well, it's so nice of you to join us. I see Kisy won." He looked over at Kisy on the back of Pinky's bike and winked at her.

When Pike stormed toward them and wrapped Pixie up in his arms, Lucifer looked away and gave them their moment. His eyes landed on Crush heading for Ginger and her bike. Lucifer jogged over and took her hand. He yanked her around and met her gaze. Looking into the eyes he loved so much, he stated, "We need to talk, and we need to do it now."

"Later," she said.

"No. Now," he turned and started for his bike, pulling her along with him.

He couldn't keep doing it. The push and pull had been fun for a while, but he was done wasting time. They needed to make a go of it, or she needed to let him go. And she didn't have long to decide because he wasn't going to keep through this.

Rock

For years, Rock had hated and loved Lace at the same time. Their relationship had been wild and crazy from the start. He had been sure he wanted her for the rest of his life, but she had been hesitant. Within two weeks of Lace agreeing to an exclusive relationship, they flew to Vegas and got hitched. When she finally let him into her heart, their sex life had went from fun and wild to intense and all-consuming. They spent more time in bed than out of it for a few months. Only their jobs and the clubs managed to make them get dressed.

Then the kids came. He didn't realize that Lace was overwhelmed with motherhood until the first time he found her blacked out drunk while she was supposed to be keeping an eye on the kids. Thankfully, the kids were okay, but it was an eye-opening experience for Rock.

He took it as a failure as a spouse that he hadn't noticed the signs. His happiness in fatherhood had blinded him to the struggles Lace was going through.

He wasn't blameless in the demise of their marriage. His reaction to her drinking was harsh and unyielding in the beginning. It brought him back to his childhood, when his mother would get drunk, and Rock was left to fend for himself. If it hadn't been for Brute's family, he would have starved. It was why he thought so highly of Brute's family and had barely shed a tear when his mother died.

The day that Joker pulled him aside and gave him a talking to about respecting Lace as the mother of his children, regardless of her addictions, was the day Rock took a good long look at his own actions and how they made the situation worse. It was also the day he began trying to talk Lace into going to rehab.

Rehab had been a bust when he finally got her to go. She came out and went back to drinking, but she added drugs to the mix. When he went to check on her at her shitty apartment and found the needles and the baggies, he filed for emergency custody and stopped letting her have any access to the children without strict supervision.

Since then, he had been in a constant state of confusion about Lace. He loved her, the person she was without the drugs, and he hated her, the person she was with the drugs. He respected her as the mother of his children, but he was disgusted by the way she lived her life. He wanted his children to know their mother, but he hated that they only remembered her as the junkie. Seeing the sadness in their eyes and their worry for her damn near killed him.

She went through cycles of being clean. She would quit the drugs and start to get her life together, but that wouldn't last long. Lace had expected him to forgive her and come back to her as soon as she was clean for a few days, but Rock didn't trust her. He couldn't let go of what she had put him and the kids through. When he wouldn't agree to commit to her, she would go back to the drugs and alcohol.

He didn't handle her clean cycles well, either. He may not have committed to her, but he had made love to her during those times. It confused the situation more and made things more difficult. It wasn't until last year that he cut her off from him completely. He became the father of her children and nothing more to her.

Rock would carry that guilt for the rest of his life. If he handled things better... if he would have tried harder to get her clean... if he would have stood by her...

"Stop," he heard Lace croak from her bed at the apartments.

He lifted his head from where it had been hanging down in front of him and looked over at her. Sitting in the chair next to her bed with his elbows resting on his knees, he had spent the last hour trying to figure out how to tell his kids that their mother was no longer going to be in their lives. She wasn't dead yet, but she was dying. The drugs in her system had made it where her body wasn't strong enough to heal the way it should.

"What?" he asked around the lump in his throat.

Lace looked so different from when he met her. Her blond hair used to be shiny and silky. Her skin used to be a milky white with a blush and her eyes had been clear and bright. Looking at her in that bed, he saw a shell of who she had been. Her hair was stringy and yellow, her eyes were glazed, and her skin was pock-marked with scars, loose in some spots and too tight in others. Her eyes were sunk in, and there were dark circles around them. She had been slowly killing herself and hadn't been aware of it.

"Stop blaming yourself. This was me," she said and gave him a sad smile as tears filled her eyes. "This was all me."

"Lace," he breathed and reached out, taking her hand in his.

"I won't let you shoulder this, Rock. You are a great father. You were a great husband. I did this."

"If I—"

"No!" She coughed and sucked in as deep of a breath as she could take. "If I hadn't done this, you wouldn't have had to deal with any of this. I don't blame you for any of this."

Rock choked back his sobs and gave her hand a squeeze.

"Just know that I love you. That never changed. I love Mia and Hunter. And I know you'll make sure they have a wonderful life."

"Lace," he moaned.

"Marry that woman and give them a family... a *real* family. You deserve Mary, and so do the kids. Tell her thank you for taking care of you and them."

He shook his head and laid his forehead against their joined hands.

"Now, go."

He shook his head again.

"Rock, go. You don't need to watch me waste away more than you already have."

"I don't want you to be alone."

"I want to be alone." She coughed again, harder this time. "Rock, go."

Rock got to his feet and bent over her. He kissed her lips firmly and let his tears fall. Then he straightened and stalked out of the room. Once the door was closed behind him, he leaned back against the wall next to the door and let the tears flow freely. As his heart was torn to shreds, he slid down the wall and onto his ass on the floor.

He thought the last several years were hard, but nothing would compare to what he faced when Lace was gone.

Chapter Twenty-Four

Axle

Looking across his desk at Crush, Axle uttered, "I think it's the only way, Crush. If you're there, the Claws will be distracted, worried about you. You don't want that and neither do I."

Crush didn't look happy, but she knew he was right. "I'll keep Ginger and Minx here with me. Any news on Lace?"

Axle sighed. "She's not doing well," he answered. "The doctor said he could make her comfortable, but he doesn't think she's going to make it. The drugs and alcohol in her system are making it too hard for her body to heal the way it should."

Crush cursed under her breath. "Rock is going to take that hard."

"Yeah, he already is. He's with her now, saying his goodbyes. I'm not having him come with us. Nails is doing pretty good, but she's pissed she's too injured to come with."

"She would crawl onto the field of battle if we let her." Crush stood and headed for the door.

Axle followed her. "Do you want me to have Flash and Keys stay here?"

Crush shook her head. "Ginger, Minx, Rock, and I can handle it."

As they reached the doorway to the main area, he asked, "What about Lucifer?"

"If you fucking try to tell me to stay here," Lucifer began, "I'll just follow."

Axle turned his head and saw Lucifer leaning back against the wall next to the opening to the hallway. "You aren't a member yet."

"I don't fucking care."

Axle rolled his eyes. "Whatever. I don't want to hear you whine if you get hurt."

Lucifer chuckled. "You wouldn't want to hear that either way."

Axle ignored him and gave out a loud whistle, bringing everyone's attention to him. "Gather around! We've got shit to talk about before we go!"

Once everyone was close and listening, he laid out the plan. "The champions are luring the assholes to the field at the Aikman Farm. We're going to hide out in the woods. Once they have them there and engaged, we're going to close them in and take them out. Sound good?"

The room erupted in howls and roars.

"Great. We'll park our bikes on the hiking trail a mile down the road. Lira's been keeping me updated. If we head out now, we should have just enough time to get our bikes hidden and hike through the woods. Mount up!"

Axle noticed Crush stop Ginger from following the others out and begin a conversation. She motioned over Vixen.

Leaving her to do what she needed to, Axle looked around. He saw Dragon and Kisy talking to his dad as they walked out of the room. Dragon had his arm around Kisy and looked at ease, but Axle knew better. Dragon was not okay with Kisy going along, but he knew that fighting his woman would be useless. That woman was a force to be reckoned with, and while she frustrated the hell out of him, Axle admired her. The look on Griff's face said he did, too. His slight smile was a rare sight, but whatever Kisy was saying had brought it out of the old burly wolf.

Still dealing with his injured arm, Striker was staying behind as well with Rock at the apartment building. Axle hated that they were losing Lace for so many reasons. Most of all of those reasons were Rock and their kids. It was going to hit them hard.

Axle didn't allow his brain to go near what Emerson was going through or what it would do to Gorgeous when Axle shared the news about Georgia. It would hit her the same way reality was hitting Rock and Emerson.

He hoped this was the last day he'd have to share news like that, but he doubted it would be.

With a resigned sigh, Axle headed out to join his club and lead them to the war that had the very real possibility of hurting or killing his family.

Dragon

Looking into Kisy's teal eyes, Dragon swallowed around the lump in his throat. He wouldn't voice his fear for her or his frustration in her decisions. It wasn't the time. Instead, he stated, "You will stay by me. We will fight together."

She gave a nod. "But you can't get distracted because you're worried about me. That will put you at risk. I won't allow that."

He raised an eyebrow and gave her a smirk. "Is that so?"

She put her hands to her hips and nodded. "Now, kiss me and let me climb on the bike behind you. Or am I riding on Pinky's bike again?"

Dragon gripped her chin and pulled her face forward as he dropped his head. He pressed his lips firmly to hers. When he pulled back, he whispered, "You belong on the back of *my* bike, Love. Understood?"

She smiled her sassy grin. "Until I get a bike of my own."

"Fucking hell," Dragon muttered and released her.

Once he was on the bike and she was mounted behind him, he turned his head and met her gaze.

"What?"

Dragon grinned at her. "By the way... *three*."

"Promises. Promises." She bit that bottom lip and Dragon sent up a prayer to the gods that they made it through the next few hours, if only so he could dish out the *consequences* she was making clear she wanted.

"Fuck. I love you."

"Love you, too. Now, let's go. Vroom vroom."

In response, Dragon faced forward and started his bike.

As he rode out of the parking lot, he saw the van pull away from the curb to follow. The humans were going to ride in it to get to the farm from the trail, since they could hike through the woods at the same speed as the shifters. Driven by Keys, they would use it to transport the injured if needed. Dragon sent up another prayer than they would have no use for it, but he didn't have high hopes.

After parking their bikes down that trail, the humans loaded up in the van. Dragon watched as Kisy stepped up into the back of it. He would find her when they got there and keep her close. They all would wait on the trail for a text from Axle before they would head to the farm.

Once the doors were closed, the shifters shifted into their animals and darted into the woods. It took them less than two minutes to travel the distance to the farm. They hung out just inside the woods and shifted.

Within five minutes, the champions arrived — some of them by just appearing out of nowhere, and others by vehicles. The ones who arrived in cars and trucks squealed into the driveway and the yard. Behind them, at least fifty bikes roared onto the scene, guns out, taking shots when they could without hitting each other.

Axle held up a hand and shook his head, letting the Howlers, the Claws, and the people waiting with them in the woods know it wasn't time yet. He dropped his hand and pulled his phone from his pocket. After sending what Dragon assumed was the text to Keys, Axle put his phone away and shifted.

Dragon shifted to wolf form and watched the fighting. The champions were holding their own as they used guns, their bodies, and their paranormal abilities to fight the bikers, and in some cases, unarm them. As was the plan, they were staying in their human forms. It was an attempt to minimize the number of people who witnessed paranormals. He supposed that part of the plan was pointless since his little tantrum through the town when he thought his mate had died, but whatever.

When the sound of the van barreling down the road filled the air, Axle let out a growl and darted out of the woods. Dragon and the rest of the shifters followed.

While most of the shifters headed straight into the fight, coming up behind the bikers, Dragon headed for the van where their humans were emerging, guns drawn. Kisy saw him right away, jogged over to him, and stayed by his side as they headed into the battle.

Once again, he sent up a litany of prayers to the gods that they protect Kisy. He couldn't lose her again. He wouldn't make it.

Trip

Fighting alongside Orion, a bear shifter, Trip tore out necks and disarmed men when he could. Once he did what he could in his wolf form, he shifted and pulled out his gun. From the corner of his eye, he saw a man raise his arm and point a gun at Orion. Unfortunately, Orion was in the middle of trying to get another fucker to release his weapon by latching on to the fucker's hand and violently shaking his head. Without a second thought, Trip raised his gun and shot the biker who was aiming at Orion. The bullet slammed into the temple of the man. Orion's gaze met Trips, and there was a small nod as he finished off the guy in front of him.

Before Trip could take in his surroundings fully, he saw another man coming for Axle and Lira to his right. He turned and headed that way, letting off a few shots in the attacker's direction.

When the attacker shot in Axle's direction, Riles came out of nowhere in wolf form and jumped in front of the bullet meant for Axle. Just as Riles went down, Trip squeezed the trigger and watched as the bullets hit the man square in the chest, causing him to fall.

As he watched the man hit the ground, Trip saw movement off to the left. He turned his head just in time to see his father dive in front of him and take a bullet to the arm. His father didn't hesitate to stab the asshole shooter in the throat. Joker and the asshole dropped to the ground at the same time.

Fuck! Dad!

After looking around and finding Lira and Orion at their backs, Axle and Trip dropped to their knees at their dad's side.

Joker rolled over and let out an annoyed sigh.

"You good?" Axle's scowled down at their father's bullet wound.

"It's a damn graze. Get back to work. This isn't over," Joker growled.

Trip snorted a laugh. Well, their father would be okay.

Rebel

It was time for them to do another round of security checks, Rebel decided. Since she was the only woman in the conference room with the ability to shift, Rebel approached Darlin', who was sitting near the door. The rest of the women and children were camped out on the floor on the other side of the room, watching a movie on the television.

"What's up?" She looked up at him.

He handed her his spare gun, handle-first, and lowered his voice as he told her, "I'm going to do some rounds. Check on things. I'll have someone at the front and back doors. You feel comfortable watching this one?"

Darlin' nodded. Her expression went from worried and contemplative to warrior in a matter of seconds. Rebel had every intention of making sure she never had to use that gun, but he had faith she would use it to protect the women and children if she had to.

With that thought in his mind, he left the room, making sure the door was shut behind him, and made his way to the main area of the library. Seeing Ruby at her desk, he approached and quietly said, "I have to do some rounds. Is anyone in here?"

She shook her head. "I decided to close for the day. It's just you guys."

He bent down and kissed her cheek. "Thank you. I owe you."

Her cheeks turned that pretty pink he loved so much, but he couldn't focus on that. He had a responsibility to his family. Instead of standing there and taking in that beautiful face, he winked at her and headed for the front door.

Vega, the Mexican dragon-shifter, was standing just inside the front door, his eyes trained on the parking lot through the windows of the door. He had dark brown hair that he kept short and deep brown eyes. He was just under six feet tall and was compact muscle from head to toe.

"Are we good?" Vega asked but didn't look away from the windows.

"Yeah. I'm just doing some rounds. Anything odd?"

"Nope."

"Thanks for helping out." Rebel gave Vega's shoulder a squeeze. Then he made his way through the library to the back door.

Ross and Ryker, his twin cousins, were sitting on either side of the door.

"Hey, Cuz," Ross uttered, and continued munching on an apple he brought with him.

"Hey. Anything odd happening?"

Ryker shook his head. "Nope."

"Okay. I'm going to do a lap of the building and double check. Stay alert. Got your weapons handy?"

The twins nodded.

"Good." He pulled his handgun from his holster and shoved his way out the back door. He looked both ways down the alley but didn't see anything. It wasn't until he was rounding the box truck they had parked along the other side of the alley to check beyond it that he heard the gunshot. The bullet whizzed past his leg near his ankle from under the truck.

Assuming the gunman was watching his movements through the space under the vehicle, Rebel jumped and perched himself on the bumper of the box truck. His heart racing, he slowly made his way across the bumper to peer around the edge. He was just about to look to find out who the gunman was when he heard the back door of the building open. His gaze swung that way to find Ryker and Ross in the open doorway.

"Stay in there," Rebel shouted. "Shut the door!"

"What's going on?" Ryker asked.

"Go back inside!"

"Come on out, boys," he heard his uncle shout from the other end of the truck. "Join the party."

Rebel saw both of the twins freeze in place, stunned, as they stared toward the front of the truck.

Fuck! They must see him.

What Rebel didn't know was *why* his uncle was shooting at him. Sure, they weren't fond of each other, but *shoot at him*? His uncle had pulled Rebel's older brother into the drug world, and that had gotten him killed. Because of that, Rebel had cut his uncle out of his life, but they didn't have this level of animosity. At least, Rebel didn't think they had.

"Ross! Ryker! Go back inside," Rebel urged. He slowly leaned to the side and peeked around the corner. A shot rang out and whizzed past him again. Rebel pulled back and flattened himself against the back of the box truck.

"The second you put on that cut, you became the enemy," his uncle shouted. "The Howlers are evil. They take what doesn't belong to them. They think they are the judge and jury. They don't own this state! Can't tell people what to do! Gonna teach them that today! Gonna teach *you* that, Port!"

Rebel hated his fucking name, but in that moment, he would let his uncle fucking run his mouth. If he was talking, he wasn't as focused on shooting. That was important, since his cousins were still standing in that fucking open doorway.

From the glimpse he took, his uncle wasn't watching under the truck anymore. He needed to get his feet back on the ground, because taking out a gunman would be hell if he had to do it from the six-inch wide bumper.

Taking a chance, Rebel jumped down and ran for his cousins. He positioned himself in front of them, turned to face his uncle, raised his gun, and aimed.

His uncle chuckled and dropped his gun hand. "You think I'm scared of your gun, boy? You think you're going to protect those traitorous little shits? They were dead to me the minute they left with the Howlers."

"You sold your kids to drug lords for your debt," Rebel spat at him. "They didn't betray you. You betrayed them."

"I didn't sell them!" His uncle's face, gaunt from drugs, was turning a dark red as he yelled.

"The drug lord you owed money to took your boys and made them slaves! They did what he wanted to protect *you*!"

"They failed!" His uncle took several steps towards him, and Rebel let off a warning shot, aiming for the ground next to his uncle's left foot. His uncle growled and rolled his shoulders forward. After a flash of eyes and another frustrated grunt from his uncle, Rebel realized he had been trying to shift, but wasn't able to. "Fuck!"

They had given him the drug, Rebel realized. That was why he was behaving the way he was and was unable to shift. His uncle was a selfish, drug-addicted asshole, but he wasn't so much of an asshole that he'd try to kill Rebel or disown his children. This was the result of the shifting blocker the champions mentioned.

Rebel's brain raced with some way to get his uncle to put down the gun. They would get him to a safe place, lock him up, and see if there was a way to reverse the effects.

"You're a piece of shit," his uncle spat at him, "and those pussies behind you are nothing more than jizz their mother should have swallowed. You all disgust me! Your father, too! Thinking his shit don't fucking stink! To see the way you all turned out... It's a good thing Patrick died."

Rebel's brain stopped thinking. His wolf took over and reacted. In two seconds, he shifted and launched himself at his uncle, who was now only a few yards away.

He bit down on anything he could reach with his fangs and yanked. He ripped piece after piece from his uncle's body, until there was nothing left but a pile of flesh, bones, and blood.

Still in wolf form and panting, Rebel turned around to look at the twins and make sure they were okay. Hating that he tore their father to pieces in front of them, even if he hadn't had control of himself at that moment, he took in their faces. They looked angry, but it didn't seem to be directed at him. They were glaring at the mess that had been their father.

His gaze shifted to the space between them, and he saw Ruby's wide eyes staring at him. Not wanting to scare her, he shifted back, but realized he just showed her shifters existed. He didn't know what to do, what to say. Knowing there was a chance for blood to still be on his face, he used his tee to wipe it off. Relief flooded him when he didn't see much on the fabric.

Rebel opened his mouth to ask the boys if they were okay, but his phone rang. When he answered it, Axle told him to bring the women back.

Fuck! He didn't have time to deal with the twins or Ruby. When you are pulled in three different directions, what do you do? He approached the twins and Ruby slowly, stopping a few feet away.

"It's fine," Ryker said reassuringly as he met Rebel's gaze. "I don't blame you. It needed to happen."

"Yup." Ross nodded, stunned, still looking at what was left of the body. "Needed to happen."

He wasn't so sure they meant that, but he'd figure that out later. "Go get the women and children ready to go. I'll bring the truck around front."

Ryker nodded his understanding and stepped past Ruby to enter the library. Ross followed him.

There was so much Rebel wanted to say to Ruby. *I'm not a monster. I won't hurt you. Please don't fear me. You're safe with me. I can explain.* But he didn't have time. Instead, he said, "I'll explain that later, okay?"

Eyes still wide, Ruby nodded and patted his arm. Rebel lifted a hand to cup her pale cheek, but when he saw that his fingertips was blood-stained, he dropped it, turned, and went to move the box truck. He hated to see her without the normal blush to her cheeks, but he didn't have time to address the million questions she no doubt had.

T.S. Tappin

Chapter Twenty-Five

Kisy

HDMC and Reapers MC members were dropping left and right, but so were people from their side. She couldn't focus on that, though. She needed to stay sharp and protect herself, so her mate wouldn't be distracted with the need to keep her safe.

In doing that, she pushed down her worry over their downed family members, aimed her weapon, and took down anyone she could without risking injuring anyone from their side.

The sounds of shouting and gunshots filled the air, along with the smell of blood and other bodily fluids. She didn't focus on that for too long, either. The things a body does when it's dying would have her gagging if she didn't lock that box in her brain to keep focused.

Growls and snarls came from her mate as he moved from one biker to the next, yanking off limbs and knocking weapons from their hands. Kisy stayed close, reaching down to grab the dropped weapons and tossing them aside when she could.

She was doing just that when the dickhead attacked her, trying to sweep her legs out from under her. Years of double-dutch muscle memory kicked in, and she jumped over the leg. Dragon turned from his target and headed in her direction, but Kisy swung around and aimed right at the man's head. She pulled the trigger, and down went the dickhead.

Just then, she heard a gunshot right behind her. Ducking and turning, she saw a bullet hit Griff in the chest as he darted in front of it to protect a distracted Dragon. Cursing, she lifted her gun and aimed for the offending gunman. He didn't see her as he aimed at Dragon. She was quicker, pulling the trigger, and took him out with a shot in the center of his forehead.

"Check on Dad," she shouted to Dragon over the noise. "I got you!"

Dragon didn't argue with her, but that was probably only because he was worried about his father. She knew they would talk about her giving him orders, later. That was fine. As long as there was a *later* for them, she'd gladly fight it out with him.

Scanning the area in front of her and to the sides, she made sure no one was coming for her mate. She'd take a hundred lives and not lose a wink of sleep to protect Dragon.

Kisy totally forgot all about Ordys, or the fact that he had been fighting close by, until she heard him shout her name. She whipped around to see a wild-eyed man with thin, gray hair and a wicked scar across the bridge of his nose coming at her with a hunting knife in his hand. The man had a mission, and that was to use that knife to end her.

For some reason, her body took that opportunity to just stop. Her muscles froze. Her brain stopped functioning. Her eyes didn't even blink, which is how she was able to clearly see when a large dragon appeared at her side. The kind of dragon with scales, a tail, and wings. It took in a deep breath, opened its jaws, and let out a deafening roar. With that roar came a stream of fire that swarmed around the man, almost instantly engulfing him in flames.

The dragon's large, dark green face turned to look at her, smoke coming out of its nostrils.

Kisy chuckled. "Yeah, that's shit's cool. Think you can do us a favor, Puff, and take out a few more? I'm getting bored."

The dragon snorted, and Kisy swore he smiled at her before he turned his head and shot more fire at another asshole.

Siren

Poindexter, the vampire Siren had been partnered with, was an arrogant fuck who refused a gun, swearing his fangs and superstrength would be more than enough. Siren internally cursed the asshole as he charged toward Poindexter, who was being ganged up on by three bikers.

The first biker was easy to take care of. Siren came up behind him and yanked him back by his greasy hair. After pulling out his knife with his other hand, he raised it to the dick's throat and ended him.

The second biker noticed him killing the first and turned to engage. Before Siren could drop the discharged biker, the second one swung a knife at him. It stabbed him in the middle of his right hand, causing him to drop his own knife, as burning pain shot up his arm.

"Motherfucker," he growled and launched himself at the asshole. With the asshole's knife still lodged between his bones, Siren wrapped his other hand around the man's neck and squeezed, taking pleasure in watching the life drain from him.

When he was finally dead, Siren rolled off the man and lifted his injured hand up to look at it. He couldn't take the knife out yet. As he was debating what to do, Poindexter approached and looked down at him.

"You okay?"

"I have a fucking knife stuck between the bones of my hand," he spat. "No, I'm not fucking okay."

Poindexter grinned. Then he looked in front of him and the grin faded. "Shit!" He jumped over Siren and took off on a run.

Siren got to his feet and looked in the direction Poindexter ran. The vampire had almost made it in time. Siren watched as a biker raised a gun, aimed in the direction of Rozzat and Bullet, and fired off several shots. After both men crumpled to the ground, Poindexter launched himself on the fucker and tore out his throat with his fangs.

"Bull!" Siren ran toward them and dropped down to the ground next to Bullet, who had a large, seeping wound to his gut, his eyes rolling back in his head, but was at least still breathing. "Fuck!" Siren scooped him into his arms and stood, ignoring the pain in his hand. "Stay with me! You hear me, Bull! Stay fucking with me!"

Then he ran for the van, only vaguely noticing the heat from what he assumed was fire behind him, because what else would produce that high of a temperature?

It wasn't until he got to the van that he looked back. There were three dragons taking out the handful of opponents left standing. It mesmerized him for a moment to see the streams of flame coming from creatures he thought were only found in high fantasy novels and movies.

Then Bullet's groan and brought his attention back to the task at hand. *Get Bullet to a doctor, STAT.*

Axle

Once the enemy had been taken out, Axle looked around. Bodies and blood were everywhere. His eyes caught on too many of his brothers and sisters on the ground, along with a number of champions. Charred corps littered blood-soaked ground and smoke left the scene in a haze. The uninjured and the barely injured were in a flurry of motion, attempting to save anyone they could. Dirt and blood streaked faces were creased with worry as they carried the dead out of the carnage. It was a scene Axle would never be able to erase from his mind.

As he lifted his father in his arms and headed for the van at a fast clip, he saw the uninjured helping the injured out of the field. His heart clenched as he saw a worried Dragon carrying an unconscious Griff toward the van. When he got to the van, he'd call Hawkin to arrange for transport and send a text out to the doctors they had waiting to help.

It was a smart suggestion from Hawkin to have medical help on standby. If his world hadn't been crashing around him, he might have thought about it on his own. There was so much he had to tackle, that some things fell through the cracks. He was failing his club. He *had failed* his club and his sister-in-law. *Fucking Gigi!* His heart skipped a beat and then clenched tight at the memory of seeing Emerson howling out his heartbreak on the screen of Keys's phone.

"Stop it," his father mumbled.

"We're almost to the van," Axle replied, distracted by the dread of having to share the news with Gorgeous.

"I'm talking about the fact that you're taking the blame for all of this."

Axle stopped next to the van and gently set his father on his feet. He met the man's hard stare, the eyes so much like his own swirling gray ones, as his father leaned back against the side of the vehicle.

"You are a great president, son." His father took a deep breath and swallowed hard. "Better than I ever was. This is not on you. It is on the men who are dead, the men you and your family took out. Don't take that on."

A lump formed in Axle's throat as tears threatened to pool in his eyes. "I didn't protect th—"

"Oh, so the club is a one-man show now? Is that what you're saying? 'Cause I could've swore it was a family who has each other's backs. A family who wins together and loses together. But, sure, take it all on yourself and take away every bit of pride your brothers and sisters have in what they do for their family."

Axle felt like a scolded four-year-old as he looked down at his feet and cleared his throat.

"You did everything you could, Ax. You *all* did *everything you could.*"

He felt his father's hand grip and squeeze his shoulder. Axle gave a nod as he fought back his emotions. Even in his thirties, hearing his father say he was proud of him in any words was an emotional thing.

"Great. Now, get me back to the compound and get me patched up. I need some whiskey."

Axle's lips twitched as he helped his father into the back of the van. Once Joker was settled on the floor, Axle looked around inside. Among the injured, he saw Siren working on Bullet. Bullet's white shirt was covered in blood and dirt, making it impossible to see how bad his injuries were from where Axle was standing.

He rounded to the side of the van and opened the doors closest to Bullet. "How bad are we looking at?"

Siren didn't even look up from what he was doing in the area of Bullet's abdomen. "Bad. We need a doctor now." Siren was using his EMT voice.

"Fuck," Axle barked and pulled out his phone. Ignoring the blood and dirt on his hands, he called Hawkin and put the phone to his ear.

"Hawkin."

"We need more transport and the doctors to meet us at the compound."

There were muffled words and Axle knew Hawkin was giving one of his crew orders. Then he asked, "Numbers?"

"Maybe a half dozen killed, and a dozen injured. Some of them are things we can handle. Some are life-threatening. I'm sending our van to the compound now with the worst."

"Our contacts at the police department and fire department are holding back on addressing what's been happening, but they can't much longer."

"Understood." Axle slammed the side doors and moved to the back. He shut the backdoors. "Thanks for your help, Hawkin." Axle ended the call and put his phone away.

After motioning Keys over, he ordered, "Bullet's hurt bad. Take the van back to the compound. Doctors will be waiting."

Keys darted for the driver's seat.

Once the van pulled away, Axle went in search of Lira. He found her in the middle of the field, helping a dozen of her champions temporarily dress wounds.

"Lira."

She looked up at Axle from where she was crouched on the ground. "Yeah?"

"Transportation is on its way for the injured."

"Great." She turned back to securing the tourniquet around Winnon's injured thigh. "I have Sol and Menzanya counting our dead and carrying them out of the carnage." She let out a shaky sigh but kept herself together. "Then once we're all out of the way, the dragons will take care of the mess."

Axle raised a brow. "Take care of the mess?"

"It takes a lot out of them, but they can make fire hot enough to incinerate bones."

Fuck. He looked over at Ordys and Rozzat, a few yards away. Ordys had a section of someone's shirt tied around his arm and was doing the same to Rozzat's calf. Neither man looked as if they had a problem with what their Lira was expecting them to do. Axle was glad the champions were on their side.

Dragon

After they helped load the dead and injured into the vans Hawkin sent to help, Dragon turned away when Kisy laid a discarded jacket over his dad. He couldn't take the visual without falling apart. He retrieved his bike and rode it back to pick Kisy up at the farm. He spent the entire ride sending up his gratitude to the gods for making it through the battle without injury.

The way that she handled herself was mesmerizing. It took everything in him to stay focused on the battle, instead of sitting back and watching her use her gun to take out their enemies. It was sexy. It made him want to pull over to the side of the road and lay her out on his bike to fuck her until she screamed his name.

They didn't have time for that, and Dragon knew it was his brain's way of avoiding his emotions. It had been the day from hell. First, they lost the most precious soul to ever grace the planet when the assholes blew up Gigi. Second, they shot Pinky and Lace. When they left the compound, they were all aware that Lace wasn't going to make it. Then he thought he lost Kisy, went insane, and ran through the streets of the town in his wolf form, only to find out that she was okay. Finally, after rescuing Crush and Pixie, they fought in a war and came out of it with multiple injuries and deaths.

Each one of the injuries and deaths weighed heavily on him, but none more than the death of his father. Griff wasn't a perfect person or father, but he had taught Dragon everything he knew, including how to protect his family.

He hated that his father gave his life in order to protect Dragon's. He was grateful to his father, but he also held a lot of guilt that he was the reason Griff was gone.

Dragon had to tell Dani. That was going to be the worst part of his entire day. Kisy had offered to tell her for him, but he owed it to his sister and his father to share that information himself. He had always been the one to break difficult news to Dani and that wasn't going to change. He would continue to be someone she could depend on, someone she could trust. He thought of it as part of his job as her brother.

He had agreed when Thrash had been insistent that they let Tweetie – Trip's mom and Axle's stepmom, but the mom who raised him – tell Dragon's mom. Tweetie could hold her and help her through it. Dragon could see how his mother would need that level of support. Griff had been her rock for the entirety of her adult life. Learning to live without him was going to be a difficult task, probably the hardest thing she ever did in her life.

Dragon must have tensed up or something, because he felt Kisy's hand gently stroke his abdomen in a supportive way while she pressed her face harder into his back. She was sensing his emotions, even though he was trying his hardest to only graze the top of them. It shouldn't surprise him that she could do that – she was his mate – but it took his breath away that she had learned to read him so quickly.

He briefly released the handgrip and caressed the back of her hand for a moment, hopefully letting her know he appreciated her support.

A few minutes later, he turned the bike into the parking lot to the clubhouse and parked around the back of the garage, to leave the close spots for the vans. When he killed the engine, Kisy's arms tightened on his waist.

"You okay?"

Dragon forced her to let him go and dismounted. Then he pulled her into his arms while she still straddled his bike. "Yeah, Love, I'm okay."

"No, you're not," she uttered into his beard as she tipped her head up to kiss his jaw.

He tipped his head down and pressed his lips to hers. "Later. Okay?"

Kisy stared up at him for a long moment, her eyes assessing him. She must have clocked his need for time, because she gave a nod and allowed him to help her off the bike.

Gripping her hips, he lifted her off it and set her feet on the ground. He tried to take her hand in his, but she lifted his arm and snuggled her way into his side. Yeah, his mate knew what he needed when he needed it, because having her as close as possible is exactly what he needed.

With his arm around her shoulders and hers around his waist, they headed into the clubhouse.

Chapter Twenty-Six

Kisy

After they helped the injured to their rooms in the apartment building, Axle had made the call for Rebel to bring the women and children back to the compound. Kisy didn't know what happened on the phone call, but Axle looked even more pissed when he got off the phone.

He paced the room while Siren and Trip stayed close and looked pensive. Cuddled up to Dragon's side, Kisy could feel how tense he was. She knew he was worried about telling Darlin' about Griff, just like the others were worried about telling Darlin', Sugar, and Gorgeous about Gigi.

Emerson was still in the basement. Dragon told her he was still unable to shift back because of his grief, and the Howlers had him locked in a room down there for his own safety.

Kisy felt bad for Emerson in so many ways. She didn't know him well, but she didn't have to know him well or at all to have sympathy for everything he was going through. She mentioned going down there to sit with him, but Dragon shot down that idea, saying Emerson wouldn't want her seeing him like that.

Instead, she hung with Dragon and kept an eye on him. It was his nature to put everyone else's safety and emotional state above his own. It was her job, as his mate, to make his a priority, especially in moments of trial or when tensions were high.

She wanted to support him, but she was also concerned that he didn't seem to be processing any of the devastation they had faced that day. None of that surprised her. It was Dragon's way to close himself off, and she'd give him the time he asked for, but she wouldn't let him hide his emotions from her. When they were alone, he was going to lean on her whether he wanted to or not.

About thirty minutes after Axle made the phone call, the front door opened, and the women and children streamed into the room. Gorgeous pushed her way through and ran over to Axle, launching herself at him. Axle caught her easily and held her tight. At the same time, all the other women headed for the arms of the men they loved. She noticed that Butterfly wasn't there, but Kisy assumed she had already headed for Bullet in the apartment building.

"Are you okay? Is everyone else okay? Where's Gigi and Emerson?"

Axle winced and closed his eyes before he buried his face in her hair. "Just a minute. I'll tell you everything," Kisy heard him say.

Ginger glanced at him with sadness in her eyes before she got the kids rounded up and escorted them out of the room, with the help of Rex and Top. As they passed Axle, Ginger quietly uttered, "I'll take them to my room and keep them occupied."

Still holding Gorgeous in his arms, Axle nodded and waited for most of the room to clear out, except for Trip, Darlin', Siren, Sugar, Rebel, Dragon, and Kisy.

Axle set Gorgeous on her feet as Siren gently pulled back from the clinch he was in with Sugar. Kisy swallowed hard around the lump that had formed in her throat. She knew the men around her were tasked with the worst possible job of delivering heartbreak to the people they loved the most. She wished she could wave a wand and make all of it okay.

Darlin' eyed Trip warily from her place in his arms, then she looked over at Dragon. "What? What happened?"

Axle cleared his throat. "The war started with... uh..." He visibly swallowed hard before he met Gorgeous's gaze with his own. "They killed Gigi in front of Emerson."

There was silence for a long moment before sobs sounded and Gorgeous let out a heart-wrenching howl and collapsed. Axle just barely caught her before she would have hit the floor.

"No," she screamed and beat at Axle's chest.

Kisy looked over at the others. She saw Sugar's face streaked with tears as Siren held her up, and Darlin' was clearly in shock, her eyes wide and her mouth open as tears fell down her cheeks as Trip kept his arms around her and fought his own tears.

"I'm so sorry," Axle choked out, his voice hoarse with emotion.

"Where's Emerson?" Sugar asked and looked up at Siren. "He needs support."

"I'll show you," Siren told her and lifted her up into his arms, bride-style.

As Siren carried Sugar out of the room, Axle lifted the sobbing Gorgeous up into his arms and did the same.

After they left the room, Dragon let go of Kisy and approached his sister. Trip released her, but stayed close, keeping his arm around her waist. Kisy stayed close as well, in case Dragon needed her support.

"Sis," Dragon began and Kisy watched his adam's apple bob a few times before he continued, "during the fighting, Dad jumped in front of me and took a hit that was meant for me. He... uh... he didn't make it."

Darlin's eyes filled with tears again as she stared up at her brother. For a long moment, she didn't say anything, and neither did Dragon. Then she was in his arms, and he was holding her tight.

"I'm sorry you had to see that," she expressed through her tears.

"I'm sorry our dad is gone because of me," Dragon replied.

Kisy was startled when Darlin' smacked the back of her brother's head. "That's fucking nonsense."

Trip let out a quiet chuckle, but Kisy saw the sadness in his eyes. Her poor family was going through it, and she would do her best to support all of them. With that in mind, she walked over and wrapped him in her arms.

"I'm so sorry, Trip," she told him as she felt his arms hug her back.

"Thanks, Kisy." He kissed the top of her head. "It's a good thing we have such an amazing family, huh? There are a lot of shoulders to lean on."

"True," she replied. "I'm pretty sure that's the best thing Griff could have given them."

A few seconds after those words left her mouth, she was pulled out of Trip's arms and Darlin' was hugging her tight.

"I am so grateful for you," Darlin' whispered, even though the guys could hear every word. "He needs you. Take care of my brother, okay?"

"You have my word," Kisy responded through tears and pulled back enough to look into Darlin's eyes. "I promise."

Darlin' gave a nod and let go of Kisy. Then she glanced over at Dragon. "Thanks for finally giving me a sister. Love you."

Dragon reached over with one of his long, beefy arms and ruffled her hair. "Love you, too, Squirt."

Darlin' rolled her eyes as she fixed her hair.

Rex

Rex didn't think it was the best plan in the world, but it was the only one he could come up with at the moment. After getting the kids settled in Ginger's room with her, Rex left to check on their injured.

He finally convinced Siren to let someone check on his hand. The bastard had wrapped it in a dirty strip of fabric from someone's tee when they got back, saying he wouldn't worry about it until after he saw Sugar. Rex understood. Siren was worried about how Sugar would take the news about Gigi, but damn, she wouldn't take him dying from infection any better.

Sugar had seemed upset, but she firmly sided with Rex and shoved Siren toward the room that the doctors were using as a triage.

Rex checked on two of the Claws — Rita and Nails. Both had been sleeping, and had their wounds wrapped up. He walked in on Joker fighting with a doctor about how to patch him up. He left them to argue, knowing that his presence wasn't going to make it any easier on the doctor.

When he checked in on Bullet, he cursed and looked him over. Bullet was laying on his bed in tiger form and sleeping. When he convinced Butterfly to let him rest earlier in the night, Bullet had still been in human form and was knocked out on drugs. The surgeon had cleaned him up and stitched Bullet back together. The surgeon didn't like leaving Bullet in that bedroom instead of a hospital, but Top had convinced him that they would keep a close eye on Bullet and showed the surgeon the door. They needed him at the compound so that his shifter healing could take care of business and not raise brows at a hospital. The Howlers could also keep Bullet protected. With the world let in on the secret of the shifters, taking one of them to a hospital to recover was only asking for something bad to happen.

With Bullet's stitches ripped and in animal form, Rex couldn't call the same surgeon. The doctor who knew of shifters was busy working on Siren's hand. Bullet's wounds needed to be taken care of, but at least they weren't bleeding as profusely as earlier. He made a decision that he would find another doctor as quickly as possible. In the meantime, he'd have Top watch for one of the doctors at the compound to become freed up. If that was the case, Top could show them back to Bullet's room.

That was when Rex remembered the veterinarian who had just moved into a house a few blocks down the road. Mama Hen had mentioned her when he stopped in to thank her for letting them use her hotel for a few days. It didn't surprise him that Mama Hen had already met the woman. She was the resident welcome committee, a kind soul, and a social butterfly, making new friends easier than most people breathed.

Supposedly, the vet was joining the local animal clinic. Maybe she'd be eager to make connections in the community and would be willing to help them out. He prayed to the gods that she was home as he hopped on his bike.

Rex knew it was a horrible idea, but it was the only one he could come up with, so it would have to do. He drove the three blocks and pulled into the driveway of a modest ranch-style house with navy siding and white trim with an attached garage and a white picket fence around the front yard.

After killing the engine, he climbed off his bike and made his way up the walk to the front door. When he raised his hand and knocked on the door, he noticed the blood and dirt on his hands. *Shit!* He hoped she assumed it was just from the hurt animal.

He heard the locks twist and disengage, before the door was pulled open. Standing in front of him was a woman in her late thirties or early forties with blond hair cut short around her perfect face. What got him, though, were the big blue eyes staring up at him, open and engaging. Rex felt like he could happily fall into them and live there forever. Mentally shaking off that ridiculous thought, he focused on what she was saying to him.

"Can I help you?" Her gaze dropped to his shirt, and he knew she was seeing the blood and dirt on his clothes. "Is there someone hurt?" Her brows drew together, no doubt assessing how that much blood and dirt ended up on a person.

"Uh... I'm a member of the Howlers MC. Our compound is down the road," he said and zipped closed his cut in an attempt to hide most of the blood and dirt.

She nodded and waved her hand in a circle in front of her that said *get on with it*. "Mama Hen told me about your club. Said you were good guys."

Rex made a mental note to bring Mama Hen a gift basket of all of her favorite things. "Yes. Well, we have a badly hurt tiger at the compound. I was wondering if you had a moment to come look at him. We didn't want to move him."

The second she heard the words *badly hurt tiger*, she shifted into doctor mode. She slipped on a pair of shoes by her door and bent over to snatch a black bag off the floor that looked a lot like one of the medical bags you saw in television shows.

She looked ridiculous and sweet in her outfit. Her shoes were those clogs that all doctors and nurses seemed to own. Hers were a bright yellow. On her long legs, she wore a pair of ratty jean cut-off shorts. Her shirt was a bright red, with the words *mutt squad* in white inverted script on the front. *Fucking adorable.*

When she saw where he was looking, she shrugged. "I make videos and post them online about how best to take care of your pets. The inverted words make it easier to film on my phone. It's most efficient."

Rex smirked at her. "I like it."

She raised a blond brow at him, putting her free hand to her hip. "Are we flirting, or are we helping your tiger?"

Rex bit back the growl that his wolf insisted on. His wolf wanted to do more than growl, though. His wolf liked the vet and wanted her closer. *Fuck!* He needed to pull his shit together.

"The tiger," he replied, and cleared his throat. He stepped back as she came out of the house and turned to face the door. "Do you know how to get to the compound?"

As she locked her front door with her key, she answered, "Just go straight down the road next to the hotel. The road dead ends there, right?"

"Yes."

"Then yes, I know the way. Want to tell me why you have a tiger when it's against the law to have an endangered species without meeting certain criteria I'm sure your club does not meet?" Her question was more of an order.

"Uh... no."

"Didn't think so," she mumbled, and turned to face him. "We'll revisit that later. See you at the compound."

"Meet you there," he replied and returned to his bike. As he mounted it and started the engine, he told his wolf they couldn't play until after she fixed up their brother. His wolf gave a whimper but laid down.

Then he backed out of the driveway and headed for the compound.

Rex pretended not to notice the doctor's skeptical looks as he led her into the apartment building, up the stairs, and down the hall. He hoped she didn't raise any of the questions in her eyes.

He wasn't that lucky, he realized, when she asked, "You were so worried about moving the injured tiger that you carried it up a flight of stairs? Tigers are heavy."

Kicking himself in the ass for not thinking through what he would say when he went to ask her to help, Rex replied, "We found him up here in the hall."

"The injured tiger came into the building and climbed the stairs while injured? And you guys managed to move an injured tiger without the tiger fighting to protect itself?"

"I guess," he mumbled and opened the door to Bullet's room. "He's in here." He looked around the door to make sure Bullet was still in tiger form. He was, so Rex stepped aside and let her in.

He tried to follow her in, but the doctor faced him and firmly stated, "Wait outside. If it wakes up, it can be aggressive. I can handle it. I have tranquilizers, but I don't need to be distracted by worrying over your safety. If you want to help, I could use some warm water and clean towels, white if you have them."

Rex nodded to the door to the bathroom. "There are clean towels in the bathroom."

"Great. Wait here." Then the doctor shut the door in his face.

Rex wouldn't call her demeanor rude, but it was abrupt and demanding. What he didn't understand is why he liked that so much.

Chapter Twenty-Seven

Kisy

When they stepped into the house, Kisy kept her eyes on Dragon. He looked like he had everything pulled together, but she knew he was on edge. It was a vibe, a flow of energy coming off him that had her worried. It was like he was standing in the middle of a rope bridge, and someone was cutting through the ropes on both ends. He looked safe and stable, but all it took was one good cut.

He approached the part of the kitchen counter that jutted out halfway, cutting the room into two spaces. After dropping his keys there, he planted his hands on the top and let his head drop down.

Kisy rounded the counter and stood across from him. She gave him a few moments, then she reached out and covered his hands with hers. She didn't say anything. Words weren't needed. She only wanted him to know she was there if he needed her.

After a while, he said, "I'm pissed."

"Okay. You have a right to feel whatever you're feeling in this moment," she said softly.

His head lifted, and his gaze locked on her. "At you." He scowled at her. "First, you deliberately put yourself in danger to protect Crush and Pixie. I thought I lost you. While I was grieving, you were risking your life!"

Kisy flinched at the loud boom his voice had become by the time he finished his last sentence. She didn't take it personally, though. The emotions he had locked down all day needed to come out. If that meant he yelled at her, she would take it.

"Then you did it again when you insisted on going to Bobby's! And *again*, when you insisted on fighting in that battle! We had an agreement!"

Staring up at him, she waited for him to go on. When he didn't, she asked, "Are you done?"

He yanked his hands out from under hers and glared at her. "No, I'm not fucking done! I can't handle you being in danger, Kisy! I can't take it! I was worried about my family, my baby sister, my brothers, my *dad*." His voice broke on the last word and his anger crumbled as he closed his eyes and his body jerked violently. "Fuck... Dad." He lifted his hands and covered his face.

Kisy rounded the counter and wrapped her arms around his waist, holding on tight. He didn't hug her back, but that was okay. She would do the hugging for the both of them if that was what he needed from her. Seeing him struggle was hard on her, but it was nothing compared to the anguish Dragon was feeling.

"He died for me," he croaked as his chest heaved with a sob.

"I bet he has no regret about that," she said carefully, not wanting to upset him, but wanting to point out that his father wouldn't have changed it if he could. She didn't know Griff well, but she knew he would have taken a hundred bullets or knives to save Dragon from one.

"I failed him. I failed all of them."

"No, Dex, you didn't."

He dropped his hands and looked down at her with pain in his watery eyes. "I did."

She cupped his face in her hands and shook her head. "You didn't fail them. You have protected them for so many years. You've done everything you could do and you continue to put their safety above your own. That is all you can do. You have never failed them."

"I failed you," he whispered as he dropped his head and rested his forehead on top of hers.

"I get to decide that, and I reject that narrative, Dex."

"I feel like I got stabbed... here." He put a hand to his heart.

"That's heartbreak," she replied, and moved one of her hands to cover the spot, gently rubbing it. "I wish I could take it away. I can't, but I'll be here for you."

"I thought I lost you," he said in a voice so low she almost didn't hear him.

"You didn't. I'm right here."

He wrapped her up tight in his arms and lifted her so he no longer had to bend down. He kissed her lips softly. "You're real, right? I'm not dreaming this and you're really dead?"

"I'm right here," she repeated and gazed into those sexy green eyes of his. "I'm here and I'm not going anywhere."

"Promise?"

"Forever, Dex."

"Love, I need you, but..."

She pressed her lips to his, fully understanding what he couldn't verbalize. She could run the show for the night and take care of him. It would be an honor to make sure his heart fully believed she was alive and with him. He didn't fail her, and she wouldn't fail him. They were a team. It was just her time to take the lead.

"Take me to bed, D, and I'll give you what you need."

Axle

After holding Gorgeous until she cried herself to sleep, he carefully laid her on their bed and covered her up. As quietly as possible, he took a shower and got dressed. His intention was to check on the injured and then spend some time holding Nugget. He needed to look into those beautiful blue eyes of his baby girl and see hope. His soul needed some good, and Nugget was wholly good.

When he made it to Bullet's room, he found Rex sitting on the floor just outside the door. He stopped and looked down at his brother. The man was a good ten years older than Axle and had the graying blond hair to prove it, currently pulled back in a ponytail at the nape of his neck, but Axle still looked at him as a brother.

"How's Bull?"

"Uh... well..." Rex scratched his bearded jaw and avoided looking up at Axle. He'd never heard Rex stammer before. That was interesting, but it also alerted him to something being wrong. "He's tiger right now."

"He shifted?"

Rex gave a nod and let out a humorless laugh. "And we didn't have a free doctor to take care of the ripped stitches."

"Okay. So, he needs to be stitched up?" Axle turned, ready to go find a doctor.

"No, not anymore."

Annoyed that Rex was dragging it out, Axle barked, "Fucking say it."

Rex cleared his throat. "I went and got the new vet from down the street."

Axle blinked. Then he blinked again. "A vet?"

"Well... he's a tiger right now." Rex shrugged. "It was the best I could come up with on short notice without having to explain to someone what shifters are or that yes, we're real and why we're not evil be—"

The door flew open, and a blond woman Axle had never seen before stormed out, saying, "Nope. Nope. Nope," under her breath as she shoved stuff into a medical bag. She was shaking her head, making her short hair wave side to side slightly.

Rex jumped up to his feet and followed the woman. "Wait!"

Curious, Axle approached the open bedroom door and stepped inside. There was Bullet, lying on his bed in human form, his head flopping side to side, but he wasn't exactly conscious.

Well, shit.

Rex

"Wait." Rex caught up with the doctor before she could step onto the stairs that would take her to the first floor. He moved in front of her and looked into her eyes. "What's wrong? What happened?"

"I'm losing my mind. That's what happened." She looked calm, but Rex could see her chest heaving with her barely contained panic.

"Maybe... but why don't you tell me what you think happened, and I'll tell you if I think you're losing your mind?"

She narrowed her eyes on him, but she answered, "That tiger just turned into a man. A man! Tell me I'm not losing touch with reality now."

He liked it when she looked at him like that. That challenging, assessing gaze and the demand in her tone made his juices flow and his cock twitch.

Rex shrugged and let his smile grow on his face. "What if I told you I could do that, too, but a wolf, not a tiger, and that you're not losing touch with reality?"

"I would tell you that *you're* losing touch with reality."

"What if I proved it?"

She set her bag down on the floor. When she straightened, she crossed her arms over that ample chest, gave him a questioning look and a nod, before she said, "Prove it."

Rex chuckled. "Okay. But promise me you won't run. I'll explain everything once I'm done."

"Yeah. Yeah. Yeah." Like she did at her front door, she waved off his words and recrossed her arms. Then she stared at him, expectantly, an order in that stance.

Gazing into her eyes, Rex allowed his wolf out. Once he was shifted, he looked up at her and waited.

She stared at him with wide eyes for a long moment. Then she breathed, "Holy motherfucking shit balls."

Rex leaned forward and dropped his head. He licked her knee and was shocked when she swatted his head.

"Bad dog!" Then, she let out a humorless laugh. "Shit! Fuck! I just swatted a wolf." Taking a few steps back, she rubbed her face with her hands.

Rex shifted back and rubbed the back of his head where she had hit him. It didn't hurt, but he used it to his advantage. "There was no need for that," he grumbled.

"Sorry. Shit." She dropped her hands and glared at him. "Why am I apologizing? You shouldn't have licked me without my consent. Consent is a thing, ya know. It's also the fucking law." She began to pace in front of him. "Not to mention, you're the one who just did the impossible and changed forms in front of me. How is that possible? Science tells us that isn't possible, but yet, you did it and so did your... friend. Do your lungs and heart work the same? Internally, are your systems the same as humans or animals? There are so many questions."

When Rex took a step in her direction, she held out a hand and ordered, "Stay."

He cursed himself for listening to the order like a fucking golden retriever, but he didn't think disregarding her order would work in his favor. Once again, he was reminded how much he like a demand coming from her beautiful mouth.

Settling in his spot, Rex crossed his arms and waited while she made pass after pass, until finally she stopped and faced him. That assessing, challenging gaze back.

"You're not losing touch with reality," he told her.

"I'm still not so sure about that."

She waved off the topic, causing Rex to chuckle. Fuck. He liked it when she did that too.

"So, when you are in wolf form, are you a wolf or a human? Are you human in general? How can you shift back and forth? Does it hurt? What does it feel like? Were you bit and turned? Are your parents like you?"

Rex held up his hands in front of him to stop her barrage of questions. "Hold up. I'd be happy to talk to you about all of this, but that's a lot of questions all at once."

She shrugged. "It's science. I'm a doctor. Science is my jam."

"Fair." Rex smiled at her. "Did you finish sewing Bullet up?"

"Bullet?"

"My brother who can shift into a tiger."

"Oh, shit!" Then she snatched up her medical bag and headed back toward Bullet's room. "I think so, but I better check."

Following her, Rex chuckled and shook his head.

Chapter Twenty-Eight

Kisy

Down in their bedroom, Dragon set Kisy on her feet, and she took his hand. She led him over to their bed and began to undress him. First, she removed his cut and hung it on the hook by the stairs, where he always put it. When she returned to him, she gripped the sides of his shirt and pulled up and off his body.

While she worked, Dragon just watched her, that green gaze traveling all over her. He was still struggling with the reality that she was alive and well. She would allow him to stare at her or anything else he needed to do for as long as he needed. She would do anything to wipe away the fear and despair that had plagued him for the time she was held prisoner.

Kisy slowly pressed kisses all over his pecs and down his abdomen, taking him in and allowing him to do the same with her touch. With every kiss, his breathing intensified, until she was on her knees in front of him and was untying his boots.

"Love," he breathed.

"Shh." She removed his left boot and sock, then moved over to the other. "Let me. Just... feel, D."

She felt his fingers slide into her waves, a loving caress from her mate.

"Yeah. Okay," he agreed and lifted his leg when she tried to remove his right boot and sock.

She reached for the button of his jeans. Looking up into his eyes, she unbuttoned and unzipped his jeans. When she pulled them over his hips, taking his boxer briefs with them, he ran his tongue along his bottom lip, his piercing twinkling in the light.

Tossing his jeans and boxer briefs aside, she ordered, "In position on your back on the bed."

Dragon raised a brow at her, his lips twitching, but he moved to the bed and did as she asked. He laid down in the middle of the bed on his back and extended his arms above his head. "Now what, Love?"

Giving him a smile, she reached to slide her prospect cut off her shoulders. Dragon bit his lip like he was stopping himself from saying something. She stopped and asked, "What?"

"Can I make a request?"

She gave a nod.

"Will you wear only that?"

Her smile grew into a grin. She laid the cut on the bed and finished disrobing. After she was done, she grabbed the cut and slid it back onto her shoulders. When she entered the bed from the foot on her knees and began to crawl toward him, he watched her.

"Fuck," he groaned, and his eyes began shining that green light at her.

She stopped crawling between his knees and straightened. "I take it you like?"

He gave a nod. "Love it, Love."

She bent forward and fisted his now hard cock in her hand, giving it a slow stroke. "And if I wore it while I rode this?"

"Dream come fucking true," he growled as his hips twitched.

"Well, just call me a dream maker," she commented and moved forward on her knees. Straddling his hips, she reached between her legs and circled her clit with the head of his cock and one end of that piercing.

His eyes continued to bathe her in that green light as he held his head up and watched every movement she made. A slow growl built and rolled out of his gritted teeth.

"I like your piercing," she panted as her climax began to build, that sweet throbbing of her clit letting her know how close she was. "I think you should get more. Should I get some?"

"Your tits," he gritted out. His chest was heaving with the intensity of his breathing.

She cupped one of her breasts with her free hand, pinching the tip between her fingers. "You want my tits pierced?"

He nodded. "Only if you want it, though."

In response, Kisy shifted the head of his cock to her entrance and slid down until he was as far as he could get inside of her. "I want it," she moaned and began to ride him, slowly and steadily.

He threw his head back on the bed and fisted his hands, but he kept them where they were. He didn't try to take over or make demands. She was surprised he had lasted so long, but she suspected he needed to give up control. Maybe he realized it as well.

She played with both of her breasts as she slid up and down his cock. The noises coming from him were familiar, but more than she had ever heard from him before. It was as if he was intent on letting her know exactly what she was making him feel. It drove her to ride him faster, harder, chasing the noises and earning new ones. The rush of pride that filled her was something she only felt when she followed each of his orders to perfection, and he gave her his satisfied smile. It was a heady feeling.

"Love, I'm close," he groaned.

She leaned forward and braced herself with her palms to his chest. Widening her stance, she ordered, "Fuck me, D. Make me come."

With his hands still above his head, he bent his knees up. Then he slammed his hips up against her, over and over, until her climax exploded inside of her, shooting pleasure through every limb.

"Can I come?"

She heard his panted question through her climax, but she could only nod in response.

"Fuck yes," he shouted as he slammed up and held his hips against her as he shot his cum deep inside of her.

When her body began to relax again, she dropped to his chest and panted. She waited for the tension to leave his body, then she ordered, "Hold me."

Without hesitation, he wrapped his arms around her and pressed a kiss to the top of her head. "Thank you, Love," he whispered.

She knew exactly what he was thanking her for. He needed to let go and just let his brain work through it. It would be an ongoing process, but what she gave him was the first step, and he wanted her to know he appreciated it.

In an attempt to lift the mood, she mumbled, "I liked being in charge. Think we could make this a regular thing?"

Dragon snorted a laugh. "Nice try, Love."

Axle

Dealing with the drama Rex had put into motion would take more give-a-damn than Axle had access to at that moment. He left the man to deal with it. Axle wasn't sure Rex realized it, but he was positive the man had just met his mate. He wondered how long it would take Rex to figure it out. Just because the man was older didn't mean he had a better grasp on that sort of thing.

Instead of taking that on, Axle stepped outside the apartment building and called Hawkin.

"Hawkin."

"How big is the news of shifters in town?"

Axle heard Hawkin sigh on the other end of the line. "Well, in town it's the biggest news story, besides the fact that explosions and gun fights filled the day. The cops want answers. The fire department does, too, but they've pulled enough camera footage from around the area to know that there was another club in town. They suspect them of it, but they want to talk to you. Outside of town, people are losing their minds about the video footage that was leaked by the assholes you took care of today."

"Leaked footage?"

"Apparently, HDMC took recordings of the shifters they had in their control and released the videos to the public." Hawkin sighed again. "From what we could find out, they didn't have any shifters with them but one. That one was taken out by Rebel at the library, and the body is gone."

Axle didn't reply, but he already knew that. It was Rebel's uncle. He had sent Claws to take care of it as soon as he talked to Rebel on the phone about it. While Rebel was bringing the women and children back to the compound, Kitty and Pumps were taking care of the evidence. He didn't know how they did it, and he didn't want to know.

He remembered the dragons taking care of the mess at the farm and decided it wouldn't be a bad idea to have one of them around, too. Axle wasn't about to pimp out one of the Claws in hopes that they would snag a dragon, so he just had to hope the Claws took a shine to one of them.

"How are the injured?"

"Healing. With the exception of Lace, the injured were able to be saved. We ended up with eight dead, though, including Riles and Dragon's dad."

"Fuck, Man. That sucks." Hawkin sounded like he really meant those words, and Axle believed that he did.

"I know you're tired of hearing this, but I need a favor, Hawkin."

"The number of markers I have in my hands from you is ridiculous, Weber."

Axle snorted. "I'm sure you'll call them in, eventually. I need you to arrange a meeting with the mayor for me. We need to reassure the town, but I need the mayor's support to be able to do that."

"Yeah. I'll call him in the morning. ASAP on the meeting, I assume."

Pacing up and down the sidewalk, Axle replied, "Yeah."

"Consider it done," Hawkin stated.

"Thanks, Hawkin." Axle leaned back against the building and took a deep breath.

"Weber?"

"Yeah?"

"I heard about Georgia. I'm so fucking sorry, man. She was a great young lady and a diamond in this town. Her loss is a heavy one."

Axle swallowed hard around the lump in his throat and nodded, even though Hawkin couldn't see him.

"Okay. That's all I'll say about it. I'll call you when I have the meeting set up." Then Hawkin ended the call.

Dragon

Dragon was shaken to his core. Raw. He didn't know how to handle the emotions running through him. The grief and anger were more than he had ever experienced in his life. But more than that, the need to give Kisy control and let her take care of him was a battle. It was a conscious decision and took a boatload amount of effort for him to let go of the constant control he kept over every situation.

Kisy wouldn't hurt him. He knew that. It was the mantra going through his head as he let go of the control, allowing her to take the reins. The entire time, he was worried he wouldn't be able to keep it up, then she looked him in the eye, and he saw nothing but love and safety shining back at him.

Dragon fully gave himself over to the experience, and it was exhilarating. He wouldn't have been able to do that with anyone else, but Kisy wasn't just anyone. She was his mate, his heart, his happiness. She was the everything that made him whole.

When it was over, his skin was too sensitive, and his emotions were exposed. Kisy sensed his uneasiness and broke the tension with her joke. It only made him love her more. He hadn't even known that was possible.

As he laid there with her asleep on his chest, he allowed the grateful tears to stream from his eyes, over his temples, and soak into the pillow under his head.

His father approved of Kisy and of Trip being with Dani. He knew they had found their happiness. That was what Griff had told Dragon as he died in Dragon's arms. His last words were for love of his children and their mates. It had been the first time in his life that his dad actually told him he loved him. Sure, Griff had expressed his pride in Dragon, he made sure Dragon knew he was loved, but he hadn't ever said the words to Dragon.

It hit him more than his father's death actually did. He knew his dad died the way he would want to – protecting someone he loved. He could accept that. He would miss him, and he felt sadness for his mom and Dani, but he wasn't really sad for his father or himself. It was the *I love you, Son* that had done him in.

After going through the grief of thinking he lost Kisy, it was too much, too many big emotions. He should have known his Kisy would take care of him. She had thrown herself fully into their relationship and his family. She was all-in and made sure he knew she wasn't going anywhere. It should have been obvious that he could lean on her.

It hadn't been until he looked in her eyes in his greatest moment of suffering that he accepted he could give her everything. So, he did. He gave her everything, and she soothed those hurts with her love. *Fuck...* That shit was powerful.

He tightened his hold on her and pressed his lips to the top of her head. When she cooed in her sleep and tried to snuggle closer, Dragon smiled and closed his eyes.

It was the best night's sleep he ever had.

Rex

Hours had passed with Rex sitting in the corner of Bullet's room, watching Doc work on his brother. In his mind, he had taken to calling the vet *Doc* because he didn't know her name. He wasn't sure he wanted to know, now. It wouldn't make a difference. She would always be Doc to him.

His wolf whined at the distance between them, even if it was only a few feet. Rex knew what it meant. He'd heard enough stories about how his brothers' animals had reacted to their mates to know that was why his wolf was behaving so oddly, but he wasn't ready to admit it out loud.

He didn't even know what she thought about shifters yet. Her reaction was so strange. It wasn't fear, but he wouldn't say it was happiness either. It intrigued him. Everything about her intrigued him. He wanted to know all of her thoughts and her hobbies and her passions. He wanted to know how she sounded in every situation, how she tasted everywhere, and her boundaries. Rex wanted to know everything that made up Doc.

"Tell me why you keep looking at me like that, Fido."

Rex smiled, but his smile turned into a grin when he heard Bullet snort a laugh. He looked over at his brother and saw Bullet open his eyes.

"Think that's funny, do ya?"

Bullet nodded and coughed, wincing at the pain it caused in his abdomen. "She... She?" He looked at the doctor and the doctor nodded, confirming her pronouns. "She called you *Fido*. Of course, I think that's funny."

Doc smiled as she lifted the bandage and checked on Bullet's stitches. "Well, listen here, Tony, you shouldn't laugh. For one, you need to take it easy. Also, you flashed your stripes at me a couple times over the hours."

"What?" Bullet looked at her like he didn't understand English, then he turned his head to look at Rex.

"You shifted. You were human when you were first worked on. Then you shifted and tore your stitches, so you were tiger when I brought in Doc. She stitched you back up. Then you shifted... and shifted... and shifted."

"Yeah, so think you can stop doing that?" Doc looked at Bullet and raised a brow. "You keep ruining my good work."

"You... shifters? You... know?"

Doc gave a humorless laugh. "I didn't until you shifted while I was bandaging your wounds. I was going to leave because I was positive I lost my mind, but Fido proved that I was still sane. Then I remembered that I took an oath, so... here I am. I'm full of questions, and Rex will answer them eventually, but you need to take it easy."

Bullet sputtered as he tried to process her words. Rex chuckled. "It's fine, Bull. Just try to stay human until your healing takes care of things. You had a rather large hole in your abdomen."

Still confused, Bullet nodded. "Where's Butterfly?"

Doc stopped in the middle of checking Bullet's vitals and turned to look at Rex. "Oh god... please don't tell me there are butterfly shifters, too." Her eyebrows shot up as her eyes widened.

Rex smiled at Doc. "Nah... just us predators. Butterfly is his mate. She was in here earlier. She introduced herself as Harlow."

"Oh." Doc let out a deep sigh. "I thought those news reports were just a quirky twilight zone-esque part of the town, but... well, I guess it is... depending on how you look at it. The physiological changes as you all shift boggles my scientific brain. How? Why? What happens to your muscle structure? And your bones... how do they lengthen and shorten to accommodate the form of an animal? And the fur... where does it come from and where does it go?"

Rex bit back a laugh as she mulled that over and put her doctor stuff back in that medical bag. Having her around was going to be fun. Now, he just needed to figure out a way to convince her to *be around*.

"I need water," Bullet commented. "Yeah. I think that's why I can't think."

Rex stood and went for a glass of water from the bathroom as the doctor replied, "Water can only help. Well, I assume. I mean, I don't know much about shifters, but you seem to have the physiology of a human when human and that of a tiger when shifted, so yeah... water."

Smiling at her words, Rex brought the glass to Bullet and helped him sit up enough to drink it. He held the glass to Bullet's lips. When Bullet was done, Rex set the glass down on the table next to the bed.

Bullet looked up at him with a knowing smirk. "She's yours, isn't she?"

Rex rolled his eyes and gave a nod. "You're not having too much trouble with thinking, are ya?"

"Fair enough," Bullet replied, and grinned.

"Uh... if you're talking about me, the answer is *Negative*. I belong to no one."

"Sure, Doc," Bullet replied, breezily, and closed his eyes.

Rex shifted his attention to the doctor and saw her looking at him with that assessing expression she always gave him. He winked at her.

Her eyes narrowed more. "You boys are insane... and not just because you can be animals whenever you want."

"Yeah, but we can also be animals in bed," Bullet mumbled as he fell back to sleep.

Rex shrugged. "He speaks truth."

Doc raised a brow. "Not if I don't give you permission to be."

And that was the moment Rex knew his future had been decided, and it included the beautiful doctor across the room.

Chapter Twenty-Nine

Axle

Axle hadn't slept a wink the night before. After making sure all of his brothers and sisters were okay and safe, he went and picked up Nugget from Ginger's room. He brought her to the room he shared with Gorgeous and sat down in the armchair in the corner. That is where he stayed with his daughter in his arms.

Nugget had woken up numerous times in the night and looked up at him with those beautiful, trusting eyes for a few moments before she drifted off to sleep, happy in the knowledge that her Dad had her. She trusted Dad to protect her and the ones she loved. Axle felt like he failed his family, but his father was right. He couldn't keep taking everything on his shoulders. It was unfair to his brothers and the Claws.

The problem was, he wasn't sure how to change his mindset. It was going to take time, but his father's words made something Crush had been trying to say click in his head. All of the times he kept the Claws out of things *for their safety* diminished their abilities and their contributions. It had been a rub between them for a long time, and it was up to him, as the club president, to make sure the Howlers changed that mindset, too. The Claws deserved that respect.

He couldn't do it alone, though. He was going to have to talk to certain members of the Howlers and get them on board to help change it. Who could he talk to? Dragon, for sure, once he had time to process everything that had happened. Skull, as the Vice President, should be included. Top and Rex, as senior members, should be involved, too.

"Ax," he heard Gorgeous utter from the bed. Her voice was rough from all her crying and screaming. Hearing it brought back all the pain from losing Georgia, but he pushed it back and looked over at her.

"Hey."

"Come lay with me."

Axle stood and carefully transferred Nugget from his arms to the bassinet they kept in their room for her. Once he knew she was still asleep and comfortable, he moved to the bed and laid down next to his woman.

Gorgeous instantly shifted into his side and wrapped her arms around his waist. There weren't any more sobs or screams, but she asked, "It's real, isn't it?"

He kissed the top of her head and sighed. "Yeah, Gorgeous, it is."

"Are you sure they're dead?"

"Yeah," he answered, wishing he could bring them back so he could kill them again.

"I love you," she said against his chest.

"More than life," he replied.

She was yanking his shirt up his body when his phone rang.

Cursing under his breath, he pulled it out of his pocket and answered it, not wanting the ringing to wake Nugget. "Weber."

"Hey. Meeting with the mayor at my office at eleven," Hawkin said on the other end of the line.

"I'll be there. I'm bringing Crush."

"Okay. That's fine, but think you can leave your VPs and your SAGs at home? It can't look aggressive if you want this to work."

Axle knew Pike was going to fight him on it. Skull would understand, but Pike was in the position he was because of his fierce protection of Axle. He'd stay out, but he wouldn't like it. "Yeah. At least in the meeting. I can't promise Pike won't follow, but he can hang in the lot."

"Fair enough."

"See you at eleven." Axle ended the call and set his phone on the nightstand.

"I need to feel your skin," Gorgeous said, "for a while, until you have to leave."

Axle returned to his feet and undressed. He'd do anything for Gorgeous, especially if it helped her with her grief. He couldn't bring Georgia back, but Axle would help her deal with Georgia's passing in any way he could. His thoughts were looping. Axle knew that, but it was the only thing keeping him from falling apart. He needed to be strong for his girls. If they were okay, he would be okay. Or at least, he hoped.

"When do you have to go?"

Axle sighed. "I have to meet with the clubs and the champions at eight. We have a couple hours."

Gorgeous nodded and snuggled closer.

Dragon

After dropping Kisy off at the compound to hang with the ol' ladies, Dragon took off with the Howlers and the Claws to meet up with Lira and the champions. They decided on the farm, since the police were still holding off on questioning them.

Dragon wasn't sure how Axle and Mick managed that, but he assumed it had something to do with fear. The police were learning that shifters were a real thing, and they weren't sure they could handle the Howlers and the Claws, since they wouldn't be able to overpower or control them. Or at least, that was Dragon's guess.

When they pulled up at the farm, Dragon was shocked. The large field behind the farmhouse looked like it had been tilled and ready for planting. He knew the ground had been scorched with dragonfire. Axle explained that a bit before they left the clubhouse, but this wasn't scorched ground.

"What the fuck?" Trip slid off his bike after he parked next to Dragon.

"That's exactly what I was thinking," Dragon uttered as he dismounted.

Lira chuckled from her spot, sitting on the rear stairs to the porch about ten feet from them. When Dragon looked over at her, she said, "It's what happens to the soil. The dragonfire has properties that nurture the soil. Think of it as burning away the bad. The tilling was done with a wave of the hand by your buddy, Orion, Trip."

Trip turned his head and looked over at the man that he had been partnered with. "Nice trick."

Orion shrugged. "Thanks."

"You becoming a farmer?" Trip asked and nodded toward the field.

Another shrug. "Maybe. I like the forests around here."

Dragon didn't bother speaking on any of that. He just joined Axle and the rest of his brothers, who were in riding form on the edge of the field.

A few minutes later, Crush and the uninjured Claws joined them. Once the girls had dismounted and made their way to the field, Lira and the champions made their way over.

"Okay. So, this is the message from the gods," Lira began.

Dragon liked that she seemed to be pretty efficient with their time.

"The world has learned of shifters, thanks to those fucking videos HDMC put out before they killed the feral shifters they were using. Rebel took out the lone survivor, right?" She looked over at Rebel, who nodded. "But those videos are not being brushed off as altered. Because of that, we are offering to station a group of champions here, if you would like. I suspect a lot of visitors to

Warden's Pass — some curious, some excited, some with nefarious goals."

Axle looked over at Crush. Then he shook his head. "You're welcome to station a group here, but this is our town. We will protect it."

Lira gave a nod. "Consider it backup."

Crush narrowed her eyes as she looked at Lira. "You know more than you're telling us."

"I can only give you what the gods have permitted me to," Lira confirmed without confirming.

"Mother fucking piece of shit gods. What good are they if—"

"Okay!" Pinky put her hand over Crush's mouth and gave a fake smile. "Thanks for the backup."

Dragon was pretty sure he heard Crush's mumbled words, "I will fuck you up for that, Pinks."

Pinky rolled her eyes.

"Anyway," Axle cut in, probably to keep Crush from killing all of them. "We appreciate your help in all of this. If you need anything from us, give Crush or me a call. But please understand that we have a lot of deep shit we're dealing with right now and could use some privacy in that."

Lira inclined her head, sadness in her eyes. "As are we. Understood."

Without another word, Axle and Crush led their clubs off the field and back to their bikes.

It was one thing to let the champions help in a crisis, but the Howlers and the Claws closed ranks when it came to dealing with death in the family. It would be handled and processed in the privacy of their ranks. Their dead deserved the respect, and they would get it, even Riles.

As that thought crossed Dragon's mind, he approached Axle. "What are we doing about the four remaining UpRiders?"

Axle sighed. "I'm meeting with them after I meet with the mayor. I think we have an obligation to help them."

Dragon nodded. "Patch over?"

"If that's what they want." Axle ran his fingers through his hair. "We'd have to vote."

"Yeah, but I don't think anyone would object. I think we should send a few Howlers to help set up the club and help them recruit, though, if we go that route."

"Something to consider," Axle mumbled as he threw a leg over his bike and settled on it. "Plan on church at two. Spread the word on that, will ya?"

"You got it, Pres," Dragon replied and turned to do just that.

Axle

As expected, Pike threw a damn fit over not being able to come in the building with Axle. He was stuck out in the parking lot with Dragon and Skull. Neither of them were okay with it, but they didn't fight it.

Pinky looked pensive as Crush walked for the front door of Milhawk Investigations. Axle wasn't sure what that was about, but he knew Pinky well enough to know there was a valid reason for her concern. Something was going on with Crush.

As they stepped into the lobby of M.I. and found it empty, Axle asked, "Why is Pinky so worried about you? The shit at the farm, and the look on her face now, tell me something's going on."

"It's none of your business," Crush replied, but she wasn't giving him the steely mind-your-business stare she normally gave him when she was putting him in his place. It was a hard glare.

"Crush," he said quietly, reminding her they were friends.

Crush didn't say or do anything for a long moment. Then she huffed out a breath and looked up at him. "Lucifer gave me an ultimatum. And... I'm..."

Axle bit the inside of his cheek to stop himself from smiling. When he had himself under control, he said, "You're scared."

Crush cringed but nodded. "He's just so... *infuriating*."

Axle chuckled. "That's because he broke through that wall of don't-give-a-damn you've surrounded yourself with. You let me in, once, but other than that, men don't get through. The fact that he was able to do that, Crush, says he's worth a shot."

"You don't even like him," she scoffed.

"That might be because I only want the best for you, and I'll feel that way about anyone until they *prove* they are *the best*." He gave her an understanding smile. "If I'm wrong and he's not worth it, the Howlers and I will pull cleanup for a change. Deal?"

A small smile twitched her lips. "Fine."

"Great. Now, let's put on our best faces and prove to the mayor that we aren't a danger to the community."

"Nothing like asking for miracles," Crush mumbled as she turned and headed for the door to the back hallway of Milhawk Investigations.

Five minutes later, they were sitting in a conference room across the table from Mayor

George Cardinalie and Hawkin. The mayor was a middle-aged man with thinning, white hair on top of his head, a large belly around his waist, and a welcoming smile on his face. He was the mayor because that smile made the community feel like they could trust him. Axle knew that smile disappeared when something serious was threatening Warden's Pass, which is why that smile was nowhere to be found in their meeting.

"Mr. Weber. Ms. Welles. I was told by Mick that you had some concerns you wanted to talk to me about."

Axle intentionally didn't say anything. He wanted to let Crush have just as much input as he did in the conversation. He needed to quit speaking for her, so he made it a point to let her speak for herself.

Crush looked over at him, curiously, before she addressed the mayor and said, "You are aware of the videos that had been leaked, I'm sure, as well as the incident from yesterday in the middle of town."

Mayor Cardinalie gave a nod. "I am aware."

"We're not going to sit here and try to tell you that none of it's true." Crush took a deep breath. "Shifters are real. Shifters are humans who have the ability to take the form of an animal. It is limited to a specific animal that comes from their family line. We cannot bite people and change them. We are just like any of you. It's just a gene we are born with, like green eyes or red hair."

The mayor cleared his throat. "My concern is... the videos showed aggressiveness, violence, a danger to people without that gene."

Crush nodded, understanding the mayor's concerns. "Yes, but that is not normal. I will not tell you that no shifters are a danger. Just as with humans, there are bad guys in the shifter community, but the shifters in the videos that were released were given a drug. It's called Variulisis. It's a drug that causes a shifter to become more aggressive with continued exposure over a long period of time. Those shifters were also eliminated."

The mayor looked over at Axle. "Are you all shifters?"

Axle shook his head. "Not all of the Howlers MC members or the Tiger's Claw members are shifters. The majority are, but not all of us."

"Are you dangerous?"

Axle looked at Crush and they exchanged a long look, before Axle returned his attention to the mayor and answered, "To you and the citizens of Warden's Pass who are good people? No. Mayor

Cardinalie, I have no illusions that you haven't been made aware of the way we have been helping the women and children of this community for decades. You know that we have bent and broken the law to make sure the women and children of Warden's Pass are safe. That is who we are."

"That is who we will continue to be," Crush added. "All we're asking for is a chance to explain that to the community. We are willing to answer questions from the town. We are willing to let them in on some secrets, if it makes them feel more comfortable with us around, but, most importantly, we would like the chance for them to understand that this isn't something new. It is who we have always been. We were born this way."

The mayor took a deep breath and looked over at Hawkin. "What do you think?"

Hawkin shrugged. "I've known them for most of my life. I've never known them to harm anyone without a reason. I trust them around myself and my crew. They are good people, Mayor Cardinalie."

It was a long moment before the mayor gave a nod. "Okay. I'll arrange a town hall meeting for tomorrow afternoon at four, at the high school to accommodate the crowd."

"Thank you," Crush said and gave him a smile.

T.S. Tappin

Chapter Thirty

Kisy

Sitting in the diner with Darlin' and Gorgeous, Kisy tried to keep the mood up. She figured she would follow their lead. If they didn't want to talk about their losses or their heartache, she wouldn't bring it up, but if they brought it up, she wouldn't run from it. They were her family now. That meant she would stick by them through it all.

Holding Cane to her chest, Darlin' looked across the table at Kisy and smiled. "I saw Dragon when he dropped you off. He seemed more... at peace than I expected."

Kisy returned her smile. "He had some stuff to process, as you know, and he still is, but he's doing okay."

"That's you," Gorgeous said and handed a toy to Nugget, who was lying in her car seat.

After a shrug, Kisy confirmed, "I might have had something to do with it."

"You had everything to do with it." Darlin' waved a hand between them. "I don't want to know how, because I already heard enough about what my brother likes to get up to in his bedroom. I just wanted to say... thank you, Kisy, and I'm glad you're my sister."

Kisy's eyes had filled with tears as Darlin' spoke. She swallowed hard around the lump in her throat and gave a nod to let Darlin' know she heard her.

She had a sister, but Kisy was not opposed to having more. And having women close to her who understood what it was like to be with a man like Dragon would come in handy.

Between Dragon and his family, they were filling holes in her life she hadn't been aware were there. She wanted it official. Sure, the mating mark took care of that, but she wanted to be able to show the world that Dragon was her forever. She decided to address it with Dragon as soon as he got back, or at least as soon as they got a moment alone.

"There you are!"

Hearing her aunt's voice, Kisy turned around and saw Auntie Hen headed her way. Her teal hair was bright and fun, just like the smile on her face.

"Auntie Hen. Hey."

"You can't show up at my hotel in handcuffs and not think I'd want all the details!" She slid in the seat next to Kisy and looked down at Nugget in her car seat on the floor. "Well, hey there, little lady."

Nugget cooed at her.

"My day is going okay. Thanks for asking."

Gorgeous giggled as Auntie Hen continued to have an animated conversation with the infant.

After wrapping up her conversation with Nugget, Auntie Hen looked over at Kisy. "Now, I've heard about everything that went down in town yesterday, and I know all of you have something to do with it all, so I want details. I ain't waiting for the rumors, either. They probably don't have a lick of truth left in them anymore. I want it straight from the horse's mouth."

"Or wolf's, or tiger's, or bear's, or mountain lion's, or—"

Kisy snorted a laugh, cutting off Darlin's words.

Gorgeous rolled her eyes but smiled. "What have you heard, Mama Hen? We'll confirm what is correct and fill in what we can."

"You think Axle will be okay with that?" Kisy asked, carefully.

Gorgeous raised a brow at her. "He's having a meeting with Mayor Cardinalie as we speak. Also, Axle is my mate, not my boss. I may not be as loud about it as you two are, but he gets put in his place just as often as Dragon and Trip. Besides, my daughter is in that community, and I have no intention of teaching her to be ashamed of who she is."

Kisy gave a nod and let the grin grow on her face. "Well, okay, go on with your bad self."

They spent the next half hour giving Auntie Hen the bullet points of what happened the day before, and the truth about shifters. To say Auntie Hen was jealous of shifters would be an understatement.

When Crush and Axle returned to the compound, they gathered the able-bodied members in the clubhouse and went over what happened during the meeting with the mayor and then the plan for the town hall meeting at the high school.

Kisy wasn't shocked to find that the Howlers and the Claws were a united front on how they wanted to handle addressing it with the community. She had learned over her time there that to the rest of the world, they would always be a united front. If there were disagreements, they handled them internally and didn't let that leak to the outside world.

What shocked her was what Crush did at the end of the explanation. She walked over to the bar and pulled a box out from behind it. As Crush ripped it open, she said, "There is someone in this room who went above and beyond what is expected of someone who is not patched into the clubs. She put herself in danger to protect us and our family." Crush turned and looked at Kisy. "The point of prospecting is to prove you can be trusted. It's to prove you will put the club above yourself. It's to prove you would do anything to protect the club and our family. You've already done that. So, give me your prospect cut."

A bit confused, Kisy stood and made her way across the room to where Crush was standing. She removed the prospect cut she received the day before and handed it to Crush.

Crush laid it on the bar and reached into the box. She pulled out a new leather cut with the Tiger's Claw MC colors on the back and a member patch on the front. She handed it to Kisy. "Your *Kisy* patch is on order, but I didn't want to make you wait for your cut since you have more than earned it. If you still want to be in the Claws, put that cut on."

Kisy turned and looked at Dragon. She was putting the cut on, no matter what, but she was happy to see him give her a slight nod. He was proud of her, and he wouldn't hold her back. With a giant grin on her face and tears in her eyes, Kisy slid that cut on her shoulders.

The second the leather settled, the room erupted into cheers, and Dragon scooped her up in his arms. He pressed his lips to hers as he slowly twirled her around in a move that was so unlike him that she broke the kiss to laugh.

Dragon

In the church room upstairs at the clubhouse, Axle sat at the head of the table, with Pike to his right and Skull to his left. Dragon sat next to Pike and Bullet sat on Dragon's other side. They tried to tell Bullet he didn't need to come, and that they would proxy his vote, but his stubborn brother wouldn't hear of it.

Bullet slowly made his way over to the clubhouse from the apartments, with Butterfly bitching at him the entire way. The fact that all of his brothers agreed with her didn't make a difference. He just shrugged and made his way up the stairs. At Butterfly's request, Dragon had followed closely behind Bullet, prepared to catch him if he started to fall. By the time they made it to the top of the stairway, Bullet was covered in sweat.

When Rex entered the room and took his seat, four seats down from Bullet, he leaned forward and looked down the table at him. "Doc said she's not stitching you back up again. Five times was enough."

Bullet snorted a laugh. "I bet she would if you asked nicely." When Rex just flipped him off, Bullet's laugh turned into a chuckle, which turned into a groan as the pain hit him.

"You deserved that," Dragon told him.

"You're supposed to be on my side," Bullet grumbled.

"Not when you're being a dumbass," Trip pointed out.

Dragon reached behind Bullet to bump fists with Trip.

"Oh, so *now* you two are friends again? Fucking traitors."

Trip rolled his eyes, and Dragon grinned.

"Fuck." Bullet shook his head, looking at Dragon with awe on his face. "I'll never get used to seeing that. I think we ought to give Kisy a fucking trophy. She deserves one for that grin."

"Okay. Enough," Axle said, but the grin on his face told Dragon he liked their banter. He waited for the voices to die down before he started the meeting. "We have a few different issues to address. First, can we just agree that Kisy is a member of the family and Dragon's mate, even though she already has her property patch, *and* he has yet to bring that shit to the table?"

The fact that every single one of his brothers said yes and looked at him like he kicked their dogs made him a little uncomfortable. "Okay. I get it. Just... a lot has been happening."

Trip boomed out a laugh. "Fuck! Screw a trophy! Buy her a fucking island! She's got him all... I dunno... discombobulated."

"Fuck you, Trip."

"And, we're back to normal," Bullet mumbled as Dragon reached behind him and smacked Trip upside the back of his head.

"Okay!" Axle rolled his eyes. "Kisy's ol' lady status is confirmed. Next, the UpRiders have made a formal request for a patch over. There are only four surviving members, all of which helped our side in the war and had been loyal to Riles. In order to do a patch over, we all have to agree...

unanimously. Also, we would need to send a small group to the UP to help them recruit and set up a proper club. Whether the group stays or returns after that's done is up to the member, meaning... if you go up there and decide to stay, that's your choice. Let's vote. Skull?"

"I'm good with it." Skull said with a shrug.

"As long as we're in charge of the restructure, I'm a yes," Score voted.

Top nodded. "Yes, and I volunteer to go if I need to."

Stretch simply said, "Yup."

And that was how it went all the way around the table. They were patching over the remaining UpRiders.

"Great. We'll discuss who is going up over the next few days and plan. Now, the town hall. Pike."

Pike sat up in his chair and cleared his throat. "I've talked to the mayor's security detail, and they have agreed to all of us being there, or at least as many as we want, but they have insisted on us being searched. So, no weapons."

There were some grumbles about being searched, but Pike ignored them.

"Dragon and I will be at the doors. We'll be watching the crowd for anyone of note. The mayor has requested that we limit the number of Howlers on stage to five. Same with the Claws. The rest can sit in the audience. There will be rows designated."

Axle spoke up again, "On the stage will be Me, Skull, Top, Rex, and Siren."

Many of his brothers nodded. They fully expected that lineup. Axle and Skull for obvious reasons. Top and Rex were the older members of the club and had the most time in the community. Siren was a trusted member of the community, since he was a former police officer and a former EMT/Firefighter. Axle was going with the most trusted members of the club. It made sense.

Pike nodded. "Axle and I have discussed this, and we think the best way to handle this is for us to be as honest as possible. We will keep the answers to the five on stage, and the others will just be there for support."

"Crush and Pinky are determining their lineup and who will join Pike and Dragon at the doors since Nails is injured." Axle gave a moment for questions and comments. When none came, he moved on, "Okay. The last item, Ginger and Top are arranging a memorial for our lost members and Georgia. The rest of the family is arriving tomorrow morning. The memorial will be tomorrow night. Whether or not there is a burial service will be left to next of kin."

"How's Emerson?" Top asked.

Axle let out a sigh. "He's back in human form, but he refuses to talk to anyone. I brought up the memorial to him, and he threw an empty bottle of whiskey at my head. He's in one of the spare rooms at the apartments. I don't expect him to come to the memorial or any other service, but we'll make sure he gets the information. So, the service will be at the clubhouse after the town hall."

"If you need help with anything," Rex began, "just let me know."

"Want to talk about that doctor you were making goo-goo eyes at?" Axle asked.

Rex flipped him off. "You're turning into quite the fucking gossip, Pres."

Dragon watched as his brothers laughed and tried to grasp any bit of happy they could. He sent up a prayer that they could have a good stretch of happy before the next disaster knocked on their door.

Kisy

Sitting in the middle of their bed at their house, Kisy watched as a shirtless Dragon carried a six-drawer tall dresser down the basement stairs. Earlier that day, when they woke up, he had looked over at her stack of clothes and frowned.

She didn't know where he got the dresser, but it was in the garage when they returned to the house. After a quick round of fucking against the wall at the bottom of the stairs, he went up to get it. He didn't even break a sweat. That shifter strength was something to marvel over, but Kisy was sweating watching him.

The man was sexy as hell. All the muscles and his quiet force of a personality made her kitty pulse. Add on the fact that he knew exactly what to do with those muscles and how to make her scream his name... *Fuck!*

"Love," he began as he set the dresser down next to the cabinet, "if you keep looking at me like that, I will tie you down and not let you cum for hours."

Kisy grinned and laid back on the bed, sliding her hands above her head. "D, I keep telling you, fucking me is not the threat you think it is."

She was staring up at the ceiling when she felt him enter the bed from the foot and crawl over her, stopping where he could look down into her face.

"That wasn't a threat." He nipped her chin. "It's a promise, Love." He slid his tongue out and caressed her bottom lip with his piercing. "Can't get enough of you."

In response, Kisy lifted her legs and wrapped them around his hips. "I'm ready and willing when you are."

That green light shined from his eyes as a growl rolled out of his mouth. He extended his hand up toward the headboard and grabbed one of the lengths of rope there, but he was stopped when there was a voice coming from the top of the stairs.

"Just a heads up, I'm here," Ordys called down. "So is your sister and your brother-in-law. Don't stop what you're doing on our account, though."

"Dexter Dole," Darlin's voice rang out, "if you get all freaky with your mate while I'm in this house, I'll tell mom about every single thing I hear!"

Dragon let go of the length of rope and dropped his head into the pillow under her head. Kissing her shoulder, he groaned.

Kisy giggled and unwrapped her legs from his waist. "We have to go up there, Dex."

"I don't wanna."

She giggled louder at Dragon sounding like a teenager. "I know, but maybe they have Cane with them."

"Fine," Dragon grumbled and climbed off her. He reached out and took her hand, pulling her to her feet. "You're putting on pants."

Kisy looked down at her bare legs. She had on underclothes and one of his tees. The hem of the tee went almost to her knees. "I'm covered."

"You'll be more covered with pants on."

She put her hands to her hips and glared at him. "I'm more covered than if I had on a pair of my shorts and one of my shirts."

Dragon crossed his arms over his chest and stared down at her. "Love, you don't know what the sight of you in my tee does to a man."

"Oh, so it's *my* responsibility to make sure some other *man* doesn't get aroused?"

Dragon took a deep breath and slowly exhaled. "For the sake of my sanity, please put on pants," he gritted out.

Kisy rolled her eyes and walked over to her clothes that were stacked on the floor across the room. She grabbed a pair of leggings and yanked them on. "Happy?"

"Yes."

She turned and stomped toward the stairs.

"And, Love?" When Kisy stopped and looked back at him, he flashed that green light from his eyes at her and uttered, "*One.*"

Kisy's clit started throbbing, and she pressed her legs together in order to appease it a bit. Dragon noticed and grinned. Feeling feisty and wanting him to be just as turned on as she was, Kisy finished her trek to the stairs and bent over, putting her palms to the third stair up. She dropped her head and looked at him from between her thighs.

The loud growl she heard from Dragon had her giggling and running up the stairs.

T.S. Tappin

Chapter Thirty-One

Dragon

An hour into the visit with his sister and Trip, Dragon realized they were staying a while. While holding Cane, he pulled out his phone and put an order for delivery. Four large pizzas ought to do it.

Ordys had been in the guest room for a while, but he came out and joined them eventually. Since the first night he stayed with them, he'd only used the room one other night. Most of his time had been spent at the apartments with Kitty. Not that Dragon blamed the man. Kitty was a gorgeous woman.

"So, I think I might be hanging around," Ordys announced as he took a sip of his beer.

Trip gave a nod. "Figured that, since I've only seen Kitty without you once since you arrived."

Ordys just smiled and shrugged.

Kisy turned in her chair at the dining table and put her bare feet in his lap. "Dex," she said, firmly.

He began to rub her feet with his one free hand and looked over at her. When he saw her looking at him with wide, intent eyes, he scowled. "What?"

Kisy dropped her voice low and, in her best Dragon impression, uttered, "The room is yours as long as you need it, Ordys." Then she bugged her eyes out at him.

Dragon rolled his eyes and sighed. "What she said."

Trip's head was looking back and forth between Kisy and Dragon, a stupid grin on his face. He opened his mouth to say something, but Darlin' put her hand over it. "What," he mumbled.

"Your input was not needed."

"Your input is rarely needed," Dragon added and dropped his head and kissed the top of Cane's head.

Trip flipped him off.

Dragon put his mouth near Cane's ear. "Your father is an idiot. Just listen to Uncle Dex, okay?"

Kisy and Darlin' giggled as Trip glared at him and got to his feet. Dragon didn't stop him from taking Cane from his arms, but he looked over at Darlin' and winked.

"If you think I'm not going to tell Cane that you are Trip's bestie, you would be wrong," Darlin' told him as she continued to giggle.

"We're not *besties*," Trip complained. "We're brothers."

"*Bestie* brothers," Kisy clarified.

After the girls and Ordys got done laughing at him and Trip, Kisy looked over at Dragon and blurted, "I want a real wedding. The whole shebang. It doesn't have to be big, but it needs to be the real thing."

Without saying a word, Dragon lifted her feet from his lap and stood up. He crossed the room and pulled open a drawer in the kitchen. After grabbing the small box he had put there, he closed the drawer and returned to his chair. He opened the box and set it on the table in front of Kisy. Then he took hold of her ankles and returned her feet to his lap.

"That's Mom's engagement ring," Darlin' said with awe in her voice.

Dragon didn't look at her. His eyes were locked on Kisy's. They were violet that day. "Marry me."

Without breaking eye contact, Kisy removed the ring from the box and slid it on the ring finger of her left hand. Two seconds later, she was straddling his lap and kissing the hell out of him.

"I think it's time for us to go," Darlin' commented.

Ordys chuckled and agreed, "Looks like I'm staying with Kitty again."

"Bye, Dragon. Bye, Kisy."

Without stopping their make out session, both Kisy and Dragon waved hands at their guests.

Next day... Rebel

When Rebel walked into the auditorium at the high school, his eyes instantly scanned the crowd for the prettiest librarian he ever met. Hell... she was the most beautiful woman he had ever met. But he didn't see her.

Disappointment filled him as he took a seat at the end of the quarantined section of the second row. The Howlers and Claws seats were actually sectioned off with caution tape. Rebel rolled his eyes and yanked the tape down. That wouldn't help their cause.

His brothers and the Claws filed in and took seats, except for the ten who would be on stage. Crush decided on Pinky, Ginger, Shortcake, and Kitty to join her. It made sense. Just like the Howlers, the most notable to the community.

As he waited for the rest of the townspeople to enter the room and take their seats, Rebel thought about Ruby. After what she saw him do in the alley of the library, he hoped she wasn't afraid of him. He didn't regret it, but he didn't want her to think the worst of him.

His wolf snarled at him. Yeah, his wolf was pissed that he might have pushed away their woman, but it's not like Rebel wouldn't do whatever he needed to do to fix it.

"Why the frown?"

Rebel jolted at the sound of her voice. He turned his head and there she was, sitting right next to him. She gave him a sweet smile.

"You're here." He cringed as soon as the words left his mouth. *No shit, Sherlock!*

Ruby giggled. "I am. Figured I ought to get to know more about the man who is going to take me out for tea."

He bit the inside of his lip to stop the grin that threatened to appear. "So, you aren't planning to lose my number?"

"Considering you have yet to give it to me..."

"Oh, shit!" He took out his phone and asked, "What's your number?"

She rattled it off, and he called her. When her phone rang, she pointedly added his number to her contact list and showed him.

"Now, to answer your question... No way."

Rebel let the grin grow as Ruby's face turned the lovely shade of red that made his cock twitch. "That makes me happy." He reached over and took her hand in his, lacing their fingers together. "Just so you know, we aren't a danger to you or anyone else in this town. You'll always be safe with me."

She gave his hand a squeeze and replied, "I know."

There was so much more he wanted to say, but the mayor was approaching the microphone in the middle of the stage. Instead of saying the words, he turned his head and leaned toward her. He pressed a kiss to her temple and stayed close to her as they listened to the town hall meeting.

Axle

They spent two hours taking questions from the audience. Axle tried to remain patient as the townsfolk asked everything from how they shift to whether or not they knew anything about aliens. The point was to prove to them that the shifters weren't a threat. They couldn't exactly do that if he snapped at them for asking stupid fucking questions.

Once the last question was answered, he held the microphone to his face and uttered, "We will now show you. Keep in mind that while we're in animal form, we are still *us*. We still think as humans for the most part. We recognize people we know and remember what happens while we are in animal form. If anyone is interested in touching our animals, we ask that you form a line and remain respectful. While we're willing to do this to make you comfortable, we're not a circus show."

As he put the microphone back in the stand, he saw that half of the town began to line up at the edge of the stage. He had Brute join them on stage, since he was a bear and no one else on the stage was a bear shifter.

Pinky, Shortcake, Axle, Siren, and Brute shifted and lined up at the edge of the stage. The rest of the members, the mayor, and Hawkin congregated on the stage as the townsfolk walked up the steps and crossed the stage. Most of them didn't touch the shifters. They just looked and seemed to be curious. The few dozen who touched them remained respectful.

All in all, Axle considered it a success. After the last of the line crossed the stage, the shifters returned to their human forms. Axle approached the mayor and Hawkin.

"Mr. Weber," Mayor Cardinalie shook Axle's hand, "thank you for doing this. I'm sure it will put the town at ease."

Axle gave a nod. "I would appreciate it if you informed us if there was a problem. If there's more we need to do, we're willing to do it... unless it's degrading or disrespectful."

The mayor nodded. "I'll keep you informed."

Axle said his goodbyes and rounded up the clubs. They were in the parking lot, mounting their bikes, when Hawkin approached.

"I have been listening to what the townspeople have been saying for the last thirty-six hours. For the most part, they have been saying that the clubs have always been an integral part of the community, and this doesn't change anything."

Axle heard the sigh of relief come out of Crush on the bike next to his. He thanked Hawkin and shook his hand. "Thanks again for setting this up."

"Just another marker on the books," Hawkin replied with a smirk and walked away.

"Well, let's just hope he's right," Crush said and started her bike.

Dragon

When they got back to the clubhouse and stepped inside, he was assaulted by a flash of red hair and hands with long red nails. Okay, *assaulted* was a bit much. His mother grabbed his face and pulled his head down so she could kiss all over his face.

"Ma," he said after a moment. "You're wearing lipstick."

"And?" She let go of him and smiled up at him. "My boy."

"And I don't want to wear lipstick." Dragon used the back of his hand to wipe away the remnants of his mother's show of affection.

When he was done, he wrapped her in a hug and kissed the top of her head. "Ma, I'm—"

She swatted his arm. "If you say you're sorry, I will beat your ass. You're not too big for that, ya know. You know he wouldn't want you to feel that way."

Dragon could tell by the way her voice cracked that she was barely holding on to her emotions. He just sighed and kissed the top of her head again. "Ready to meet my mate?"

"I already spied." His mom pulled out of his arms and grinned up at him. "She's got all the curves and sass I knew your mate would have. I knew you'd never pick a little thing. You need someone you can toss around, and she has enough fluff to her to take it."

"Ma!" Dragon cringed as he looked around and saw all of his brothers and the Claws looking at him with amusement on their faces.

"What? It's the same reason your father gave me a sec—"

Dragon put his hand over his mother's mouth. "Please... for the love of the gods... do not finish that sentence. Do you want to formally meet Kisy or not?"

She nodded, but amusement twinkled in her eyes.

"Promise you won't talk about my sex life or your sex life in that meeting?"

His mother shrugged, and he knew that was the best he was going to get. He sighed with resignation, removed the hand from her mouth, and escorted her outside. He knew Kisy was hanging out at the diner because she had texted him that was where she'd be, but when they stepped outside, Kisy was headed across the street.

He met her on the sidewalk in front of the clubhouse and kissed her lips. "Hey."

"Hey, Dex. Meeting go okay?"

"About as good as could be expected," he replied and turned to face his mother. "Kisy, this is my mom, Bonnie Dole, but she goes by BonBon. Mom, this is Kaitlyn Neilson, but she goes by Kisy."

His mother winked up at him before she pulled Kisy into a hug. "Nice to meet you! I've heard a lot about you from Darlin' and Trip."

"Fuck my life," Dragon mumbled when he heard Trip had been talking to his mother. That could mean nothing but disaster.

"Oh, stop. And I heard you've been mean to that boy. You need to let up."

Dragon clenched his jaw to stop himself from going on a damn tirade about all of the things Trip had done with the sole intention of pissing him off. It wouldn't do any good. He'd just wait until all of this was over and beat the hell out of Trip. That would make him feel better.

Obviously sensing his tension, Kisy pulled out of the hug and changed the subject. "Cane is a total ham. I could pinch his chubby cheeks all day."

The second the Grammy in his mom was triggered, all thoughts of Trip and Dragon were whisked away.

Dragon caught Kisy's gaze over his mom's head and flicked his top lip with his tongue ring, letting her know he'd give her his thanks later. He knew she got his meaning when she pressed her thighs together and visibly swallowed hard.

While the women chatted about his fucking adorable nephew, Dragon steered them back toward the clubhouse so they could get the memorial underway.

While their dead deserved it, the emotion was heavy in the air. Dragon was ready for it to be over. If he had to be raw for much longer, he couldn't be held responsible for what he did. And Trip had a way of making himself the perfect target.

Dragon knew his mother was yanking his chain about Trip, trying to keep his mind off his father, but it was confirmed when he spied Trip chuckling and giving his mother a fist bump.

When Trip lifted his gaze and saw Dragon staring at him, he stopped chuckling.

Dragon made a cutting motion at his throat.

Kisy smacked his arm and giggled. "Stop it. You're not going to kill Trip."

"I wouldn't bet money on that." He wrapped his arms around her and pulled her into him as he shifted his attention to the bar.

Standing on top of the bar, Top – the club's chaplain – was waiting for the noise to die down. Around him were photos of each of the members they lost. *Gigi. Griff. Lace. Ivy. Lash.* Just past the photos was a painting done by Ginger that included the names *Riles, Storme,* and *Marya* within the beautiful, abstract sunrise.

The crowd noise slowly faded as the room realized Top was waiting, and everyone turned to face his direction. Top cleared his throat and said, "Today is a day we never wanted to have. It's a day that will always live in our souls and bring sadness every time we remember it, but remembering our lost family is what keeps them with us. It is what teaches the next generation about the ones who came before. It shows them how to live and how not to live. It is important that we keep them close and let their memory live on."

There was a hushed agreement that rolled through the room.

"Speak of their triumphs. Speak of their failures. Speak of their contributions to this family and the world. Their most recent contributions were their lives, but that cannot be the only thing we speak of."

A smattering of applause was heard in the room.

"So, to those we lost, we love you. We appreciate everything you brought to our world. You will not be forgotten."

Top climbed down from the bar top and picked up a handful of white roses from where they laid on the back counter. After rounding to the front of the bar, he laid a rose in front of each photo and laid three roses in front of the painting.

As music began to play quietly in the background, every adult member of the clubs and their families took their share of roses from the table at the end of the bar and did the same as Top.

Dragon felt the emotions building in his throat as he set a rose in front of Gigi's photo, and it only got worse with each rose after that. He managed to hold tight to it, but Kisy was another story.

By the end of the rows of photos, Kisy was a blubbering mess. Dragon knew her emotions were not only for herself, but also for every member of his family. Her heart went out to every person affected by the losses.

Fuck! Every time he thought he couldn't love her more, she went and proved him wrong.

He cupped her face in his hands and used his thumbs to wipe away her tears. "I love you," he told her quietly.

"Love you, too," she mumbled through her crying.

Dragon wanted to smile at the love she was showing him and everyone that meant anything to him, but he wrapped her in his arms and held her close instead.

Emerson

Stumbling down the back hallway that connected the apartment building to the clubhouse, Emerson took a deep breath and slowed his steps. He needed another bottle from the bar, and he wasn't going to get that if he fell and hit his head on something. When he started moving again, he did so taking careful steps and with his hand on the wall to guide him.

His heart hurt so fucking bad. How in the fuck could his heart hurt? How could it hurt if Gigi was his heart? She was his everything. And how did he feel so empty when his heart must still be there in order for it to hurt? But Gigi *was* gone. He knew it. He saw it happen.

As his eyes filled with tears again, he reached the mouth of the hall and glanced around the main room of the clubhouse. He didn't see anyone. Grateful that the place was empty, he turned left and headed behind the bar to grab another bottle. As he walked, he spotted the line-up of 8x10 frames on the bar top. He couldn't see what was in them, since they were facing the other way, but he could see the petals of the flowers sticking out from the side of the frames.

After snatching the closest full bottle he could find, he glanced down at it. Vodka. Guess it was vodka's turn to attempt to numb his pain. Whiskey and Rum hadn't managed it.

With the bottle in hand, he used his free hand to guide him around the end of the bar. He looked at the first 8x10 frame and nearly dropped the bottle. His Gigi was smiling out at him, those beautiful blue eyes shining.

His heart squeezed, and his chest heaved with the sharp intake of breath. She was gone. His Gigi, his mate... *gone*.

Reaching out, he grabbed the frame and pressed it against his bare chest. Holding it tight to him, he carefully made his way back down the hallway.

His Gigi was gone.

Tears streamed down his face, he turned at the end of the hallway and headed for the apartment building and his room. He'd never again get to see her smile at him or giggle in that adorable way she always did. He'd never hear her say his name or tell him she loved him again.

What was the point of living without her? Why was he hanging on to this life? Because Gigi would want him to. Plain and simple, his mate would want him to fight his grief and stay alive. So that's what he would do.

But that didn't mean he had to open himself up and risk experiencing that pain again. He would shuffle around the earth until the gods decided it was time for him to die, but he would do it alone.

His hold on the picture tightened. Hopefully, Gigi would be waiting for him wherever he ended up.

Top

As Top watched Emerson shuffle down the hall with a bottle of vodka in one hand and the picture of Gigi in the other, he recognized the display. When Connie died, Top had spent days doing the exact same thing. He hadn't told her or the club, but she had been his mate.

Rex had found him in a drunken stupor and made him take a shower and clean up his act. Then Rex told him that we're not just given one person to be their mate. They're given more than that, and it's just about the mate we find. Rex had lectured him about how pissed Connie would be if he closed himself off and didn't allow any other mates in.

That was going to be the lesson Emerson had to learn. It would be harder for Emerson, though, than for Top. Emerson had completed the mating, where he hadn't. For Connie and for Gigi, Top made a vow to help Emerson through it, no matter how long he took.

Top turned his head up. I'll take care of him, girls. I promise.

Chapter Thirty-two

Kisy

Dragon climbed up on the bar top, surprising the shit out of Kisy. When she saw the microphone in his hand, she thought she'd finally lost her mind and gone full-on delusional. But when the music started to play and Dragon began singing out the words to Keith Sweat's *Nobody*, Kisy was sure that everyone in the place had joined her in her world of make believe.

The man could shift into an animal. Most of the people in that room could do the same. It would make sense that none of it was reality, and she was just experiencing a mental breakdown of some sort.

As her crooning mate hopped down from the bar top and continued to serenade her while he did a sexy walk in her direction, Kisy was ready to sign herself into a mental institution.

When he reached her, he leaned forward and said into the microphone, "Kisy, wake up."

Kisy jolted and opened her eyes to see Dragon standing on the side of the bed, looking down at her. *Fuck!* She had been dreaming.

Dragon raised an eyebrow at her. "You were smiling."

"Then why did you wake me up? That dream was the best shit I'd witnessed in forever," she complained on a grumble.

"The best?"

She made a noncommittal noise. Then a yawn hit her.

"It's tattoo day. Ginger is at the shop getting set up."

A sudden burst of energy hit her system, and she popped up out of bed, nearly knocking Dragon over with her dash to get dressed. "I'm up! I'm up! Get dressed! Let's go!"

Snatching a clean set of clothes from the dresser Dragon had bought her and brought down, Kisy ran into the bathroom. She attempted to yank on underwear with one hand as she brushed her teeth.

"You know," Dragon began as he leaned against the doorjamb, "that would probably go smoother if you did one thing at a time."

Kisy rolled her eyes at him but stopped yanking and finished brushing her teeth. After rinsing her mouth, she went to finish pulling up her panties, but Dragon beat her to it.

Kneeling behind her, he slowly pulled the panties up her legs as his lips, tongue, and that piercing worshiped the skin of her ass and lower back.

Kisy's breath caught as she gripped the edge of the vanity and closed her eyes, soaking in his touch. He could light a fire in her with only a caress or a word or even a look. The man was *hot*.

"Breathe, Love," he ordered as he settled her panties on her hips. Then he was on his feet and strolling out of the bathroom, giving her a wink over his shoulder.

"Not fair!" Kisy pouted as she put on her bra and finished getting dressed.

"I'll make it up to you later," Dragon called back.

Kisy didn't miss the chuckle vibrating his voice.

The tattoo she designed for Dragon was simple. It was her full name, Kaitlyn, in bold, flowery script with a dragon with its body and tail wrapped protectively around the word. She insisted the dragon be the green of Dragon's eyes and his nickname for her *Love* was hidden in the design of its scales. She had him get it on the left side of his neck, right where her mating mark would be if she was a shifter. Kisy fucking loved it.

She also loved the fact that he got Kisy on his chest, over his heart, in the same script. She told him he didn't need to do that, but he told her he wanted it, so she agreed.

Once he was done, the other ol' ladies, along with Crush and Pinky showed up at the tattoo shop. Ginger had Dragon do whatever she needed him to in order to tattoo his kiss mark on Kisy. Then he kissed Kisy and left her to bond with the women.

She got the Howlers MC colors on her inner right thigh. On her inner left thigh, she got the word Dragon in script with Dragon's kiss mark under it. They weren't large, only a couple inches by a couple inches each. They were going to hurt like a bitch, rubbing together when she walked, but Dragon would lick them and use the properties in his shifter saliva to help them heal quicker. That experience would make it worth it.

"He'll have to borrow Rock's truck if he plans to take you back to the house tonight," Ginger commented with a smile as she cleaned up the tattoos.

"I don't think they'll make it that far," Gorgeous uttered and yelped when Darlin' smacked her arm. "Damn it, Dani! That shit hurt."

"Then stop talking about my brother fucking!"

"I didn't say anything about that!"

Kisy giggled as she watched the two women. Pixie moved to the seat closer to Kisy and rolled her eyes. "Those two can be more like sisters than best friends."

"I like it," Kisy replied. "But Gorgeous isn't wrong. As soon as Dragon sees these, he's going to carry me up to our room here and—"

"LALALALALALALALALALALA," Darlin' blurted as she plugged her ears with her fingers.

Sugar grinned at Kisy. "I like you."

"I like you, too," Kisy replied.

From her position leaned back against the wall by the door to the room, Crush asked, "Where are you getting your TC colors?"

The question brought proud tears to Kisy's eyes. She looked from Crush to Pinky standing next to Crush and back. "Full-back piece," she answered.

"Righteous," Pinky said, and grinned as she nodded her approval.

"Kick ass," Peanut agreed.

Ginger smiled at her as she stood and pulled off her nitrile gloves. "That will be an honor to do for you, Kisy. Give your body a week and I'll get you taken care of."

Kisy looked around the room at all of the women who had become her sisters in such a short period of time. Her gaze landed on Butterfly standing over on the other side of the doorway from Crush. Her new best friend blew her a kiss.

"Thank you... to all of you. I didn't always fit in with my family, and now I have a new family that feels more like home than home ever did."

"Oh, fuck," Pixie uttered as tears started streaming down her face. "Fucking pregnancy hormones!"

Dragon

Two and a half hours after he left her in the tattoo parlor with the women, Kisy was carried into the main room of the clubhouse by Pinky and Crush. Each of them had an arm around her back and another under one of her knees. With her arms over their shoulders, Kisy was laughing her ass off at some joke Dragon didn't hear.

Trailing behind the trio were the rest of the ol' ladies and Ginger.

"What in the hell did you do to my mate?" Dragon asked as they sat Kisy down on the table in front of him.

"Nothing," Crush said on a laugh. "We didn't want your lips rubbing all over the Howlers colors."

Pinky snorted. "Could you imagine Dragon kissing the Howlers' asses?"

And just like that, the whole lot of them devolved into giggles.

Dragon locked gazes with Kisy. "Explain. What in the fuck are they talking about?"

"It'll be easier to show you," She commented and pointed down to her legging-covered thighs.

Curious, Dragon stood and scooped her up. He noticed that she kept a few inches between her thighs. He didn't say another word as he carried her out of the room and into the female bathroom. After setting her on the counter of the sink, he turned and locked the door.

When he turned his head back to look at her, she was already carefully peeling her leggings off. He helped her by pulling off the knee-high boots she had on her feet. After she removed the leggings and dropped them to the floor, she put her heels to the end of the counter and spread her knees.

The sight before him short-circuited his brain for so many reasons. The first of which was just the fact that his mate was in that position. He instantly wanted to drop to his knees and fuck her with his tongue until she came all over his face and beard. When he saw the two tattoos on her thighs, he did drop to his knees on that hard tile floor.

For a long moment, he just stared at one tattoo and then the other.

"Do you like them?"

At the sound of Kisy's hesitant question, Dragon looked up at her. His eyes began to glow that green light as he leaned forward and extended his tongue. He spent a long time just licking along those exquisite tattoos, helping them heal. When he had those tattoos thoroughly covered with his saliva, her chest was heaving with her hard pants. Her skin was a pretty pink blush, and the gusset of her panties were soaked with her juices.

In a low, rough voice, he said, "You have two seconds to stop me or I'm going to eat you out right now."

When his mate just stared down at him, Dragon extended his fangs and took a hold of the gusset of her panties with them. He yanked, and those panties tore from her body. She gasped and laid her head back against the mirror behind her.

"You will not be quiet, Love," he ordered. Then he devoured her.

He wasn't gentle or slow. He slid his tongue deep and let that piercing do its thing as his thumb circled her clit. Once his chin and beard were covered in her arousal, he began to fuck her with his tongue, his thumb not letting up on her clit.

It didn't take long for his Love to open those beautiful lips and scream his name.

Kisy

Her heart felt like it was going to jump out of her chest. Kisy looked down at her mate, who still had his face buried between her thighs. As soon as she was breathing again, his tongue moved up to her clit, and that piercing began to flick against it as he fucked her with two fingers in her pussy.

"D," she moaned and lifted her hips, pressing herself harder against him.

In response, Dragon growled against her clit, setting her off again. Pleasure coiled in her pelvic area and exploded through her body. Her vision blinked out and was replaced with lights. Her hearing narrowed to the sound of her heart beating out of control.

When her climax finally crested and began to ease, she realized she had the fingers of both of her hands buried in his hair and gripping. Dragon had his free arm around her with his hand pressing against her back, holding her up.

This time, he lifted his head and looked up at her, his beard drenched with the proof of her climaxes.

She released her grip on his hair and tried to get her breathing under control. When she couldn't, she panted out, "I take it... you like... them."

Dragon stood and began to unfasten his pants. "Do they hurt?"

She gingerly touched them and was surprised to find that they felt healed. A bit shocked, she shook her head. "They're healed, I think."

"Makes sense. With my shifter saliva on them, they wouldn't take long to heal. And I've been eating you out for almost an hour, Love." He grinned as he pulled his hard cock from his jeans and stepped closer.

"What?" She shook her head again. "That can't be possible. I came twice, and they were quick."

"You came three times, and the second one took some time." He chuckled. "Someone is in a fuck fog."

She reached down between them and fisted his cock. "Are you going to keep me here for a while?"

He forced her hand away and slammed inside of her. "It's going to be a long night for you, Love." He pulled her hips closer until her ass was barely on the counter, before he set about fucking her hard and fast.

She was moaning loudly when he dropped his head to her shoulder and sucked hard on his mating mark. Another climax hit and she screamed.

"Fuck yes, Love. Let the world know you're mine," Dragon gritted out as he continued thrusting, that piercing in his dick caressing exactly where she needed it to.

"I love you," she breathed.

"Fucking love you, too." He pressed his forehead to hers, his hair falling forward and creating a little cocoon for them. "Love you, too," he repeated.

He slid his arms around her waist as Kisy slid her arms around his shoulders. They gazed into each other's eyes until she felt that tingle begin again in her pelvis.

"D," she panted.

"Give it to me," he growled. "Right there with ya, Love."

Two thrusts later, Dragon slammed his lips to hers as she had yet another climax, and he emptied himself inside of her.

He had just stopped twitching when there was a knock on the bathroom door and his mother's voice rang out. "While I've been there and understand what is coursing through your veins right now, you have quite the audience out here, kids."

Dragon groaned as his dick instantly lost any of its vigor. Kisy giggled as Dragon went about getting paper towels to clean them up.

"Be right out, Mom."

There was humor in his mother's voice when she replied, "Thanks for making my son so happy, Kisy."

"Mom," Dragon barked.

"Okay! Okay. It's just sex, but fine. Hurry up." Then they heard her footsteps as she walked away from the door.

"Fuck my life," Dragon grumbled.

"She just wants you to be happy," Kisy commented, thinking he looked just as sexy with the scowl on his face as he did when he grinned at her.

"If that was true, she wouldn't have tried to ruin the best orgasm I ever had by trying to talk to me," he complained as he rinsed his face and beard with water from the sink.

She knew better than to take the paper towel from where he set it on the counter and try to clean herself up. Dragon would take offense to that, since he thought of it as his duty to clean her up after sex.

Once his face was rinsed and he had dried it, he grabbed the remaining paper towel and returned to his spot between her thighs. Gazing in her eyes, he gently ran the towel along her slit, making sure to be as thorough as possible.

As usual, by the time he was done, she was ready to go again.

With a knowing grin, he retrieved her leggings and handed them to her. Once she had them on, he helped her put on her boots and lifted her off the counter.

He gave her one last kiss and unlocked the door. "Don't think for one second that the appreciation for those tats is done," he commented as he opened the door.

Kisy went to step through, but he smacked her ass. She stopped and looked over her shoulder at him. With a smile, she replied, "You said it was going to be a long night. I'm going to hold you to that."

His growl made her giggle as she strutted down the hall with him trailing behind her.

Chapter Thirty-Three

The next day... Dragon

After fucking Kisy until her limbs were numb, Dragon tucked her into bed in their room at the apartment building and made his way down to his bike. He had a mission to complete by the time she slept off her sated happiness.

He mounted his bike, pulled out his phone, and sent a quick text to Ranger to meet him at the dealership. After putting his phone away, he started the bike and roared out of the parking lot, with his gut full of excitement.

Three hours later, he and Ranger pulled back into the parking lot of the clubhouse. Attempting to contain his excitement, he thanked Ranger and offered to give him a ride back to his truck, but Ranger waved him off.

"Go get her, Brother."

Dragon gave him a handshake, backslap hug, before he practically jogged over to the apartment building and up the stairs. When he got to their room, he found her still naked and asleep in their bed.

He bent over and kissed her lips, holding himself up with his palms in the bed on either side of her. "Kisy," he uttered and kissed her again.

"Dex, I love you, but if you try to fuck me right now, I just might riot." She still hadn't opened her eyes.

Dragon chuckled. "I bought you a present."

One of her eyes peeled open and looked at him. "A present?"

"Yeah. Consider it a mating present or an engagement present." He smacked her bare ass. "Come on. You can go back to sleep afterward."

"It better be fucking good," she grumbled as she climbed out of bed and started getting dressed in the clothes she wore the day before. Instead of her shirt, though, she grabbed one of his from the dresser.

"We'll have to stock the dresser with some of my clothes."

"Not your shirts," he said. When she looked over at him, he shrugged. "I like it when you wear my tees."

Dragon's Kiss

She gave him a sweet smile and pulled on her boots.

After she pulled her hair back in a ponytail, he took her hand and led her out to the parking lot of the clubhouse. At first, she was confused. Then when he stopped her next to the new bike he bought her, she turned and looked up at him with shock on her face.

"I figured this way you won't have to steal mine anymore. We can have it painted or—" His words were cut off by Kisy's tongue as she jumped him and kissed the hell out of him.

"Again?"

His mother's voice was like nails on a chalkboard when he had his mate's ass in his hands and her tongue down his throat. He wrenched his mouth free and turned his head to glare at his grinning mother.

Kisy began to giggle, so he pulled a hand back and slapped her ass.

"I'm getting ready to head to the airport. Thought my boy might want to say goodbye."

Dragon set Kisy back on her feet and walked over to his mother, Kisy following closely behind him. He wrapped his mother in a hug. "It was good to see you."

"My heart can rest easy now," she replied and pulled back to cup his face in her hands. "I will miss him, but as long as you and your sister are happy and safe, I'll be just fine."

"You could always move back, Ma," he said.

She smiled up at him. "And deal with the snow? Nah. I'll come visit, though. Gotta make sure Cane knows who Grammy is." Then she released him and turned to face Kisy, taking Kisy's hands in her own and sighed. "Thank you for putting that beautiful grin on my grumpy boy's face. I'm forever in your debt."

Kisy blushed. "Well, considering he wouldn't be in my life if it wasn't for you, I think we're even."

His mother gave a nod and hugged Kisy.

"Do you need a ride?"

His mother released Kisy and faced him again. "No, thank you. Trip is taking me. You stay here and celebrate with your mate. Considering she's wearing my ring, I'll expect an invitation soon."

He nodded and watched as she walked away.

Kisy slipped her hand in his and gave it a squeeze. "She loves you. I think she left Dani with you because she knew it was what was best for the both of you. You needed to take care of Dani and Dani needed to be here with you."

Dragon cleared his throat and gave a nod.

"Want to go for a ride?"

With a smile, Dragon pulled the key to her bike out of his pocket and handed them over.

"Squeeee," she shouted and snatched it from him.

One week later... Dragon

After checking in with the crew cleaning up the wreckage that was Heat, Dragon headed back to the clubhouse. They were grateful that Heat was empty when it was blown up, but it was one of their big moneymakers. The Howlers and the Claws needed it rebuilt and fast, but first, they needed to get the lot cleared out.

Axle had spent a few days on the phone with the insurance company and had met with the police chief to explain what happened. He didn't share everything, but he shared enough. The police chief and insurance companies were still investigating the fire and the claim, but the scene had finally been released that morning, which is why Dragon had to show up and make sure the crew knew what needed to be done.

He wasn't sure if they were going to rebuild Heat the way it was or if they were going to revamp the entire business. There was talk of widening the scope of Heat around the clubhouse.

Ultimately, it would come down to whatever the clubs voted on, since it was a business they owned together.

Dragon hoped they widened the scope and considered making it more than a strip club. Time would tell.

After backing into his usual spot, Dragon headed into the clubhouse. When he stepped through the door, he was confronted with something he never expected to see and never wanted to see again – Trip on his knees with his hands tied behind his back with Ranger and Kisy standing over him.

"What the fuck?" Dragon stopped in his tracks and blinked hard, hoping he was just seeing things.

Kisy grinned. "Trip wanted tips. I told him that I got out of the ropes at the office building. He asked me how. I told him it's not uncommon that my hands are tied."

"Oh, fuck me," he groaned and scrubbed his face with his hands.

Kisy didn't even stop in her explanation. "He wanted to know how to tie someone up without hurting them and–"

"Kisy!" Dragon held up a hand to stop her from speaking further.

"What?" She put her hands to her hips and glared at him. "I told him if he was going to tie anyone up, he had to know what it was like to be tied up. Then *you* walked in and got judgy."

Ranger snorted a laugh and turned around. He walked a few yards away before he burst out in full belly laughs.

"*One*," Dragon growled at her. Then he pulled his phone out of his pocket, opened the camera app, and snapped a few pictures.

"Hey!" Trip protested, trying to get to his feet.

Dragon approached Kisy and gave her a kiss. "Continue."

As Ranger continued to laugh and Kisy began to giggle, Trip cursed Dragon's name, but Dragon just walked out.

A few hours later… Kisy

Lying on her stomach in the tattoo shop without a shirt on, Kisy took a deep breath and looked over at Ginger. Ginger gave her an understanding smile and asked, "Full-back?"

"How about half that size and on the top half… like in the middle?"

Ginger gave a nod. "Okay. I'll make the stencil and put it on you. Then you can tell me if it works for you. Deal?"

"Yeah."

Ginger placed a hand on her shoulder. "If it's the pain you're worried about, this won't be as bad as the inner thigh. If it's the permanence of the club colors, you already accepted that. This is just a visual representation of your commitment. You have to get the club colors, but the size and the location is up to you. We can make it smaller and put it in a different place if you don't like the stencil."

Kisy nodded and took another deep breath. While Ginger went about doing what she needed to do, Kisy rested her chin on her folded arms. It was the meaning behind the tattoo. She wasn't second-guessing her commitment to the Claws or to joining the family. She wasn't even second-guessing the tattoo. She was just overwhelmed with everything that she had been blessed with. Her brain was still processing the way her life had turned around.

A month before, she was working for a drug lord and sex-trafficker and had no idea. The fact that she had moved to a new town, got a new job, learned about shifters, got mated, got engaged, had been kidnapped, and fought in a war was a lot to take in.

She didn't regret any decision that had brought her to that moment, but she could recognize that getting on the back of Dragon's bike could have turned out to be the worst decision she made. He could have been a killer, but she had been being chased by two killers on the order of another killer. Lesser of the evils.

Lucky for her, Dragon turned out to be a Dom who wanted nothing more than to give her everything she always wanted. He filled all the holes in her life with his love and filled her pussy perfectly with his pierced cock while he ordered her to come for him. He was perfect for her. She sent a *thank you* to the gods as the smile grew on her face.

"Seems our Kisy just worked through the nervousness," Pinky commented as she and Crush walked into the room.

"Ginger, she's good," Crush called down the hall. "Smiling like a loon in here."

Kisy's smile turned to a grin. "Just thinking about Dragon's pierced cock and how well he can use it."

Pinky whistled as Crush chuckled and uttered, "Yeah... she's fine."

T.S. Tappin

Mattyx, God of Positivity

Sitting in their realm on the large hammock on the balcony of the home they shared with their twin, Mattyx, God of Positivity, felt it when the soul of their Pangloss Eyne champion was released.

Storme was a good champion, a dependable Pangloss Eyne. The moment his soul was released from his body, a wave of sorrow came over Mattyx.

After climbing out of the hammock, they got dressed in a plain pair of white slacks and a light blue button-up shirt. Barefoot, they made their way down to the beach just outside the home. They didn't have to wait long.

Three waves later, the soul of Storme floated in from the sea and stopped in front of Mattyx.

"Thank you, my champion," Mattyx expressed. "You have a decision to make. You may move on to your end or reenter the world anew. What will it be, Pangloss Eyne?"

Storme's soul moved back a foot, letting Mattyx know he wanted to reenter.

Mattyx lifted a hand and cupped the cheek of Storme's soul. With a smile and a push of power, they sent the soul back over the sea. The soul would get a new body and a new existence, with no memory of the life it had already lived.

"Be well," they whispered as they watched the soul disappear into the distance.

From their side, Rue uttered, "Colvyr just did the same with Marya's soul." Mattyx wasn't sure when they arrived at the shore, but that wasn't a surprise. Rue moved like the wind.

Mattyx sent a rush of sadness to their brother and received the same in return.

It was sad that their champions weren't successful in their mission, but their effort would be honored, regardless. Their efforts and their sacrifices were not demanded of them but were given freely.

"You win some. You lose some," Rue said in their deadpan way.

"In the end, good always wins," Mattyx retorted.

Rue shrugged. "Depends on your perspective."

Mattyx just shook their head and went back to appreciating the view.

"You know, this is just the beginning. We have a responsibility to help now."

"I know."

Rue's voice didn't change when they said, "That shifter blocker is going to be a problem."

"Yup," they agreed.

There was a deep sigh. "Give them a few days. Then we'll call in the Dolor Ayre and the Panglass Eyne to make a plan."

As much as their twin hated it, their involvement was necessary, but limited. It was time for the gods to be gods again.

A Glimpse at What's to Come...

Rex

Terrence "Rex" Piccolo loved it when his daughter came home to visit. The fact that Neveah lived in a big city on her own at the age of nineteen drove him up the wall with worry. She was a pretty girl — a model and a singer represented by an up-and-coming talent agency. She was doing quite well for herself and had yet to touch the money he sent her every week. He sent it anyway, because that's what fathers who had the means did.

Yes, he loved it when she came home to visit. What he didn't love is when she brought her trio of best friends with her. Two of the three were growing boys who would eat him out of house and home, but his daughter and her friend Kennedy required copious amounts of ice cream.

While it did a number on his bank account, it also made him breathe a little easier. A model in the big city could develop a number of issues with eating and weight. His girl had yet to show signs of any of that. She ate and she enjoyed her food. He'd buy her as much ice cream as she wanted.

He left the four young adults at his house while he made a run to the grocery store. Their visit had been a surprise, so he didn't have his pantry stocked the way it normally would be, but he always told his girl she didn't need to ask to come home. She could just show up. That's what she did.

As Rex parked his truck in a spot in the middle of the parking lot in front of their local grocery store, he reflected on some of the choices he made as a parent. One of the things he had always done was tell Neveah that her friends were always welcome at his home. It drove Neveah's mother crazy, because she didn't have the same rule.

When Neveah was in high school, he would come home to find eight or nine teenagers hanging out in his living room. Was his house always a disaster that he spent hours cleaning? Yes. Did he know what his daughter and her friends were up to? Also, yes. That made it all worth it.

Her friends trusted him. They came to him for advice. They told him their struggles and their successes. They told him about their heartbreaks and their first dates. He knew it all, but in return for that trust, he gave them the best advice he could, and he kept their secrets unless it was a safety issue.

When he got out of his truck, he snagged a row of carts from the corral and pushed them toward the front of the store, making a mental list of what he needed to get.

Neveah liked chocolate ice cream. Kennedy liked the salted caramel. Hunter and Devin requested beef jerky and peanuts. He also needed to get the ingredients for meals. He decided on Hamburgers, Chicken Chili, and Taco Lasagna for dinners. For lunches, he added lunch meat, bread, cheese, and the makings of salads to his mental list. French Toast and cereal would work for breakfast.

Stepping into the store, he took one of the carts and left the rest. He gave a nod to the older woman who was working the register. She was a sweet woman, but she didn't take any shit. He liked that. He also liked that when he came through the line, she was able to efficiently ring up the order and have a conversation without holding things up.

After getting the return nod and smile, he took a left and headed for the produce section. After grabbing lettuce, tomatoes, potatoes, avocado, onions, and green peppers, he grabbed lunch meat from the deli section and headed for the bread section in the back left corner of the store. Rex had just put two loaves of white bread and two packages of hamburger buns in his cart when he heard a familiar voice coming from his right.

"Ah." A loud, deep sigh. "There's nothing like tender meat."

Rex snort laughed as he turned and saw Doc standing in front of the meat section with a package of high-priced steaks in one hand and a container of meat tenderizer in the other. She put both in her cart. When she went to turn back to the meat section, her gaze lifted and met his own.

She was wearing a set of scrubs, light blue with cats and dogs all over them.

Rex headed in her direction. "You're a meat lover, are ya?"

Doc straightened and turned her body to face him. "Who can deny good sausage or a slab of beef? Not I."

Smiling, Rex stopped his cart next to hers. He grabbed two large packages of hamburger and a package containing four large chicken breasts.

"A breast man, I see."

Rex gave a nod. "But I also like a good rump... roast."

As he went to put them in his cart, she asked, "Are you one of those *I-grill-all-my-meat* types?"

Rex put the items in his cart, looked down at his crotch, and then looked over at Doc. "Well... not *all* my meat."

As Doc laughed, Rex reached around her and grabbed a container of chorizo and two packages of bacon. As he set the items down with the rest, he looked over at her cart. She had various meat products, veggies, and fruit.

"Are you a once-a-weeker, or a multiple times a week type?"

She raised an eyebrow. "If you're asking how often I like meat, I'm not sure that's appropriate grocery store conversation."

Grinning, Rex commented, "We could always have it over dinner. How about some *tenderized meat* and veggies?"

"Are you asking me out?"

Rex shrugged. "I'm asking you in."

She looked over at him with amusement in his eyes. "I am all for letting the dogs in the house."

"I'm a wolf, Doc."

"Okay, Fido." Doc pushed her cart forward toward the dairy section. "And if I agree to this date, does this mean I have to cook for you?"

Walking next to her, pushing his own cart, Rex answered, "No. I'm very capable of cooking. I would just need to know if there are any no-gos in the culinary department."

Doc looked surprised that he knew how to cook, if her widened eyes and lifted brows told him anything.

"What?"

"You grocery shop and you cook?"

Rex stopped his cart and turned his body, so he was facing her. "I'm a single forty-one-year-old man with a grown daughter. It was shop and cook or starve. I happen to like to eat, so I learned."

Her surprise turned back to amusement. "You may not know it, but your sex-quotient just went up, Fido."

"Does that mean you're going to come over for dinner?"

"It means I'll consider it."

"Okay. Well, let's do this." He pulled his wallet out of his back pocket and retrieved a business card. Handing it to her, he said, "This is my personal cell. Text me your no-go foods and what evening you're free. I'll respond with my address and a time. Then I'll dazzle you with my cooking skills and my charming personality."

"You're awfully confident," she replied, but she took the card and slid it in her pocket.

They made their way to the dairy section. Rex noticed her eyeing his cart.

"My daughter came home for a visit and brought three of her friends with her. So, here I am, doing a grocery run to feed them. They are all nineteen, two of them young men, so they eat a lot."

"But I bet your daughter loves the fact that you're willing to take in her and her friends and feed them. Not all parents would be cool with that."

Rex shrugged and grabbed two dozen eggs. As he set them in the cart, he replied, "If they're at my house, I know what they are doing. If buying them food is the cost for my peace of mind, I'm cool with that."

The smile she gave him hit him in the gut and made his wolf stand up and take notice. She kept her eyes on him as she reached down and grabbed a dozen eggs. Holding them up, she said, "That's Egg-cellent."

Rex chuckled and grabbed the three kinds of cheese he needed – the supersized bag of shredded Colby-jack, two packages of sliced Colby-jack, and a block of Pepperjack. As he dropped them in his cart, he uttered, "That's so cheesy."

The belly laugh that came from her was the cutest thing he'd ever heard. *Fuck...* he was in trouble. His wolf let out a whine and swished his tail, letting Rex know he agreed with that assessment.

While she laughed and grabbed what she needed, he grabbed sour cream and milk. Together, they moved to the next aisle of frozen items.

As he opened one door of the freezer and grabbed the ice cream that the girls requested, she said, "You scream. I scream. We all scream for ice cream."

Rex set the pints down in the cart and raised an eyebrow at her. "You give me the sign. You and I will be screaming, but it won't be over ice cream."

As she stared at him with her mouth open, he pushed his cart down the aisle and around to the next one. He was grabbing a variety of cereal when she joined him. He bit his lip to stop himself from laughing at her expression as he grabbed a bottle of syrup.

She reached up and grabbed a box of bran cereal, eyeing the syrup in his hand. "That's awfully saucy of you."

Chuckling, he followed her to the ethnic foods aisle. He grabbed two cans of refried beans, a package of soft flour tortilla shells, taco seasoning, salsa, and two jars of taco sauce. "Now, *this* is saucy."

She held up a bag of dried black beans. "Bean there, done that."

They were both laughing as they moved to the canned foods and pasta aisle. He grabbed mushrooms and lasagna noodles, while she loaded her cart with different kinds of pasta.

"You can make lasagna?"

He shrugged. "Yes, but this is for taco lasagna. Neveah, my daughter, loves it. She requests it every time she's in town."

"Taco lasagna?"

"Yes. If you like American tacos, you'd like taco lasagna."

"My brain is having trouble computing it."

He smiled at her. "I'll prove it. Come over for dinner and I'll make it."

"You'd eat it twice in a week?"

"I'd eat it every day," he replied as his gaze traveled down her body and back up.

"Heel, Fido," she said and pushed her cart down the aisle. "I'll text you... or not."

When they got to the end of the aisle, he had to stop and grab snacks. She smiled at him over her shoulder as she kept pushing her cart toward the front of the store.

He made a stop in the paper products aisle to grab paper towels and more toilet paper. Then he headed for the registers. When he reached the front of the store, he found her unloading her cart onto a belt and the older cashier ringing things up.

Rex moved to the next aisle and did the same. Grinning like a fool, he told his wolf he was sure they would be having dinner with Doc and to have patience.

Find her on the Web:

TikTok: Booksbytt
Instagram: Booksbytt
Goodreads: T.S. Tappin
YouTube: Books by TT
BookBub: T.S. Tappin
Website:
www.tstappin.com
Merch Store:
Books-by-tt.creator-spring.com

Any emails can be sent to
Booksbytt@gmail.com

About the Author

T.S. Tappin is a storyteller who spends most of her days playing chauffeur to her children (Tyler, Gabby, & Hailee, not to mention all of Hailee's friends who also call Tara "Mom"), strong (probably stronger than he wanted) partner to her significant other (Mark), cuddler to her American Bulldog/Pitbull (Champ), or cleaner of other people's messes (for work and at home). Reading and Writing are her favorite ways to spend her spare time, but she doesn't have much of that with three busy teenagers in the house. She loves every moment of it. She's that mom in the stands yelling and cheering and generally making an embarrassment of herself. She's a very proud Wrestling-Baseball-Softball-Dance-Cheer-Theater-Robotics-QuizBowl-DECA-Esports-Choir-NHS-Rockstar-Crew Mom!

For More Information

On the Howlers MC or Tiger's Claw MC, go to www.tstappin.com or find T.S. Tappin on any social media using the handle BooksByTT.

Your honest review would be appreciated. This book is on Amazon, GoodReads, and BookBub.

If you have any questions, T.S. Tappin can be reached at BooksByTT@gmail.com

Thank you for Reading!
Dream Big. Dream Often. Dream Always.

Printed in Great Britain
by Amazon